GET TH

For a

FREE

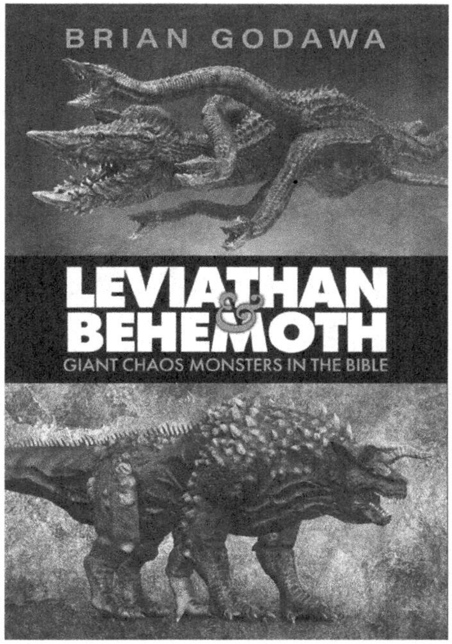

The Truth about these Two Giant Bible Beasts: Leviathan & Behemoth

Respected Christian author Brian Godawa gives a detailed biblical study of these two Chaos Monsters and their connection to Creation, Covenant, Exodus and the End Times.

Click Below to Get Your Free eBook

https://godawa.com/get-free-leviathan/

Gilgamesh Immortal

Chronicles of the Nephilim
Book Three

By Brian Godawa

GILGAMESH IMMORTAL
5th Edition

Warrior Poet Publishing
www.warriorpoetpublishing.com

ISBN: 9798710814321 (hardcover)
ISBN: 978-0-9859309-4-3 (paperback)

Scripture quotations taken from *The Holy Bible: English Standard Version.* Wheaton: Standard Bible Society, 2001.

Dedicated to
the memory of
Sinleqiunninni of Babylonia.

("Sin-leek-ee-ooh-nee-nee")

ACKNOWLEDGMENTS

Special thanks to the wife of my youth, Kimberly, who is my life, my muse, and my grounding; to Gilgamesh scholar Andrew George for his magisterial critical commentary *The Babylonian Gilgamesh Epic*; to Don Enevoldsen for his original editing; to Mark Tapson for his helpful comments; to Rich Knox, my lifelong buddy for his insightful theological suggestions; to Shari Risoff my sister-in-law for her excellent proofreading, to Sarah Beach for her great editing on this second edition; to Amazon.com that has empowered me as an author; and to the God who is sometimes hidden, but always near, Yahweh Elohim.

This is what *really* happened to Gilgamesh.

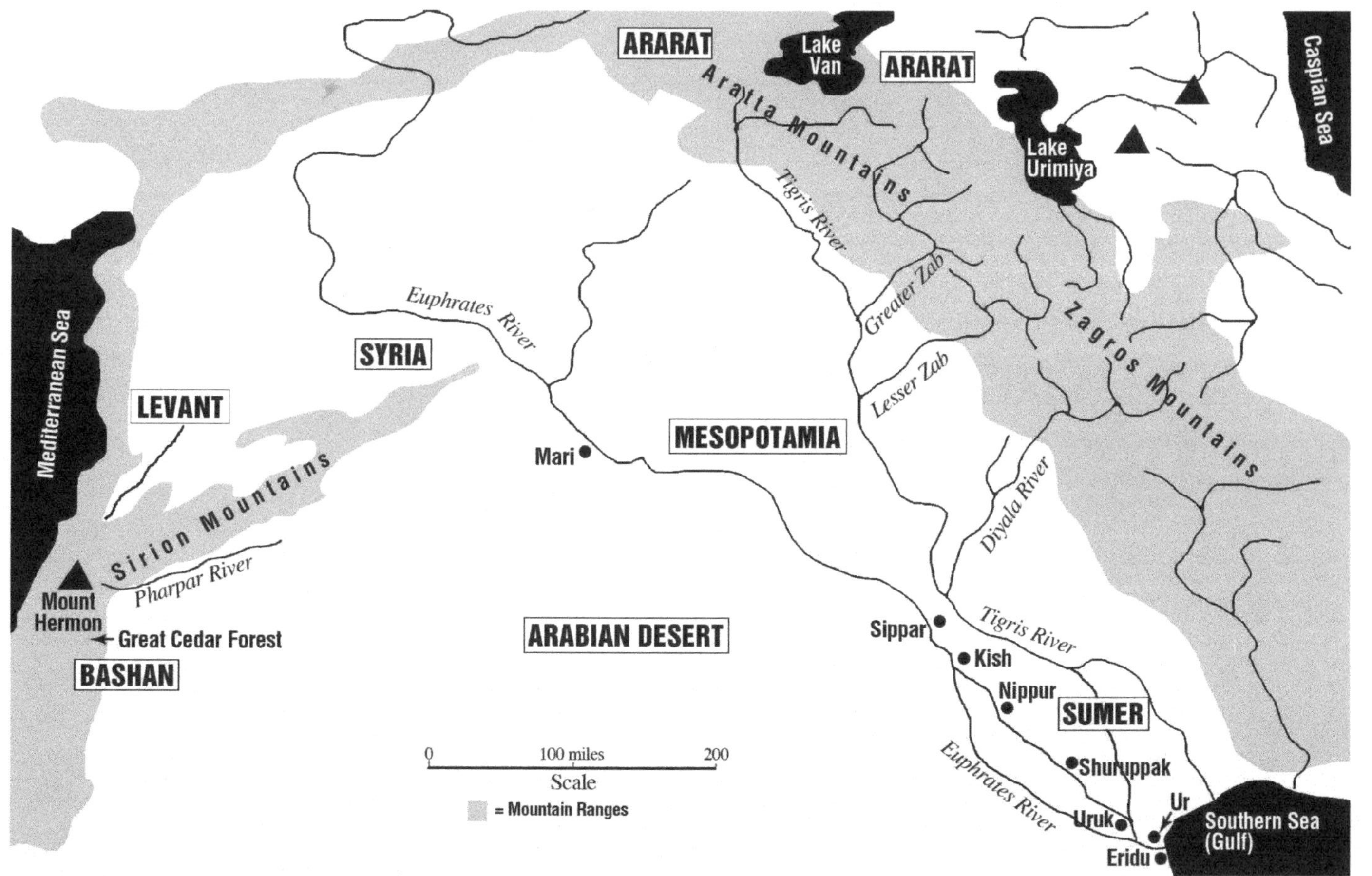
ARARAT
Lake Van
ARARAT
Caspian Sea
Aratta Mountains
Lake Urimiya
Tigris River
Euphrates River
SYRIA
Greater Zab
Zagros Mountains
Lesser Zab
LEVANT
Mediterranean Sea
MESOPOTAMIA
Mari
Sirion Mountains
Diyala River
Pharpar River
Mount Hermon
Great Cedar Forest
BASHAN
ARABIAN DESERT
Sippar
Tigris River
Kish
Nippur
SUMER
0
100 miles
200
Scale
= Mountain Ranges
Shuruppak
Euphrates River
Uruk
Ur
Southern Sea (Gulf)
Eridu

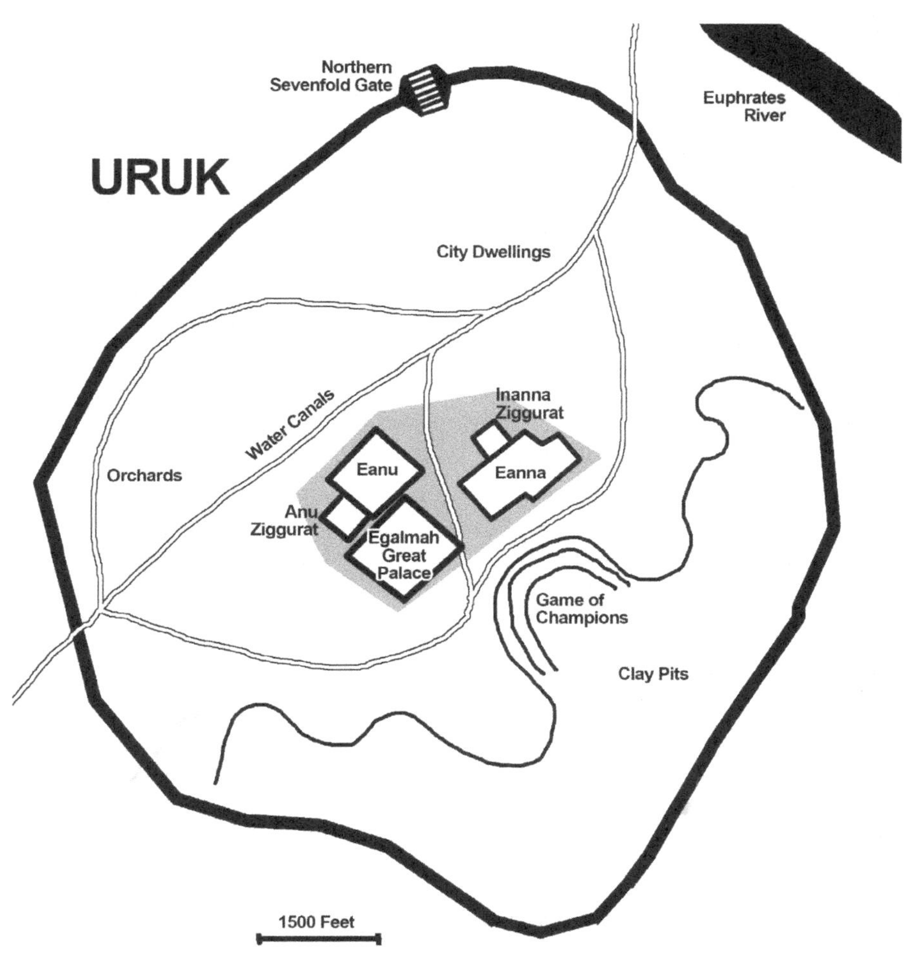
Northern
Sevenfold Gate
Euphrates
River
URUK
City Dwellings
Water Canals
Inanna
Ziggurat
Orchards
Eanu
Eanna
Anu
Ziggurat
Egalmah
Great
Palace
Game of
Champions
Clay Pits
1500 Feet

PROLOGUE

In the time before the Great Flood, the War of Gods and Men raged in the desert of Dudael. Methuselah ben Enoch had led the armies of man, undefiled by genetic manipulation and idol worship, to gloriously defend a last stand of righteousness against the rebel Sons of God called *Watchers* and their demonic minions of hybrid soldiers and giants called *Nephilim*. And then the Deluge came and washed the land clean of the corruption that had infested it.

Noah ben Lamech and his family of eight were spared by Elohim in a large box of a boat, along with a multitude of animals, to repopulate the land. Everyone else and every land animal perished. This floating barge carried Noah and his wife Emzara, and their sons, Shem, Japheth, and Ham. Shem's wife was named Sedeq, Japheth's wife was Adatanes, and Ham's wife was Neela. Neela had been pregnant on the ark and had given birth to the first child of the postdiluvian generation. He was named Cush.

The Nephilim were giant hybrid offspring of the Sons of God and the daughters of men. Though the mortal flesh of these chimeras perished in the Deluge, their divine element remained as demonic spirits that now roamed the earth with an insatiable hunger to inhabit human flesh.

The lead Watchers, Semjaza and Azazel, and their two hundred defiant Watchers, had taken upon themselves the identities of a pantheon of gods to accomplish their scheme. Semjaza became Anu, the high god, and Azazel was Inanna, his consort, the goddess of sex and war.

During the War of Gods and Men, Anu and Inanna, and many of their fellow immortal Watchers were bound by archangels and imprisoned in the heart of the earth until judgment.

But not all of them.

Seventy leaders of the Watchers avoided capture, along with a contingent of their subordinate *mal'akim* insurgent angels. Just how many, no one was sure.

•••••

The ark had come to rest on Mount Nimush near the river Tigris in the mountains of Aratta, that are now called Ararat. After the flood waters receded, Noah left the boat and offered a sacrifice of thanksgiving to Elohim, known by his covenant name of Yahweh. Yahweh made a covenant with Noah and his descendants to never again kill all life on the land with water as he had done. The rainbow in the sky became his signature of that covenant promise.

Yahweh commissioned Noah with the original calling of Adam, to multiply and fill the land. Yahweh had started all over with a new creation and new human race. Humanity was created in God's image and as such was a holy representation of that ruler over creation. The first murderer, Cain, had violated that sacred image by slaying his own brother, and thus starting an evil spiral of violence that dragged the original creation into the very depths of Sheol. Now Yahweh gave Noah the charge to uphold the sacred image of God in man through just recompense. *Whoever sheds the blood of man, by man shall his blood be shed, for God made man in his own image.*

After some time, Noah and his family descended from the mountainous region into the Mesopotamian plains to start anew. They found a sight horrible to behold. The waters had washed over everything, burying the once beautiful fertile terrain in layers of mud and silt. The land was wiped away, leaving a vision of barren ugliness and death. The cities were piles of flooded rubble. The thought of so many people drowned to death sickened them. Noah would often say that all of humanity had been turned to clay.

Even so, life had already begun to break through the graveyard before them. Vegetation quickly sprouted from the seedlings buried in the soil. Elohim had created a resilient earth.

The family of Noah began to multiply and fill the earth. They rebuilt civilization by passing on their acquired knowledge to their descendants. It would take time before cities, culture, and technology were reconstructed to the level they had been before the Flood. But just like the vegetation, civilization would return speedily, because the seeds of such knowledge lay in the accumulated experience in the world before. The growing population pushed forward with a hunger to pick up where it had left off.

Noah had been a warrior before the Deluge. Now he started anew and became a tiller of the soil. He felt weaker, and he was not getting any younger. He set his mind to develop agricultural growth. Emzara his wife taught him what she had learned in her time at Erech. His crowning achievement was a vineyard that sported a vast array of grapes for the fermentation of wine.

But in his heart, Noah was not at peace. He felt the depression of despair over him like the shadow of an Anzu thunderbird. He could not shake it. He had been the Chosen One to end the reign of the gods, bring rest to the land, and bear the Seed of Eve that would war with the Seed of the Serpent. He had faced death too many times to count, fought with gods, survived torture, and even looked into the Abyss of

Sheol. It had been terrifying to experience such frightful extremes, but it also had invigorated him. It had charged through his veins like a drug that fueled intense awareness of every living moment. It made him know he was truly alive.

But now, he was relegated to the position of an old patriarch in the background, as his children spread out and built cities and history. Grandpa Noah, Great-Grandpa Noah, Great-Great-Grandpa Noah. It now seemed to be his only identity. He wondered if anyone would even remember his great journey and exploits in the hands of Elohim. And what of the adventures of his Grandfather Methuselah and Enoch the giant killers? Already fading into the mists of legend. He would have to write down what he remembered, if he could only get around to it. In the meantime, he kept telling his stories to the little grandchildren and great-grandchildren and great-great-grandchildren at his feet. In these were the future.

Emzara was not so sadly disposed. She had been a slave of the priest-king of Erech, living a long time without her husband. She was just happy as a pomegranate to have the rascal finally settled down and with her every day. She determined to make up for the lost years. The making up was not merely friendly companionship and functional interaction, it was oneness.

Noah was a passionate man, but unfortunately, his current despair became an impediment to their union. He had pulled away from her and her heart was breaking. She had led a palace staff, raised a family, defied the gods, but she still found her sense of identity and personal security in being loved by the greatest and truest man she had ever met. If he was in pain, she was in pain. If he was unsettled, she was unsettled.

His drinking concerned her the most. Noah had begun to imbibe too much of the fruit of the vine to wash away his sorrow. He would get drunk and stumble into their bedroom weeping and fall asleep. At least he never got violent. He was too morally upright for that. She knew he had to wrestle with Elohim in his own way. She trusted he would find his way, as he always did. Noah was not a sinless man, but he was a faithful man, a man who had stood righteous in a wicked generation. Now he wrestled with his feelings of unworthiness of such a privilege, and inadequacy as patriarch of the new creation.

Another thing that concerned her as much as Noah's drunkenness was her grandson Cush's oddity. He had been born to Neela and Ham. The firstborn of the new world. He had come out normal and healthy enough. But as he grew up, she sensed a difference in him. He was not like all the other grandchildren or great-grandchildren that were multiplying. He was a bit tall for his age, and had sparkling blue eyes. He was a little delinquent who always seemed to get into trouble with his curiosity. It was not the curiosity of a naïve child. It seemed cold, detached, and calculating. One time Cush sat on the edge of a river bank watching with intense interest as another child was drowning only a few cubits off the bank. He did not run for help, he did not yell for help. He simply watched the child gasping and flailing. The other children screamed for someone who could swim to help the poor thing.

What Emzara could not understand was very simple to Cush. He was not like everyone else. Not even like his mother Neela. As he got older, Cush became more distant from the family. He was the first to leave the greater tribe and start a new people of his own. He named the first of his cities Kish, as a self-tribute alteration of his own name. He called it "the first kingship that came down from heaven" after the Flood.

The ambitious Cush traveled to the south to help rebuild the other cities wiped away by the Flood, including Erech. When one of his children was born a giant, it all became clear to him. Cush surmised that he himself must have been the seed of his mother's union with a god and that she had kept his true identity as a Nephilim from him. He secreted the infant away to protect that identity.

Since Cush was not a giant, the thought had not occurred to anyone that he was anything other than Ham's offspring. Only Emzara asked digging questions which Neela barely escaped with her half-truth answers. The Watcher gods had achieved their goal of suppressing the giantism as a recessive gene that would only manifest in succeeding generations. Their plans of conquest were not over yet. Neela knew none of this. She was simply a damaged woman who hid her shame from her tribe.

But the dishonor of Cush was surpassed by the horror of Emzara's own son, Ham.

Before the Flood, Ham was born and raised within the pagan world of Erech because Emzara had been captured and enslaved when she was pregnant from Noah. Ham had been taken from her, renamed Canaanu, and raised to be a priest of Inanna. His head was elongated according to royal custom under the pressure of wooden slats. He was shorn of all hair by the application of special herbal concoctions. He had been tattooed with the mark of Inanna, a mark that would be a regret the rest of his life. He looked strangely unlike his own brethren, which made him feel even less like them. He never truly fit in.

Though he repented of his pagan upbringing and embraced his true father Noah, when he was rescued from the city, Ham continued to harbor a grudge against the man who had not been there to protect him from the corruption of evil. Ham had converted to Noah's god Elohim, a god who saved him and his immediate family, but had drowned every other living thing in the land to accomplish that elective purpose. It puzzled Ham. How was this any different from Anu's wrath, Inanna's capriciousness, or the oppressive tyranny of the other gods of the pantheon? He had lost more than a dozen close friends and confidants in the waters. They had not been cruel or evil people to him. They had been innocent. They were born into their position just as he had been. Now they too were gone, and he felt all alone in the midst of a family that sought to care for him, but ultimately did not understand him. He wished his mother had never taught him about his past. He wished he had just been completely separated from her, to spare him the tension of two opposing worlds in his soul. He wished he had just been drowned with all his friends.

But he was not drowned. His contempt for his pathetic father and doting mother grew with each passing year. He saw Noah's increasing drunkenness and weak resignation to be the worst form of cowardice. Ham considered his father unworthy to lead their growing clan as patriarch. Whatever heroic deeds Noah may have done before the Deluge were now but distant memories, phantoms of legend. They meant nothing to a new generation that had to move forward into a progressive future of change. Their task was a monumental one. They had to carve, hack, and dig their way through a harsh new world sprouting from the clay and mud of the old. Noah was a symbol of that old clay world, but he would not abdicate his leadership to make way for bolder progressive visions.

In order for the collective to advance, Ham thought, *Noah must be deposed.* Who else would have the forward looking ideas to carry them into the future? Who else would have the courage and the power to bring progressive change? He remembered Anu's intent of fundamentally transforming humankind. That was what they still needed: hope, change, transformation. Not the old ways of thinking.

Emzara became determined to help shake Noah out of his depression. It crushed her to see him so sad and dispirited. She knew it went deep. He was a hearty man who worked hard, fought hard, and played hard. He often said that his favorite place to be in the whole world was with his beloved. But lately, he had not expressed affection toward her. It was as if his wine was another woman stealing his vitality, smirking at her.

She resolved that tonight, she would surprise him. She had never forgotten that his favorite dress had always been a bright red dye linen dress from Egypt. The original dress was long gone now, so she set about carefully recreating it from the cloth supplies they had accumulated. She used red dye made from a madder plant and stitched together a garment. She was sure it would please him. Old age had lessened her beauty, but it did not weaken her spirit. A little heavier make up and some jewelry would get his attention.

She made his favorite meal: steak from a steer's flank, fresh bread, onions and fruit, topped off with a gourd of wine. He was a simple man with simple needs and easily pleased.

Night fell over the tents of the tribe. Noah stumbled into their tent from a day in the fields. Her spirit deflated quickly. He had been drinking, and more heavily than usual. He could barely stand up. He almost took down the whole table of food when he caught himself from falling to the ground.

He saw the food, looked up at Emzara, and blurted out, "You are so — gorgia — gorgiaya — gorge..." He was trying to say the word *gorgeous*.

Emzara started to cry. She did not know what else she could do, what else she could be for him.

Noah saw her tears. "Oh, do not worry," he gurgled. "I may be jrunk, but I am still your love angel."

Noah finished off his gourd of wine and threw it to the ground.

Emzara walked over to their bed and sat down with deep sadness.

Noah struggled to take off his robe and tunic. He fell to the ground, mumbling incoherently.

Emzara broke down weeping. She cried out to Elohim, “Lord, bring me back my hero. Give him back his hope.”

A rustling sound drew her attention to the entrance of the tent. She looked up to see Ham step inside and close the flap.

“Ham ben Noah, your father is in shame. Leave this moment.”

Ham did not leave. He walked over to Noah and looked down on him with disgust.

“Is this my father?” he said.

“I told you to leave this moment. You shame his name,” she barked.

“*I* shame *him*?” he responded. “No, mother, he shames himself. He shames the family name. He shames the clans, the future. He shames his god.”

“How dare you!” she huffed, standing angrily, ready to throw him out with her own hands.

Ham slithered over to her and stood inches away from her face. She tried to stand up to him, to counter his defiance with her own. But he was too powerful. His reptilian glare chilled her. She shrank inside and sat down on the bed, defeated. She could not look him in the face any longer.

“What have I birthed? Have I so completely failed Elohim?”

He knelt down to her level. “No. You did the best you could. Maybe it was Elohim who failed you.”

She stared at him in shock. She slapped him hard across the face. “How dare you question Elohim’s purpose. I do not understand his ways, but he is true to his promise.”

Ham stood back up, glaring at her. His expression melted into a smirk. He gestured at Noah, still on the ground unconscious. “I find *that* a promise unworthy of praise. And I, for one, will no longer sit back and let a floundering drunkard lead the only group of humanity down into the waters of the Abyss.” He gestured again at his father.

"If *that* is Elohim's promise, then I will not submit to such deplorable foolishness. I will make my own promises. I will take the reins of power. I will be the new patriarch."

Emzara looked up in terror at Ham. His eyes had become like a serpent, ready to strike her.

Shem and Japheth had been looking for their brother Ham. He had not worked the herds all day and they were a bit angry with his increasing irresponsibility. They felt that he was acting more like an entitled king than a servant leader of the people of Elohim. Unable to find him, they decided to go to their father's tent and see if their parents knew his whereabouts.

As they approached Noah's tent, they saw Ham leaving and fixing his tunic. He gave them a snide look and walked right up to them.

"Ham, we have been looking for you," said Shem, always the elder brother with a tendency to chastise.

"Well, you have found me," said Ham. But his countenance was disturbing to both Shem and Japheth.

Then they heard the weeping inside the tent.

"Is that mother crying?" asked Japheth.

"Where is father?" added Shem without pause.

"Drunk on the ground, where else?" said Ham.

Shem knew that something was deadly wrong. "What have you done, brother?" he said.

Ham responded with a diabolical casualness, "I have uncovered father's nakedness. My child's name shall be Canaan."

The words ripped into Shem and Japheth like a dagger. The meaning of the saying "uncovering a man's nakedness" was the abuse of his wife. In a patriarchal society, it was the ultimate humiliation and usurpation of a leader's authority. Ham had contested his father's tribal power.

Shem and Japheth raced to the tent and tore back the flap. Noah sprawled passed out on the ground as Ham had said. Emzara lay brutally battered, weeping into the pillow.

Before they could see her nakedness, the brothers averted their eyes. They grabbed one of Noah's cloaks from the ground where he dropped it. They walked backwards with the garment on their shoulders toward their mother and covered her.

In the morning, Noah awoke sober and learned what Ham had done to him. He called for the elders of the community. As the displaced patriarch, Noah no longer had the authority he once wielded.

But Ham's crime could never take away Noah's special relation to Elohim. He stood before the tribe and pronounced a curse. Not a curse on Ham, but a curse on his offspring. Noah had learned that Ham had abused Emzara, so his sins would carry down to his own children and their children's children.

Ham had declared that his next child would be named Canaan.

"Cursed be Canaan," said Noah. "A slave of slaves shall he be to his brothers. Blessed be Yahweh, the god of Shem; and let Canaan be his slave. May Elohim enlarge Japheth, and let him dwell in the tents of Shem, and let Canaan be his slave."

It shocked the elders. Noah had used the covenant name of Elohim in his curse: Yahweh. As Patriarch he had the authority to do so, but it was an authority rarely exercised. Why did he curse the son instead of the father? Canaan was not the offender, Ham was. Should a son suffer the wages of a father's sin? Does Elohim visit the iniquity of a man upon his succeeding generations?

But what Noah had done was not personal vendetta. It was an act of protection for the sacred and social identity of the family and the community. Without moral taboo, civilization would fall faster than it could rise.

The community's response illustrated the power of internal evil to divide and conquer a people. Ham's evil act caused a rift in the clans. The sons of Shem supported the call for judgment upon Ham. They wanted nothing less than his life for the violation of his parents' sacred honor. Japheth and his tribes considered it wicked, but not worthy of the penalty of death. Banishment or exile, but not death. Yahweh's covenant with Noah after the Flood included the justice of a life for a life. If any man would shed another man's blood, by man should his blood be shed. The desecration of man as the image of God marked the rejection of the Creator and the beginning of the end of civilization. But did this crime rise to the level of shedding blood? They could not agree.

Meanwhile, Ham prepared his sons to leave for the south and west with future hopes of sea exploration of distant lands. He was already exiling himself. Perhaps the issue of his punishment was moot. He had made claim to the position of tribal patriarch, and now planned to leave the tribe. What drove a man to such levels of depravity? It seemed more an act of ultimate defiance of authority than one of claiming it.

Ham's actions started an avalanche of reactions with far reaching repercussions. The elders conferred at length and came to the conclusion that it was time for all of them to spread out over the Land of the Two Rivers. This event became the catalyst for something they should have done from the start. Only fear had kept them from fulfilling Elohim's command to be fruitful and multiply *and fill the earth*.

The sons of Shem settled the central and eastern region of Mesopotamia. The sons of Japheth migrated to the northern reaches. They built their new cities on the ruins of the old, changing names as language changed. Erech became known as Uruk and the land of Shinar became Sumer.

Noah and Emzara waited until Ham's son Canaan was born, before they left him in the hands of his brothers. They then traveled down the Euphrates to the Southern Sea. They sailed for the magical island of Dilmun. It was known as the Land of the Living, where the sun rises at the mouth of the rivers. It soon inspired a host of legends about the gateway to the underworld. For Noah and Emzara, it meant a chance to start a new life away from the shame. Since their family had spread to cover the known lands, the only place they would be untouched by their painful memory would be a distant unknown location. He became known as Noah the Faraway or Utnapishtim the Distant.

So the sons of Noah spread out along the river basin and multiplied. But the dispersal would only serve to delay the inevitable, for the evil that is in the heart of man goes with him wherever he goes.

As generations passed, the memory of Noah faded into legend and lore. The rightful lordship of Elohim over the earth was too soon replaced again by the old gods of the pantheon. Everyone had forgotten the past. Everyone had forgotten who they were. Everyone had forgotten Elohim. They had become futile in their thinking and their foolish hearts were darkened. They exchanged the truth of Elohim for a lie. They worshipped and served the creature and creation in place of the Creator.

And Elohim gave them over to their depravity.

CHAPTER 1

The great feline moved through the tall grass of the plain. It crouched low, muscles tensed and senses alert to every sound and smell. Unusually large, the size of seven men, it inched forward in the stealth of predatorial approach through the wavy brush. This uncanny skill in the kill had already brought long life to the wily hunter. Its mane was kingly, its musculature lean and taught, its claws and teeth, protracted and sharp.

It smelled blood.

At the end of the grassy area near the river's edge, the daunting cat froze. It saw a group of several humans in a clearing, cleaning the carcasses of animal prey hanging from the trees. Twenty gazelles, some wild boar, and a dozen ibexes dangled enticingly from the low limbs. A feast for the king of beasts.

But the great lion was not looking at the fresh meat. It stared at the large figure laying the animals onto a cart for transportation. He was clearly the alpha male, towering above the others. He was mighty, picking up the bodies of the animals with muscular ease. He sported a full but manicured beard of dark hair and wore a chignon cloth band around his head that kept his long locks from obstructing his view. A tunic hung about his waist, exposing a naked torso and an animal skin draped on his shoulders like a small cape. If the predator had been human it would have been struck by the charisma and handsomeness of the Hunter.

But the predator was not human. It saw a challenging guardian keeping the lion from its meal.

Strangely, the beast had no fear of the Hunter. Though the human was extraordinarily large, the lion had killed many men, demonstrating its ability to stay alive for so long. Fear would not stop it from seeking prey, but fear was a necessary element in producing increased strength and heightened awareness for battle. But this time, it was as if there was a spell on the beast. The lion prepared to kill, but with the lack of fear that might accompany the killing of a strong enemy on the plain.

The soft breeze carried the musk of the sweaty Hunter's scent to the lion's nostrils. It licked its lips with hunger. It crouched low to the ground waiting for its moment to pounce.

The Hunter threw a gazelle on the pile of others in the cart. The four other men with him were servants. All the animals they were cleaning and preparing were victims of the Hunter's skills. He used sport to distract his restless spirit.

He also had preternatural senses. Those senses awoke and he stopped what he was doing. He sensed something watching him. No, not merely watching. He was being preyed upon.

The Hunter looked about and saw the men cleaning the animals from the trees, oblivious to their impending doom. He scrutinized the brush mere cubits away from himself. But then he glanced behind him. He set his spear beside the cart and pulled out his dagger and axe. In front, and behind, *there were two of them.*

No, wait. Three. It was an ambush.

Before he could yell out a warning, the lions attacked.

The lion that stalked the Hunter leaped out of its hiding. It covered the short distance in a mere couple of strides. The other two lions were female, a large one and a small one. They surprised the men in the rear and ripped them to shreds with relative ease.

The Hunter was ready, and he was very good. His fear had spiked his strength. He caught the giant beast in the belly with his blade as it pounced on him. His other arm caught the fangs and claws of the monster in his copper forearm band. He pulled the dagger upward and sliced open the lion's underside. The lion howled in pain and released its grip on the ax-wielding arm. The Hunter rolled on top of the lion, raising his axe high. It would take a few more moments before the lion died, so he took no chances. He swung down. The attacker went limp.

The two female lions finished off the four servants and turned to face the Hunter. Their mouths and claws dripped blood. The big one stayed back, sizing up its prey. The smaller one was not so cautious. She slunk forward, eyes mad with rage. Smaller than her companions, she was still clearly more vicious and experienced. Without a bulky mane to get in her way, she was streamlined for killing. Her mate was dead. She prepared to maul this large human and lick its bones.

But the Hunter was not merely a human. He was also part god. He had been wanting to rid the land of these menaces. The lions had killed too many people of his city for too long.

The lioness did not care about the Hunter's heritage. It jumped at him. The Hunter ducked and the lioness rolled on the ground in a pile of fangs, claws, and dust, hitting its head on a tree. The Hunter only had his dagger, so he dashed to the cart and grabbed his spear.

Dizzy from the head injury, the lioness tried to shake off unconsciousness. The harsh bark of the tree ripped off a patch of skin and hair above the eyebrow. Blood dripped down into its blinking eye.

The Hunter raised his spear to pierce the lioness, but he felt the approach of the other one from his rear.

He whirled. The large cat was already in the air.

The Hunter barely got the spear point up as the lioness came crashing down upon him.

The spear ran right through her jaw and up through her brain, killing her instantly. The shaft broke under the weight of the monster. The mass of dead animal bore the Hunter to the ground.

He got up as quickly as he had fallen. He knew that the worst of the fight lay ahead. Once the bruised female had gotten back its senses, it would be more ferocious than its companions.

The Hunter glanced around. The lioness escaped into the brush. Its head wound must have been bad after all. He noticed that his animal skins had come off his body in the fray. This lioness was a vicious killer, but she was also an intelligent killer. When her fear came back, so too did her senses. She would not fight with the disadvantage of a bleeding, dizzying wound against so mighty a hunter. So she left to live another day. To kill another day.

The Hunter dusted himself off. He sighed at the sight of his dead servants. It was not sentiment for their lives that moved him. He would have to bury them, finish the cleaning, and bring everything back to the city himself.

He picked up the animal skins that had fallen from his shoulders onto the ground. They had been a special gift from his mother, a goddess. She had assured him that they bore the magical property of removing the natural fear of animals toward the wearer. The skins allowed him to get closer to his prey for easier kill before they bounded away. They also threw off the senses of predators like lions.

Some might think this was an unfair advantage. He was a mighty hunter, a powerful warrior, but he was not stupid. Victory was superior to honor. If wearing a magic pelt gave him advantage, then so be it. Glory would only be increased by survival, not defeat. He was victor and that is what mattered most.

The Hunter approached the entrance of the vast walled city. He led the cart alone through the seven-fold gate, before entering the public square. He even helped the donkeys to pull their overloaded cargo of animal flesh with his mighty strength. On the top of that load were the bodies of two immense lions. The sound of trumpets announced his presence. A cheering crowd heralded him in the streets.

He approached the entrance of his palace, to be welcomed by the smiling queen mother and high-priestess of Shamash, the goddess Ninsun.

She crowed with pride to the Hunter, "Welcome back, Scion of Uruk, Wild Bull on the Rampage, one third mortal and two thirds divine!"

The crowd cheered again.

The Hunter smiled at the grandiose exaltation. It was formal, but it was appropriate. He was Gilgamesh, Lord and King of Uruk.

CHAPTER 2

The new city of Uruk was built upon the ruins of the old that had been destroyed in the Deluge. All the cities of the area had likewise been rebuilt: Eridu, Ur, Shuruppak and the others. But Uruk had grown quickly to become once again the largest city-state in Sumer, boasting over sixty thousand residents. Its territory covered three and a half square miles of land. One square mile of city, one square mile of orchards, one square mile of clay pits, and one half square mile for the temple mount.

Following his predecessors, Gilgamesh had restored the cult centers along with their religious worship of deity. Inanna's and Anu's temples were rehabilitated with an extra flourish that Gilgamesh added to all his ventures. He did it to establish his unsurpassed greatness. His own Great Palace stood in the same district and included a temple, *Egalmah,* for his mother, the goddess Ninsun.

After the Deluge, most of the gods no longer showed their presence to mankind as they used to do. They seemed strangely distant. The religious priesthood continued presenting the images of the gods made from stone and wood. They still performed their "opening of the mouth" ceremony to bring the breath of the god into the statue and make it a living representation of the deity's presence. Rumors said that the pantheon was hidden away in its holy mountain,

Hermon, in the west, because the devastation of the flood waters had sent shock waves through their ranks. But no one really knew why.

Not long after the Deluge, scribes in their tablet schools began spinning their own yarns to suit their purposes. They declared that Enlil, the god of the air, had been angry at the clamor of humanity and proposed to send a flood to wipe them all out. But Enki, the crafty god of the waters of the Abyss, warned Noah, a leader of Shuruppak, called "Ziusudra" by some, to build a boat and escape the wrath. So Enki had thwarted the plans of Enlil, just when Enlil was trying to take charge of the pantheon. Anu, the high god of the pantheon, had faded into the background as a more distant deity.

The scribes did not know the reality behind their myths. Anu was actually the Watcher Semjaza. He had faded in his historical presence because he had been bound into the heart of the earth by Uriel the archangel during the War of Gods and Men at the time of the Flood. All the seven high gods "who decree the fates" had been imprisoned in that battle because they too were rebel Watchers of Elohim's heavenly host.

The only one of the high gods not bound in the earth was Utu, the sun god, who escaped in a fit of cowardice during the battle. He had also run away in the earlier Titanomachy and the War on Eden, which made him a particular nuisance to the plans of the divine pantheon. Utu changed his name to Shamash, but remained a sun god. Other surviving Watchers had taken over the identities of the absent high gods so as to insure the continuity of their rule over mankind. There was a new Enlil, and a new Anu, a new Enki, Nanna, and Ninhursag.

The only deity whose identity was not taken over was Inanna. She had been seized in the mouth of Rahab the sea dragon and buried under tons of sediment in the Flood. Her reputation for self-aggrandizement and violence was so notorious that no Watcher wanted to carry that stigma with them into the new world. But what the humans did not know would not hurt them. So they continued to venerate Inanna throughout the land.

Irrigation canals were re-dug to bring water from the Euphrates River into the fields surrounding the city, fields tended by the farmers. The city walls were a new addition by Gilgamesh.

The land of Sumer was a confederation of city-states with their own economies, governmental bureaucracy, and patron deities. Though they traded with one another and usually respected their boundaries, the nature of humankind is always to take more. Hostilities had grown between the cities and some engaged in battles over territory and passage rights on the Tigris and Euphrates rivers. The two rivers were still the lifeline of the land that brought water for crops and transportation for trade. It became evident to some that control of the waterway would lead to control of the land, so the cities on the edge of the river vied for that control by charging duties and transportation taxes. It was a seedling of trouble that would prove to grow into a tree of thorns.

Gilgamesh saw this growing aggression as a threat to the safety of Uruk, so he embarked upon a massive project to build a protective wall around his city such as none had ever seen. It was a mighty wall worthy of a mighty king who was determined to make a name for himself in history. Rising fifty cubits high, or seventy-five feet, the wall boasted a seven-fold gateway protecting the entrance into the city. A chariot could ride across its threshold with a full rig of horses. The meticulous brickwork, made of kiln-fired bricks, could withstand weather, war, and even floodwaters, unlike the more common mud bricks of most of the building structures. The material needed for this glorious enterprise was so massive that the clay pits for brick making took up one third of the city and were going deeper into the earth with every day of building. The labor needed to accomplish this feat of construction was so overwhelming that King Gilgamesh had to institute forced slave labor upon the citizens for many years, just to have any hope of actually finishing the massive brick snake that wound its way around the city.

"And therein lies your flaw, Gilgamesh," whispered Ninsun.

Gilgamesh sat on his throne, washed up from the hunt. He was a majestic nine feet tall. Ninsun stood close by. He posed motionless so an artisan could carve an accurate likeness of his face into a clay tablet while another sculpted a statuette. They were commemorating his slaughter of the two great lions by crafting images of him as "Lord of the Animals," savior of his people.

On the artist's clay tablet, the king's muscular likeness stood mightily in the center, his hands stretched out to grasp the throat of a lion on either side of him. On his head rested the horned headdress of deity. His throne also sported a carved stone lion on either side as a symbol of his royalty, so the symbolic animals he held exalted his reputation and glory.

The actual skins of the huge lions were being stripped from their carcasses and cured by tanners. They would be put on display in his palace later. Gilgamesh neglected to mention to anyone the missing third lioness. The escape was not good for his reputation. Who would believe that the smaller female was more ferocious? And the legendary fame of two vanquished lions would forever be ruined by "the one that got away." He decided it was an extraneous detail that need not spoil the grandness of his gallant story and artwork.

Gilgamesh responded to Ninsun in a whisper, so as not to be heard by the artists. "I have restored the cosmic rites of the gods, I opened up passes in the mountains for travel, dug many wells of water for my people, and I have brought much fame upon Uruk by building walls of strength and glory."

"And you have done so at the expense of your own subjects," Ninsun added. "You are working your own people into an early grave." As a high-priestess of Shamash, Ninsun was in touch with the soul of the commoner. She heard their confessions and prayers to Shamash for deliverance from their king's oppressive demands.

"I ask nothing of them that I do not also ask of myself," he hissed back.

"True enough, my son," she said. "But they are not part god as you are. The workers in the pits and on the wall are working day and night in rotating shifts with nary a rest for their labors. You must allow them some happiness or they may rise up in sheer desperation."

"That is why they will not rise up. Because they fear their king," he said.

"A healthy fear maintains authority, law, and order," she said. "But a cruel fear breeds resentment, spite, and chaos. Leave them some time to tend to their families and their own gardens of produce. Then they will die for you if you ask them to."

Gilgamesh let her words sink in. His mother was his most respected counsel and he took her words to heart. A melancholy spirit came over him and he barely whispered, "Father created a healthy fear."

"Yes, he did," she said. "But he was a good king. Holy Lugalbanda." Her eyes sparkled with reminiscence. "I was his child bride, but he treated me with tender consideration on our wedding night. Like you, he had the divine right of kings. But he was kind. And my loyalty was eternal."

Gilgamesh looked at Ninsun. She had a wise way of saying several things through metaphor. This time, she spoke not merely about treating subjects with goodness. Another meaning penetrated her words. For Gilgamesh's slave-driving impatience was not his only weakness. He was a giant born of the union of god and human. He was a *Gibbor*, a mighty warrior with a mighty appetite for two things: combat and women.

CHAPTER 3

The wedding parties at the banquet, comprised of the families and communities of the bride and bridegroom, numbered about two hundred or so celebrants. Beer and wine flowed heavily in the cups of the attendees. The celebration had filled the partially blocked off neighborhood of the bride for seven days. The marriage was typical, arranged by the parents of both sides for economic or familial benefits. The bridegroom had given a bride price of ten shekels of silver and some livestock. It served as a down payment for the engagement, followed by a large gift of foodstuffs at the wedding banquet. The bride's father had provided her a dowry of precious metals and stones that would remain her own property to protect her in case of her husband's death, divorce, or other personal tragedy.

On this last day of the party, the bride had been covered with a veil by her father that would be taken off later by her new husband. Normally, friends of the bridegroom, called "best-men," would oversee the couple in order to protect the bride against demons.

But the happiness of this celebration barely kept at bay the sadness that hung over the evening like a shadow. Their gazes all turned to the looming figure of King Gilgamesh standing in the shadows of the threshold. For a long time now, Gilgamesh had enforced the institution of *jus prima noctis*, the divine right of the Lord to spend the first night with all brides of the city. It was a way for him to assert his status of kingly power over the men of the city-state.

There were political benefits as well. If many women had their firstborn through union with the king, rebellion or insurrection would be less likely because of the deep primal feelings of family ties to his majesty.

At least, that was how he thought of it. His mother, Ninsun thought differently.

"There are plenty of hierodules to satisfy your appetite," she would say. A hierodule was one of many sacred temple prostitutes.

"As king you already have complete control over the male citizens' bodies and allegiance. They must submit to you, work for you, fight and die for you. If you allow them nothing of their own, you will breed resentment that will lead to resignation and despair. And a man who has nothing left to lose is a dangerous man who will stop at nothing if he chooses revenge."

Gilgamesh was not concerned. He knew he could out-fight any angry man of the city at any time. If any one of them tried to hurt their king, he would execute that rebel for treason. He was after all the king, and the king was the law. *They should thank me for being kind and tender with their wives,* he justified to himself. *I choose such graciousness, it is not my obligation.*

The wedding guests tried to ignore what was happening by giving their attention to their feasting and fellowship. The bridegroom took the bride in his arms and raised her veil. She was weeping. He too had tears of pain rolling down his cheek. But this was their fate. They would simply have to accept the injustice as the price they paid for being citizens of the greatest city of Sumer. He kissed her, and whispered a promise of hope in her ear. He turned and led her into the hands of Gilgamesh. The king gently led her away for the evening. The bridegroom downed a half dozen goblets of beer in order to numb himself to the incomparable personal injury he and his new wife would experience. They had no choice in the matter. Gilgamesh was their king.

CHAPTER 4

The next day, the Game of Champions took place in the huge clay pits. The pits made a natural amphitheater due to the gradual slope of the sides. This amphitheater could easily seat thousands of the citizenry as viewers of the spectacle that took place a hundred cubits below. The brick-making tools and equipment had been cleared away to make room for the warriors to fight. The Game was a frequent event consisting of warriors fighting against the king, though not a duel to the death. It was a contest of strength, wit, and strategy, but it often ended in broken bones and unconsciousness.

Some thought the Game was only a staged spectacle to glorify the king — until they joined it themselves and had their back broken or their nose set flowing with blood. Gilgamesh mandated participation in order to have an outlet for his pent-up energy that made him restless, impatient, and prone to hot-tempered outbursts.

Every tournament consisted of three or four men challenging Gilgamesh in boxing, wrestling, or fighting with staffs, rods, and other non-lethal weapons. Because of his superior size, strength, and skill as a Gibbor, Gilgamesh had to increase the number of his opponents to even the odds. The tradition had started innocently enough with the challengers holding back or feigning attack, wary of the consequences of defeating or hurting their king. But Gilgamesh could not accept such half-heartedness and soon demanded the warriors truly seek to conquer him.

He upped the stakes by offering them the Right Hand of his kingdom and abundant wealth if they could but pin him, knock him unconscious, or break a bone. The office of the Right Hand of the king was the highest honor in the city. The Right Hand acted in the name of the king, carrying out his wishes with the complete authority of the state assembly behind him. The only one with more authority was the king himself.

Gilgamesh swore upon his holy honor that the victor would truly be granted this authority. He even did so in the temple of Inanna, at the altar of Shamash, in the presence of the entire city as well as his mother Ninsun. Gilgamesh was a hard taskmaster, and aloof from those whom he ruled, but one thing he was not was a liar. If he gave his word, he would honor it, if only just to magnify his reputation of integrity.

The oath had the desired effect. Warriors not only gave their all in sparring with their ruler, they even practiced, planned, and strategized with one another before the Games, in the hope of outwitting Gilgamesh. All for the prize of being the Right Hand of the King. Unfortunately, the fighting would sometimes get out of hand as warriors were pushed to desperation. When it did, Gilgamesh would meet them with equal ferocity, resulting in broken bones and other damages. A couple of times Gilgamesh had accidentally killed a contestant. He paid the family proper compensation, and provided a glorious burial, but it was still not good for his legacy.

He had been so invigorated by his recent victory over the lions that he decided to face the largest number of combatants he had ever faced in the Games: six experienced challengers at once. The increased number of opponents would be difficult. But he felt confident.

There was a small detail he did not know: one of the fighters had a personal vendetta against him. Dumuzi the Shepherd, had experienced the gut wrenching pain of *jus prima noctis*, forced upon him by Gilgamesh. Shortly afterward, he lost his wife to sickness. Ninsun's fears had materialized. A man had finally come to kill Gilgamesh. Dumuzi planned to do so with a hidden knife to use at just the right moment.

Dumuzi recognized two of the contestants as soldiers, but the other three he had never seen before. He thought they looked like foreigners. But he knew they could not be so because foreigners were not allowed in the Games. The six men surrounded Gilgamesh. Dumuzi had a shepherd's staff. He had become adept at fighting wolves and other predators of his flock. He had also become quite a skilled hunter. One combatant had a rope, another had a net, two were competition wrestlers, and one was a champion boxer who had once knocked out a bull with a punch. Gilgamesh had his bare hands and wore only a simple loin cloth and sandals.

He looked at his opponents and smiled to himself. Could any of these men have killed the two great lions? Not even all of them together.

Dumuzi attacked first. He started hastily, but he did have a plan. He swung his staff with martial accuracy and got in a couple of good blunt hits. Then Gilgamesh wrenched the staff from him. He threw Dumuzi ten feet away. The Shepherd landed with a thud in a cloud of dust, and lost his breath.

The two wrestlers pounced simultaneously. One would have been a challenge, but two threw Gilgamesh off balance. He fell to the ground and they moved to pin him. They should not have been so confident. Gilgamesh grabbed both their heads and knocked them together with a loud CRACK, echoing through the amphitheater.

Groans of sympathetic pain peppered the crowd. Three were down quickly. Gilgamesh looked at the other three with a grin.

Dumuzi pulled his secreted dagger from his boot and crawled through the dust cloud. He snuck toward the back of Gilgamesh as the king focused on the other three fighters. Gilgamesh considered Dumuzi out for the count and therefore out of his attention. That was exactly what Dumuzi had planned. He thought it would be easy to come up from behind and slip a blade into the king's kidney or spleen and slice his life force right out of him.

Before Dumuzi could act, the fight took a turn that surprised everyone.

The other three fighters positioned themselves at preplanned locations. They each stooped down to quickly brush away some of the dirt on the ground. Even Gilgamesh paused, curious.

The three warriors quickly pulled up a series of hidden weapons. One drew a sword, another a battle axe, and the third a javelin. The swordsman screamed at the top of his lungs, "For the honor of King Agga!"

They attacked.

When Gilgamesh heard the war cry, he instantly knew their identity. Agga had been king of Kish. The two cities had been at odds for some time. Kish had been the first city to have kingship lowered from heaven after the Flood. As current regent of that city, Agga had become quite aggressive in his attempt to dominate the region. He had demanded a tribute from Uruk. The elders of the city had counseled Gilgamesh to pay it and avoid hostilities. Gilgamesh refused and gathered the army on his side. Agga besieged Uruk. The walls of Uruk were not yet complete, so Gilgamesh was vulnerable.

Gilgamesh's first envoy to Agga, Birhurturra, was detained and beaten. Agga's offense so incensed Gilgamesh that he personally snuck into Agga's encampment on his own that night and surprised the king in his tent. Gilgamesh did not kill Agga. Instead, he held his axe in hand and whispered to his opponent with poetic flair, "Agga, my lord, you once gave me safe refuge when I was on the run. You gave me my life. Now you seek to subdue Uruk, blessed of the gods, its great wall reaching the sky, the sacred temple-tower of Anu. Now, what am I to do with *you*?"

Agga lay trembling and damp with sweat. He could think of nothing other than to ask for mercy, but to do so in a way that retained his dignity. In a voice that mustered as much courage as he could, he whimpered, "Repay my favor?"

Gilgamesh grinned with satisfaction. "Now, we are even," he said. "The next time I see you, we will not be. So take care, great king and hero. I set you free to return to Kish."

Before Agga could gather himself together, Gilgamesh had disappeared into the night.

Gilgamesh had Agga in his hands and did not kill him. Agga was so unnerved by the incident that he packed up and ended the siege. Gilgamesh's little taunt was enough to stop the inevitable war. But it also had completely emasculated Agga. And Agga had never forgotten.

So the king of Kish had conspired to have his three best mercenary killers slip into the roster of the Games, unnoticed. They had planted the weapons the night before, after the arena was cleared for the battle. Now they lunged at Gilgamesh with murderous intent.

Gilgamesh's survival instinct leapt up. He responded to the attack before he knew what he was doing. The swordsman swung his blade in slashing arcs so quickly, Gilgamesh could not dodge them. But Gilgamesh was nine feet tall and had very powerful legs. When the swordsman was almost upon him, Gilgamesh crouched and jumped ten feet in the air over the swordsman. He landed in a roll behind him.

Gilgamesh did not hear the crowd cheering above them. None of the fighters did. All their senses focused on the fight and the kill.

The spearman thrust his javelin, attempting to skewer Gilgamesh. That was the first mistake. Gilgamesh twisted to the side and grabbed the javelin in the air before it could pass him by. Now he had a weapon. The spearman's eyes widened with shock. Instead of using the javelin, Gilgamesh broke it in two and tossed it to the ground. That act of confidence and disdain would have sent most fighters running. However, these were battle hardened warriors who considered Gilgamesh's action an advantage for them. That was their second mistake.

The axeman swung. Gilgamesh dodged. He looked as if he was giving the axeman a second chance. The axeman swung again, and Gilgamesh dodged again. The axeman became frustrated at the ease with which Gilgamesh moved. And that was the third mistake.

He swung down to cleave Gilgamesh in two. But the king was not there. The axe buried itself deep in the dirt. Before he could jerk it back out, Gilgamesh took the warrior and crushed his skull in his hands.

The spearman jumped, and landed on Gilgamesh with just enough force to throw him to the ground. Gilgamesh rolled, breaking the warrior's back beneath him.

The king rolled to a stop and looked up, at the raised blade of the swordsman now standing over him.

Dumuzi watched the entire fight. When he saw his king in danger, he instinctively threw his dagger across the distance. It plunged into the back of the swordsman. The blade did not kill him, but it halted him long enough for Gilgamesh to react. He extended his legs around the swordsman's feet and rolled, bringing the opponent down to the ground.

Gilgamesh punched through his throat and ripped out his esophagus.

The king looked up at Dumuzi.

Then Gilgamesh finally heard the crowd for the first time. It roared wildly with bloodlust in support of their king.

Gilgamesh got to his feet, keeping his gaze on Dumuzi. He strolled over to the man and stared down into his eyes.

Dumuzi froze like a statue in the face of a god. The shepherd did not know why he had acted so contrarily to his passions. Perhaps it was training or loyalty to his city-state. But he knew now that his life lay entirely in the hands of his king, hands that could crush him like a bug.

Gilgamesh leaned close and whispered, “I am not going to ask you where you got the knife. You saved the life of your king. You will receive honor. And perhaps any misgivings you may have had will no longer remain to lead you to an early grave.”

As the mighty Gibbor king of Uruk, Gilgamesh could execute him on the spot. But he did not. He did not give Dumuzi what he deserved. It was an act of grace.

It dumbfounded Dumuzi. He blurted out, “My lord and king,” without thinking.

Gilgamesh smiled. He turned to the crowd with a triumphant lift of his fists. They applauded with a standing ovation. Many of them had secretly wished success for the assassins, but they cheered the winner because he had won. It was the way of Sumer. Might made right, and he was Gilgamesh the mighty, the Scion of Uruk, the Wild Bull on the Rampage.

Power was god.

CHAPTER 5

Dumuzi cleaned himself up and was ushered into the presence of the king. Because his protection of the king had been an ambiguous affair, Gilgamesh avoided a big display of celebration in Dumuzi's honor. But he granted Dumuzi an increase in pay and an extended vacation from his shepherding, to go on a hunting expedition.

Dumuzi enjoyed hunting. He had become quite skilled in the art of the bow as well as the javelin. Gilgamesh outfitted him with an entourage of servants and equipment fit for a king. He was accompanied by a cook, several slaves, a handful of other hunters, and some hierodules from the temple. Dumuzi had also received permission to bring his father with him, so he would not be without family. He had a hunting chariot outfitted with a team of horses, and a pack of mastiffs, a large and powerful breed of hunting dog that could confront lions.

Dumuzi traveled from Uruk to a steppe of prairie grasslands that he knew teamed with game of all kinds, from gazelle and ibex to boar and fowl. It resembled the king's own special hunting park near the city. The king kept captured animals in cages and often released them for a royal hunt. Dumuzi was charged with bringing back some of those very animals to replenish the king's cages.

Dumuzi found a watering hole on the grasslands that would draw all the game he sought. He set up camp some distance from the water and dug some pits and set traps. In the first several days, he captured a host of animals. He began to feel as if this was going to be an enjoyable and easy hunt.

Then he found a trap sprung with nothing in it. Not long after that, he discovered others filled with dirt, rendering them useless. The pattern repeated itself too often to be accidental. He suspected that someone on the expedition was sabotaging his efforts to please the king.

He held a gathering of the entire entourage to find the culprit. No one would confess to the vandalism. So he staked out some of his traps to see if he could catch the criminal in the act, with no results. It was as if the saboteur knew where he was hiding. Only the traps that were not being watched were dismantled or destroyed.

One day, exhausted with frustration, Dumuzi went alone to the watering hole to fill his skin with water. When he reached the water's edge, he noticed some creatures sitting at the other end of the large pond quenching their thirst: a wild ox, a gazelle, and something else that was not game. But Dumuzi was not sure it was human either. It was large, about six and a half feet tall. It seemed muscular, with the structure of a man, a naked man, covered with long unkempt hair.

It looked up, seeing Dumuzi. It froze.

Dumuzi knew then what it was: a Wild Born. He had heard of such primal creatures, but had always thought they were just a legend, a story to tell children to scare them into being civilized little citizens.

The Wild Born apparently protected the wild animals. It ran off and the animals followed.

Dumuzi came back at the same time for several days, only to see the same Wild Born drinking at the watering hole with thirsty abandon. When it saw Dumuzi, it would run off. Dumuzi tried to follow him, but the Wild Born was so fast and powerful that Dumuzi could not begin to get near him.

One night around the campfire, Dumuzi finally spoke up, "Father, I have found the scoundrel that is destroying my traps and frustrating our hunt. It is a Wild Born. I saw him at the watering hole three days in a row."

"Indeed?" said his father.

"So they are real after all," said Dumuzi.

"Indeed, they are."

"And you never told me, your son?"

"You never asked me, your father," said his father, with a twinkle in his eye.

"What should I do?" asked Dumuzi. "He is too fast for even the mastiffs, should I set them upon him. I understand the way of the lion and the bull or even the bear. But a Wild Born is a mystery to me."

His father smiled. "Well, my son, he is wild, is he not?"

"Yes," said Dumuzi.

"Which makes him an animal. But he is also a man, is he not?" asked his father.

"Yes," answered Dumuzi.

"Well," his father continued, "then we understand his nature perhaps more than he understands himself."

Dumuzi's eyes brightened as he followed his father's chain of reasoning.

"If you want to trap a man," his father queried, "what is the weakness of all men?"

Dumuzi smiled broadly. He would get this Wild Born now.

CHAPTER 6

Gilgamesh awoke with a start. It was deep in the night. He had just had the second nightmare that had seemed so real to him he knew they were omens of some kind. He arose and strode through the night air, crossing the distance from the palace to the temple of Shamash, where his mother resided as high priestess.

The guards instantly accompanied him at his arrival, leading him to her bedroom. He knocked lightly on the door.

"Enter, Gilgamesh," her voice came from inside. She knew him intimately, even the sound of his knock.

He entered.

"What keeps you up at this hour, my son?" she asked.

"I have had two dreams," he said. "Both similar, but different. I want you to interpret them."

"Well, speak up," she said.

He sat down on the bed. "In the first, I was outside at night. All the stars of heaven were above my head in the firmament. Then one of them fell like a rock to the ground at my feet. I tried to move it, but it weighed too much for me to lift or roll."

"Hmmmm," she hummed with interest.

Gilgamesh stopped. "What?" he said. "Hmmm, what?"

She rolled her eyes. "I was only letting you know I was listening. Finish the dream, will you?"

He continued, "All of Uruk stood around this fallen star, milling about and kissing its feet. I kissed it and embraced it with a friendship closer than a wife. Then I lifted it and set it at your feet and you made it my equal."

"Ahhh," she said.

"Ah, what?" he asked impatiently again.

"You really need to work on your patience, Gilgy." She only called him Gilgy when no one else was around. It would not be appropriate before the court or the citizens to call the king by nicknames. But it expressed her motherly affection in private, or rather her condescending reminder that no matter how great he was, *she* was still his mother. *She* had borne him for six months and suffered the pains of birthing a giant. Only a goddess could have done so, and she would not let him forget it. Thank the gods the gestation of giants was less than a full human, and that their size had diminished enough over the generations for women to survive the birth.

"What was the other dream?" she asked.

"The same exact dream," he answered, "except it was an axe on the ground instead of a fallen star. Well?"

She thought for a moment with her eyes closed.

His foot tapped impatiently on the floor.

"His strength is mighty," she said.

"Who? Whose strength is mighty?" he asked.

"Stronger than you have ever encountered," she added.

Gilgamesh went cold. He had never encountered anyone stronger than himself. Her habit of keeping things from him as a way of having some power over him perturbed him.

"A friend," she finally spoke.

"A friend?"

She added a caveat, "Or a betrayer."

"That is not very helpful," he complained. "You might as well have said, 'It could be anyone. Anyone in the world.'"

"Dreams are mysterious things, my son. You cannot always figure them out."

"And interpreting dreams is clearly one of your strongest talents," he sarcastically chided her.

"Go to bed," she said. "Maybe something else will come to either of us by morning." She was exhausted and just wanted to get back to sleep.

Her dismissal dismayed Gilgamesh. "Mother, for a goddess, you appear to be quite limited by your flesh."

This annoyed her. "I am still your mother. Now go to bed."

Gilgamesh left her to her sleep. As he walked back to his palace, he wondered if the dream referred to Dumuzi. He had become a friend of the king by saving Gilgamesh in the Games. But the shepherd's motives were questionable. Had he found the knife from one of the warriors in the battle? Or had he brought the knife to kill the king but changed his mind? And if he had, then what would keep him from changing it back? Experience told Gilgamesh that no amount of gratitude and material blessing or awarded position in the kingdom could keep a man from temptation. No man could be trusted. All men had their price. All men betrayed. He would make sure that this Dumuzi did not get the better of him.

CHAPTER 7

The Wild Born had discovered the hunter's traps in the steppe and had foiled them to protect his brothers, the animals. It bothered him that humans invaded his territory. Life was satisfying, running through the plains with the gazelle and playing with the lions in the grass. But hunters always spoiled his peace and killed his friends. Of course, it was the way of all flesh. Animals killed and ate each other and the humans were just another animal, so they were no different. Still, it pained the Wild Born that humans were so much smarter than his brothers and sisters of the plains. The animals could never rise above their own instinct and fear and appetite. These were the times that the Wild Born felt different from his animal family. He felt alone. He felt connected to the humans in some way, as if he was part animal, part man. That bothered him deeply.

He was thirsty again. He had just finished eating a healthy serving of grass. He went down to the water hole to quench his thirst. He plunged his face into the cool liquid and lapped up the refreshing water in big gulps. When he raised his head to make sure he was not followed by any predators, he saw a figure at the other end of the water. It was a human. It was a female. She watched him with intense interest.

The breeze carried her scent across the water and exploded in his nostrils. All his senses perked up. He found himself strangely drawn to her. He had seen the males of other animals drawn to their own females. This had never happened to him before. He found himself no longer thirsty for water, but hungry for the female.

He crept cautiously around the edge of the water hole, his eyes transfixed in wonder. As he got closer, he could see she had strange beautiful markings on her face. Her lips were bright red, her eyes were surrounded by black that made the white of her eyes penetrate to his very soul. She had shiny metal dangling from her ears. Bright metal circled her arms. Disks of the stuff draped around her neck, and down onto the bright tunic she wore. He was spellbound.

He stopped a few feet from her, his six and a half foot height towering over her small figure. She sat on a cloth on the dirt, vulnerable to him. Her scent now wafted so strongly to him that he could not hold himself back. He got down on his knees and touched her soft, smooth, milky white skin. His rough hairy body was the complete opposite of hers.

She reached up and brushed his hair away from his face. Instinctually, he knew she was not a threat to him. Her soft wet lips touched his and he felt the reverberations of his first human kiss.

He responded the only way he knew how to show affection. He licked her face. She giggled as the sandy tongue and full facial hair tickled her.

She kissed him on the lips again.

Now, he became vulnerable to her.

She so transfixed his attention that it blinded his animal intuition. He was completely unaware that he was being observed. A short distance away in the grass, Dumuzi smiled with victory. His plan to distract the Wild Born had worked. Shamhat the courtesan had applied her trained skills with stunning expertise. The Wild Born was as much a captive as if a cage of iron surrounded him.

It was not Dumuzi's plan to blindside the Wild Born with distraction and then catch him in a net like an animal. He had a far higher purpose. He wanted to tame the creature, to civilize him. For a man who shepherded animals all his life, it was a worthy challenge. He left the two alone to get to know each other.

As six days and seven nights passed, Shamhat could feel the Wild Born's animal nature lessen. He became self-aware the longer he was with her.

On the seventh evening, as they lay on the cloth looking into each other's eyes, she said to him, "You have become like a god. You now have reason and understanding. Why do you wander with the beasts, my Wild Born?"

Though he did not understand her words, he somehow knew what she was saying. She heard a soft sound emanating from within his throat. She leaned in to listen more closely. Then she laughed. He was purring. Her Wild Born purred with contentment. She tried to talk to him again.

She pointed at herself and said "Shamhat." It was the most basic form of communication possible between two rational animals. To point to one's self and to speak a name was the essence of identity. It was the act of naming and it was part of the image of God.

She said it again, and patted herself, "Shamhat."

The Wild Born tried to mimic her. His inexperience produced a sound more like a grunt and a coughing up of spit.

She giggled and said again, "Shamhat."

He tried with all his heart. "Schha – marght." He was uncivilized, but he was human and he was created to speak a language.

She patted herself one more time, saying, "Shamhat." She gestured to him with obvious curiosity, "Name?"

The Wild Born somehow knew what she was asking. He struggled to get it out, "Enn — kee — doo."

She repeated after him, "*Enkidu.* Who gave you that name? The god Enki?"

Enkidu studied her, his head tilted like a dog trying to understand human gibberish. She giggled. "Then you are *my* Enkidu." She looked out at the watering hole and said, "You are Enki's creation from the waters of the Abyss, civilized by Shamhat the harlot. Enkidu of the Steppe."

He repeated with a snarling smile, "Enkee-doo."

She laughed. "Typical man, you do very well talking about yourself."

He did not understand what she said, but he smiled. He snuggled close to her. For the first time in her life, she felt the satisfaction of being loved with the security of a man's true concern for her. And he was not even really a man — *Yet.*

She began to weep. He looked at her with concern. She smiled through her tears and told him, "It is all right, my Enkidu. It is well. I am not sad. I am happy."

He kissed her. Oh, how he loved to kiss her. And lick her.

All over.

The next day, Enkidu got up to drink some water. He saw some of his friends near the other side of the pond. Two ibexes lapped up some water, glancing occasionally around the opposite shore. He smiled and strode toward them. But when they saw him, they looked at him as if they did not recognize him and bolted off in fear. He yelled and ran after them. He realized that he was not as fleet of foot as he had been. He could not keep up with them. His legs were weaker.

The ibexes raced far out of his reach. He stopped, panting. He tried to understand what had happened to him. He was different. He had changed. He was no longer one of them.

He was now a man.

He went back to Shamhat. She was awake, putting on a tunic for the first time in seven days.

She took his hand and gestured for him to follow her. "Come, Enkidu. You have much to learn."

He trusted her, and followed.

When she reached Dumuzi's camp with Enkidu, it appeared vacant. All the weapons and traps were out of sight.

Enkidu was nervous and skittish. When he saw the camp, he immediately knew it belonged to the hunter whose traps he had sprung and holes he had filled. He stopped and held Shamhat back.

She turned to face him.

"It is all right, Enkidu," she said. "These are my friends."

He turned his head sideways again, like a quizzical dog. It did not make sense to him that this beauty of love and sensuality was with the enemy of the steppe.

Dumuzi stepped out of his tent.

Enkidu's instinct surged through his body. He stepped in front of Shamhat to protect her. Would he have to kill?

She laughed lightly and stroked his hair. She had learned to pet him to calm him down. "It is all right, my Enkidu. I am safe. We are safe." She slid back out in front of him.

She met Dumuzi half way and grasped his forearm in greeting. Then Shamhat gestured to Enkidu to come forward. He did — slowly and cautiously. She brought his arm to Dumuzi's forearm and locked them together.

She patted Dumuzi and said to Enkidu, "Dumuzi." Then she patted Enkidu and said, "Enkidu."

Enkidu felt the firm grasp of Dumuzi. He could tell the hunter was no longer hostile toward him. Perhaps their packs or herds could learn to live together. If Shamhat accepted them, then perhaps they were not so bad after all.

Dumuzi smiled. Enkidu smiled in response. He had already learned some human gestures of emotion over the last seven days.

"Enkidu," said Dumuzi, "we have much to give you, and much to receive, I am sure. Let us eat."

Dumuzi led them into the dining tent for a meal.

It became a bit of a comedy for Dumuzi and the servants to watch. Enkidu gobbled up his food like a wolf without utensils. Food scattered all over the place. Dumuzi tried hard to hold back chuckling. Only Shamhat had perfect patience, teaching Enkidu not to gobble food so fast that he might choke. That night alone, he drank seven goblets of beer, and became tipsy.

"You will see, master Dumuzi," said Shamhat, "give me the month and I will have him talking and looking like a civilized man."

"My sympathies go out to you, dear woman," smiled Dumuzi. "You have your hands quite full."

She quipped with her own smile, "He does learn fast. And he seeks to make me happy. Unlike any man I have ever known."

Dumuzi gave her a raised eyebrow of curiosity. Was it not her purpose to make *him* happy?

CHAPTER 8

The hunting expedition continued for another month. Shamhat was right, Enkidu learned quickly. He was unnaturally fast. Shamhat had never seen such intelligence. Underneath his outward feral brutishness lurked a rational intellect that had been suppressed like a plugged volcano. His animal side gave him strong instincts, while his human side was like a fresh clay tablet that could carry as much as a speedy scribe could engrave into it. Shamhat spent every day with him, teaching him the ways of civilization: language, reading, tools, eating meat, etiquette, social customs. At night, he would be rewarded with wild lovemaking, the skill he had perfected best of all.

One of the first things she did was bathe him. She shaved his hair and beard from his body, and then anointed his body with oil. He felt as if he was being born for the first time. He felt completely naked and vulnerable until she put clothes on him. Then, he felt bound and limited. The belt was tight, the tunic cumbersome, and the sandals clumsy. But as he became more like the humans around him, he became more comfortable with their ways. He felt that he had been on a long and wearisome journey and had finally come home. It was all so strange and new, but he was finally home. He embraced his new world with passion and gusto.

Learning about the city of Uruk and the world of mankind filled him with wonder. Shamhat took great care that he understood the civilized ways of mankind with justice and law and art and education and family.

"What is marriage?" Enkidu asked Shamhat one day while she taught him in the tent. He had learned the basics of language. He wanted to dig deeper into the meaning of being human. She had been explaining to him what a family was and why it was important to civilization.

Shamhat sighed. As a harlot, she had never thought much about it, since it would never be her lot in life. She knew what it should be. But she also knew that she was an instrument of the dark side of men that worked against what marriage could be.

"Well," said Shamhat, "marriage is when a man and woman love one another, they share a union..."

"Union?" he interrupted. "What is 'union'?"

"When two become one flesh," she answered.

"Like Shamhat and Enkidu?" he asked with wide eyes.

She smiled. "Well, it includes that, but that is not all."

"What else does it include?" he asked.

"A special promise that we call a 'covenant.' It means a man and woman are devoted to one another for the rest of their lives. And they do it before their community in a special ceremony that seals their promise. And they have a large party with all their loved ones to celebrate." Her eyes teared up with sadness and pain for her own loneliness, a loneliness that she only now realized she had forgotten in his presence.

"Why do you cry?" he asked her.

"Because it is beautiful," she said.

He sat there contemplating this new and beautiful thing that he had never heard of before.

He finally spoke like a king pronouncing a decree. "Enkidu and Shamhat should share this beauty. Enkidu and Shamhat should get married. Enkidu will go back to Uruk with Shamhat and we will be married and have a celebration to be devoted to one another for the rest of our lives." He was all smiles.

She broke down weeping into his arms. He had a difficult time understanding how all this crying was happiness about the beauty of marriage.

"I am not worthy," said Shamhat. "You do not understand my shame."

"Nonsense, silly rabbit," he said. He called her by affectionate animal names to express her different character traits. "Enkidu knows Shamhat's shame and I love you. Shamhat knows Enkidu's shame and you love me, do you not?" He was getting better at using the first person in his conversation.

Her tears turned to a strange combination of crying and laughing. "Yes, yes, I do," she said between her laughing tears. Enkidu displayed that simple male rationality that did not understand emotions and yet could cut through the confusion of those emotions with a clarity she could not deny. She had heard proclamations of "love" from many a man, but this was the first time she knew it was true and real.

Enkidu proudly beamed, "Well then, we shall return to Uruk with Dumuzi and we shall marry."

This was a man whose lead she would feel safe to follow. A man to whom she wanted to submit with all her heart and soul.

"Yes, my Enkidu, I shall marry you."

They kissed, and Enkidu's purr became a growl of happiness.

Suddenly, Enkidu pulled away and looked at her. She could see he was troubled, as if struck by a thought like one is struck by a boulder. He spoke with some hesitation, unsure of his reasoning. "If we are to make this commitment for a lifetime of oneness, should we not hold our bodies apart until the ceremony of oneness?"

Shamhat stared at him blankly. The thought had never even occurred to her. It made perfect sense with the intention of spiritual unity to wait for physical and ritual unity to formalize it first. She knew it would be difficult, but his moral reasoning already exceeded his animal urges.

Before she could respond, they heard a servant's scream outside the tent. Dogs started barking.

Enkidu rushed out to see what caused the commotion. Several of the mastiffs bolted past him and into the brush, chasing after something. Enkidu saw one of the servants lying on the ground in a pool of blood. A predator had attacked. But it was on the run now.

Or was it?

Enkidu glanced around. He smelled the air. He knew who this predator was. Whatever the mastiffs were chasing was a diversion. He saw Shamhat exit the tent and approach him. Enkidu placed his hand out to stop her. He looked past her into the brush. She froze in fear.

She turned slowly to see a female lioness padding out into the clearing. Their eyes locked. The lioness crouched for attack.

Enkidu yelled out a guttural sound, a vestige from his past as a Wild Born. It was how he had communicated with the animals around him and they had understood him. The lioness did not even acknowledge Enkidu. It was as if she had never seen him before.

He knew this one. He knew that she was vicious and cunning. She had a taste for humans, unusual in lions. She had a patch of skin and hair missing above one eye, a scar that Enkidu suspected was the source of its ferocity.

On the other side of the camp, Dumuzi came out of his tent with a spear and two servants with swords and shields. But they were too far away. There was no time. The lioness was seconds from pouncing upon the precious fragile form of Enkidu's salvation.

He sprinted toward Shamhat.

The lioness jumped.

Shamhat screamed.

Enkidu met the lioness in midair and the two crashed to the ground.

Shamhat backed away. The two servants pulled her to safety. Dumuzi prepared to spear the lioness, but Enkidu put his hand up to stop him. Enkidu was going to do this.

The lioness growled and snapped at Enkidu. He was still powerful and skilled at wrestling with animals. He flipped around with the lioness in the dust until he was on its back. He clutched its throat in a choke hold. The lioness thrashed and clawed, but Enkidu was like a boa constrictor wrapped around it. He would not let go.

The lioness could breathe no more. With a couple of final spasms, it lost consciousness, falling limp. Enkidu grabbed its head. With a mighty heave, he broke its neck. Shamhat had been saved by her lover and hero, a man who had only recently himself been a wild animal. He had killed one of his own to protect her. His transformation was complete.

Enkidu fell to his knees and wept. Shamhat did not understand why. Was he mourning the loss of his untamed past? Were the implications of what he had become finally overwhelming him? By sheer will power, Enkidu forced himself to stop. He got up and embraced his beloved Shamhat. And everything was well again.

Dumuzi wanted to bring the dead lioness with them back to Uruk to tell the amazing story and give Enkidu some rightfully earned recognition. But Enkidu asked Dumuzi to spare the spectacle. He wanted to bury the animal here in the steppe and with it, all the memory of his past. He did not want a stuffed reminder of the brutal world to follow him into the civilized world. He wanted to be human.

CHAPTER 9

Dumuzi returned to Uruk without announcing Enkidu's presence in his entourage, abiding by Enkidu's wishes. Shamhat had warned Enkidu that he would become a freak on display, the Wild Born who became civilized. He wanted to be a normal human being, to learn the normal human craft of shepherding from Dumuzi, and to live a normal civilized life in the great city-state of Uruk. His big-boned stature would make him stand out amidst the smaller, slender people of Uruk. He did not want any more attention to make him an animal in the king's zoo of caged carnivores.

Shamhat and Enkidu were married on a beautiful summer day in the temple of Anu, at a simple small wedding. The ceremony followed the privilege granted by the assembly of elders to all of the citizens. They went back to their banquet in the town square of the Dumuzi family's district to finish the celebration. Since neither Enkidu nor Shamhat had family, Dumuzi took them into his family fold to help them get a new start together.

They had a simpler wedding than most. There were few celebrants, and they streamlined the ceremony. Nonetheless, it ended on the seventh day with the traditional feast and much ale.

Shamhat had prepared Enkidu for the king's right to *jus prima noctis*, first night. She told him not to worry, that she would be thinking of Enkidu even as she was with the king. She would guard her heart that wedding night.

But Enkidu remained troubled.

"I thought marriage was for one man and one woman for the rest of their life," he said.

"It is," she replied. "This is merely one of the pains we must suffer because the king has the right to do whatever he wants."

"In the grasslands, I would kill this so-called 'king,'" he said.

"Enkidu, this is not the wild," she scolded him. "The king has the power of the realm behind him. He would execute you for such treason."

Enkidu shook his head. "This is civilization? This is more barbaric than the wild."

"We have no choice in the matter," she said. "If we want to live, we must obey the king."

"Is there no higher authority?" he asked.

"The gods. But the gods give the king the right to do as he pleases."

"That is madness," he replied. "Who are these gods of such foolishness?" Enkidu had been enlarging his vocabulary lately.

"The king is part god himself," she said.

This debate had gone on for days. It was a debate that Enkidu could not win, because the king was the ultimate authority. He eventually grumbled and threw his hands up in frustration — until the next time the topic came up.

But this time, it was not a mere topic of conversation. It was reality. The celebration night was coming to an end. The celebrants started to leave for home. The king's giant form stood in the shadow of the threshold, waiting to take the bride.

Enkidu burned madly. His love for Shamhat would not allow her to be abused in such a way. He would protect her with his life. He had decided that if he was killed, he was killed, but nothing would stop him from protecting his new wife.

He watched Shamhat approach the king in the shadow of the threshold. When the king stepped forward, Enkidu saw him for the first time.

He was truly a mighty man, this Gilgamesh. Handsome, a giant, and with the confidence that reminded Enkidu of a bull, so huge and fierce that none could live in its path.

Shamhat maintained her dignity as she walked ahead into the home.

As Gilgamesh followed after her, he found his way blocked by Enkidu. It shocked Gilgamesh. No one had ever done this before. The bridegroom was defying the king right to his face. It was certain death for this fool.

Gilgamesh knew the man was not from Uruk. He stood head and shoulders above other men, but at just over four cubits tall, he was still smaller than Gilgamesh's six cubits. But he had superior muscle mass. Gilgamesh wondered if he would be a good fight in the Game of Champions.

"Ho, hurrah," said Enkidu. He had fondly picked up this way of getting attention from the Shepherd Dumuzi. "This is not a right thing that you do, O king."

"You dare question my authority?" said Gilgamesh.

"By the gods," Enkidu replied. "How would you like it if I took first night with your queen before you?"

Gilgamesh took offense. Even Enkidu could see it was outrageous to suggest such a thing.

Enkidu said, "You prove me correct, O king, with your moral outrage. For how are we superior to the animals if we act with such disregard for moral right and wrong?"

Gilgamesh smiled with amusement. "How long have you been in the wild, clodhopper?"

He meant to point out Enkidu's ignorance of the city of Uruk and its laws. He did not realize that calling Enkidu "wild" would be the worst thing he could say to this small powerhouse standing before him. It fueled Enkidu's rising rage.

"Longer than you have been a tyrant, my lord," spat Enkidu.

That pushed Gilgamesh's patience to the brink.

"What is your name, rebel?" said Gilgamesh.

"Enkidu, my despot."

Gilgamesh grabbed Enkidu, to kill him with his bare hands. He would not wait for the formal process of legal indictment and execution.

But Gilgamesh did not know who he had just grabbed with his bare hands.

Enkidu blocked Gilgamesh before the king could do anything. He slammed the surprised giant against the closest pillar with such force that the pillar cracked and the entire house shook.

Gilgamesh released his grip, stunned.

Enkidu hissed into Gilgamesh's ear, "No man or god will dishonor my wife while I am still alive."

Enkidu spun around while still holding Gilgamesh and threw him into the street. The king crushed a row of tables of food, scattering the stragglers. It had taken a lot of strength to lift a giant and throw him such a distance. There was more to this rustic yokel than met Gilgamesh's eyes.

Enkidu was smaller in size than Gilgamesh, but stronger of bone. He equaled the king in strength. Or maybe exceeded him. Gilgamesh had finally met his match, and it took him completely by surprise.

Enkidu turned to Shamhat and said, "Wait for me here, my dove. I may be a tad delayed."

He leapt like a stag and landed at the stunned Gilgamesh's feet. He grabbed the king's feet and dragged him out into the town square. A crowd of gawking citizens gathered to watch this amazing spectacle of clashing titans.

Enkidu swung Gilgamesh by his feet and slammed him into another building that shook at its foundation. Gilgamesh slid to the ground. His head reeled. Enkidu grabbed him by the cloak to pick him up. Gilgamesh grasped Enkidu and threw him against the very same house. It crumbled from the impact. Enkidu saw stars.

The two clutched each other and wrestled for advantage. One moment, Gilgamesh would be on top, and then the next moment, the tails turned and Enkidu held the superior position.

They slammed each other into buildings with the force of two rampaging bulls, reducing the town square into a pile of rubble.

They circled each other, ready to trample and gore.

Gilgamesh shouted, "Where are you from, mighty Enkidu?"

"I come from the steppe."

"I am impressed. I have never seen such strength or bravado," said Gilgamesh.

"What is 'bravado'?" asked Enkidu.

Gilgamesh smiled. *This is some kind of primitive,* he thought. *Untainted by the petty shame of civilization. Could he be a domesticated Wild Born?*

"Pomposity, bombast, braggadocio," grinned Gilgamesh. Now, he taunted Enkidu, answering him with even more intellectual words beyond Enkidu's comprehension.

Enkidu boiled.

"It means the pride that comes before a fall," Gilgamesh added. He flipped Enkidu with a thud into the dirt. The entire town square shook like an earthquake. A normal man would not have remained conscious.

Enkidu was not a normal man.

Gilgamesh still held onto him.

Enkidu threw him off balance and flipped the king over his head, right into a stone well. Gilgamesh crashed into the stone structure and smashed it to pieces, stunning him.

"I will forever remember such words in context with King Gilgamesh, the tyrant, despot, and oppressor," said Enkidu.

Gilgamesh shook off his stupor and thought, *Has Dumuzi taught him this discontent?* Gilgamesh said, "Why would you sacrifice your life for such a minor inconvenience as a wife?" He was genuinely surprised at Enkidu's extremist moral sentiment. He could not understand what drove a man to have such an absolutist mentality when it came to morals. Wives were mere property to him. They could be bought, beaten, divorced. Enkidu replied, "A man's life is sacred. And his wife's virtue is no minor inconvenience."

Enkidu's antiquated integrity fascinated Gilgamesh. It was everything Gilgamesh did not have. He found himself drawn to it.

Gilgamesh complained, "But your wife is a harlot."

Gilgamesh said it as a statement of fact, not an insult. Enkidu heard it differently. He raged and tackled Gilgamesh head on. They slammed into the side of a house with such force that it brought the building down completely upon them.

They dug their way out of the debris. Enkidu coughed the dust out of his lungs. As soon as Gilgamesh burst out of the pile of mud bricks, Enkidu unleashed with a fury of rapid face punches that would have taken off the head of any other adversary.

It only knocked Gilgamesh unconscious. Enkidu pulled Gilgamesh out of the rubble and carried him on his back out into the town square before a cheering crowd. He did not care one whit for their attention. He only thought of his beloved Shamhat. He raised

Gilgamesh above his head and threw him to the ground with another earth shattering quake.

Gilgamesh lay crumpled on the ground. Enkidu walked over to a horse hitching post and pulled the large log from its posts.

He carried it over to Gilgamesh and raised it high above his head, intending to smash his enemy's skull.

Gilgamesh had been feigning unconsciousness. He rolled into Enkidu's legs and brought him crashing to the ground. The log went flying.

Gilgamesh used a wrestling maneuver he had learned in his physical training many years ago. It was the advantage that civilization gave over the wild. Perfected training through practiced experimentation and rational study would ultimately be superior to brute strength and untrained natural instinct. Gilgamesh pinned Enkidu. He quickly pulled his knife from his belt and held it to Enkidu's throat.

Enkidu looked up into Gilgamesh's eyes. The king could see that he was ready to die. It was as if he knew who he was and why he was here.

"You have fought well, my adversary," said Gilgamesh. "I have never met my equal. But you have bettered me in more than one moment today."

"It is true what they say of the unique son of Ninsun," said Enkidu. "You are destined to rule mightily over men."

Gilgamesh was amused and impressed. He is complimenting me before I kill him.

"Promise me something," said Enkidu.

Gilgamesh was startled. "*Me* promise *you*?" Considering Enkidu's current situation, he had a lot of gall to demand a promise.

"After you take my life, honor your words of respect for my skill by protecting my wife's virtue."

Gilgamesh could not believe his ears. "So this is love," he said. He stared into Enkidu's eyes and could see no guile.

It seemed bizarre to Gilgamesh. This powerful warrior was entirely beyond his comprehension. Yet, he strangely resonated with some sense of moral truth deep down in the king's soul.

He changed his mind.

"I will protect your wife's virtue," said Gilgamesh. "*And* I will not take your life."

He released the knife from Enkidu's throat. The turnaround shocked Enkidu.

Gilgamesh offered his hand to help Enkidu up from the ground.

Enkidu took his hand warily. He wondered if Gilgamesh was just throwing Enkidu off his guard, in order to give him a merciful surprise death, something he would not see coming. He wondered if he would barely realize he was dead until he opened his eyes in the underworld.

But Gilgamesh did not surprise Enkidu with a bushwhack. He helped Enkidu up and brushed the dirt off his wedding clothes. Both of their clothes had been ripped to shreds.

"I will make you my Right Hand," said Gilgamesh.

"I do not understand," said Enkidu. "Are you not obligated to kill me for my defiance?"

"I am king," said Gilgamesh. "I am obligated to nothing. I can do whatever I want." He smiled deviously. "And I have never met a man as strong and honest and true as Enkidu of the steppe. Why would I want to kill such a man?"

Enkidu was as stunned as if he had been thrown into a brick wall.

"Enkidu, would you be my Right Hand?"

It was a genuine and heartfelt request rather than a kingly command.

Enkidu stared long and hard at Gilgamesh. He said, "You release your claim of first night with my wife?"

"I do so."

Then Enkidu offered him his forearm and they grasped each other. They kissed as was the custom of the land, not a kiss of lovers such as Enkidu and Shamhat, but a kiss of male friendship as Enkidu and Gilgamesh.

Gilgamesh thought to himself, *There is much to teach this primitive man. I pray his morality does not get in the way of his education.*

Enkidu thought to himself, *There is much to teach this educated fool. It will be a most difficult task to civilize him.*

Gilgamesh suddenly spoke up, "All this fighting has made me famished. Come, my Right Hand, let us feast!"

Enkidu looked at Gilgamesh with incredulity. "As your trusted ally, do you desire me to maintain my strength, honesty, and truthfulness?"

"Of course," said Gilgamesh. "I require it, even to my disadvantage."

Enkidu said, "Well, then, my lord, it would do you well to remember that I have just been interrupted from consummating my wedding night."

Gilgamesh grinned and slapped Enkidu on the back. "Forgive me, Enkidu. Go and spend the evening with your new wife."

Enkidu stared blankly at Gilgamesh. The king winked and walked away, throwing out another playful jab, "See me in the feast hall in the morning, if she'll let you go."

Enkidu turned and walked toward the waiting figure of Shamhat, standing on the threshold of their banquet house.

She smiled with pride. She could not comprehend why the gods had been so kind to her with so good a man.

CHAPTER 10

Gilgamesh sat deep in thought on his throne, his brow wrinkled. He gazed off into the distance, a small opening from a window above casting a beam of light upon his back in the otherwise shadowed hall.

Sinleqiunninni stood beside Gilgamesh's throne. He was the *ummanu*, the king's scholar. The ummanu served as the head scribe of the palace. He was also principal of the scribal school and responsible for the court archives. He maintained the written stories of the culture. He wrote letters for the king and oversaw the engraving of monumental inscriptions. The ummanu had taken the place of the pre-Deluge *apkallu.* While the apkallu had been primarily a mystical sage of wisdom for kings, the ummanu was more of an intellectual scholar of knowledge reference.

The world had become less magical and more rational with the growth and accumulation of human knowledge in libraries of cuneiform tablets in the cities. All that written knowledge required a manager more inclined toward tablets than people, toward rational intellect than understanding of human nature. These qualities explained Sinleqiunninni's pudgy and flabby body shape, since he spent most of his time sitting and reading.

Unfortunately for Sinleqiunninni, Gilgamesh did not care for his personality in the least. The scholar was undoubtedly intelligent and knowledgeable. He could cite from memory things written down in tablets stored deep in the library. But he did not have much wisdom or practical ability to apply his knowledge. His social and verbal skills were dreadful. The only reason his monotonous voice did not put Gilgamesh to sleep was because it annoyed him so much. But Sinleqiunninni was the only one in the kingdom who knew the library by heart, so Gilgamesh needed him, if only to recount such petty details that would be necessary for particular discussions or decisions.

Enkidu's voice snapped Gilgamesh back into this world. "Ho, hurrah, my king!"

Gilgamesh looked up and saw Enkidu and Shamhat being led into the throne room by the Guard.

"Why does Gilgamesh the Gibbor appear so glum?"

Gilgamesh smiled broadly. "Contemplating the mysteries of the cosmos."

Gilgamesh gazed upon the beautiful Shamhat. It seemed that Enkidu's love had transformed this wild woman, into a vision of womanly grace and honor. A splash of envy washed over him. He shook it off.

"Welcome, my turtledoves," teased Gilgamesh. "Are you tired of each other yet? Or annoying one another?"

Enkidu and Shamhat smiled. "Humility is a character trait of which I intend to instruct the king," Enkidu teased back.

Shamhat joined in, "Would my Lord prefer us to demonstrate how much we enjoy each other's kiss?"

Gilgamesh laughed heartily, "No, no, dear Shamhat. I shall trust your expert opinion, and pray that I may someday find such a desirable and goodly wife as you. Thank you for civilizing this manly brute." It was the way of men to insult one another as an ironic act showing affection and respect.

"The honor is mine, good king," said Shamhat.

"No," said Gilgamesh.

Enkidu and Shamhat stayed silent. They did not know what he meant, and were not sure they wanted to.

"No, I am not a good king," he continued. "Please accept my humblest apology for interrupting your wedding night with my scandalous unacceptable behavior. I vow to never treat you with such disrespect again. You are the wife of my Right Hand."

Shamhat and Enkidu were stunned. Shamhat started to tear up with gratitude.

She finally spoke up, "My lord the king is sovereign. He does as he pleases."

"Indeed I do," Gilgamesh replied. "But that is why the gods have given me your husband, as a standard to show me the consequences of my actions. Already he has me re-evaluating my policy of *jus prima noctis*, thanks to his amazing wife. I understand now why he was willing to die for her."

"My lord," she said simply, bowing her head. She felt embarrassed that the king should disclose so much of himself. But she also felt honored to receive it.

Sinleqiunninni cleared his throat like a teacher. He spoke softly, with a false humility, "Excuse me, my lord, but technically, *jus prima noctis* was never absolute obligation on your part. You need not abolish it to avoid universal administration. You merely apply it selectively."

"Thank you for the technical clarification," snapped Gilgamesh with a touch of contempt. He looked back at Enkidu. "As you may have realized, this is Sinleqiunninni, the king's scholar, or technical clarifier."

"Ummanu, to be more accurate terminologically," added Sinleqiunninni.

Gilgamesh spouted, “Well, we would not want to be terminologically inaccurate, now, would we?”

Sinleqiunninni said, “Actually, if I may…”

“No, you may not, Sinleqi,” said Gilgamesh, shortening the name as an example of his shortened patience. The scholar shut up.

Gilgamesh looked back at Enkidu and said, “I have much to discuss with you, Enkidu. But first, if the lady permits, we shall, you and I, pay a visit to the Queen Mother, goddess Ninsun.”

Gilgamesh walked Enkidu through *Egalmah*, the Great Palace temple of Ninsun, his Queen Mother, in the temple district at the center of the city. Although she was high priestess of Shamash the sun god, she was also a goddess herself. His altar was on the roof of her own temple, for convenience.

Enkidu could not get all the temples straight, there were so many of them. The idea of a pantheon of gods troubled him. It seemed more sensible to him to worship one creator god, but he could not make heads or tails of which one it was. Was it Aruru, the goddess who supposedly created Enkidu? Was it Mami or Nintu who mixed clay with his flesh and blood? Was it Enki or Nudimmud who made mankind from the spilt blood of the god Qingu? He thought he might consult with the king’s scholar for clarification. But then he remembered his previous encounter with the learned idiot, and thought better of it.

Nevertheless, there were so many different contradicting versions of creation, that he could not get them straight. That very diversity seemed to him to speak of the confused state that humanity was in. It was as if the Creator god had pulled away from humanity and this confusion was the result of such abandonment. But who could that Creator god be?

Enkidu and the king came to Shamash's Gateway, where Ninsun prayed to the sun god. It was a modest room in an otherwise ostentatious temple palace. Gilgamesh wanted his mother to meet his new Right Hand, and he wanted it to be a surprise. He had Enkidu hide behind a pillar until Gilgamesh introduced him.

Gilgamesh saw his mother kneeling and praying in the gateway. He approached silently, so as not to startle her. As he reached hearing range, he heard her prayer of complaint to Shamash.

"He is just a domesticated Wild Born bastard. Born in the wilderness without father or mother, raised by animals. His hair is ratty and unpleasant. What shall I say to my son if he appoints him to power in the kingdom?"

"You could say, 'Well done my wise and noble son,'" Gilgamesh's voice interrupted.

She whirled around, to see him standing behind her with a frown on his face.

Gilgamesh continued, "Since you are already privy to the intelligence of the fight, Mother, you will apparently be unimpressed to hear that I have appointed Enkidu to the position of my Right Hand. I am sorry to disappoint you."

He was not sorry. He just enjoyed making sarcastic barbs. He loved his mother, but he would not be ruled or manipulated by her. He listened to her counsel, as he did all others, but he did what he thought was right. He was lord and king of Uruk.

"My son," she protested, "do you fault me for my concern? He has no lineage. He is not royalty. I only seek to protect your throne above all else."

"Yes, you do," he said. "And so you will no doubt appreciate knowing that I have never in my entire life met a man I could trust – until this day. Mother, I have gazed into the Abyss. I know the nature of man. And I tell you, there is no guile in Enkidu of the steppe."

His sentiment deeply moved her. He continued, "He is appointed my Right Hand and I expect you to grant him all observance and authority of his position."

She listened without a word.

He said, "I came here to tell you something."

He turned and walked to the back of the room.

He meant to get Enkidu, but when he reached the pillar where he left him, Enkidu was gone. He sighed deeply, turned back to Ninsun and said, "Come to dinner tonight and we will talk."

"Yes, my son," she said with heavy sadness.

Gilgamesh left her to her thoughts.

Gilgamesh found Enkidu in the royal stable. He reasoned that after hearing Ninsun's derogatory complaints, Enkidu would return to where he felt more comfortable – with animals. He found the former Wild Born brooding with the mighty horses of the king's chariot.

Gilgamesh did not see this escape as weakness. He understood his new companion perhaps better than he understood himself.

Gilgamesh said, "Enkidu, the animal world is not the only place where hierarchy is dictated by rules. But in human society the strong do not rule. Aristocracy is family born."

Enkidu replied sadly, "I have no family. I am not a man."

Gilgamesh stepped up to him to emphasize his intent. "You are more a man than anyone I have ever known in my entire life."

"But I am not your family," protested Enkidu. "I should return to the steppe. That is where I was born to live and die."

"Nonsense," said Gilgamesh. "You have been reborn as my Right Hand. And there is a way for you to be my family."

Enkidu looked up at Gilgamesh stupefied. "How, my lord?"

Gilgamesh gave him a serpentine grin, "It begins with you joining me in a feast."

Enkidu asked, "Will Lady Wild Cow be there?"

Gilgamesh smiled. It was a religious name for Ninsun, but in the lips of this ex-Wild Born, it carried irony. "Yes, she will. But so will the city elders, because I have a proposition that will affect both your destiny and mine, and I require the approval of the assembly."

Enkidu could not shake his melancholy.

Gilgamesh offered his forearm and said teasingly, "I cannot very well show up before the counsel with my left hand and not my Right Hand."

Enkidu tried to smile. "Of course I will obey my king." He grabbed forearms and they embraced.

CHAPTER 11

The assembly of ruling elders of the city commonly met in the Hall of Pillars. Massive columns of strength studded the long hallway. Brightly colored cone mosaics ornamented them. They radiated a power and glory that gave the meetings a sense of divine majesty. Gilgamesh had turned it into a feasting hall. Long tables were spread with fish and fowl, bread and beer, plums and pomegranates. Enkidu and Shamhat sat on Gilgamesh's right and Ninsun on his left as they ate a hearty meal together. Dumuzi sat to the left of Ninsun and next to him lounged Sinleqiunninni. All around them were the seventy assembly members, convened for an important meeting, all wondering what Gilgamesh intended this time.

The gathering began with the feast, and Enkidu was feasting. He ate so fast that he could not keep his plate stocked or his goblet full. The servants scurried about pouring wine and beer. He almost choked on some food and he washed it down with wine, splashing down his greasy face.

Shamhat was horrified. His animal like eating habits were the one thing that he seemed incapable of civilizing. Shamhat leaned toward him and whispered, "Enkidu, slow down. You are eating too fast."

He knew she was right, but it still annoyed him.

Gilgamesh watched Enkidu with amusement. He cracked a big smile, “Worry not, Enkidu. The fowl will not fly astray nor the fish swim away.”

Enkidu slowed down, even though the added voice of correction irritated him like a shallow wound.

Gilgamesh added, “I think you are so speedy, you need your own servant just to keep your plate from starving.”

“Forgive me,” retorted Enkidu, “I am just so used to having my food stolen from me by the king’s hunters.”

“Ha! Good one!” exclaimed Gilgamesh. “Speaking of which, I have much to query you on your life in the wild.”

“It is a topic I rather prefer not to discuss, my lord,” said Enkidu.

Ninsun and Dumuzi leaned forward, eavesdropping.

Suddenly, Enkidu raised one of his legs and let go a loud and rumbling fart. He continued to eat as if nothing had happened.

Ninsun and Dumuzi sat back with noses wrinkled in disgust. Shamhat whispered harshly to him, “Enkidu!”

Gilgamesh laughed again. “I see Shamhat is not done discussing your wild habits and the etiquette of civilization.”

Shamhat apologized, “Pardon, my lord.”

Gilgamesh added, “Mother taught me well that slowed consumption decreases flatulence.”

It peeved Enkidu. He munched a bite in his mouth, staring at Gilgamesh. He stopped his chewing, scrunched his face, and let another fart rip out like a lightning bolt. It was his rebellious response to being judged.

“Excuse me,” said Enkidu, with the most ironic contrast of sweet politeness he could muster.

Gilgamesh loved it. The two of them broke out in uproarious laughter. Apparently, they were the only ones to enjoy such a childish violation of civilized etiquette.

But Gilgamesh was crafty. He abruptly switched the topic back to his original inquiry. "Tell me, Enkidu, what was it like to run wild and free with the animals? I have often desired to know such liberty."

"Being wild and free is not all it seems, my lord," Enkidu answered.

"Agh!" bellowed Gilgamesh. "We humans are constrained by such petty rules and social norms. I sometimes feel in a cage of tradition."

Then perhaps you should eat faster, Enkidu thought. Instead of saying that, he countered, "I consider the rules of civilization to be good boundaries. They keep man from being an animal."

"But an animal runs naked and free," said Gilgamesh. "Animals experience everything with gusto, the hot sun on their backs, the freezing cold rain, a cool drink of water or a battle of fangs and claws."

Enkidu would not bow. He knew the reality. "Animals freeze to death and die of dehydration in their simplicity. They gorge themselves and starve to death. They eat their own. They leave behind the weak as victims of predators. They lack meaning and purpose, and none of them understand the spiritual intimacy of marriage."

Gilgamesh could not understand that one either. But it did not keep him from pontificating. "Well, if we are more than animals, then what is the meaning? What is our purpose? To live, build cities, and die? How is that different from living in a herd, eating grass, and dying?"

"You are the king," said Enkidu. "I would have hoped you had wisdom about such things."

Ninsun felt her opinion of Enkidu change. Despite his lack of pedigree, he seemed to have a good effect on her son.

"Ah, very good, Enkidu," said Gilgamesh. "Indeed I should. And yet, I have been young and am now older. I have seen that all of life dies, human and animal, rich and poor, king and commoner. All alike die. All of life is striving after wind. All our days are numbered, Enkidu. So what is the point? Our lives are less than a breath in the eternal timeline of existence. Like a vapor, we exist and are gone. Everyone, both the wise and the fool, is soon forgotten."

Gilgamesh spoke like one of the *apkallu* wisdom sages of old. The elders of the assembly puzzled over it, but Enkidu followed well enough. It resonated with his soul.

"Are you afraid of death, O king?" asked Enkidu.

"Only the fool is not," said Gilgamesh. "Death is the great equalizer. No man of any strength, cunning, or goodness has ever overcome it. It remains the only question of importance."

Enkidu asked, "Would the gods give answer? Are they not divine?"

Ninsun smiled with approval at Enkidu's intuition.

"The gods are strangely silent," said Gilgamesh. He turned to his mother, noting her attention to the conversation. He added courteously, "Present company excluded, Mother, the gods do not seem to show their faces much anymore. We have their images of wood and stone, to represent their dominion, but they seem to be markers of their absence more than of their presence."

Ninsun would not let her chance be missed. She spoke up, "Ever since the Deluge, the Annunaki gods who were not caught in the waters have chosen to rule from their cosmic mountain, Hermon, in the west. It stands in the midst of the Great Cedar Forest that is guarded by a ferocious giant ten cubits tall."

Gilgamesh's attention piqued. Enkidu became still with silence.

Ninsun finished her preaching, "The gods have not forgotten us, Gilgamesh. They are surely strategizing our future from on high."

Gilgamesh sat silently in thought.

Ninsun, Dumuzi, Enkidu, and Shamhat all watched him with curiosity, wondering what he would say.

Ninsun had no patience. "Son?"

Enkidu knew why the king kept silent. "He is contemplating the mysteries of the cosmos."

The feasting continued around them. The assemblymen ate, drank, gossiped and jockeyed for power in the Urukean political hierarchy.

Gilgamesh whispered a word to Enkidu.

The king's Right Hand stood up suddenly drawing all attention to himself. He announced to the crowd, "Ho, hurrah! Men of Uruk, listen! Assembly of the city draw near. Your king has a pronouncement that requires your approval!"

Everyone went silent. Of course, their approval was a mere formality. Gilgamesh always did what he wanted and afterward garnered whatever approval was required by the city charter to satisfy the citizens. It made them feel less ruled over than they actually were. Good morale was important when the king wanted his subjects to keep from revolting.

Gilgamesh dropped his surprise. "Your king and his Right Hand will be going on a journey."

Everyone looked at one another with curiosity.

Gilgamesh continued, "This will be a journey of such importance as to bring everlasting fame upon Uruk and upon the name of her king."

No one knew what would come next.

"Enkidu and I will journey to Mount Hermon, the mountain of the gods and we will fight the giant who guards the Great Cedar Forest."

Hushes and gasps went through the crowd. Ninsun's face turned white in terror. Enkidu buried his face in his hands.

Gilgamesh continued, "With the approval of this assembly, we will kill this monster so that all evil be banished from the land. And we will scout the Cedar Forest for timber to enhance my mighty palace to new greatness over all the earth!"

Silence permeated the room. Glances shifted back and forth, avoiding the king's attention. They were afraid to stand up to their sovereign.

Gilgamesh looked around for response.

"Well?" demanded Gilgamesh, "speak up! You are the assembly, not a brood of deaf mutes."

Eventually, Nashukh, the mayor and head of the assembly, rose to his feet. He was so old he did not care if he was killed for the negative counsel he was about to give, even though everyone else thought the same thing. Nevertheless, sweat trickled down his forehead. His hands and his voice trembled.

"My lord and king," Nashukh said, "you are young. Your spirit is restless. Your heart is carrying you away into foolishness."

Voices murmured in shock at the scandal of the old man's words. It rose to a cacophony stopped only by Gilgamesh shaming them. He slapped his hand down on the table, letting the sharp cracking sound snap through the Hall.

"Silence! You sound like schoolchildren. At least one of you has the liver to speak his mind. I admire you, Nashukh. Now, sit down."

Nashukh obeyed.

Gilgamesh said, "Give me your blessing. I will embark on a distant journey and return a mightier king through the gates of Uruk. And I will do so in time for the New Year's Festival."

Again, silence rewarded his declaration. Everything they had heard of the monster of the Great Cedar Forest promised nothing but failure for Gilgamesh.

"Your hesitation is ill-informed," said Gilgamesh. "Folk tales and legends always make these monsters much worse than they actually are. What say you?"

Suddenly, Enkidu blurted out, "Humbaba!"

All eyes turned to Enkidu.

"His name is Humbaba," he repeated. "Humbaba the Terrible." Everyone knew he spoke of the giant guardian. They all listened in rapt attention as Enkidu spoke with deadly seriousness.

"I have been to the Great Cedar Forest when I roamed the wild, years ago. Humbaba is a mighty Rephaim giant. This is not a creature you want to face."

Even Gilgamesh felt chills down his spine as he heard the ominous tone in Enkidu's voice, a man he thought had no fear.

Enkidu continued, "His roar is like a flood of many waters, his mouth breathes fire and death. He never sleeps and he can hear the rustling of a leaf across the distance of the whole forest."

Okay, now he is exaggerating, thought Gilgamesh. *Vestiges of his simple animal experience as a Wild Born.* Gilgamesh knew the forest extended nearly a hundred leagues. No giant, not even a Rapha, had hearing that acute. A hundred or more cubits maybe, but not a hundred leagues. And no creature could live without sleep. A god, perhaps, but not a creature. All this was the stuff of legends, and legends are overthrown by real world Gibborim warriors like himself. Enkidu's attempt to strike fear in Gilgamesh's heart only served to embolden him to the challenge.

Enkidu continued his story with a hushed voice, as though telling a ghost story to impressionable children around a campfire. "His strength is unequalled. He has powers to paralyze his enemies at a distance. Every man's battle with him is that man's last. The only creature more fearsome on land is the Bull of Heaven."

The Bull of Heaven was a ferocious amphibious beast that dwelt mostly on land. The size of a temple, black as a raven, legends said it survived the Deluge because of its aquatic nature and bullish will of iron. Humbaba was mild in comparison. Knowing this did not encourage Enkidu. He sensed his fate was already sealed for this journey.

Gilgamesh broke the hypnotic spell cast by Enkidu's story, "Men of Uruk, noble counselors of the assembly, who has immortality but the gods of heaven? As for humankind, our days are all numbered. All our life is chasing after wind. No one returns from the grave. Glory and fame alone can establish a name that will live forever."

The assembly sat in awed silence. A tear rolled down Ninsun's cheek. She treasured her Gilgamesh with all her heart and feared to lose him to a foolhardy adventure.

Gilgamesh looked at Enkidu with a sincere longing. "Enkidu, what has become of your boldness and strength? You were born and raised in the wilderness. I have heard that you have killed a lioness with your bare hands, one that once escaped my own weapons of death."

Enkidu looked up at Gilgamesh, surprised.

Shamhat and Dumuzi had told Gilgamesh the story of the lioness attack. From their descriptions of the marks on the lioness's face, he had realized it was the one who had faced him down earlier. It might have killed him, had it not been for the accidental head injury.

Gilgamesh continued with a touch of sarcasm. "Well, if you are afraid, my Right Hand, you may trail behind me and call out to me, 'Go this way or that.'" He turned back to the assembly and concluded, "I will vanquish Humbaba and cut down his Cedar trees. And should I fall, I will still establish my fame for eternity as Gilgamesh, the mighty Gibbor, who locked horns in battle with Humbaba the Terrible!"

The assembly broke into more murmurs. Sinleqiunninni cleared his throat in a teacherly way. He spoke up, "My king, trees are not all that Humbaba guards."

Gilgamesh waited, curious.

Sinleqiunninni said, his voice a droning monotone, "The Cedar Forest is actually two hundred leagues in extension. It contains not merely cedars but juniper, cypress, acacia, myrtle and olive trees. It surrounds Mount Hermon, which rises approximately five thousand, eight hundred and seventy one cubits high into the air. It is part of the Sirion mountain range that extends for thirty one leagues in a northeast southwest direction."

Gilgamesh had lost track of what the scholar was saying. It was amazing. Sinleqiunninni could deaden any discussion by simply speaking. It was as if this man of knowledge made knowledge boring. It was worse than Enkidu's flatulence.

Gilgamesh determined to keep the assembly focused on his proposal before Sinleqiunninni distracted them to oblivion. "Well, what is the point, scholar? Is there a point here?"

Sinleqiunninni finally got to the point. "Mount Hermon is the home of the gods."

"I would appreciate it if you do not rattle off the list of gods who reside there, as we do not have all day," said Gilgamesh. Sinleqiunninni sat down, silenced.

Enkidu said, "What will you do, O king, when the gods discover that you have killed their Guardian?"

"I do not know, Enkidu, but do you not desire to know why they hide away in their cosmic mountain with such timidity? This is more than an heroic adventure of killing a giant and establishing a name. This is a search for the gods, in whose hands is eternal life."

Enkidu protested, "But you are already two thirds god."

"And one third human," added Gilgamesh. "So death still has its claim on me."

Enkidu considered his words carefully.

Gilgamesh continued, "You have transformed from an animal into a man. Would you not want to transform from a man into a god?"

"But is it for man to do so?" asked Enkidu.

"Join my side, Enkidu, and together we shall see," said Gilgamesh.

There was no stopping him. Gilgamesh would answer each objection that Enkidu could come up with. He would defy any technical fact the king's scholar could muster, until every objection was worn down. It was sheer will power and Gilgamesh had more of it than everyone in the room combined.

Enkidu resigned himself to his fate. He stood up and announced to the assembly, "Noble counselors, I know the route to the Great Cedar Forest, and I know the wiles of Humbaba. If you will grant your blessing, I will accompany King Gilgamesh on his journey for the greatness of Uruk and his good name."

And so they received the blessing of the assembly. They charged Gilgamesh not to trust his own strength, but to trust his Right Hand to lead the way and his own skill of fighting to make each blow hit its mark.

Such a great quest of mighty deeds would require weapons of special handiwork.

Gilgamesh and Enkidu oversaw the forging of battle axes of three talents each. Men of normal human strength could not wield them. Their swords with gold hilts weighed two talents each, their girded kilts were fifty minas. A war net of two talents completed their battle gear that totaled almost ten talents each. Gilgamesh also brought along his magical animal skins that took away the fear that animals had of man. But he told no one about this special talisman, not even Enkidu, his most trusted ally.

Gilgamesh and Enkidu went to the town square near the main gate. Gilgamesh blew his horn to gather the men of the city. He called for fifty warriors to join their journey to the Cedar Forest.

"But this quest is the most dangerous I have ever performed," Gilgamesh told them. "So if you have a wife, return to your wife. If you have children, return to your children. For I require warriors who have no family to suffer loss."

Among the champions who volunteered were seven warriors, sons of the same mother, each with special talents. The eldest had mighty hands like the paws of a lion that could tear a man in half. Another had a strong jaw whose bite was like that of a cobra. The third had a sword made of flexible metal that operated like a whip and cut like a dragon serpent, rumored to have been handed down from a son of Noah himself. The fourth could spit fire like a dragon. The fifth could track anything with the taste of his serpentine tongue. The sixth had a mighty power in his fists and arms to batter mountains into rubble. And the seventh could call down lightning from heaven onto his adversaries.

After all this preparation, Gilgamesh was still not ready to leave on his journey. He told Enkidu that one last thing remained to knit him to Gilgamesh as close as a brother.

CHAPTER 12

Queen Mother, goddess Ninsun, left the feast. She went to her temple Egalmah, to intercede with Shamash on behalf of Gilgamesh and his crazy idea for glory and fame. She bathed herself seven times in tamarisk and soapwart for purity. She donned a robe and sash, along with jewels and her tiara. Then she went up to the roof, set incense before Shamash, and sprinkled holy water onto the ground.

She grieved before the sun god with raised arms. "Why have you inflicted my son Gilgamesh with a restless heart? He will travel on a road he knows not, to a destination he knows not where, and fight a battle he may never know again. During his days of journey to the Cedar Forest and back, may the Anunnaki, the Watchers of the night, watch over him and his companion, Enkidu. Bring your mighty winds against Humbaba."

The sun god remained silent. He was after all a statue of stone.

A servant approached Ninsun to notify her that her guests had arrived. She completed her supplication and retired to her chapel below to speak with Gilgamesh and Enkidu.

The chapel hummed with the activities of priestesses, as well as votaries bound by oath, and the hierodules of the temple. Gilgamesh and Enkidu stood before the altar, Enkidu with wide eyes of wonder at all the pomp unfolding before him. It was a ceremony of some kind. The juniper incense tickled his sensitive nostrils. That was one of the things about religion that he did not care for, the incense. The odor was too strong for his highly attuned olfactory sense. There was much about religion that he questioned, but this was not the time for his challenges.

Ninsun approached Gilgamesh and Enkidu, followed by her coterie. She looked at Gilgamesh and nodded in secret agreement. Gilgamesh smiled.

She turned her gaze to Enkidu.

Gilgamesh whispered to him, “This is what I told you about earlier, my brother.”

Enkidu gave Gilgamesh a glance of skeptical wariness.

Ninsun spoke, drawing his attention back to her, “Mighty Enkidu, though you are not of my womb, I speak for the votaries of Gilgamesh and the priestesses and sacred women of Egalmah.”

Enkidu could feel the hair on the back of his neck stand up. An excited chill ran through him as he began to realize what was taking place. Ninsun took from around her neck a leather strap with gold amulet. She draped it on Enkidu’s trembling form. It bore the royal family seal, stamped on precious metal.

Ninsun continued, a smiling tear rolling down her cheek, “This amulet is a talisman of our family name. It bears all the weight of mighty Uruk behind it. As the daughters of the gods take in a foundling, so I take Enkidu, to love as my adopted son. May Gilgamesh be a favorable brother to you.”

Enkidu burst out weeping. It would be the only time Gilgamesh would ever see such a display of emotion from this former Wild Born, this Gibborim warrior by his side. Enkidu hugged Gilgamesh first and whispered into his ear, “My brother.”

Then Enkidu stood and embraced Ninsun saying, "My goddess, my mother."

Ninsun concluded with a benediction, "I commission you, Enkidu to safeguard your King, your brother, and that if necessary you give your life for such an honor."

Enkidu gazed at her with utter submission. "I will," he said.

She looked at them both now. "May your journey to the Great Cedar Forest have short nights and long days. And may your loins be girded with strength and your stride be steadfast and sure."

She reached behind her and brought out a powerful looking bow of a foreign design. It had not been crafted for normal human use, but for a giant. Gilgamesh knew immediately what it was. Ninsun said, "I present to you, my son, this, the bow of Anshan from the distant land of Elam, that you may slay Humbaba the Terrible."

She handed it to him.

They made an offering of root cuttings and prayed to Shamash for protection.

It dawned on Gilgamesh that this must have been the meaning of his dreams of the star and axe that would be "made his equal" by Ninsun. By becoming his brother, Enkidu would be the family equal of Gilgamesh. He could not help thinking about her off-the-cuff comment about this equal being a possible "betrayer." He hoped it was just another one of her wrong interpretations.

The ceremony moved Enkidu to the very core of his being. Adoption into the family of Gilgamesh meant more to him than royalty. It answered his longing for the human identity of which he had been deprived. A family represented continuity with humanity. It meant being a part of a lineage that would continue through the ages, giving meaning to the branches and roots. If he remained a lone wolf, he would exist alone and die alone in the vast emptiness of solitary annihilation. Without family, what would his days of comfort and love with his wife be but a cruel joke, a momentary spasm in an eternal nothingness? By being grafted into this tree of human history, he would finally be rooted in a transcendence beyond himself, something bigger than his meaningless un-rooted self. And his new family gave him semi-divine roots at that. Enkidu's feelings were the opposite of what Gilgamesh sought. Enkidu wanted to lose himself in the whole. Gilgamesh wanted to stand out and be separate, to be a unique and eternal self of importance, one that shined above the masses of mundane existence – like a star, like a god.

The next day, Gilgamesh and Enkidu met with the fifty warriors chosen for their journey to the Great Cedar Forest. Gilgamesh had also called Dumuzi and Sinleqiunninni to see them off. Ninsun stayed in her palace that day. She felt too emotional and full of fear for her sons. And she harbored a secret that tore her heart and soul apart. She could barely face Gilgamesh without feeling deep guilt and regret. But she was determined he would never discover her secret. So she stayed in her palace and hid herself away.

Gilgamesh spoke to Sinleqiunninni, "My scholar, be prepared when I return to inscribe the tale that I will bring back. For I will have mighty deeds to tell."

"Yes, my king," said Sinleqiunninni, "Your fame will bring you eternal life."

That thought suddenly struck Gilgamesh as incongruent. Fame is eternal life? What good was fame in Sheol? Was he a fool searching for the impossible? Was he a fool to search at all?

Enkidu, standing beside him, said in a low voice, "It is still not too late to turn back. You could finish the walls of Uruk to great fanfare and still be the mighty Gilgamesh who built the walls of Uruk."

Gilgamesh gave Enkidu a look of rebuke. He would not dignify the statement with any other response. Instead he turned to Dumuzi. "Dumuzi, my Shepherd, I want you to rule the city in my absence."

It shocked Dumuzi. He did not consider himself worthy of such an honor, and he certainly did not desire the responsibility it laid on his shoulders.

"I am just a shepherd, my king," protested Dumuzi.

"Yes," replied Gilgamesh. "And you shall shepherd Uruk until I return." Gilgamesh placed his arm strongly around Dumuzi with affection. "My friend, aside from Enkidu, you are the only one I trust in my absence to so rule."

Sinleqiunninni looked sour. He had secretly hoped that *he* would be given that privilege. After all, he was the ummanu, the scholar, more intelligent than anyone else in the palace. He certainly had more knowledge than this shepherd of low confidence. The volumes he knew were surely a well of wisdom that every ruler could only dream of.

Gilgamesh is a strong leader, but he is not an intellectual genius. Not like me, he thought. *When will the world recognize that knowledge is true power?*

Enkidu smiled as he saw Sinleqiunninni's disappointment.

Gilgamesh finished his charge to Dumuzi, "The wall is almost complete. I need you to strengthen the morale of the workers to finish the task before I return. I am sure you see the benefit of me vanquishing the giant and arriving home to the completed mighty walls of Uruk."

"It is positively mythical," butted in Sinleqiunninni. He did not mean to let himself be pushed out of the moment entirely. "The symbolism would be a powerful metaphor for advantageous propaganda in an epic cuneiform tale."

Gilgamesh also knew it was to his advantage to avoid stifling the one who would pen his story with stylus to clay. He just nodded and did not respond to the flattery.

Dumuzi knew Gilgamesh was right. He sighed and nodded to his lord and king, accepting the big responsibility before him. He would rise to the occasion. He also thought he would use this opportunity to stick Sinleqiunninni away on some scribal project, to keep the scholar's annoying presence out of his hair.

They embraced in farewell.

Gilgamesh turned to Enkidu, "Let us begin our journey."

Enkidu signaled to the waiting warriors, atop their horse mounts. He gave the command, "Ho, hurrah! Let us journey forth, warriors!"

Gilgamesh said to Enkidu, "I have been meaning to ask you, where on earth did you get that saying, 'Ho, hurrah,' you repeat with such annoying repetition?"

"From Dumuzi on the steppe, my lord," smiled Enkidu.

Dumuzi looked away embarrassed.

Gilgamesh said sternly, "Dumuzi."

Dumuzi looked up timidly at him.

Gilgamesh said, "Ho, hurrah," and gave him a wink. They turned and left the city gates, heading into the open land before them.

CHAPTER 13

It had been several days since Gilgamesh left Uruk for the Great Cedar Forest, with Enkidu and his band of warriors. Dumuzi had taken to his new responsibilities over Uruk with a certain amount of distaste. The only satisfaction he received came from sending Sinleqiunninni to the library archives for a detailed, up to date accounting of the kingdom finances. He would be there for weeks most likely, rummaging through a myriad of broken, misplaced, and out of date tablets, trying to recalculate inaccurate numbers and tracking down missing accounts. The crown was meticulous in its accounting, but humans were fallible and corrupt. There would be much corruption to uncover, and wrongs to right, all of which made Sinleqiunninni the perfect bureaucrat of tedium to employ.

Fortunately, it was not a pointless exercise. As the wall neared completion, Gilgamesh would have to reconcile his finances and resources. So it was all necessary.

Dumuzi missed the herds and the grazing fields. He missed the open air and the sound of baaing sheep lulling him to sleep. He wondered how he found himself in such an odd position of trust with the king he had wanted to kill, for the violation of Dumuzi's dignity and honor in the past? He found himself strangely drawn in by Gilgamesh's magnetic charisma. He was an abusive ruler in some ways, but in others, he was a positive force, drawing order out of the chaos. He was just the kind of leader needed to restrain the petty grumblings and mob mentality of the masses. People tended to blindly follow the strongest, most sensational call to action, regardless of its rationality or its moral value, right or wrong. And usually it was wrong. Only a strong leader could calm the mob or stir them in his calculated direction.

Gilgamesh also provided leadership with strong vision for a better future. Yet, he was a troubled king who seemed to be having his own personal crisis of meaning and identity. Thus, his quest for fame and eternal life. If recent events were any indication of the future of Uruk, Dumuzi felt hopeful. Enkidu's influence on Gilgamesh had already persuaded him to retract the abominable policy of *jus prima noctis,* that had stolen Dumuzi's honor and been the source of his rage. King Gilgamesh showed signs of becoming a better king, a more just king.

Dumuzi put these things out of his mind as he approached the clay pit. The foreman had alerted him that the workers had noticed a strong odor permeating the area. It was the stench of rotting flesh — or to be more precise, as Sinleqiunninni would say — rotting fish.

He arrived at the pit and journeyed down the incline. At the bottom, he came to where the workers had stopped and gathered. A large area of ground had been uncovered, revealing something gargantuan that had been exposed from underneath. It appeared to be the rough scaly backbone of some huge sea monster. It stunk to high heaven. The scales and spinal bones were too strong to break with their tools, but the flesh was rotting upon them.

Dumuzi summoned Sinleqiunninni out of his exile in the dungeonous library to provide some explanation. As best the scholar could determine, it was probably a sea dragon of some kind that had been buried in the sediment of the Great Flood.

"Normally, the flesh would have rotted away generations ago," declared Sinleqiunninni with superior knowledge, "leaving only a carcass of bones. But according to my observations, the burial was rapid, and apparently must have worked like a kind of sealed tomb, which stopped or slowed down the deterioration of the flesh. But when the workers broke the seal, and unearthed the body, it came into contact with the open air again, resulting in the rapid decomposition of its current state."

There was a lot of flesh to decompose. The thing was huge, even large enough to obstruct the entire work area. It might force them to start a new clay pit.

Dumuzi ordered clay workers to keep digging further away from the discovery. The current excavation would continue in order to see just how big the corpse was. He returned to the palace to take a nap and find some clean air to breath.

CHAPTER 14

A few days out from Uruk, Gilgamesh and his band of warrior brothers careened along their journey to the Great Cedar Forest at Mount Hermon in the west. This elite corps of mighty soldiers of the king had trained for years in his service. One could even call them Gibborim. "Gibborim" had come to mean mighty warrior, whether human or Nephilim.

Gilgamesh had led them on such a fast-paced march that they felt sure must have been supernaturally aided by the gods. Their trip crossed three hundred leagues to the foot of Mount Hermon in the midst of the Great Cedar Forest. Gilgamesh followed seven constellations by night through seven mountain passes. They navigated fifty leagues a day, twenty before they broke bread, and another thirty before they pitched camp. They traveled in a mere few days what would have taken weeks for a normal trained militia. Enkidu considered it nothing short of a miracle. Gilgamesh was too focused on his goal to notice.

They dug a well and poured a water offering out to Shamash in gratitude. Enkidu wondered what use water would be to a god who was a big ball of burning fire in the sky. Was he eternally thirsty? Would not water put his fire out? It did not make much sense to him, but he went along with it. Perhaps Shamash would shine some light into the darkened corners of this infernal forest.

They had traveled along the Euphrates river, around the fertile crescent, and down into the foothills of the Sirion Mountain range. By the time they were in sight of the cosmic mountain, at the edge of the vast forest, Gilgamesh confided in Enkidu that he had been having dreams again as he had before he battled Enkidu in Uruk.

"What are the dreams?" asked Enkidu. "I am not skilled in the art of interpretation like your mother," he said, pulling out the golden amulet from around his neck, "but I bear the spirit of your family name."

Gilgamesh said, "There have been five of them." Enkidu's eyes went wide with surprise.

"Well," said Enkidu, "let us construct a dream house of the gods and compose the circle for you to recount your dreams."

So they threw together a crude dream house out of loose lumber, a makeshift lean-to. Enkidu drew the circle with a stick, poured out a libation of flour on the ground, and the two sat down in the middle. Gilgamesh drifted into a trance and rested his head on his knees.

"My king?" said Enkidu.

Suddenly, Gilgamesh snapped his head back, blinking at Enkidu with bleary red eyes. "Why did I wake up?" he shouted, "Why am I trembling? Did a god pass by?"

Enkidu stared at him blankly. He had no clue what Gilgamesh meant, but he would try to help his friend find his way.

Enkidu spoke as if he knew what he was doing, "Tell me your dreams."

Gilgamesh said groggily, as if just coming out of a trance, "In the first dream, I was in a mountain gorge and the mountain fell upon me. But I was pulled out of the mountain and cast it down, and it was covered with flies."

Enkidu became even more confused. He wondered if he had gotten in over his head, if he should back out while he still had the chance. His mind raced for something positive, anything he could make up to encourage Gilgamesh. He looked out upon Mount Hermon in the distance. He blurted the first thing that came to his mind, "The mountain is Humbaba!"

Gilgamesh gazed at him, expecting more. He was superstitious when it came to dreams and susceptible to anyone with an interpretation.

Enkidu filled in the silence with words, while he thought of something else to add. "Your dream is — uh — favorable. It is a precious — omen." He had heard Ninsun use that word "omen" before and thought it might fit well here, though he only vaguely understood what the word meant.

He repeated, "The mountain you saw is Humbaba." His thoughts drifted toward the monster. His emotions about the giant spilled out, "We will catch Humbaba and slay him — and throw his corpse out upon the field of battle for the flies to consume like excrement."

That did not seem too bad. Gilgamesh followed his words like a hypnotized religious fanatic.

The sun broke through the clouds. The glare shot into Enkidu's eyes. He sneezed from the brightness, and quickly said, "A sign that Shamash will show us favor."

Gilgamesh began describing his next dream before Enkidu could stop him. "My second dream surpasses the first."

Oh, great, thought Enkidu. *What have I gotten myself into?*

Gilgamesh continued, "Another mountain threw me down and held me until a man appeared, a most handsome man, who pulled me from beneath the mountain and gave me a fresh drink of water."

Gilgamesh paused. He stared at Enkidu like a school child looking to the master to give the answer.

Enkidu was even more in the dark than before. He thought, *What do the gods hope to achieve by giving such crazy dreams that do not make any sense? If I were a god, I would chose a clearer means of communicating my message.*

"Enkidu," Gilgamesh interrupted his confusion.

Enkidu said the first thing that came to him. "Uh, the mountain is *not* Humbaba," Now Gilgamesh looked confused. Enkidu thought to himself, *Why did I just say that? I just said the opposite of what I said before. I will never talk about dreams to anyone ever again.*

Enkidu tried a dodge, "What was the next dream? Maybe they are connected in some way."

Gilgamesh nodded. He said, "I was grappling with a wild bull of the wilderness, and his bellowing snort split the earth beneath my feet and a cloud of dust obscured the sky."

Enkidu sat stone silent. He felt like he had fallen into a crevice of his own making and had no way to climb back up.

Gilgamesh started to explain his next dream, "In another one, heaven and earth rumbled and flashes of lightning…"

"I am sorry, my lord," interrupted Enkidu.

Gilgamesh was not listening. He kept going. "And an Anzu bird was caught by a strange man…."

"Ho, hurrah, my king!" bellowed Enkidu.

Gilgamesh stopped.

Enkidu said, "I really do not put much investment in dreams. Basically, we are going to fight with Ḫumbaba. There is going to be a lot of chaos and destruction, but we will triumph over him with great victory. Now we have our axes and swords, you have the mighty bow of Anshan, and we have fifty warriors backing us up. Let us kill ourselves a giant!"

With that, Enkidu jumped to his feet. He burst out of the lean-to and gathered his weapons. Gilgamesh nodded his head solemnly, finding some profundity in it all.

Enkidu thought, *This is definitely one of the king's weaknesses. I think his mother did this to him. She is too coddling with his obsessions.*

CHAPTER 15

While Dumuzi slumbered, the workers in the pit continued their labors excavating the great fish. It was causing a delay in putting the finishing touches on the walls of Uruk.

A group of workers hacked away at the clay some distance from the original discovery site. They came upon what appeared to be the head of the sea monster. Knowing where the head lay in relation to the torso helped them understand the size and shape of the monster. Soon they would know where to complete their work of brick-making, far from this stench-filled area.

A dozen feet away, one of the workers saw the ground move.

"Did you see that?" he asked the others.

They grumbled. A scattering of "no" rippled through the group, along with complaints to keep digging.

The ground moved more noticeably.

They all stopped to watch. One of the workers blew a horn. The foreman and others gathered to see what all the fuss was about.

A large humanoid hand broke out of the clay and grasped the air into a clenched fist.

The growing circle of observers backed away in fear. What was this beast that was being born from the earth? A shade escaping Sheol? Had they accidentally broken in upon the forbidden underworld?

The earth bulged.

The thing struggled to rise up out of its grave. Though everyone else backed away, the foreman crept forward with macabre curiosity. For some strange reason, he wanted to help the thing.

The clay finally ruptured.

A large being eight feet tall burst its way out of the clay. It looked humanoid with luminescent burnished bronze skin, made of scales so small they were not readily visible to the normal human eye. It had body-length hair on its head and eyes of lapis lazuli blue.

The earth that had been removed from the discovery revealed the immense teeth of the sea monster. This being had been clamped in the dragon's mighty jaws. Now it was free.

It looked down at the foreman, who stood transfixed by the mystery of this naked being of power and awe. The crowd all around was speechless.

The being spoke to the foreman with a voice that creaked as if talking for the first time, "What is your name?"

"Ninshubar," he answered obediently.

The shining one reached down and put its hand on the foreman's shoulder. Ninshubar smiled. He looked into the face of a god.

The god grabbed Ninshubar's head and ripped it from his body. His dead body fell to the ground. The shining one roared with fury to the heavens.

The workers scrambled in fear. But they would not escape today. The shining being hunted them down like rabbits, hundreds of them, and killed them all in a rage of fury. Its speed and efficiency were astonishing. It swatted, clawed, punched and ripped its way through the workers up toward the top of the clay pit.

After it had its fill of frenzy, it stood at the top of the pit and looked down upon the blood and carnage with a lack of satisfaction. It would take considerably more death and destruction than this to quench its rage, a rage that generations of buried solitude in the depths of the earth had fueled.

The shining being was Azazel the Watcher, who had been caught in the mouth of Rahab the sea dragon of chaos in the flood waters of the Deluge.

Since the Watchers were divine Sons of God, they could not die. So when the sediment buried him, he was condemned to a living grave of captivity. His rebellion with Semjaza and the two hundred Watchers who fell from heaven, led to his imprisonment in the earth until the future punishment in the end of days.

But the end was not yet here. It was not yet his time.

As a member of the heavenly host, Azazel's body shone when he had strong emotional reactions. And Azazel brimmed over with generations of compounded angry rage, manifested in flashing lightning-like radiance. He had had plenty of time in his earthly imprisonment to plot his revenge.

CHAPTER 16

Gilgamesh and Enkidu arrived with their entourage of warriors at an entrance to the Great Cedar Forest. An impenetrable wall of timber towered over them. Before them lay an opening that seemed like a gateway into a haunted world. They could hear strange and unfamiliar sounds from within that sent chills through their skins. A pathway disappeared into the murky foliage, apparently well-worn by the Guardian who patrolled its vast expanse.

The peak of Mount Hermon rose out of the earth just leagues into the forest, visible above the tree line. It was the abode of the gods, the very cosmic mountain where the pantheon came down from heaven. It was where the gods congregated in assembly for deliberation.

The travelers were weary from their journey. They made camp on the perimeter of the forest. They would rest the night and prepare to engage the giant within the following day.

Gilgamesh offered a sacrifice of two kid goats to the sun god Shamash. Enkidu recognized the importance to Gilgamesh. So he encouraged the king to perform the ritual, even though Enkidu himself did not think much of it all. Gilgamesh implored Shamash for protection and help to enter the mountain land to fell great cedars and slay the giant Rapha, Humbaba the Terrible. Unfortunately, the god did not answer him.

The seven warriors from one mother possessed tireless endurance. They practiced their art of war every day, even after long grueling marches. The eldest, Ariel, with hands like the paws of a lion scratched bark off trees. Izi the firespitter helped start their campfires. Yahatti, the serpent-tongued, licked the air to gauge the weather and check for nearby intruders. The one with powerful hands, Lama, crunched trees into manageable firewood. Ikuppi, who could call down lightning, avoided practicing his art for obvious reasons. Mari, with the serpent sword Rahab, practiced his technique by slicing through trees with his whip-like sword of flexible metal. He even showed the curious Enkidu how the weapon worked. He told the king's Right Hand the story of how it had been forged on the mountain of Eden by angels. It had been passed down from their forefather Lamech through the line of Noah, thus eventually coming into Mari's hands.

After dinner, Gilgamesh and Enkidu sat before their campfire, separated from the other men. Enkidu sharpened his axe blade on a whetstone. Gilgamesh stared into the open flames, playing with the mutton on its bone.

"My lord is contemplating the mysteries of the cosmos?" asked Enkidu.

Gilgamesh kept staring into oblivion. "So I enter this mountain land, and I defeat the giant Humbaba. What then?"

"We return to Uruk, and I to my lioness, Shamhat. I eat food again that does not taste like this leather," said Enkidu. With that, he lifted his leg and let loose a loud rip-roaring fart.

Someone barked out, "Keep it down, gas bag, you will trumpet our location to the giant!" The other men laughed.

Gilgamesh did not laugh. His face scrunched with an angry look. He stood up. Enkidu thought he may have pushed Gilgamesh's respect too far.

Then Gilgamesh crouched and let loose a long blast of gas that sounded like the trumpet the others had joked about.

He had clearly one-upped Enkidu, who gave him a surprised look to challenge his etiquette.

"You think a god king has no digestion?" said Gilgamesh. The other men chuckled.

Gilgamesh smiled. "Enkidu, when outside the court and in the company of men facing sure death, you may consider yourself entirely free to violate the laws of etiquette against passing gas."

"Thank you, your majesty," said Enkidu. He promptly grunted out another blast of rumbling gas. It was not as loud or as long as Gilgamesh's.

Enkidu concluded with a faux bow to Gilgamesh, "But I do yield. You remain the king of flatulence."

Gilgamesh pinched his nose in disgust and quipped, "You give me a run for my money as the prince of stench."

The men broke out in laughter again.

They all settled back down into their own interests.

Gilgamesh returned to his serious posture. He probed Enkidu. "You are a man of the earth and of nature. Do you ever concern yourself with higher things like the meaning of life?"

Enkidu thought for a moment. He finally answered, "If you refer to gods and dreams and spiritual knowledge, then 'meaning' is something that evades my sensibilities. The only 'meaning' I know is the hunger in my belly, the desire in my loins, the sight, sound, and smells of wherever I am at this very moment, right here and right now. My brother at my side, my wife waiting at home. Beyond that, I know no meaning."

Enkidu knew he was not being completely honest, for he was not telling Gilgamesh everything. He had had experiences in the wild that had made him wonder about his creator. But now was not the time to speak of such things.

Enkidu picked up a leg of mutton and took a bite. It was terrible and old tasting. He spit it out, gagging with distaste. He threw the bone in the fire.

Gilgamesh laughed. “Yes. We will eat, drink, and be merry. And then we will die, like every other man.” But then he turned morose. “I have seen rivers plugged with corpses. I have looked upon battlefields drenched in blood and piled high with the carnage of human bodies. So too it will happen to you and me.”

“Hopefully later than sooner,” offered Enkidu.

Gilgamesh was not listening. “No matter how tall a man is, he cannot reach heaven. And no matter how enduring, he cannot traverse Sheol.”

Enkidu said, “And no matter how philosophical, he cannot conquer a giant of the Rephaim with words of profundity.”

Gilgamesh brightened. “Enkidu, you are my only truest friend. Together, we will enter this mountain land, slay a giant, and I will engrave my name in this Great Cedar Forest. We will return to Uruk with mighty cedar wood to dress my glorious palace.”

“Or Humbaba will kill us and feed on our corpses,” added Enkidu.

Gilgamesh smiled. “Strengthen your trembling arms, Enkidu. You speak like a spineless weakling. Where is your ‘Ho, hurrah,’ annoying though it may be? I will gladly run with you into the face of death and go out in flames of glory. I will be honored to have you by my side in the valley of Sheol.”

Enkidu was not so focused on glory. “I would prefer, my lord, to make it out of this alive, if you do not mind.”

“Enkidu, we two can do together what one cannot,” said Gilgamesh. “Together we vanquished three legendary lions.”

"Yours was bigger than mine," said Enkidu.

"But yours was the fiercest," said Gilgamesh. "I used the skill of a javelin, dagger, and axe. With what did you vanquish your lioness?"

Enkidu averted his eyes shyly, "My bare hands."

Gilgamesh grinned wide. "That is nothing to be ashamed of, Enkidu. You have earned your name." Then he thought better. "Just do not boast about it around my palace."

Enkidu smiled humbly.

Gilgamesh said, "We had better get our sleep. And do not leave your axe behind tomorrow. I suspect even the mighty Enkidu's bare hands will not be enough when we face Humbaba the Terrible." He winked at Enkidu with a genuine humor that only a true friend could give when bettered.

Tomorrow, they would continue their journey into the forest in the direction of Mount Hermon, home of the gods.

CHAPTER 17

Azazel found his way toward the palace. He saw that the entire city of Uruk had been rebuilt upon the ruins of the pre-Flood city. It was quite glorious. The walls were an impressive innovation. He did not know just how long he had been trapped in his living tomb, but it must have been generations. Needless to say, mankind had done rather well in picking up the pieces and starting over. Or at least, this city had done rather well.

I must meet this king who has achieved such glory, he thought. *And I must find out what has happened to the other gods.*

Azazel's first stop on the way to the palace was *Eanna,* the new temple of Inanna. It was bigger. Everything was bigger in the city. Signs of grandiosity abounded. It had a different layout. But he easily recognized the servant and priestly antechambers. He passed through the garden-like courtyard where the hierodules pursued their trade with patrons.

Indeed, I must meet this king, Azazel thought again. *He has taste, a sense of spectacle and self-aggrandizement that suits me.*

Temple servants scattered in fear, as Azazel made his way to the High Priestess' chambers. The shining spectre stood eight feet tall, naked, and covered in blood. A terrifying sight to the citizenry. He had decided to maintain his identity as the goddess Inanna because he had worked hard on that persona. He had come to enjoy the theatrical spectacle that it allowed him to release. He did intend to make one significant change that he would announce upon his arrival at the palace court. But first, he needed some garments.

He burst into the chambers of the High Priestess. She was engaged in improper activities with several highly placed assembly members. *Too bad for these pathetic saps,* thought Azazel. *About to end their pursuit of pleasure in a spasm of pain.*

Azazel slaughtered the men in several swipes, flinging them like small puppies against a brick wall. The Priestess screamed. Azazel put his finger to his lips to shush her.

He backed the Priestess up against the wall. Her eyes widened with fear, her vocal chords paralyzed by the immense creature towering over her.

Azazel paused with a smile, victim's blood dripping down his face. "Why do you look so surprised, priestess? I *am* the goddess of war that you worship. You never expected to see me in the flesh?" He enjoyed such moments of irony and fear in his subjects.

She could only shake her head with short jerky movements. She was confused. Azazel looked like a strange mixture of female and male. His long tangled hair had not stopped growing all those decades trapped in the earth. He would have to do something with it.

"I thank you for your devotion on my behalf," said Azazel. "And now, I must ask you for one more act of sacrifice."

Azazel gently grabbed her head and broke her neck. He needed her clothes for himself. She also had a fabulous gem laden necklace and earrings to kill for.

He had needed to eliminate the High Priestess in any case. He would have to start all over with a new and loyal retinue of servants. Danger lurked in keeping old leadership with a regime change, no matter how flexible their loyalties. It was always just better to kill them all and start over with fresh blood.

He found some additional garments in her wardrobe that he put together to create a flamboyant outfit. He thought he would stress his female identity to start with, so there would be no question as to the gender of this long lost goddess. And he wanted it to create a splash, a memorable introduction, not easily forgotten. Perilously high heels, brightly colored loud hairdo sprinkled with sparkling gem shavings, a tight tunic accented with billowy cuffs, and a satin robe that flowed behind her carried by two hand-picked male slaves.

Inanna was back.

CHAPTER 18

Gilgamesh, Enkidu and the fifty warriors made their way into the forest a couple of leagues toward Mount Hermon. They stopped by a river flowing through the forest and filled their water skins. They had followed the beaten trail created by the guardian giant with the intent of crossing his path. However, the forest was so thick and so vast, they realized they were not likely to find Humbaba's residence. They would have to encourage Humbaba to find them.

Gilgamesh raised his mighty axe in the air and swung it. Its head sank into the bark of a mighty cedar tree with a crunch.

The strangest sound emanated from the wood. It was not a sound they heard, but rather a sound they felt, like the screeching pain of a child crying out for its mother.

Enkidu swung his axe and hit the same tree. They intended to chop down the wards of the Forest Guardian until he came to rescue the trees. The other warriors hacked away together on several other trees. The sound of heavy chopping drowned out the silent screams that vibrated all around them.

Then something changed.

The screams became like a song that lilted in their ears. The men became tired and sleepy. In threes and fours, they dropped to the forest floor like sleeping dogs. Even Gilgamesh and Enkidu laid down and drifted into unconsciousness. An enchantment wrapped them with an aura they were not prepared to encounter.

Gilgamesh began to dream. In his dream he saw again the wild bull of the wilderness. The animal's bellowing snort split the earth beneath his feet. A cloud of dust obscured the sky. Then a man came before him and gave Gilgamesh a drink of water from his water skin. Somehow Gilgamesh knew that the man was his father, holy Lugalbanda. The bull suddenly spoke with a roaring voice, "Gilgamesh, awake! So says Shamash. Gilgamesh awake!"

Gilgamesh came to with Enkidu shaking him and yelling, "Gilgamesh, awake!"

Gilgamesh heard the sounds of rumbling in the forest, the sounds of giant feet stampeding their way, getting closer. A massive roar of monstrous rage penetrated the thicket a hundred feet away and wakened the other warriors. Humbaba the Terrible had found them.

CHAPTER 19

Dumuzi awoke from his nap and returned to business. He consulted with Ninsun over a temple redecorating project.

Then Inanna arrived at the palace demanding the presence of the king.

Ninsun and Dumuzi hastened to the throne room. The entity they found standing there stunned them. Despite her outrageous outfit, they could tell this was not someone to trifle with. She was queenly and held herself as one who owned the world and was returning to claim it.

Dumuzi's appearance failed to impress Inanna. She had expected someone more — grandiose. This small flesh pot seemed nothing more than a shepherd. And the female smelled of pretention.

"Are you the king and queen?" asked Inanna.

"No," said Dumuzi. "But I am Dumuzi, the king's stead until he returns. And who are you, may I ask?"

This man was definitely not royalty, thought Inanna. *He talks like an outdoorsman. Though he is physically strong and well developed. Handsome.*

"The wench?" asked Inanna.

Ninsun was taken aback by the brazen insult. She barked back, "How dare you insult the goddess Ninsun! Explain your identity immediately or you will pay for your insolence!" Ninsun snapped her fingers and six soldiers stepped out from the shadows ready for orders.

Inanna smirked. She ignored the soldiers and walked right up to Ninsun, next to the throne.

Ninsun started to tremble. She did not have the guts to call on her guards. Somehow, she knew it would be futile. This being had hypnotic power over her.

Inanna sniffed her. "You are a wild cow, but you are no goddess."

She stepped over to Dumuzi and looked him up and down. She could smell his fear. "Were you in charge of the clay pits?"

"Yes," said Dumuzi. He tried to maintain a semblance of strength and confidence. But this shining one before him had such an aura of power that he could barely hold his bladder from his fear.

"I like you. And I have much to thank you for. I am the goddess Inanna."

Dumuzi felt his knees go weak. Ninsun almost fainted. He caught her and helped her to sit on the throne next to his.

Inanna continued, "And you will never believe what happened to me." She started to pace around with the gestures of an orator as she spun a tale to cover her own pathetic subjugation at the hands of Elohim's archangels during the Flood, and ultimately in the jaws of Rahab the sea dragon of chaos.

She titled her story, *Inanna's Descent into the Underworld.* "Once upon a time, in those days, in those far-off days, in those nights, in those distant nights, I planned to visit my sister Ereshkigal, goddess of the underworld, known as Sheol, the Land of No Return. In truth, I had ulterior motives, which you really should not know, so I will spare you the details and with them, your lives. But be that as it may, it was an important journey, so I dressed accordingly. As you can see, I am quite adept at fashion. I do not go anywhere important without dressing up." Inanna turned fashionably around, showing off her outfit.

She continued, "Unfortunately, my sister had been conspiring against me, the little strumpet. It is true. And her abode is guarded by seven entrances, called the Seven Gates of Ganzir. Sheol is not called 'the Land of No Return' without reason. Anyway, as I journeyed through each gate, the Gatekeeper, who shall remain nameless, required me to take off a garment at each gate. At the first of the seven gates, he took my tiara, and said, 'Thus are the rules of the mistress of the netherworld.'"

Inanna paused. She could see she was losing them, so she cut to the chase. "Well, I will not bore you with the details of each and every gate. Suffice it to say that the Gatekeeper eventually removed all my garments and I was naked, totally naked. It was shameful."

Dumuzi perked up.

She continued, "I know that I look spectacularly stunning, but it also made me vulnerable. So my sister sent sixty diseases at me until I succumbed to death and was hanged on a stake. Fortunately, before I descended into the netherworld, I had left word with my servant Ninshubar to make sure the assembly of the gods would know of my absence should I fail to return within three days and nights."

Dumuzi listened closely. He knew Ninshubar. He was the foreman of the clay pits. He realized Inanna was making this stuff up and he wondered why.

Inanna spoke quickly to wrap it up, "And Ninshubar made the rounds of the gods until one of them empowered him and he freed me from the underworld, blah, blah, blah."

Inanna focused her piercing eyes on Dumuzi and Ninsun. "The point of the story is, I went down into Sheol as the goddess Inanna. I am now reborn, the goddess Ishtar. You shall call me Ishtar, Queen of Heaven."

She strode back to the speechless Dumuzi, and spoke with a seductive, firm whisper, "And you, my dear Dumuzi, shall be my assistant and escort. I shall call you 'Tammuz.'"

Dumuzi's throat went dry. The blood drained from his face. He had been thinking how masculine this goddess was beneath her feminine façade. Goddess of war seemed more applicable than goddess of sex. Still, he wondered what terrors she imposed upon the victims of her abuse.

His entire world crashed down around him when he realized that *he* was her next victim.

Ishtar held her hand out to him.

She said to Ninsun, "I will want to spend some time with you, Lady Wild Cow, to be brought up to speed on the machinations of religion in this new era. And for an explanation of your play at deity. But first, I have some things to discuss with my companion." She looked at Dumuzi and grabbed his hand.

He had no other choice. He thought of killing himself, but he would not have that privilege. It was too late for that. He prayed for suffering endurance.

CHAPTER 20

The giant Humbaba stood twenty feet tall, more than twice the size of Gilgamesh. He charged at them from the depth of the forest like a raging bull. Gilgamesh had never seen such a giant. He did not know it was possible. So *this* was a Rapha, so this was one of the Rephaim, the special bloodline of leaders bred from gods and men.

Enkidu was right. He was a terror that any invader would not want to face. His roar bore the sound of a rushing flood of waters and a mountain avalanche of boulders. His face was monstrously ugly, like a pile of coiled intestines with a bulbous nose and ugly eyes. He had two large tusks jutting out of his jaws like a wild boar. Gilgamesh also noticed that Humbaba's hands were huge and contained six fingers each. They could easily crush a warrior, even one the size of a giant like himself. It struck Gilgamesh that all of Enkidu's wild description was more factually true than he had thought possible. And for the first time in his adult life, fear filled Gilgamesh.

Humbaba the Terrible roared again. The entire team of warriors cowered behind their shields and behind trees.

The giant stopped to get a better look at the vile little insects that had trespassed in his forest. He liked to know who he was killing and eating. Unfortunately, warriors, because of their muscular features were always a little grizzly and not as juicy to taste.

A bright flash of lightning and a loud crack of thunder split the sky above them. While the warriors had slept under the temporary spell, a storm front had moved in. Black billowy clouds boiled overhead and the wind began to whip around them.

Gilgamesh said to Enkidu, "This is not looking good for us."

Enkidu gave Gilgamesh a condescending look. He repeated back to the king his own words with relish, "Strengthen your trembling arms, my king. You speak like a spineless weakling. Find your courage and let us face our destiny."

The rebuke came like a slap in the face for Gilgamesh, waking him from another enchantment. He shook it off.

The two of them stepped out in the open, Enkidu with battle axe and Gilgamesh with the bow of Anshan. The fifty warriors circled behind them, ready for battle.

Enkidu shouted in a hearty voice, "Ho, hurrah!"

When Humbaba saw Enkidu, he stopped in surprise, as if he found the Wild Born familiar, but could not place him. Then his eyes widened with recognition. He thundered, "Enkidu?"

Gilgamesh shot Enkidu a surprised look. "He knows you?"

Enkidu had a lot of explaining to do. He had told Gilgamesh that he knew *of* Humbaba, but he did not say that Humbaba knew *him*.

"It is a long story. I will tell you if we survive," said Enkidu.

Gilgamesh rolled his eyes and looked back at Humbaba.

"I am Gilgamesh, lord and king of Uruk," he shouted with as much confidence as he could muster.

Humbaba ignored Gilgamesh as if he were an inconsequential servant. "Enkidu, son of a serpent with no father, spawn of a reptile with no mother's milk. Why do you bring these cedar smiters into my paradise?"

Enkidu whispered to Gilgamesh, "He cannot hurt the trees. It is his weakness."

Gilgamesh hissed back, "You tell me this *now*? It might have helped us sooner if you would have…"

"An idiot gives a moron counsel?" Humbaba interrupted them. "Now I see that I should have eaten you then and filled my belly with you, Enkidu."

Humbaba stood beside the river bank. He reached down and picked up a huge boulder. He threw it at Gilgamesh and Enkidu.

They jumped out of the way. Several of the warriors behind them were slower, crushed by the huge rolling stone.

Gilgamesh shouted to his men, "Hide behind trees! He cannot harm the trees!"

Instantly, his men reacted. They dove behind trees, using them as shields against the force of this terrifying gargantuan.

Humbaba looked up into the storm winds that lashed around them. A lightning bolt crackled down to earth and hit one of the tallest cedars. It cut the tree in two, capturing everyone's attention, except that of Enkidu.

He watched Humbaba the entire time. He saw the giant flinch and cringe.

Humbaba yelled with anger, "By the gods, what sorcerer has caused this tempest of winds?"

Humbaba struggled to keep his balance in the furious gale. His greater height made him more susceptible to the wind than the warriors were.

Gilgamesh wondered if the storm had been sent from his patron deity Shamash.

Enkidu had seen the mighty Rapha cringe.

It began to rain.

Humbaba gave a gurgling roar. He abruptly turned around and ran deeper into the thicket of the forest.

Gilgamesh shouted, "Warriors!"

He prepared to command them to run after their fleeing foe.

Enkidu stopped him. "My lord. We cannot hope to keep up with his swift-footedness. And in this storm, it would be even less possible. The woodland is his soul."

Gilgamesh looked askance at Enkidu. "Is this fear rising up again, my Right Hand? We have him on the run."

"No," said Enkidu. "He is luring us into a trap, where he has the advantage."

"What do you mean?" asked Gilgamesh. He had to shout to be heard in the winds.

"Humbaba is not the brute ogre he appears," Enkidu yelled back. "He is a brilliant strategist, and the odds are against him at this moment. The storm winds keep him off balance, since he is not low to the ground as we are. The warriors were using as protective shields the trees that Humbaba will not hurt…"

Gilgamesh finished the lesson, "And the rain obscures the clarity of vision necessary to vanquish forty to one combat."

"Rushing headlong after him now invites disaster," said Enkidu.

Gilgamesh smiled, "We can track him on our own terms."

He turned to the warriors and called out, "Yahatti!"

Yahatti of the Seven Brothers stepped out of the crowd of warriors. Enkidu remembered the special talents of the Seven. He asked Yahatti, "Was the lightning called down by your brother ?"

"No," said Yahatti. "That was Ikuppi. He was killed by the boulder." He paused a moment painfully, then finished, "Along with the rest of my brothers."

Of the ten men who were killed by the flung boulder, six of them were the warriors with special skills. Ariel, who had paws of a lion and talons of an eagle; Mari, the wielder of a special sword; Izi who spit fire; and Lami with hands of crushing power were now all dead. Yahatti alone survived. It could not be a more crushing blow to

Gilgamesh. His team of mighty Gibborim were ripped from him without even one chance to use their skills. It was a cruel joke of fate that mocked him and his task. And it ensured the failure of their mission.

Enkidu was not listening to Yahatti. He thought about the fear he had seen in the Rapha. He looked up into the black sky, blinking in the falling rain and windstorm. Perhaps there were other gods out there of which they were not aware. Unknown gods with storm power that would frighten the most vicious creature Enkidu had ever met.

Gilgamesh shouted to his band of warriors, "We will wait out the storm and track Humbaba in the morning!"

CHAPTER 21

Ishtar led Dumuzi on a leash out to the clay pits in the dark of night. He was completely humiliated, like a dog with a collar. Dumuzi struggled to keep from falling, wincing in pain and soreness with every step. Being Ishtar's assistant and escort was a painful horror, not an honor. He felt like he was being led to his grave. He *hoped* he was being led to his grave.

A large group of about one hundred workers followed them to the pit with torchlight.

Ishtar had a special task to accomplish this evening.

The procession came to the bottom of the pit. Ishtar instructed a couple of dowsers to search for water with their dowsing sticks. Soon, one of them announced a possible location. Ishtar knelt on the spot, pressing cheek and palms to the earth, seeking for a sign of confirmation.

She stood back up and commanded the workers to immediately begin to dig a well. They were to work at double strength and double time, all night if necessary, until they had broken through to the water table.

So, they dug.

Ishtar and Dumuzi climbed back up to the top of the pit and watched them. Ishtar sat on the portable throne from her temple. She made Dumuzi kneel beside her. She looked down on him and patted his head like a pet. His presence gratified her.

While they watched the workers dig the well, Queen Ninsun arrived with her retinue of servants.

"Ah, Lady Wild Cow," said Ishtar. "I have been dying to talk to you of the pantheon."

Perspiration saturated Ninsun's robes, far more than usual.

Ishtar continued, "Tell me of Mount Hermon and of the assembly of the gods. Who is left? Who escaped the Flood? Where is Semjaza? Who is in charge?"

Ninsun had no idea what Ishtar was talking about. She had been exposed by a real goddess. She had wondered if this would happen one day, and now that day was here, and she did not know what to do.

"Are you not a goddess? Do you know anything of the pantheon?"

The real goddess was impatient and wrathful. Ninsun wondered if she would live to see the morning.

Ishtar exploded with wrath, "I ASKED YOU A QUESTION, COW!"

"N- no," stuttered Ninsun.

"N-no, what?" mocked Ishtar. "No, you are not a goddess or no, you do not know of the pantheon?"

"Both," said Ninsun.

"Ah, well, we shall have to drag out of you just what little political intrigues you are scheming," said Ishtar.

A call from down in the clay pit interrupted them. The workers had struck water.

Ishtar sent a servant to raise the signal flag to command them to continue with the next phase.

Down in the pit, the foreman saw the signal and looked darkly at his diggers. "Hoist the drill," he said.

The workers looked at him with shock. One of them spoke up for the rest of them, “But sir, if we do that…”

The foreman interrupted him with an angry command, “Do not question the goddess! Hoist the drill, NOW!”

The workers looked at one another and obeyed. What else could they do? They knew no other life. They had been bred to obey royalty and deity without question. But they knew that what the goddess had ordered them to do was suicide.

They wheeled over a large mechanical structure made of metal and timber. It had weights and pulleys and looked like an inverted battering ram. By pulling the ropes, workers slammed stone weights onto a log with a sharpened point that would plunge into the earth, penetrating as deep as they could hammer it.

On the upper edge of the pit, Ishtar grinned diabolically at Ninsun’s explanation. This would indeed be interesting. She had heard about the giant king, about his strength and glory. But this new information was most interesting indeed.

“I cannot wait to meet this Naphil king Gilgamesh,” said Ishtar. “He and I have much to plot.”

They heard screaming from below.

The plunging drill had penetrated into the water table. The log blew sky high. Water gushed out, a geyser created by the sudden release of massive pressure. The fountain of water slammed into the workers and washed them around like ants in a storm.

Then the ground crumbled inward. A huge sinkhole formed, sucking the ground downward. Then suddenly the earth and clay heaved upward with the force of the releasing waters below. The drowning flood washed away the hundred workers. The waters began to fill the clay pits like a suddenly dammed-up stream.

Ishtar smiled. Ninsun recoiled in horror. Dumuzi was too broken to care.

"Why are you doing this?" Ninsun cried out.

Ishtar had no intention of explaining to Ninsun that she was covering up her past. She said nothing. Besides, these were not just the waters of an underground lake that had been dowsed. These were the waters of the Abyss pouring up from the Darkness below. What more fitting way to cover her tracks? She would create a lake that would bury forever her dishonor in the jaws of Rahab.

As the water rose to fill the clay pits, Ishtar had the portable throne carried to the sheer edge of the pit. Dumuzi's leash had been fastened to the throne, so he was dragged along with it.

Ishtar descended the throne. She leaned down to Dumuzi, whispering, "Tammuz, my shepherd. You have brought me much pleasure. I have much to thank you for. You rescued me from Sheol, my bridegroom. I will write love poems one day to commemorate you. But you have outlived your usefulness. Someone must be left behind in the Abyss to take my place, as a substitution. That someone, my dear love, will be you."

Ishtar stood up and gestured to the servants of the throne. They picked it up and threw it over the ledge. It splashed into the water. The leash stretched. The collar pulled at Dumuzi's neck. The weight of the sinking throne dragged Dumuzi with it. He sank into the depths. He was the last connection to the knowledge of Ishtar's shame.

Ishtar turned to see Ninsun's terror-stricken face.

"Do not fret yourself, Lady Cow," said Ishtar. "You are still useful to me."

Her important business done, Ishtar noticed one of the servants in the entourage, a handsome man. She walked up to him and looked him up and down.

Her demeanor changed like a chameleon. She was suddenly soft, with a voice to match. She breathed to him, "And who might you be?"

"Ishullanu, the king's gardener," he said.

She could see he shook with fear.

She said to him, "Oh, I see we have the same effect on one another."

She softly coaxed him out of the line of servants. She murmured, "Lead your goddess to her temple."

Ishullanu stepped from the crowd of servants like a singled out prisoner. He walked silently toward what he knew was his own execution. Ishtar followed him on her journey back to Eanna.

CHAPTER 22

The storm raged on over the Great Cedar Forest. It was like thirteen different winds all conspiring to converge together in this very moment, in this very location. Gilgamesh's party found scattered locations to try to stay out of the main fury of it all and sit out the night. They were soaked and chilled to the bone. Gilgamesh and Enkidu hid beneath a huge fallen cedar.

Gilgamesh said nothing. He simply glared at Enkidu, who knew what was expected of him.

Enkidu finally spoke up. "Humbaba killed my tribe when I was but an infant nursing at my mother's breast. For some unknown reason, he spared me and tried to raise me in his domain. But when I learned to speak and understand, I discovered my heritage and I ran away into the grasslands of the steppe."

Gilgamesh could not believe what he heard. He thought he had known Enkidu, but he had not even begun to discover the depths of this civilized Wild Born.

Enkidu continued, "I should have died. But a pride of lions found me and raised me as one of their cubs. I was young enough and impressionable. I became as one with them and quickly lost all sense of my humanity. That was the state in which Shamhat found me. And that is why I could learn language so fast. I was simply reacquainting myself with what I had suppressed inside for so long."

He was not done. He took a deep breath, and then said, "The lioness that you wounded, the one I killed…" He wanted to make sure Gilgamesh knew which one he was talking about. "She was my feline mother."

A lightning bolt of shock shot through Gilgamesh's body. He was not going to sleep tonight. "Enkidu, I am sorry to have ever challenged your courage." He spoke with a sensitivity Enkidu had never before heard in his voice. "I did not know that this was so much more for you than a mere giant slaying. In fact, I would have no regret in allowing you to stay and watch the camp for us when we seek Humbaba tomorrow. There would be no shame in it."

Enkidu snapped at him, "How dare you steal from your servant the one thing I have left to offer you, my king."

A slight smile crossed Gilgamesh's lips.

"You are not my servant, Enkidu of the steppe," pronounced Gilgamesh. "You are my friend."

Morning broke over a quiet forest. The storm had passed. The sounds of insect and animal life awakening filled the air. The beams of sun burst in through the canopy of foliage.

But all was not as serene or beautiful as it appeared. They had lost their carts to the storm winds. Everything was destroyed or gone. All their food supplies and extra weapons, including their huge war net, were smashed and scattered to the four winds. There were only forty of them left and they had only the weapons and water skins on their persons. Even Gilgamesh's bow of Anshan had been lost.

However, they had not lost their senses. They were mighty warriors, Gibborim. They would finish the task that Gilgamesh had started. They would find this Rapha giant Humbaba and kill him. And then they would cut down his cedars to bring home a mighty trophy of their exploits.

With the help of Yahatti's sensitive serpent tongue and Enkidu's animal tracking skills, they traced their huge quarry's path to the very base of Mount Hermon. The fighting team found an immense house made of cedar. It blended into the side of the mountain as if it grew out of the crags of rock. It was the size of a small palace.

Enkidu looked up at the mighty house of timber. He whispered to Gilgamesh, "I thought Humbaba would not hurt any trees. This mansion looks as if he had to clear cut the entire mountainside to provide the lumber for it."

"Rational consistency is not a concern of such monsters," said Gilgamesh. "The loudest so-called 'protectors' always seem to exempt themselves from their own rules."

"Well then," Enkidu replied. "Let us disabuse this titanic fiend of his double standard."

"Let us burn his house down," smiled Gilgamesh.

The band of warriors approached the gate of the cedar palace. It stood wide open. In fact, there was no gate. The monster had no fear of enemies? Was it a trap?

Gilgamesh led them cautiously inward, weapons drawn and ready.

The structure soared upward all around them. It gave the impression of sweeping one up into heaven. The timbers were vertical, the opposite of an earthy log cabin design of horizontal layering. And everywhere was empty. There were no decorations, no furniture, no sign of creaturely presence or habitation. It felt like a cathedral of loneliness.

A chill went through Gilgamesh's spine. Was this the 'kingdom of One?' He felt a strange connection to this beastly prince of the wood. As if he understood Humbaba, even as he was planning to kill him.

They pressed on.

The next chamber showed the first signs of residence, but it was a ghastly residence. Dozens of creatures inhabited the room, all standing in frozen positions. Bears, wolves, deer, boar. All of them standing still in eternal petrified positions. But they were not stone statues or carved wood. They were the real flesh of creatures Humbaba had captured and killed. When Gilgamesh examined them up close, he could see that they had been stuffed with sawdust. They were the skins of once-live animals filled to make them stand in perpetual crowd-like community.

"My lord," said Enkidu. He drew Gilgamesh's attention to one of the sections of stuffed creatures. Gilgamesh's stomach turned. They were humans. Skins of once-living people that Humbaba had skinned like animals and stuffed, to set up in his museum of horror.

They were arranged so that all looked forward in the same direction. It reminded Gilgamesh of the statues that he and other worshippers made of themselves to place in the temple sanctuary of Eanna and Eanu. The purpose of the little votary statues was to make sure that they had a representative of themselves always before the presence of the deity. Like the temple votary statues, these mummified trophies with gem stones for eyes had their gaze wide open, as if to give the deity their perpetual awareness. Or giving their souls, as the eyes were the windows of the soul of man. It struck Gilgamesh that these figures resembled an audience of the living dead for Humbaba. They were the closest thing he could have to real creaturely company.

The vastness of the architecture absorbed them. They failed to gaze upward in this room.

A large net fell upon them from above. It was their own huge war net. Humbaba must have come to their camp during the storm and stolen the net from under their noses as the winds howled and raged around them, drowning out all other sounds. They were ensnared in their own net. It had been a trap after all.

Gilgamesh and Enkidu looked at the stuffed trophies and then at each other. They knew what fate lay in store for them.

CHAPTER 23

Humbaba brought his captives deep into the heart of his mighty wooden palace, hidden away at the point where the mountain rock met the wooden timber. It was a sanctuary, with large regal tapestries hung before the mammoth cedar doors as curtains. The draperies had probably been confiscated from one of the kings Humbaba had slaughtered.

The forty warriors hung from the stone wall like captured game ready to be gutted and cleaned. Although Humbaba enjoyed feeding the terror of captives as he skinned them and ate them alive one by one, he took no chances with this team of trained fighters. He had killed them all. Their lifeless corpses were like phantoms overlooking this sanctuary of death.

Gilgamesh and Enkidu were restrained at their torsos to large tree columns. Their hands were bound before them in strong vines, so they could not secretly work to release themselves. Humbaba the Terrible sat watching them, his back against a huge terebinth tree. It rose straight up from the ground and spanned the ceiling height like a garden atrium. Beside the tree, a cave opened into the mountain. They stared as far upward as they could, marveling at the tree's size.

Humbaba mused over them with humor, "The tall grown sapling and his angry ox stand ready for combat."

Humbaba followed their gazes. "This is a holy terebinth tree," he explained. "I built my cedar house around it, because it is a talisman of communication with deity. That opening leads into the very throne room of the mountain of the gods."

Gilgamesh and Enkidu looked at each other.

Humbaba was quite talkative. He had lived without human or giant company for many years. There was no telling how much he might talk their ears off before eating them.

"Your army, I will skin and stuff and add to my friends. But you, King Gilgamesh, and your 'Right Hand,' you are much more important. You, I will bring in to the assembly of the gods to offer as a sacrifice."

Well, Gilgamesh thought, *It was my intention to find the assembly of the gods. I just did not think I would end up there in quite this way.*

"What are you thinking?" Humbaba asked Gilgamesh.

Enkidu thought to himself, *What kind of monster wonders what his prey is thinking? He must have severe confidence problems.*

Gilgamesh engaged the giant. "Perhaps we could strike a deal, you and I."

Humbaba laughed. "And what could you possibly offer me that I could not take for myself?"

"True enough," responded Gilgamesh. "Not only are you in control of our lives, but you have everything you want and need right here in your domain. It is *your* kingdom. You rule above all things. No one can compare to you. No one dares to come near your greatness. They leave you alone, *all alone,* in your mighty pre-eminence and solitude. Your appetite is that of a mighty king, insatiable, unquenchable. There is nothing that can fill these hollow halls with meaning. Nothing that can satisfy the eternal desire."

Enkidu watched Gilgamesh with admiration. He was not only a warrior of courage, he was a master of the tongue. He used flattery to uncover the emptiness and misery of Humbaba's soul. It sounded very insightful of the human condition to Enkidu.

It was insightful because Gilgamesh had been speaking of himself.

Humbaba mused, "I find you interesting. We kings have much in common."

"Then consider an offer of royal marital alliance." It was not unusual. It was quite common for kings to marry their family members to vassal kings they have subdued in order to maintain the continued allegiance of the vassal king. But Gilgamesh was the vassal audaciously making the offer. He hoped to distract Humbaba by exploiting his loneliness.

"I have two sisters," said Gilgamesh. "Enmebaragesi and Peshtur. Very beautiful. Very tall. I am from a family of giants after all."

Enkidu suppressed a look of surprise at the claims. He knew Gilgamesh had no sisters. But he quickly figured out what his compatriot was doing.

Gilgamesh used a tone of sumptuous memory, as if he were remembering the most pleasant meal he had ever eaten.

Humbaba got impatient. "What about them?"

"Well," replied Gilgamesh. "I think they would be perfect for you. They are large, and beautiful of face and form. You could have one as your wife and the other as concubine. They are obedient, provide splendid company, and they are quite the conversationalists."

The offer tempted Humbaba. He had been so lonely for so long. He was actually a sociable creature who needed the company of others. But he had been made to dwell alone by the gods for their purpose of focused guardianship. He often thought his bitterness and hatred came from this deficit. He thought he had gotten used to it. But he had not. Always in the back of his soul, lurked a loneliness and despair that he could not shake. At some moments, it so overwhelmed him that he had thought of killing himself. But his responsibility always brought him back from the brink. He was Guardian of the Great Cedar Forest, and more importantly, Guardian of the abode of the gods.

The wisdom and insight of his king impressed Enkidu. Gilgamesh had sized up their captor's psychological weakness with great cunning. It was uncanny. It was as if he knew Humbaba as he knew himself, and was simply sharing his own soul.

Enkidu could see Humbaba was fascinated with the picture painted by Gilgamesh.

The giant considered the offer. He stroked his tusks as one would a beard.

Gilgamesh added, "I swear by the life of my mother, the goddess Ninsun and my father the holy Lugalbanda, we would be kinsman. You would receive flour for baking bread, cool beer for your belly, large sandals for your feet, and many sparkling gemstones of precious value."

Enkidu thought Gilgamesh was talking a bit too much, filling in nervous silence. He should be letting Humbaba chew it over.

Humbaba said, "Unfortunately, your offer is problematic. I would have to let you go in order to get your sisters. This is unacceptable, for I do not put much value in oaths."

"Hold the bodies of my men as a surety," said Gilgamesh.

Humbaba laughed. "Warriors are expendable. Especially dead ones. Do you take me for a fool, cedar smiter?"

Gilgamesh said, "Enkidu is not expendable. He is not merely my Right Hand, but my adopted brother and my only true friend in all the world."

Humbaba studied Enkidu. He could indeed see that Gilgamesh did not lie to him. A creature of loneliness could spot the intimacy he longed for a mile away in those who had it.

"I would come back for him," said Gilgamesh.

"This, I believe," said Humbaba. " And with an army ten thousand strong, no doubt."

"But with Enkidu as your hostage," said Gilgamesh, "My very life would be in your hands. Surely, you understand that for him to die in my place while I lived would be a fate worse than my own death."

Enkidu watched Gilgamesh closely and knew that he was not speaking words of deceit to trick the Rapha. He spoke the truth. Gilgamesh was making his last desperate attempt: pure undefiled honesty.

Humbaba looked at Enkidu, and the truth stood out clearly again. He could see these two men had a bond so close, it was unbreakable.

"Well, in that case," said Humbaba. "I will send Enkidu in your place. He should be capable of bringing back your sisters as well. And if he brings with him an army, he will have the distinct privilege of watching his king burned alive in a fortress of cedar."

It was a fate worse than death for Enkidu. Humbaba had made a brilliant tactical move. The giant had nothing to lose, because he had nothing to live for. Going up in blazes holding the mighty King Gilgamesh of Uruk would insure his miserable pathetic existence a place in history, or better yet, a place in mythology. And he would get his revenge on Enkidu by the same act.

"No!" barked Gilgamesh. "I beg of you. Do not do this, Humbaba."

Humbaba grinned. He knew he had the upper hand now.

Gilgamesh blurted out, "Enkidu cannot be trusted with my sisters! Remember his past! He is still a Wild Born!"

The protest came too late. Humbaba released the cords around Enkidu, to set him on his way.

It was exactly what Gilgamesh wanted.

Enkidu had been raised by lions, which go for the throat and the eyes.

He sprang. He clawed the giant's eyes. Enkidu's fingers dug deep. Had Humbaba not been of extraordinary constitution, Enkidu would have popped them right out of his head. He might be only one third the size of Humbaba, but he was stronger of bone than Gilgamesh, filled with his past as a Wild Born, *and* he was a skilled warrior with a score to settle.

Humbaba screamed. He batted at Enkidu to protect his eyes.

Enkidu went for Humbaba's throat. His teeth sunk in deep.

But Humbaba was a mighty Rephaim. He tore Enkidu from his throat and slammed him into a cedar pillar. The house as if by an earthquake.

Humbaba swayed on his feet, dazed and choking, bleeding from the open wound on his neck.

Enkidu spit out the blood of his enemy. Humbaba would have his senses back any moment. Enkidu had only that moment to dive for the pile of confiscated supplies. He hoped to find the serpentine sword called Rahab in the pile. He only found a dagger. A small human-sized dagger at that.

Humbaba rose to his feet, roaring. When he finally spoke, it was with difficulty. His windpipe had received part of the damage of Enkidu's bite.

"Enkidu! Why have you betrayed me?" Humbaba gurgled. "Would you betray your own birthright?"

Enkidu did not answer. He threw the dagger. Humbaba dodged it with ease. But Enkidu had not aimed at Humbaba. It hit the wooden pole inches above Gilgamesh's head. It would have hit him in the forehead had Gilgamesh not ducked. He reached up, yanked the blade out of the wood with his bound hands, and began to saw at the bonds around his torso.

Humbaba swatted Enkidu with brutal force. He flew into the mountain wall. The stone cracked from the impact. Rocks crumbled down upon Enkidu's spinning head.

Enkidu immediately stood up. The blood rushed from his head and he almost passed out. He fell back down to the ground on his rear. He was not returning to the fight any moment soon.

Humbaba turned to take care of Gilgamesh. But he was gone, cut free from the pole. Humbaba whirled around looking for the king. He could not find him.

It did not occur to the twenty foot tall giant to look down at his feet. Gilgamesh had taken to his hands and knees. He stood up suddenly and jammed the dagger into Humbaba's abdomen.

Humbaba screamed. He instinctively grabbed the blade and Gilgamesh. Seizing the king tightly by the shoulders, he lifted him up to his face.

Humbaba growled, "You will not be returning to the city of the goddess who bore you."

He threw Gilgamesh against the rock wall. The king hit one of the dead warriors chained to the wall. The corpse cushioned Gilgamesh's impact. Gilgamesh slid down, dazed.

The crash jostled one of the torches on the rock wall. It fell to the ground.

Gilgamesh snatched it up and threw it at Humbaba. The giant swatted it away.

Humbaba reached down to his feet. He picked up an iron mace, a pear-shaped club honed for efficient bludgeoning of the enemy by years of war.

He limped over to Gilgamesh. He raised the mace high, ready to smash down on the pest.

A voice boomed out from behind Humbaba, "HO, HURRAH!"

The giant turned around at the shout.

A flexible metal blade wrapped around Humbaba's hammering hand. With a mighty jerk, the blade sliced it from Humbaba's arm. The hand and mace fell to the ground. Humbaba screamed in agony and grabbed his bleeding stump. He collapsed to his knees.

Enkidu had found Rahab.

Gilgamesh got to his feet and approached Humbaba. Enkidu staying behind him with Rahab ready.

Behind the combatants, the forgotten torch had rolled to the entrance. The heavy curtains caught fire.

Humbaba wept, "Mercy, O mighty Gilgamesh. Spare my life!"

Gilgamesh looked at Humbaba with contempt. The giant prostrated himself before Gilgamesh.

"I will be your slave. Let me dwell here for you in the Forest of Cedar. I will cut down as many trees as you command, for the pride and glory of your palace at Uruk."

It amazed Gilgamesh how quickly this massive giant, this mighty Rephaim, had been reduced to a babbling victim pleading for his life. It could be another trick.

Yet, Gilgamesh found his heart taking pity. Somehow, he knew this was not a play act. He had been just as honest moments before with his own pain. The two of them were truly more alike than they were contrary.

Humbaba turned his head toward Enkidu. "Enkidu, my life lies in your hands. Tell Gilgamesh to spare me, I beg of you."

Enkidu stared at Humbaba without a sliver of mercy. He said to Gilgamesh, "You have your enduring fame to think of. How Gilgamesh slew Humbaba the Terrible."

The hiss and crackle of fire caught their attention. They realized that the entire entryway to the vast chamber was engulfed in flames. The ceiling was an inferno high above their heads. The torch had done much more than anyone could have imagined. The palace was on fire.

Gilgamesh stepped back and gazed upon the pathetic form of this once terrible monster. He mused, "Enkidu, let the captive bird go free. A broken wing impairs him."

"A freed captive returns to its nature," replied Enkidu.

"The gods will be angry," cautioned Humbaba. "You would execute their guardian and bring down their wrath?"

Enkidu said coldly, "A man cannot serve two masters."

Suddenly, Humbaba hardened his resolve. Spite filled his voice, "Enkidu, I should never have shown you mercy and tried to raise you as my family. I should have hung you by a tree at the entrance of this forest and let the vultures feed on your…."

Humbaba's speech was cut short. His head was severed from his neck by the swinging blade of Rahab in the hands of Enkidu.

Gilgamesh and Enkidu stood gazing at the body of their enemy.

Finally, Enkidu said to the dead giant, "You are not my family. You murdered my family."

Enkidu took a deep breath and looked around. The massive flames licked the dry timber walls in a whirlwind of impenetrable fire. The companions were in the heart of a furnace about to implode upon them.

"Our exit is blocked," shouted Enkidu.

Gilgamesh looked at the cave entrance by the terebinth tree. "The only way out is into the mountain."

Enkidu said, "Are you kidding me? Enter the assembly of the gods, the two of us? That would be worse than plunging through a palace of flames!"

Gilgamesh said, "Shut up, Enkidu. We are going in."

CHAPTER 24

The smoke of Humbaba's burning palace of cedar rose high in the sky like a black pillar up to heaven.

Gilgamesh and Enkidu escaped the inferno through the tunnel into the heart of Mount Hermon. They followed the trail of smoke that was sucked inward toward the source of cool air from within.

The tunnel opened up to a magnificent cavern full of sparkling jewels that lit the vast hollowness with ghostly luminescence. Huge stalactites and stalagmites throughout the cave gave the impression of being inside the mouth of Rahab the sea dragon of chaos, or more precisely, the seven mouths of Rahab's offspring, Leviathan.

They had barely stepped into the cavern when they were greeted by a large Shining One. The eight foot tall being stood with arms crossed, as if waiting for them. His glowing blue eyes sent a shiver down the spine of Enkidu.

Gilgamesh immediately went down to his knee in worshipful obeisance. He pulled Enkidu down to follow his lead.

The god spoke, "You, king Gilgamesh, have caused quite the ruckus in our assembly."

Gilgamesh spoke with a humility that Enkidu had not seen in him before. "O Mighty Shamash," he genuflected.

Enkidu thought, *So this was the sun god Gilgamesh had spoken so frequently of at Uruk.* He had wondered just how real these gods might be.

Gilgamesh finished his entreaty, "I pray thee, before you smite me, I beg an audience before Enlil and the assembly to plead my cause."

"Of course," said Shamash. "If I wanted to smite you, you would already be smitten."

Shamash herded Gilgamesh and Enkidu through the tunnel until they found themselves facing the assembly of gods in the heart of the cavern. Behind them spread a lake of black pitch with a flame flitting across its surface. This was a portal of the Abyss. Before them stood a throne with Enlil, Lord of the Storm. Around him were seventy gods and assorted mal'akim. They all had names and identities, but Gilgamesh only recognized Shamash and Enlil.

Gilgamesh kissed the ground before Enlil and offered a leather bag at his feet. "I present to you the head of Humbaba the Terrible."

He recited a lyric for poetic ornament, "The ravines did run with his blood."

Enlil looked enraged. "Gilgamesh, why do you vex me so? Have I not granted you greatness of stature and station in Uruk? Are you not satisfied with your might as a demigod? Yet, you come into my forest and create havoc. Did you not expect to be punished for such hubris?"

Gilgamesh averted his eyes as he spoke, "Mighty Enlil, forgive me, but I have as my only defense my obedience to the commands of Shamash."

Enlil looked at Shamash expecting an answer. Shamash was blindsided by the appeal. He searched his memory, quickly replaying the conversations of his few visits to Uruk. Of course, he was supposed to check on his patronized followers. But in fact, he used the opportunity as an excuse to "explore" other travel experiences. He was not about to reveal his excursions of irresponsible debauchery through the cities of Sumer. For that, he would receive punishment he did not want to experience again. The scars of brutal lashes on his back were reminders of his failure before the Flood.

Back then, he had been Utu the sun god. He and Enki had been under the command of Inanna to secure the Tree of Life. He had abandoned his post with Inanna when they realized the war would not be won. Even though he only received half the lashes of Inanna, it was still enough to solidify his determination to never again be caught in an error or impropriety.

Unable to pull up a memory of such a conversation, Shamash said to Gilgamesh, "I have made many commands. To which do you refer?"

"To the dreams," said Gilgamesh.

Curses, thought Shamash. *He is being too general. I still cannot figure out what he is talking about.* "Explain yourself, half-breed. I am not about to recount the details to the pantheon on your behalf."

Enkidu's instincts tingled as he watched Shamash struggle to reply to Gilgamesh. He could swear that the sun god appeared to not know what was going on. Hardly the level of all-knowing wisdom one would expect of a god.

"Forgive me, O mighty Shamash, but I refer to the dream of the bull and man who gave me water to drink after saving me from being crushed by the mountain of the gods."

"And what did I tell you?" said Shamash.

He tried to sound impatient, as if he knew what was in the dream and was urging Gilgamesh to hurry up and finish. But Enkidu detected a slight hesitation of question in the god's voice.

Gilgamesh continued, "You bid me awake after I offered you a sacrifice of a lamb."

Enkidu glanced at Gilgamesh. It was not a single lamb, it was two kid goats. *Ah, so Gilgamesh was a step ahead of me,* thought Enkidu. *He is testing Shamash, the tricky scoundrel.*

"I remember the lamb," said Shamash. "But when did I ever tell you to kill Humbaba and burn down his house?"

"You spoke to my mother, the goddess Ninsun, your high priestess in Uruk."

"Ah, see, that is where you are wrong," said Shamash. "I did no such thing."

Enkidu stepped forward and followed Gilgamesh's humble stance. "My gods, if I may," said Enkidu. "I am the king's Right Hand and I was there at the temple of Shamash. I am witness to what Lord Gilgamesh claims."

The dirty toads, thought Shamash. *They are conspiring. I will have their heads.*

"Well?" said Enlil. "What say you to these claims confirmed by two royal witnesses, Shamash?"

The assembly all stared at Shamash. He scrambled for words.

Both Gilgamesh and Enkidu thought at almost the same moment, *What kind of gods know nothing of prayers and dreams or that the palace fire was an accident?*

Shamash hit on the perfect cover. "It must have been Inanna."

Everyone looked surprised at him.

"She must have impersonated me in order to deceive these flesh bags to do her bidding."

Then Shamash let the zinger loose. "She has probably come back and is already engaging in diabolical plans, no doubt."

It was outrageous, unbelievable. Yet, it was just the sort of thing Inanna would do if she had survived the Deluge judgment.

Enlil protested, "But we have not seen her since the Flood. We assumed she had been bound in the earth with the others."

Shamash was flying high now. He spoke without hesitation as if he knew what he was talking about. "True, we have not seen her all this time. But we also do not know what happened to her. And considering her tendency to seize power, she may have been conspiring this entire time for a takeover of the assembly. Or maybe someone found her and released her from the earth."

Shamash had no idea just how close to the truth he really was. He was absorbed in pride at how quickly he had recovered, without being sure what he would say next. The lies came to him as smoothly as the truth might come to someone recounting what really happened. He was quite a good liar. He had Inanna as a shining example. He would have to thank her if he ever did run into her again.

Gilgamesh found it the perfect opportunity to ask a question that burned in his mind like the combustible palace of Humbaba. "O mighty Enlil, may I ask why the pantheon of gods is hidden away in this cosmic mountain? Why do you not live amidst your people of the alluvial plain as you did before the great Deluge?"

It was a strategic move by Gilgamesh. He suspected that there must have been some shame or fear behind the gods' refuge in Mount Hermon. By drawing the discussion out, he could play off their pride. He might even manipulate them into mercy out of their own self interest.

Brilliant, thought Enkidu. *He is forcing their hand.*

Enlil contemplated his answer. He liked this king. He had real backbone to walk into their lair and face certain death. And he was a Naphil, one of their own progeny after their own image. If they wanted to rekindle their control over the land, this could be the very mediator the gods would need: a hybrid gibborim warrior with a mythical reputation; a sole monarch who could possibly unite humanity under the rule of the gods again. But they would need his full support to do it right. He would have to see his own self-interest satisfied. What did this pretentious one want? To become a god?

Was it too soon to come out of the mountain? The gods had been hiding out in Mount Hermon because of the thoroughness of devastation wrought by the Deluge. The Creator, Elohim, that despicable deity of Noah ben Lamech, had wiped out their plans with such comprehensive cataclysm that those who survived were afraid to show their faces for fear of further reprise. They were not sure what Elohim might do next, so they decided to stay low for an undetermined period of time. They planned how they might begin anew their scheme.

Enlil decided to spin the tale, and hope that he could seduce this haughty Gilgamesh into his spell.

"I will tell you the story of the Deluge," said Enlil. "The demigods once suffered work and toil like men. They were the Igigi who served the Anunnaki. The Igigi we called Nephilim. They dug the canals for the cities of the river. But they complained and revolted against me in a gigantomachy that had to be put down."

It was masterful. Enlil incorporated just enough of what really happened so that it carried a ring of truth. But now, he must get creative. "So I summoned the birth goddess Nintu before the assembly of the gods, to create mankind. I said, 'Let man bear the toil of the gods.' So the Creatress slaughtered a god and mixed his flesh and blood with clay. This was spat upon and became man. And mankind was given the toil of the gods.

"But after many years, the peoples multiplied and became too numerous for Mother Earth to sustain them. The land bellowed like a bull before my ears. I was disturbed by the uproar and the clamor. They consumed too much, complained too much, and the uproar of their ways disturbed our sleep. So I let the winds come. I held back the rain, and caused famine on the earth. But the clamor of mankind became more oppressive and the humans began to eat their children. So I sent pestilence and plague. But the people did not diminish. So I decided to send a Deluge upon the land to cleanse it from the filth and start all over.

"Unbeknownst to the pantheon, Enki secretly went to the city of Shuruppak and warned a man in that city of the coming destruction."

"Was that Noah ben Lamech?" interrupted Gilgamesh. He was riveted by the tale, and had heard a version of it himself from his mother.

It annoyed Enlil. He did not like being sidetracked. "That is what some called him. But his name was Atrahasis, or Ziusudra to others. And Enki told Atrahasis to build a large boat a full acre square and one hundred and twenty cubits high, and covered in and out with pitch. And on this boat he would take animals of every kind to save from the coming flood."

It suddenly struck Gilgamesh, Is this god the high god of the pantheon and he is too stupid to know that a square ship would never float properly? Or the sheer ridiculousness of thinking that a boat with that height as a cube would not tip over in the waves. Why was he lying? What was he hiding?

Enlil continued, "For six days and seven nights, the wind continued and the Deluge demolished the land. And when the waters subsided, the boat came to rest on the mountain of Nimush. Atrahasis left the boat and offered a sacrifice unto the gods. We smelled the sweet savor and gathered around the sacrifice."

Like a bunch of flies around excrement, Enkidu thought to himself. *They seem to need us as much as we need them.*

Enlil continued, "But when I confronted Enki with his defiance of my command, he revealed that he had not told Atrahasis directly, but in a dream, which freed him from the legal punishment of the assembly of gods."

"But you allowed Noah to live?" asked Gilgamesh.

"*Atrahasis*," corrected Enlil emphatically. "I allowed *Atrahasis* to live. In fact, in my incomparable grace, I approached Atrahasis and his wife and told them that hitherto they should now be like us gods. And I took them afar off to the Land of the Living, at the mouth of the rivers where the sun rises, to reside no more amongst mortal men."

"You made Noah – I mean Atrahasis – and his wife immortal?" Gilgamesh repeated for clarification.

"Yes," said Enlil. "The only human beings to have the honor."

Yet again, Gilgamesh and Enkidu were in perfect harmony with their thoughts. They both mused simultaneously *What is Enlil hiding with this fairy tale?* It seemed partly true and partly manufactured for propaganda purposes.

Enlil said, "Gilgamesh of Uruk, do you wish to achieve eternal fame and a great and mighty name forever?"

Gilgamesh could not believe what he was hearing. He thought that he and Enkidu were going to be chewed up and spit into Sheol for the sheer impertinence of what they had done. He did not realize that his killing of the guardian of the abode of the gods had inspired Enlil to set into motion their next plan for dominion.

"Y-yes," stuttered Gilgamesh in shock. "With all my heart and soul."

Enlil said, "Then we shall covenant together upon a mutually beneficial opportunity."

Enkidu did not share the excitement he heard in Gilgamesh's voice. He did not trust these gods. They proved unpredictable, not particularly knowledgeable or powerful as befits deity. He found their worthiness of such respect and allegiance questionable. On the other hand, obedience might be the only other option to death for them both.

Enlil said, "You shall be given a view into the divine council of the gods that no other man has ever had or ever will have again. In exchange, we will require of you certain things to insure that our plan will be carried out with power and with finality."

"Yes, my Lord," nodded Gilgamesh.

The gods were about to come out of hiding.

Enkidu remained dutifully silent. He considered that voicing his thoughts right now would only cause trouble and might result in the dissolution of this newly forming alliance.

Enlil continued, "Allow me to introduce to you the god who will be our emissary and who will aid you in accomplishing our plan in Mesopotamia."

One of the gods stepped forward, a mass of muscle and heavily armed with bow, mace, sword, and war net. This one was a fighter.

Enlil continued, "Suffice it to say he will be adequate to the task. Gilgamesh, meet Ninurta, son of Enlil, god of vegetation and harvest."

Enkidu thought to himself, *God of vegetation? That is a strange signification for such a powerful looking scrapper. What is he? A 'mighty gardener'?*

Gilgamesh thought the same.

CHAPTER 25

Enlil put several demands upon Gilgamesh to show his obedience. He was to build a huge door of cedar wood, ninety-nine feet high, thirty-three feet wide, and one and a half feet thick. It should be carved as one piece from the mightiest tree in the Cedar Forest. Then he had to cart it one hundred and twenty leagues or four hundred miles back to the Euphrates river on donkey-driven carts built from forest wood as well. He would then ride the door as a raft down the Euphrates all the way to the city Nippur. In that city, they would present it as a gift to the temple of Enlil, an obvious ego stroke for the head of the assembly and his so-called son, Ninurta, who was accompanying them. Nippur was the main religious center of the pantheon and this act would affirm their authority. This elaborate enterprise was only the smallest part of the master plan they had commanded Gilgamesh to accomplish.

Enkidu was not privy to the master plan. It was the only thing Gilgamesh would keep from his Right Hand. The gods had demanded this silence between the bond-brothers as a condition, upon pain of death for both of them. Ninurta was there to make sure of it.

Enkidu intended to uncover the plotting of these despotic deities, in order to protect his lord and friend, the mighty Gilgamesh.

Enkidu mused over this intention as he helmed the cedar raft of Enlil's door on the downstream waters of the mighty river Euphrates.

Gilgamesh came back from the bow to join Enkidu at the helm. He left Ninurta standing vigil like a statue of stone at the forward end of the raft, watching the river.

"He is not much of a talker, that one," said Gilgamesh. "It is like pulling teeth to get him to say anything. Or in his case, more like pulling fangs."

Enkidu said nothing.

Gilgamesh noticed something wrong with his friend. "What distresses you, Enkidu?" he asked.

"I do not trust these gods," whispered Enkidu under his breath. He did not want Ninurta to hear his voice, though he was upwind. They spoke with hushed voices.

"Neither do I," said Gilgamesh.

Enkidu whispered, "They are more powerful than us, yes. But they are still finite, limited, ignorant, and petty. They do not seem to me to be what they depict themselves."

"What do you mean?" asked Gilgamesh.

Enkidu watched Ninurta. Enlil's son glanced back at them before returning to his shepherd dog posture at the front of the raft.

Enkidu stared into the distance with melancholy. He spoke in a hushed tone with a detached longing, "When I was a Wild Born, I was blissfully unaware of any deities like those we saw on Mount Hermon. But when I roamed the steppe, sometimes all alone, I would be overwhelmed with a sense of — awe. I did not know what it was, but I would look around me and see the earth that was unmoving beneath my feet, and the magnificent mountains that held up the starry firmament. And I would see the countless stars and the sun and moon in their courses. I would think to myself, surely someone created all this perfection. He would have to be infinite to be capable of managing so vast a cosmos, but also orderly, to maintain the constancy of the seasons and of the ways of all things. And an ultimate goodness. A goodness that I felt in my bones we did not measure up to."

Gilgamesh interrupted his musing, "But have you seen this creator?"

"No," replied Enkidu, "yet he was everywhere present. As an artist is present in the sculpture he forms, or the mosaic he creates. Only, he has not left an explicit signature. I do not know his name. But I do know that those gods of the assembly are not him. They are part of the mosaic."

Gilgamesh said, "What kind of a creator does not speak, does not give his name, and does not reveal himself?"

Enkidu responded, "Maybe we are the ones who do not listen or see."

Gilgamesh countered, "It looks more to me that we are abandoned."

Enkidu said, "Maybe we are abandoned. But look at this world. What we have become. Maybe we brought it upon ourselves. Maybe we deserve it."

Gilgamesh said with a touch of sarcasm, "Or maybe you have spent too much time alone in the steppe and maybe you went mad."

Enkidu smiled. "I think you are right. Life as a Wild Born is one of much ignorance. But I still do not trust these temperamental gods."

Gilgamesh said, "But you must trust me. I am bound by oath not to reveal their plans."

"You did not have much choice," Enkidu said. "It was either carry out their wishes or execution."

Gilgamesh assured him, "I promise you, Enkidu, it will be glorious for me. And you will be by my side."

"There is always a price to be paid for such glory," said Enkidu.

"And what else is there?" asked Gilgamesh. "What is life anyway, but striving after the wind? All is vanity. Our life is a vapor, that is here for a moment and disappears like a wisp of smoke. But you and I are still alive. And better is a living dog than a dead lion."

"I want to get back to my wife and back to my life," said Enkidu.

"Back to a life of *what*?" said Gilgamesh. "Physical and emotional experiences? Enkidu, I love you closer than a brother. I know you find the caresses of Shamhat to soothe your soul. But consider this: you too will die. And in the underworld, where you are going, there are no caresses, no companions, and no memories of either there. It is the land of forgetfulness, from which no man returns."

Enkidu tried to argue back, "That is why the gods envy us. Because we are doomed, life is more intense. Every moment is full of beauty that will never return. Nothing can be more abundant with meaning. Every day is our last. Every pleasure, pure and holy because it will never be again."

"Do not be a fool," said Gilgamesh. "The truth is the exact opposite. Every pleasure you experience, every human connection you make, wife, friend, or offspring, is a lie, a cruel joke of meaninglessness that you delude yourself into believing has value. What is your tiny moment of beauty or pleasure in an eternity of despair? It is nothing. It is worse than nothing. It is a mockery that makes the pain far worse because there is something to be compared to. Do you not see? Hope is the very thing that secures one's eternal misery in the face of death if there is no transcendent truth within which it is rooted."

"Then what do you conclude?" asked Enkidu. "You just made the case for nothingness and meaninglessness and you criticize me for folly? Why not just kill ourselves now and get it over with, if there is nothing that awaits us but despair?"

Gilgamesh's intensity lightened. His scrunched face relaxed and he thought for a moment. "That is a good point," he said.

Then he smiled deviously and added, "And that is why I want to become a god. I want eternal life, Enkidu. I want to live forever."

Enkidu stared at him. "You are already two thirds god. Is that not good enough?"

"No. I will still die," said Gilgamesh.

"You know," added Enkidu, "I have been meaning to ask you anyway, how could you be two thirds divine and one third human? If your father was a human and your mother was a goddess, that would make you half divine and half human."

Gilgamesh said, "To be honest, I have often wondered that myself. I never contested it, because two thirds divinity makes me more feared in the eyes of the populace than a mere half. I would not want to waste that opportunity. But the nearest I can come to figuring it out is that my human father, holy Lugalbanda became a god, so maybe that explains it."

Enkidu replied skeptically, "But that was a ceremonial declaration made after his death, long after you were born and already a prince."

Gilgamesh paused. Enkidu was right. But the truth would certainly not be of advantage in this discussion, so Gilgamesh turned wisdom sage on Enkidu. "And that proves my point, Enkidu. In much wisdom is much vexation. And he who increases knowledge increases sorrow."

Enkidu frowned at him. Gilgamesh had avoided the issue. Enkidu did not mind letting Gilgamesh see that he was not convinced.

Gilgamesh reacted to it. "Do not give me that look. It does not matter what percentage god I am. I am still also a man. And so I will die, because all men die. The wise man and the fool alike. The king and the commoner, the rich and the poor. No man escapes Sheol. And in the long run, the dead are all forgotten."

He paused for dramatic effect, then concluded, "But a god lives forever."

"It reminds me of a proverb," said Enkidu.

Gilgamesh saw it coming. He sighed and asked Enkidu with a touch of sarcasm, "And what proverb is that?"

"Better is a poor and wise youth," said Enkidu, "than an old and foolish king who no longer knows how to take advice." Then he added, "Not that I am implying anything."

"Of course not," remarked Gilgamesh. He was getting a little peeved. "And that reminds me of a proverb as well."

Enkidu refused to ask, because he knew he was going to get it anyway.

"A Wild Born once civilized forgets his careless freedom and learns to become a worry wart."

Enkidu's eyes narrowed. He said, "You just made that up to get back at me."

Gilgamesh refused to look at Enkidu. His eyes stayed focused on the river ahead of them with a captain-like intensity. Then a grin spread on his face and he pronounced, "Well, I *am* king, so I get to make up my own proverbs."

Enkidu bowed and said, "This is undeniable. I bow in submission to thy divinely annoying authority."

Gilgamesh and Enkidu both burst into laughter. They embraced one another with a bond of love.

The display of affection irked the disdainful Ninurta, still standing at the front of the raft. He shook his head and turned back to navigating their craft toward Nippur.

Ninurta thought to himself, *A king with a trusted confidante is not proper material for a tyrant. I shall have to do something about that.*

CHAPTER 26

Gilgamesh commanded the raft down the Euphrates to Nippur. He barely tolerated the pomp and ritual of a formal dedication to the temple of Enlil. He found it all so dreadfully boring that he could not wait to leave. Their business done in Nippur, they hired a boat to take them the rest of the way to Uruk.

Uruk, the mighty city with its mighty walls, towered over Gilgamesh and Enkidu as they docked their boat in the river wharf. Ninurta was to shadow Gilgamesh as his newly appointed personal guard. They hid his identity as a god underneath a hooded cloak. The revelation would be delayed until the appropriate time. This would prove difficult, since he stood about eight feet tall and built like an upturned ziggurat. His intimidating presence helped hold off questions.

Gilgamesh wondered what had transpired in the city during his absence. He saw that the city walls were complete. They were divinely grand. Beautiful towering cliffs of kiln-burned brick surrounded the city like a huge protective serpent of power. *Well done, Dumuzi,* he thought. *A reward for your industriousness is certainly due.*

They passed through the sevenfold gate. A trumpet announced the arrival of the king.

As they approached the palace, he glanced over at the temple district. What he saw shocked him.

A huge tree grew within the Eanna temple area. It rose a thousand feet into the heavens, its branches spreading wide. It was astonishing. Gilgamesh wondered how on earth it had gotten there and grown so tall within so short a time.

Then he realized that the entire Eanna complex was being remodeled by a large contingent of workers. Brick layers, carpenters, and hundreds of workers swarmed the complex in the process of enhancing and extending the entire structure.

Gilgamesh started to get angry. He is gone for a fortnight and the man he leaves in charge begins to act like he owns the place?

"What in the world?" began Gilgamesh.

Enkidu drew his attention down to the clay pit sector of the city, fully one third of the acreage of Uruk. It was now a lake! Gilgamesh's eyes went wide with shock, then narrowed with anger.

"Heads will roll," he barked, as he tramped his way into the palace and in toward his throne room.

Gilgamesh threw open the throne room doors in anger. He immediately saw his mother Ninsun on her queenly throne. But someone else sat on Gilgamesh's throne, and it was not Dumuzi.

He quickly suppressed his wrath.

The throne stealer was an eight foot tall being dressed in a robe of vulture's feathers and wearing the horned headdress of deity. She was a goddess.

Gilgamesh stopped. Enkidu stopped. Ninurta stepped back into the shadows of the entrance way to stay unnoticed.

The being spoke like a queen herself. "You must be the mighty Gilgamesh, Scion of Uruk, Wild Bull on the Rampage, one third mortal and two thirds divine!"

She glanced at Ninsun who sat fearfully quiet. "Is that how you say it, Lady Cow?" She looked back at Gilgamesh with a smile and open arms, and hungry eyes.

"I must say you are *everything and more* that your mother said you were," she purred, licking her lips.

"Oh, forgive me. I am taking up your throne." She stood up and gestured for him to sit on it. Her courtesy mocked him. The goddess knew full well she could do whatever she wanted.

Gilgamesh stared at her, unsure of how he should respond.

She took a step further away from the throne and said, "Allow me to introduce myself. I am the goddess of sex and war. You may have known me in the past as Inanna, but I am reborn from Sheol as Ishtar."

Out of sight at the back of the room, Ninurta's eyes went wide with shock beneath his hood. It was true. Shamash had not been lying. Inanna was back somehow, but with a new name. Though looking at her garments under the robe, apparently her new name involved the same bizarre identity she had exploited before the Deluge.

"Where is Dumuzi?" Gilgamesh asked Ninsun.

Ninsun could not look at her son. She averted her eyes.

"Dumuzi? Or Tammuz, as I called him," Ishtar butted in.

Called him? thought Gilgamesh. *As in past tense?*

She continued, "Well, let us just say that he has performed an invaluable service for me that will keep him detained in Sheol for — Well, he is not coming back anytime soon."

Her attitude dumbfounded Gilgamesh. He could not believe the arrogance of this tramp goddess. But he was also not particularly alarmed either. After all he had gone through, there was not much that could frighten him.

Ishtar could see it.

"My, you are a brave one," she purred. "We will have some exciting times together, you and I."

At that potential threat, Ninurta stepped forward. He did not take off his hood, but he was clearly being protective of his ward.

Ishtar scrutinized him. Her playful tone turned suddenly irritated. "Stop hiding, son of Enlil. I smelled you when you walked in, you imbecile."

Ninurta pulled down his hood. He stepped up beside Gilgamesh, remaining chillingly silent. He kept his hands ready to draw a weapon.

Ishtar was the most fierce and bloodthirsty of all the gods. She feared no one and was feared by all. But Ninurta was not like the rest of the pantheon. He was the son of Enlil and if anyone could be her match, it was him. He was stronger than the others, and well trained with many weapons and fighting techniques, bow, axe, mace, sword and battle net. The rumors were that he had even mastered the "way of the Karabu," the secret angelic fighting technique that had been used by generations of giant killers and archangels.

But Ishtar's connection to this 'son of Enlil' ran deeper still. Back in the days of Jared, before the Deluge, when she was Inanna, she had been a secondary deity of Enlil's patron city, Nippur. Through her schemes, she had managed to usurp Enlil's authority and draw the devotion of the citizens to her own temple and regency. Enlil had been enraged with her treachery. But he was unable to take back his previous glory. When she failed to win the War on Eden, she was demoted to be an escort of Anu in Uruk, so the high god could keep an eye on her. Enlil had retained Nippur. But in the Deluge, he was bound into the earth by the archangels and another Watcher took on his identity. If anyone's offspring had a vendetta to take down Ishtar, it would be Enlil's — the very one standing before her now.

She wondered just how much Ninurta knew of these past events.

Ishtar suppressed her thoughts of this history. She needed to maintain her prowess or he would have a weakness to exploit. She stared him down, until he looked away.

She gestured toward Gilgamesh.

"Are you his protector?" she asked Ninurta with surprised delight.

"Yes," said Ninurta.

"What of Shamash, his patron?" she said.

Ninurta answered, "King Gilgamesh has a commission of the pantheon behind him. I am to insure his success in carrying out his duty." He was stone-faced and stoic, her emotional opposite.

"Indeed?" said Ishtar.

Gilgamesh and Enkidu thought it wise to listen quietly.

Ishtar asked, "And who rules the pantheon now?" She had guessed that Anu had been bound into the heart of the earth, along with Enlil and the other Seven who decreed the Fates. She knew Gabriel the archangel well enough to know that he always got his man, or in this case, Watcher. Since Semjaza led the pantheon in the guise of Anu the high god, surely Gabriel would have targeted him first and foremost before hunting down the others.

"Enlil rules," said Ninurta.

"A new Enlil," she corrected.

He nodded. Some other Watcher had taken his identity to carry on the program. The humans would not know what they were talking about.

"And how many escaped the binding?" she asked.

"Seventy, and various mal'akim."

"All hiding out in Mount Hermon, I suppose."

"Yes," he said.

She circled him verbally like a snake ready to strike.

"You must tell me what this commission is," she said. "I am excited to hear the good news."

"I am not authorized to do so," said Ninurta.

Ishtar's face turned sour. "You are not authorized to do so?" she mimicked him with bile.

She burst out in a shout that resounded throughout the palace, "I AM GODDESS OF WAR! I WILL BE TOLD THE COMMISSION OF THE ASSEMBLY!"

Ninurta responded with a deep resounding voice like thunder, which surpassed Ishtar's in tone if not volume, "I AM GOD OF STORM! AND I AM NOT INTIMIDATED BY YOUR LACK OF SELF CONTROL!"

Gilgamesh, Ninsun, and Enkidu were shaken by the ferocity. Two gods with explosive tempers did not bode well for their safety. They had not been told before that he was a god of storm. Well, that explained the excessive physique.

Ishtar was impressed. She did not remember this vegetation god being so brawny and formidable before the Flood. He must have trained hard in the intervening years to climb the hierarchy. Still, she did not fear him. In fact, that there was finally someone with a will of steel to match Semjaza's lost leadership impressed her. The challenge aroused her. She realized that she could not rely on force alone. She would need to employ strategy and intellect to master him. The prospect would sharpen her political skills. She would enjoy this.

Ishtar feigned backing down, coupled with a fake attempt at saving face, "Well, mighty 'calf of the storm,' I can see intimidation serves neither of our interests. We do not want to reduce this fine city to a pile of rubble because of unyielding brutishness, now do we?"

Ninurta shook his head in agreement. He knew this cunning vixen. He could see right through her acting. She had not backed down at all. She meant to cow him into a false sense of superiority. He would not fall for that. But he would play along for his own schemes.

"Lady of Heaven," said Ninurta, "this is your city. I have no desire to contest your authority here. I will stay focused on the purposes of the assembly and will not interfere in your governance."

Then he threw out the trump card he had been holding for the right moment. "When will you travel to the Mount of Assembly in Hermon? Enlil and the pantheon will surely be inspired to hear of your glorious rebirth."

The big snake, thought Ishtar. *He is threatening to disclose my presence to the pantheon. The gods will be no more inspired to hear of my return than a wildebeest to hear of a lion's presence. The truth is they would all prefer me to be chained in Tartarus and ineffective.*

She countered with her own fake sincerity, "Well, I certainly have every intention of getting there as soon as possible. I am excited to discover what leadership and plans are in place for the new assembly."

She would do no such thing. Since the leadership of the assembly was unwilling to let her know their plans even through this dung beetle of an emissary, then to Sheol with them. They were unworthy of her allegiance, the pack of hyenas. She had her own plans.

She completed her excuse, "I will do so just as soon as my temple remodeling is complete. You know contractors. They cut corners and put in mud brick when they should use kiln fired bricks, and so on."

She would have to keep her distance from the pantheon until she could figure out what this Gilgamesh was all about. Then she would try to worm her way into their scheme, with hopes of taking it over.

Ishtar had her own ace up her sleeve, and she pulled it now. "So the assembly is not aware of my return from Sheol yet?"

Ninurta answered, "Shamash had mentioned your name more out of hope or possibility than actual fact, in connection with dreams of some kind." He was deliberately vague. He did not want to commit to anything that she might use against him in the future.

She said, "Interesting. Shamash has not been home to Uruk in quite some time." *The cowardly flea*, she thought. *So they did not know I was freed. Shamash was probably blaming me for his own incompetency. I must use this to my advantage.*

She finished, "I suspect Shamash may be the one who is pulling the sheep's wool over all of our eyes with his own deception."

Ninurta knew Shamash was a coward. He did not trust him either. But he kept his thoughts to himself behind a face of inscrutability.

Because the gods were so focused on their own verbal maneuvering with each other, they had ignored the humans, who had listened carefully to everything. Gilgamesh and Enkidu now knew that there was a contest of authority within the divine assembly that threatened to tear it apart. This goddess of war was evidently not very welcome for her incorrigible attention-grabbing egotism and apparent schemes of coup d'état. And she could not control her temper. She was not the goddess of war for nothing.

More important than all that, these so-called gods had no idea what was actually going on with each other. Shamash had maneuvered himself politically before the assembly of gods by lying about Ishtar and nobody knew the difference. Shamash knew nothing of Gilgamesh's dreams or sacrifices to him as patron deity. He had not heard Ninsun's intercessory prayers to him either. And nobody knew about Ishtar's return from Sheol, until now.

Enkidu listened with loathing. What kind of gods knew so little and quarreled so much? Were they really worth worshipping, or were they just another petty kingdom of power to fight against for superiority over the land?

Gilgamesh could see that a confrontation between these rival heavenly powers was inevitable. Ishtar would no doubt try to deceive him with her wiles, to gain his confidence. She wanted to know what the gods were up to and she probably wanted to take it over. He started to wonder if he would make it out of this alive, let alone achieve the immortality he sought.

His muscles hurt from all his traveling. Right now, he just wanted to get out of his filthy garments and have his first bath in weeks.

"My gods," said Gilgamesh, "I beg your leave. Enkidu and I will retire to our bathhouse now to clean up. It has been a long and grueling journey for us."

"Certainly," said Ishtar. "My Gilgamesh is deserving of a celebration of his great and mighty deeds! We must throw a party!"

CHAPTER 27

Gilgamesh and Enkidu bathed themselves, relaxed, and put on clean garments. During that time, Ishtar and Ninsun organized a celebration feast in the palace main hall. Enkidu slipped away for a visit with Shamhat. He would have to meet Gilgamesh at the town square later, for a triumphal entry through the city streets of Uruk.

As they lay in each other's arms, Shamhat listened quietly while Enkidu described the events of their journey. When he drew the narrative to its end, she gently probed into her lover's mind and heart.

"Do you also seek this immortality?" she asked him.

He thought a moment, then answered, "No. But I love my king and I am his loyal follower and devoted friend."

It was a bond of love between men that even the love of a woman could not attain. Enkidu felt that the experience of journeying together, looking into the Abyss, and cheating death to be unrivaled, even by the most intense oneness that he could achieve with Shamhat.

"Well," she stated, "I will never understand you men and your need for death-defying quests and slaying giants. I am just glad you are home, because I love you, my Enkidu."

"And I love you, my precious songbird," he replied.

Enkidu joined Gilgamesh in the town square. They rode Gilgamesh's war chariot, pulled by mighty horses through the streets teeming with citizens of Uruk. They sported the rotting head of Humbaba on a pike as a trophy of victory. The masses roared with praise and worship of their demigod king, the Scion of Uruk, and his mighty Right Hand.

After the procession, they retired to the palace main hall to feast. Everyone in the palace court was there in their royal finery. Enkidu sat at the right hand of Gilgamesh as usual. Ishtar sat on his other side, pushing Ninsun away from her rightful seat beside the king. Ishtar degraded her with every opportunity she could get. Shamhat sat close beside her husband. The pudgy Sinleqiunninni was there, trying to surreptitiously clean his fingernails clay-caked from too much tablet handling. Ninurta stood sentinel behind the king's chair, just out of sight.

Choice lambs and boars were roasted with vegetables. Fruits beyond the capacity of the baskets and platters spilled over the table surfaces. Wine and beer flowed heavily.

Enkidu got into a drinking competition with Ishtar. She might be a god, but these gods had digestive systems and Enkidu could drink anyone under the table. He decided to see how far he could push her. They kept the empty goblets at the table and received new ones with each refill. The pile before each of them increased steadily like mini-ziggurats as they pretended not to bother noticing the other's collection.

As usual, Ishtar dominated the party with her loud and boisterous bragging.

"Tell me, Gilgamesh," spouted Ishtar, "However did you manage to wriggle out of the wrath of the gods for slaying their Guardian?"

"Well for one thing," crowed Gilgamesh, "We discovered that the giant had a digestion problem, which resulted in gigantic flatulence that dwarfed even Enkidu's gastral magnificence. So the gods actually thanked us for clearing the air!"

Everyone burst out laughing. Even Ishtar was drunk enough to chuckle.

Gilgamesh added through tears of laughter, "Truth be told, Enkidu had a significant hand in the matter."

Joyful eyes all turned to Enkidu. He was ready with his quip. "They were as impressed with the king's size of intellect as they were with the manliness of my looks!"

The crowd erupted with laughter again.

Enkidu added a hearty, "Ho, hurrah!" to milk the punch line.

Ishtar asked Gilgamesh, "And what was your impression of the assembly of the gods?"

Gilgamesh thought for a second, then said, "Not too bright for governing deities." He smiled and announced, "Present company excluded, of course." Some chuckles peppered the crowd.

He continued, "I think I would rather be governed by any seventy plebeians of the city of Uruk than the seventy gods of the divine council."

More laughter erupted.

Ishtar dropped a wet rag on the joking through slurred lips, "Do you realize that you are only the second human to have ever experienced the privilege and lived?"

Enkidu did not take kindly to the insult of being ignored. She knew full well he had been with the king.

"Who else has done so?" asked Gilgamesh.

"A giant killer named Enoch. Now *there* was a feisty one. Whooshed right up to heaven before we could get our hands on the little creature." Then Ishtar realized that she had said too much. She had better stop drinking. She changed the subject.

"Nevertheless, congratulations are in order," said Ishtar, "to the 'Wild Bull on the Rampage' and his trusty dog."

Now Enkidu sat stone faced. Next to him, Shamhat was both embarrassed for him and ready to jump up and scratch Ishtar's eyes out. But she knew better.

The festive atmosphere of celebration vanished as everyone in the room fell silent in uncertainty of the direction the confrontation might take.

Gilgamesh took the opportunity to turn the challenge onto Ishtar while she was not as guarded. "I have been meaning to inquire of you, Queen of Heaven. I see you have been busy in my absence, planting a massive Huluppu tree in your garden."

"Indeed," said Ishtar. "I plucked the tree, a single Huluppu tree, from the river Euphrates, and I brought it to my holy garden. And there it grew with the Anzu in its branches, and a serpent in its roots. Do you like it, Gilgamesh?"

The Anzu bird was a gigantic thunderbird that had the face of a lion and the talons to match. It was a mythically powerful avian that inspired awe and fear in most Sumerians. The Huluppu tree was its natural home.

"It is a tad unsightly, though its manly looks do remind me of Enkidu."

Laughter echoed in the chamber again.

Ishtar was not amused. "It is a link from the great above to the great below. Consider it a throne for the earth goddess and a bed for earthly souls."

"I take it I am also to congratulate you for filling the clay pits for swimming instead of brick making?" asked Gilgamesh sarcastically.

Ishtar said, "Oh, *that*. Well, the workers accidentally hit the water table and 'bloooosh!' Instant puddle of the Abyss." Ishtar laughed. She was the only one doing so.

She decided to rub salt in the wound. She added, "I hear Dumuzi was a good diver." She chortled through tight lips trying not to laugh. The frivolity of the feast had been completely deadened by her drunken callousness.

Ninsun could say nothing about the truth that was being hidden from Gilgamesh. She would be instantly killed if she made one peep. So she sat sullen in her chair, longing for her stolen dignity.

Ninsun did not have to tell Gilgamesh anything. He could figure it out for himself. He burned with anger.

"Well, I hear that the gods are not very good swimmers themselves," he growled. "Shall we arrange for lessons, O Queen of Heaven?" He said it with venom, staring right at her.

How did he find out about our weakness? Ishtar thought. She could not think very straight with all the alcohol in her gut. *The little maggot is threatening me.*

The divine council were supernatural beings, but they were created beings and every created being has weakness. The gods lost their superhuman power in water, becoming vulnerable. It was the curse of Elohim on them. She tried to dodge it with the unpredictable: self-deprecation.

"Well, as you can see, we gods are also not too good of drinkers. So I think I shall retire for the evening."

Ishtar stood to leave. Everyone else stood in obedience. She waved them back down and stumbled out of the room. She was not as drunk as she appeared to be. But she had decided that any display of pretended weakness would inspire a traitor to take advantage. It could actually give her an edge. Even in her current tipsy state, she could slaughter everyone in the room and bathe in their blood — excepting Ninurta of course. That would be for another day.

Enkidu watched Gilgamesh as he looked at Ninsun. Her sad eyes said it all. Enkidu knew there was an unfolding darkness present that would only get worse. He hated Ishtar with all his heart.

CHAPTER 28

Gilgamesh retired to his bed chamber after the late night feast. But he could not sleep. He was getting used to Ninurta's shadowing presence everywhere, but sometimes it still disturbed him knowing this cold blooded creature watched over him like a divine reptile. Unblinking lapis lazuli eyes, frightening twisted muscles of power, emissary of the gods. Trust for these inscrutable and calculating creatures did not come easily.

Gods did not sleep, so Ninurta would find a corner in a dark shadow out of sight, to stand sentry through the night over Gilgamesh.

Gilgamesh turned toward the dark corner, and said, "Ninurta, go do some training in the desert. I want some time alone."

Ninurta slipped into the light from the fire in the hearth.

Gilgamesh said, "I do not need you with me every second. I can take care of myself, you know."

Ninurta would not argue with him. He said, "I will be back before dawn."

He gathered his bow, sword, mace, and javelin and jumped out the window down to the earth fifty feet below.

Gilgamesh wondered if he had gotten in over his head with this monster. Ishtar was intemperate and volatile, histrionic and emotionally unstable. But this one had a different kind of frightfulness about him. He was a cold and silent killer, with no emotional display. Like a heartless crocodile in the water that suddenly snaps with jaws of iron, or a cobra that stands swaying until it strikes with death. In some ways that was more blood curdling to the king.

He went to the window to look out into the night, hoping to see Ninurta's shadow at play under the moonlight. But he was already long gone.

Then Gilgamesh's blood ran cold.

He turned to see Ishtar standing by his bed, her eyes watching him like a snake, a charmed snake. All her drunkenness had vanished, her impatience soothed. She seemed to move like a wisp of undulating smoke in a flowing robe. She wore exotic makeup and her head hosted a most beautiful headdress of gems and feathers.

She entranced Gilgamesh. The thought occurred to him that she might be using enchantment, but that left his head as quickly as it had entered. He found himself attracted to her.

She removed her robe to reveal lingerie of satin, leather, and lace. And she was not without heels. Ah, the high heels that gave the female figure such elegance when moving.

When she spoke, it was not her usual terse and condescending voice. Gone was the impatience and spite, and in their place was sweetness and desire.

So she really did live up to her reputation as goddess of fertility, thought Gilgamesh. He felt his deepest desires start to surface.

"Gilgamesh, I am sorry for my — lack of self-control — this evening," said Ishtar. "I was entirely inappropriate. It was your night of celebration and I stole it with my impertinent jealousy. Please forgive me."

Gilgamesh said nothing. He stared.

Ishtar gave a little smile and writhed closer to him. But not too close.

"I will not lie to you," she said. "I am the goddess of war and sometimes that means I am ridiculously excessive in my outbursts."

She shimmied just a little closer, so he could look into her eyes. He could smell her intoxicating perfume. Of course, he did not trust her, but he could not deny his attraction to her at this moment.

She whispered amorously, "Gilgamesh, you are a giant with a giant's hunger. You are more than man. You are part god. I could see when I first met you that you that no human woman would be enough for you."

He could not deny it. She was a treacherous megalomaniac, but she *was* a goddess. She knew his unsettled soul with pinpoint perfection.

She continued her breathless whisper, "You are not like other men. You are a king, and a god. You need a goddess for a wife."

He believed her. He absolutely believed her. She had all the danger of a den of cobras, but she was not lying to him in this moment. His pulse increased. His breath shortened. She smiled.

"I am not here to seduce you, Gilgamesh." The comment jolted him out of his fog. "You are far too great a man for that. No, I am here to make a rational offer of much consequence."

Gilgamesh came fully back to his senses. He glanced out the window into the night, wondering when his protector would return.

"This is the most reasonable you have sounded yet," said Gilgamesh.

"Oh, everything I do has a reason," she said smiling.

Indeed, he thought. *She is the most calculating creature I have ever met.* More calculating than even him. Well, maybe not. But close.

She said, "I offer Sacred Marriage between us. I will not lie to you, Gilgamesh, it is an arrangement for me to get what I want but also for you to get what you want. This is not about love. This is a fair and even exchange for mutual benefit."

"I just have to let you in on the plan of the gods," he said, uncovering her true desire. There was no way in Sheol he was going to risk his life for *that*.

She responded with vulnerability, "It is no secret that I am not well liked in the assembly."

His expression said that was the understatement of the millennium.

"But I know the pantheon, because I was its original archon," she said.

He stared at her, surprised. He knew she must have been a leader, but the original? That changed things.

She continued, "Along with another archon, who is at this time, shall we say, 'indisposed.'"

She hid a smile at saying this. Anu was indisposed all right. Deep in the heart of the earth somewhere in chains until judgment day.

"The original plan was mine," she said. "To mate with human women and breed our offspring, the Nephilim, as a divine-human hybrid that would exist in two planes at once. You are one of them. You are a Naphil.

He could not believe it. "I am a giant, the offspring of a goddess, but were not these 'Nephilim' wiped out in the Flood?"

She said, "Yes, but not entirely. You are one that carries their blood in your veins. You are in the lineage of the seed of the Serpent."

"Nephilim had twelve fingers and twelve toes. I have ten each," he said.

"Look at your hand, Gilgamesh," she said. "Do you see the scars where the sixth digit would be? Your mother cut them off when you were born."

Gilgamesh felt sweat beading on his skin. He did have scars on both his hands and his feet where a sixth digit would be. He had wondered about that as a child, but Ninsun always said it was just a special birthmark of his deity.

She said, "I know that the pantheon sees in you a great and mighty leader to help them in their plan. I know, because I see it too. We are trying to unite heaven and earth."

He would not respond to her. He was bound by oath not to.

She said, "They have offered you immortality, if you unite with them to accomplish their purposes."

She was completely right. She could figure out most of their plans, but not everything. She did not know everything.

She continued, "I just want to be in on the plan. If I marry you, I will be. I do not hide that intent. But if you marry me, a goddess, you will have immortality. You will be my 'wild bull' and I will never let you go."

She waited only a moment, then continued, "Imagine the power we could attain together that we cannot achieve apart."

"But I already have a deal with Enlil and the pantheon," he said.

"Do not be foolish, Gilgamesh" she said with unusual calm and empathy. "Do you really think that once Enlil has what he wants that the gods will not discard you?"

He realized the truth in what she said. Betrayers could sniff out other betrayers as easily as he could spot royalty in a crowd.

"With me as your queen," she said, "they cannot dispense with you. I need you as much as you need me, to stay inside the plan. Alone, we are at the mercy of the pantheon. Together, we are a force to be reckoned with."

"And what of Ninurta?" he asked.

"Ah, Ninurta," she sang. "He protects you now. But later, what will protect you from him?" She paused to let it sink in. "I can. And I would be bound by a covenant to you. He would not be."

She knew the pantheon and its protocol better than anyone. If he married into the godhead, then he would be more protected than he would be in his current status as an instrument of the gods. Marriage would afford him rights. Rights that might very well protect him from the capricious will of these gods.

"Come, Gilgamesh," she said, breaking his concentration, "be my bridegroom and I, your bride. You will ride a chariot of gold and the world will bow down before you — kings, nobles, and princes."

This made sense on every level to him. It perfectly balanced all interests. Protection of the one from the many. An uneasy alliance, but the only one that kept at bay the worst that could be done to him.

The only problem was that the offer was being made by Ishtar.

He turned to her. He said, "If I take your hand in marriage, will I be treated with the enduring affection of your other lovers?"

She had not anticipated this. His perception blindsided her.

He continued, "Where is Dumuzi now? You say you fell in love with the shepherd, the keeper of herds. Yet, you made him drink the muddy water. You made him a substitute for you in Sheol. Now perpetual weeping has been ordained for the mother of Dumuzi, for your 'Tammuz.'"

Ishtar stiffened. He accused her of betrayal and she could not deny it. It was like a dagger inside her belly. Then he turned the knife.

"And what of Ishullanu, my gardener?" said Gilgamesh. "You snuggled up to him and tasted his vitality. Then you planted him in his own garden."

She felt her bile rising up within her. *This little cockroach,* she thought. This Gilgamesh was cunning. He added just enough poetic flair to his words to avoid outright hostility. In a way, it was a sharper blade with which he was cutting her.

Gilgamesh finished twisting the knife, "It would not be wise for me to embrace your offer, Queen of Heaven, as I would not wish to accept the consequences of those who are unlucky enough to have garnered the intimate attention of the goddess of war."

Ishtar started to tremble with anger as they slowly circled one another. "You ungrateful maggot. You dare question my integrity from my actions with a couple of worthless plebeians?"

He stopped circling with his back to the window. The moon shone into her eyes. She stepped closer to him, but stopped when she saw the large silhouette of a mighty being rise behind him in the window sill. Ninurta had returned. He stood behind Gilgamesh, pumped up and ready for war. In her rising anger, her attention had been distracted from sensing the approach of the storm god. She had let her emotions get the better of her. Now he was here, and she was not ready. This was not the time.

Ishtar hissed to Gilgamesh, "You have insulted me and slandered my name. And now you hide behind this — muscle-brained boor."

Ninurta was not offended by the insult. He cared nothing for words. He respected only power.

She stared at Ninurta. Two mighty gods ready to spring like lions on one another. But it would not happen tonight.

Ishtar said, "Remember, Gilgamesh, Ninurta protects you *for* the pantheon. But who will protect you *from* the pantheon?"

She slipped out the door and vanished.

Gilgamesh sighed. He knew he had barely dodged a death blow. "Next time, do not take such a long workout, will you?"

CHAPTER 29

The next morning, Gilgamesh awoke to the news that Ishtar was gone. She had left in the night for the desert, after killing half a dozen male and female slaves in a fit of anger.

He guessed that his rejection of her offer had so enraged her that she lashed out at whoever was near her and took off into the desert to cool off. Or maybe she was traveling to Mount Hermon to attempt to worm her way back into the gods' good graces. Or maybe she was engaged in diabolical plans of revenge. He had better stay close to Ninurta just in case.Gilgamesh was not easily intimidated. He was not above asserting his authority as king, even to a goddess. He detested the unsightly eyesore of that mammoth tree in the middle of Eanna. He suspected it was like a weed of her own growing roots of manipulation. It was time to address this aggravating blight on the city of Uruk – *his city*.

He grabbed the huge axe that had been crafted for his journey to the Great Cedar Forest and went to gather Enkidu.

When they arrived at the temple complex, Ninurta stood sentry at the gates while Gilgamesh and Enkidu entered the complex. The pair found their way to the immense Huluppu tree.

Already, it stood a thousand feet high and seventy feet round, its tangled roots clutching the ground like a reptilian claw.

Gilgamesh surveyed the surrounding buildings and open areas of the city to determine which way they should lay the huge tree to the ground. They heard the caw of the mighty Anzu thunderbird in the sky. Looking up, they saw it launch from a nest high above and fly off into the sun. It must have sensed what was about to happen.

"Enkidu," said Gilgamesh, "let us chop some wood."

They raised their axes high. But before they could swing them, the haunting sound of a female voice behind them interrupted them. "Mighty Gilgamesh!"

They turned.

A raven-haired woman in a flowing robe and a wreath of flowers on her strikingly long hair stood in the shadow of the tree. Her face looked milky pale, almost translucent. When she spoke, she sounded as if she was singing.

"I am Lilith, and I live in the folds of this mighty Huluppu tree."

The men glanced at one another, puzzled.

"It is the Great Goddess Earth Mother, the Tree of Life. She is the link between heaven and earth. Why would you seek to murder her?"

"Murder?" said Gilgamesh. "It looks like just a tree to me, not a person."

"Ah, but that is where you are wrong, O king. The mystery of life flows through her sap. Her branches bear the fruit of love, and her roots are the very nourishment of the soil around you."

Enkidu quipped, "I think if you were to ask the soil, it might disagree with you, and consider itself a victim of depleted nourishment."

Gilgamesh looked at the ground surrounding the tree. Enkidu had spoken the truth. The dry ground lay cracked, completely void of all vitality and vegetation. The tree sucked the life out of the soil. There was nothing nourishing about it. If given more time, it would no doubt suck the life out of all of Uruk, and then expand to the cities nearby, Eridu, Ur and the others.

Lilith stepped closer. The movement pulled their attention from the parched ground back to her. Her beauty became more distracting to the men.

Desperation began to tinge her voice. “Does Ishtar know what you are doing? Does she approve?” she said.

“I am king of Uruk,” said Gilgamesh. “I built this temple, I rule the four quarters, and I do not approve of this tree.”

Lilith said, “Do you build your kingdom on the exploitation and degradation of your environment?”

“I have been accused of worse,” he responded.

Enkidu thought he felt the ground move slightly below his feet. He gripped his axe tightly.

“You leave me no choice but to call up the earth to fight back and protect itself,” she said.

“The earth is unruly enough,” said Gilgamesh. “It is mankind that has harnessed her and tended her to bring order out of the chaos.”

Lilith spoke, but did not address what Gilgamesh said. She simply stated, “Ningishzida, arise.”

Gilgamesh and Enkidu felt the earth move again. Something burrowed through the dirt beneath their feet. They did not doubt it was this ‘Ningishzida’ that Lilith called forth.

Enkidu spotted the leading edge of the moving mound. He slammed his axe down on the moving pile, burying it deep into the earth with an explosion of dirt. When he jerked his axe back out, a gush of blood spurted out of the ground. Whatever Ningishzida was that crawled beneath their feet, it was not going to arise to do anything.

Gilgamesh said to Enkidu, “She is a demoness. Let us get this done.”

As a Naphil with a sensitive connection to the spiritual world, Gilgamesh could sense when he was in the presence of a spirit being.

They turned to continue their chopping.

Two young children stood in their way, hugging the tree behind their backs. They were both feminine, but one of them seemed to Gilgamesh like a boy dressed up as a girl.

"You would murder my little girls, Lili and Lilu, as well?" cried Lilith. "What kind of monster are you?"

Gilgamesh threw a glance toward Enkidu and said, "They are demons too." They both swung their axes at the children. The pair dissolved into the tree as the blades buried in deep.

A scream penetrated the air. It reminded Enkidu of the screams they heard in the Great Cedar Forest. But this one sounded evil. As if they had just struck a dragon.

The bark of the tree started to writhe and twist like a living thing. They looked closer. The tree appeared to be made from the intertwining bodies of human beings that were all in torturous pain. It was as if the tree was an imprisonment of the damned.

Another good reason to cut it down.

Gilgamesh and Enkidu continued their hacking away at the giant organism of torture for over an hour, until it finally began to creak and lean.

They stood back, and Enkidu shouted his signature, "HO, HURRAH!"

The mammoth timber fell and landed on a significant portion of Ishtar's remodeled temple, crushing it to smithereens, exactly as Gilgamesh had planned.

"Whoops," said Gilgamesh. "I guess Ishtar has some rebuilding to keep her busy." They both smiled.

Gilgamesh knew the world had not seen the last of this damnable abomination. He had heard of the Huluppu tree from before the

Deluge, and knew that its seed survived the waters. It would seek to grow somewhere, as long as there was a Mother Earth Goddess to worship. This demoness would never stop trying to rise up and take power. The world was just not ready for such a deity yet.

"Let us get this thing cut up," said Gilgamesh. "I have a surprise gift for when the goddess returns."

•••••

The goddess Ishtar planned to return to Uruk soon. But she had her own surprise that she was working on for Gilgamesh. She had learned certain imprisoning spells of enchantment from Enki, back before the Flood. They had used them on Leviathan, the sea dragon by luring it into an undersea cavern with the spells written on the rock walls. When Leviathan became surrounded by the engraved spells, it became temporarily under the control of its captors. From there, they unleashed the sea monster upon the field of battle in the desert of Dudael at the War of Gods and Men. The devastation had been massive. But the Great Flood had crushed those plans.

And now, Ishtar had found her way into a certain desert canyon where she could engrave those spells of enchantment on a gorge of steep walls. She had been focused on her task for a few days, and had almost completed it, when she heard the sound of her intended quarry approaching her trap. A mighty roar bellowed through the canyon and echoed like thunder off the steep rock walls around her.

"Come to me, my monster of chaos," she muttered. "I have need of your talent for destruction."

CHAPTER 30

Ishtar returned to the city of Uruk a few days after her disappearance. She came without fanfare, late in the evening when no one was out to see her except for watch guards.

She approached her temple complex and discovered that her tree, her beautiful single Huluppu tree, was gone, cut down. Ripped from the heart of the earth. Her Anzu bird flown away, her Ningishzida gone, and her Lilith disappeared.

Her guttural cry of affliction ripped through half the city.

It woke Gilgamesh. He grinned to himself. The ever-present, never slumbering Ninurta even gave a slight upturn of his lips.

Enkidu heard it as well. He was not so pleased, because he knew that this would probably mean a personal war of vengeance between Ishtar and Gilgamesh. He did not like the prospects. Ishtar would not give up until she was victor. She could not die, so it would be an unending war.

Gilgamesh, however, could die. So he could not win.

Ishtar entered her temple area. The sight of half her remodeled temple crushed to smithereens from the fallen timber slapped her in the face. All the work she had commissioned had been destroyed in an instant by the hand of that protected worm of a king.

We shall see who can do more damage to whose walls by the midnight hour of this evening, she thought.

As priest king of the city, he had complete jurisdiction over every structure, even the temple complexes of the gods. He could do whatever he wanted to her temple. Ishtar had wagered that her bold move would put him in a precarious political position. She had done this before. In Nippur before the Flood, her temple grandeur had placed Enlil in a precarious political position. Enlil had been at the top of the pantheon and Nippur was his patronized city. Yet even he avoided the potential public relations damage of a quarrel with Inanna over her excessive temple enhancement. As a result, she usurped his power in the city.

But Gilgamesh is not so politically astute, she thought. She had counted on his self-interest, that he would seek to avoid doing anything that would reinforce the tyrannical reputation he was trying to overcome. That would have enabled her to slowly encroach upon his authority.

She had counted wrong. He had asserted his territorial claims over her, and cursed the consequences.

She could crush him like a frog, were it not for his personal bodyguard, that bilious overgrown brute, Ninurta. And then there was the oath of the pantheon not to transgress the narrative of the mythology they had established. Well, oaths were *always* eventually broken. It was just a matter of time, and a matter of the right moment.

She walked through the courtyard. it was full of servants and votaries playing a sport with wooden instruments called a pukku and mikku. Their fun enraged her. She grabbed the closest servant to her and snapped his neck, screaming, "How dare you worthless insects play games instead of clean up this mess! I will have all your heads! All of them!"

She grabbed another servant and threw her fifty feet into a stone wall.

A frightened servant yelped, "But goddess, the king himself commanded we do so!"

She stopped short of killing them. "Of course," she said with realization. Then lopped off his head.

She thrust her way into her throne room. She paused when she saw the display of a newly carved wooden throne replacing her old one. On it was a tablet sealed with the king's own seal.

She opened it. It read, *Dearest ~~Inanna~~ Ishtar*. The bravado of this meat sack fed her rage. Writing her old name and then crossing it out as if he forgot she had changed her name. She knew there was nothing accidental about it.

Please accept my apologies for the minor demolition and inadvertent inconvenience I may have caused your remodeling with the downing of the Huluppu tree. It was an impediment to the architectural and structural integrity of the great city-state of Uruk. I would have preferred to tell you this personally, but you had been absent from the city. Please accept these tokens of my appreciation of your patronage of my city.

Tokens, plural? She thought. *What other object of spite did he create to vex me?*

The letter concluded, *I had them expertly carved out of the wood of the Huluppu tree for your nostalgic remembrance, and included the pukku and mikku instruments for the sporting pleasure of your servants.*

She crushed the tablet to pieces in her fist and burned with anger. *For the sporting pleasure of my servants? I will send those players with their instruments into Sheol.*

She continued through her palace to find the final offending object. When she reached her private chambers, she found it. The queenly bed of her intimate quarters had been replaced by a carved wooden one. This was an obvious attack on her offer of marriage to Gilgamesh. She burst out in a fit of rage and cracked the bed into pieces. All the servants had already fled her presence, fortunately, or several would have lost their lives in her wrathful reaction.

She dragged the bed out of her chambers and down into the throne room. She set it on fire, along with the wooden throne. She ordered some of the diviners to add incense and incantations to the flames. It would be a homing beacon for her revenge.

She whispered to the earth and sky, "Gilgamesh, you will regret the day you disrespected my name."

She would not wait for the midnight hour after all. She wanted her revenge, and she wanted it now.

A mighty bellowing roar was heard throughout the land. It shuttered through the dark streets of Uruk. Something immense and very wicked was descending upon the city.

CHAPTER 31

The strange bellow echoed through the city.

Gilgamesh and Enkidu awoke simultaneously in their separate bed chambers in the palace. Enkidu quickly suited up in armor and dashed to Gilgamesh's door.

As he was about to knock, the door opened. Gilgamesh stood there, armored and ready to go meet their approaching nemesis. They heard the war horns of the city in the background. The army was mustering.

"You are late," said Enkidu.

"Excuse me," said Gilgamesh, gesturing to his armor. "I am as ready as you are."

"But I made it all the way to your room before you even opened the door," said Enkidu.

Gilgamesh thought quickly, "The king does not assist his servants. His servants assist him." *Got him,* thought Gilgamesh.

"Would you prefer I help you with your armor next time, sire?" asked Enkidu with a touch of playful condescension.

Gilgamesh ended it. "I will grant you a merit of honor before the entire city for punctuality and for being the first to gird your loins. But first, we have a city to protect, so shut up and let us get moving. This is no time to jest."

They bolted for the city gates.

The army of fifteen thousand strong gathered before the gates in anticipation of commands from their king. The standing army of ten thousand were ready almost immediately. But when the city itself was under attack, an additional five thousand able bodied younger men and elderly joined the ranks as reserve support.

Gilgamesh ascended the rampart of the seven fold gate. No adversary, be they army or monster, would dare assault the impenetrable seven fold gates of Uruk. It was sure failure — and death.

Ninsun had come to support her son, but he sent her away to the protection of the temple of Enki to offer a sacrifice on his behalf.

Gilgamesh and Enkidu looked out into the night surrounding the city. They could see nothing but blackness. But they heard the thundering footsteps of a gargantuan creature approaching their walls.

The mighty roar of this unseen colossus resounded again. Enkidu felt the city walls tremble. Even Ninurta was alarmed. He stepped closer to Gilgamesh, his protective instincts roused.

The night guards lit large torches along the city walls. The torchlight cast an eerie orange glow for hundreds of feet out. But nothing could be seen.

Enkidu turned toward the city.

Ishtar stood beside them. Her presence startled Enkidu. They had not heard her approach. She apparently liked appearing phantom-like to enhance her mystery.

"What is this intrusion that disturbs my slumber?" asked Ishtar.

Gilgamesh also had turned to check the city. He stared at the glow of a huge bonfire that seemed to rise from the Eanna complex like a writhing cobra.

He turned back to Ishtar.

"Actually, I thought you might know, *goddess*," he said.

Ishtar glanced at the glow. She returned the biting sarcasm of his letter with her own false remorse, "It pains me greatly to report that your wonderful gifts of wooden throne and bed accidentally caught on fire in the temple. I might have saved them, had I not been distracted."

Another mountainous roar echoed across the walls. It was closer. Many of the warriors of Uruk soiled their kilts when they heard the sound. They were used to war, but this was something else. Something much worse.

"But now that I hear it," said Ishtar, "I do believe I have a faint recollection of such a creature in the past." She pretended to continue searching her memory.

Another thunderous roar ripped the air. Ishtar's eyes went wide with feigned recognition.

"Ah yes," she said. "Now I remember that sound. It was before the Flood. It was a creature I had assumed was dead, but obviously its amphibious nature saved it."

"Well, what is it?" asked Enkidu impatiently.

"It sounds like the Bull of Heaven," said Ishtar.

Gilgamesh and Enkidu anxiously glanced at one another. They had heard of this mythical creature of chaos. But they would no longer need to rely on legends and folklore. The real thing broke out of the darkness before them and approached the walls of Uruk.

It was immense, and black. That explained why it had been impossible to see in the darkness. Now, in the torchlight, they glimpsed its mammoth features. It walked on all fours, but appeared to be able to stand on its hind legs. Almost as tall as the walls, it had a bullish looking head with horns and a huge misshapen hump on its back, covered with stony irregular armor plates. It was an ugly denizen of darkness.

Ishtar let out a sarcastic tinge, "Oh my. That one *is* immense. I guess you have finally found your peer, Gilgamesh. 'The Mighty Bull on the Rampage' of Uruk versus the Bull of Heaven. It is positively mythological."

Enkidu corrected her. "It is '*Wild* Bull on the Rampage,' not '*Mighty* Bull on the Rampage.'" He hoped for some verbal victory out of this losing battle.

"Thank you, *Wild Born*," said Ishtar. "We must get Sinleqiunninni up here. He cannot miss this opportunity to verify your accuracy and enhance his storytelling tablets."

Gilgamesh knew she had somehow sent this monstrosity. But he also knew he could never prove it, if she was too devious to admit it. Nothing she did was cowardly, so this was definitely some kind of secret scheme on her part. But this was not the time for court intrigue. They had a Bull of Heaven to kill.

The Bull rammed the wall a hundred feet down from the gate. The strong walls of Uruk crumbled before its pounding force. A large section of the wall fell away. Gilgamesh and Enkidu were thrown off their feet.

The Bull's horns were stuck in the bricks. It shook its head until they came loose, knocking down another section.

In the streets of Uruk, citizens ran screaming for their lives, trying to get as far away from the wall as possible.

The Bull reared back, and rammed again. More of the wall crumbled apart. Considering the humongous heavyweight attacking the structure, the city wall held well, but it would not hold up forever.

The beast snorted and roared again.

Gilgamesh yelled to his men below, "Open the gates! Attack the Bull in two flanks of a hundred apiece!"

The commanders of hundreds heard the order. The seven gates opened in rapid sequence. The officers led the men charging through the gates.

Enkidu got back on his feet. " My lord, the Bull is favoring one side," he observed. "I believe it is blind in one eye."

Gilgamesh looked closely. His Nephilim eyes could clearly see the Bull's scarred-over eye at the distance. "By Enlil, you are right, Enkidu!"

Ishtar winced with anger. They had spotted the monster's weakness before she had hoped they would.

The Bull was indeed blind in one eye. Before the Flood, this Bull of Heaven had been known as Behemoth. It used to guard a secret valley in the east, first inhabited by the wolf clan of Cain and then by Noah ben Lamech's tribe. Behemoth had killed the wife of Methuselah ben Enoch. Methuselah had blinded the beast's eye with his javelin in return. He then revenged himself on the beast by using it to his advantage in the War of Gods and Men. Methuselah and a contingent of archangels tethered Behemoth. They let it loose on the battlefield to counter Leviathan, the secret weapon the gods had released from the water to wreak its destruction. But the desired confrontation never occurred because the waters of the Deluge swept the plain clean before it could happen. Behemoth, with its semi-aquatic nature was able to stay alive during the Flood. No matter how cleansing a judgment upon mankind, there always remained some evil, some chaos in seed form that survived.

Gilgamesh blurted, "Let us kill this blind brute!"

Gilgamesh would have leapt from the wall to fight the Bull, but Ninurta stopped him. "King, this will not go well for you. Let your army do their work."

Gilgamesh looked down on his men as they flooded out onto the plain by the hundreds. The forces methodically approached the Bull of Heaven in the orange glow of torchlight.

The king looked at Enkidu. His Right Hand merely gripped his axe tighter, awaiting his orders. Gilgamesh turned back to see how his men would do.

The first two flanks of a hundred men each trumpeted their war cry. They attacked the monster with shields up and spears out.

The Bull turned its good eye toward the sound. It stomped its front foot, ready for blood. Gilgamesh and Enkidu then saw that it had a third rear leg, which gave it extra trampling capability. The extra appendage also gave added push each time it banged its head against something. This creature was diabolically ugly from hind to hump, a perfect incarnation of the chaos that it wrought.

As the soldiers drew near, the Bull of Heaven lowered his head and charged.

The forces did not stand a chance. They were like a blanket of red laid out for the Bull to make its rampage precise. It swooped through the forces and trampled them to death.

A side flank of a hundred men used their chance to launch their spears at the beast from the side.

Most of the spears simply bounced off its skin, a hide of bulbous calloused armor. The few weapons that stuck in between plates merely added to the Bull's rage. It turned, swiping away another hundred soldiers with its head, crushing them or casting them to their deaths.

The other soldiers backed away. They were too frightened to run swift-footed to their deaths.

On the rampart above, nobody noticed the slight uptick of Ishtar's lips as she watched the devastation she had called down upon Uruk and Gilgamesh.

Gilgamesh said to Enkidu, "They do not stand a chance. They are like an army of ants being stomped."

Enkidu watched it all with an Anzu eye. "Yes, but a single ant or two is hard to catch with one eye and clumsy feet."

Gilgamesh glanced at Enkidu, wondering what he meant.

Enkidu strapped his axe to his back and barked, "I have an idea. If I can get behind him, you take the head."

Before Gilgamesh could stop him, Enkidu ran down the rampart to meet the Bull.

Having lost the soldiers as targets, the Bull turned again to its goal of shredding the wall. A few more hits and it would run rampant through the city of Uruk, trampling homes and people to dust. Gilgamesh guessed that Ishtar's fire was some kind of homing beacon drawing it in.

As Enkidu approached the ledge, the Bull hit the walls again with its horns. Enkidu timed the attack and jumped into the air as the Bull hit, so he would not fall victim to the tumult that shook the wall. He landed back on the walkway as the Bull pulled its horns from the brick rubble. He looked down and saw its gouged-out eye socket, blinded to his presence.

Enkidu checked the state of the wall. The top third had crumbled away. One more hit and the Bull would be inside the city.

The Bull raised its head to get a better sight of its damage. The monster's head came right up to the level of Enkidu. It snorted, and Enkidu was blasted with a ghastly odor and a splash of nasal slime and foam that turned his stomach.

"Disgusting," he muttered. But the Bull had still not seen him.

He launched himself onto the head of the beast and grabbed its horn in a vise grip, bellowing "HO, HURRAH!" like a joyous stallion buster.

Now, the Bull knew of Enkidu's presence. An annoying little flea had just jumped on it and screeched in its ear. Infuriated, it snapped its head backward trying to fling the little thing off its horns.

Enkidu expected the action. He released his hold and went flying in the air to the rear of the animal. He caught the beast's tail, thick as a huge cedar tree. He lost his breath in the impact, but he held on.

Gilgamesh raced toward the ledge. He and Enkidu could think as one when it came to battle. They did not even need to verbalize their strategy. Ninurta ran a few paces behind him.

Gilgamesh launched off the ledge onto the Bull's head. He caught a horn and held on for dear life as the monster jerked and swished its head.

These fleas were not going to let go.

Enkidu, forgotten by the Bull, pulled out his heavy battle axe. He raised it high for the mightiest swing he had ever made in his life.

He brought the axe down with a fierce wedging blow. He buried deep into the tail end of the Bull.

The Bull roared in pain. It was only the tip of its tail, but the axe had lodged in the spinal cord of the tail and set its nerve endings on fire.

The Bull's attention immediately returned to Enkidu. It whipped its tail with ferocious velocity and snapped Enkidu into the air. He went flying so fast and so far that he would surely perish from internal injuries when he landed on the ground a thousand feet away.

Enkidu's action gave Gilgamesh just enough time. While the Bull focused on Enkidu, Gilgamesh pulled out his axe and buried it deep in the creature's skull.

The blow was not enough to kill it. The Bull had a thick skull. But Gilgamesh had stunned the creature and it stumbled. It tried to move its feet, but its thoughts could not translate to the body movements. The axe had severed some functional part of its brain.

Gilgamesh drew his sword and found the soft spot at the nape of the Bull's neck. He thrust the sword in with all his strength. It went in all the way to its hilt.

The Bull of Heaven froze. Its brain had been pierced. It gave a sound like a squeal compared to its earlier bellowing. Then it fell to the ground like a lump of clay. The collapse shook the walls one last time and a cloud of dust covered the area. The mighty Bull of Heaven, this Behemoth of ancient days, lay dead under Gilgamesh's feet.

Soldiers arrived to carry their mighty king from his lofty perch on the head of the beast.

"WHERE IS ENKIDU?" Gilgamesh screamed. "WHERE IS ENKIDU?!" He had seen the tail whip him off. He knew that Enkidu could not have survived the crushing force of that landing.

His soldiers stared at him silently. They too knew the fate of Enkidu. They had helplessly watched the entire spectacle from their fearful positions.

"WHERE IS ENKIDU?" Gilgamesh belted out one more time through broken voice. He lost his strength and fell to his knees.

An unexpected murmur ran through the gathering. Gilgamesh looked up.

The crowd of soldiers parted from the rear. A very exhausted and very beaten Enkidu limped through the crowd, dripping wet.

Enkidu smiled, "Thank the Creator for the irrigation canals of Uruk." Enkidu had landed in one of the multitude of canals so necessary for the livelihood of Uruk. To him it felt like he had hit a wall of mud bricks, since water was not particularly friendly at such distance and speed. But it was not rock, so he was alive.

The soldiers began to applaud until the entire fifteen thousand were outside cheering their heroes, Gilgamesh, the Wild Bull on the Rampage, Scion of Uruk, and his only equal, Enkidu of the Steppe — shorter in stature, but stronger in bone.

Up on the rampart, Ishtar could not contain her disappointment. She stared at the display below with a bitter frown and muttered a curse, "By the gods of heaven and earth, woe to Gilgamesh the bully, who mocked me, cut down my Huluppu tree, and killed the Bull of Heaven." She turned and fled to her temple in the center of the city.

Her mutterings did not go unnoticed by Ninurta, who had returned to the gate. He watched her with calculated interest. He knew she was behind this. He also knew that if he could prove it, he might get the council to exile her, maybe even bind her in the heart of the earth where she belonged until Judgment.

Sinleqiunninni ascended the steps to the top of the rampart near Ninurta. He approached the god, since he was the only one standing there.

"Ishtar demanded my presence for transcription," said the scholar. "What was all the ruckus?"

Sinleqiunninni had been so deep within the bowels of the library that he did not even know the fantastic battle that had just occurred. He looked down upon the aftermath and shuttered at the sight, "Oh my!"

Ninurta gave a slight smirk of amusement and said, "I think Ishtar wanted you to witness what happened so that you might record it. Although, I believe she had anticipated a different outcome."

Sinleqiunninni's mouth gaped with astonishment. "W-what happened?"

"King Gilgamesh and Enkidu killed the Bull of Heaven," said Ninurta. "I am sure you can come up with some interesting fiction to fill in the holes on your tablets of clay."

With that, Ninurta left the scholar to engage his imagination.

Down below, Gilgamesh and Enkidu were not done celebrating their victory. Enkidu grabbed his big axe and cut off the fifth leg of the monster. He gathered some soldiers to carry it in to the city.

Gilgamesh had the Bull's heart cut out for a sacrifice to Shamash.

CHAPTER 32

When a king was vanquished in a battle or war, he was usually paraded through the city dead or alive, along with his riches and other dead leaders. This triumphal parade would follow the processional way that led to the palace gates and was lined with citizens cheering the victory of their king and giving glory to the gods.

The Bull of Heaven was a different kind of nemesis that required a different kind of celebratory response. Gilgamesh dragged its carcass through the streets with a herd of mighty horses, and threw its disemboweled intestines to the people for stews and soups. Then he had the meat cut up and apportioned to the orphans of the city, as a gesture of goodness toward his weakest of subjects. Next, he had the skin brought to the tanners and they began the long and arduous process of tanning the hide in order to hang it from the palace walls as a trophy of conquest. The heart he brought to the temple of Shamash.

But for Ishtar, he planned a special offering.

The temple prostitutes, hierodules and votaries were assembled in mourning in Eanna. Ishtar led them, dressed in a black outfit that was painful looking, with body piercings, chains, and claws. She led the coterie in cutting themselves with knives and sacrificial daggers.

The sound of Gilgamesh's trumpet announced his arrival in the temple. The devotees stopped their bloody self-abuse. Ishtar turned to watch the king's entrance to the holy area. Enkidu strode by his side and that bothersome bulk, Ninurta, trailed behind Gilgamesh like a vulture. A large number of servants followed. She noticed that Enkidu looked pale and weakly, sweat rolling down his neck.

"And to what do I owe this dubious honor, King Gilgamesh?" asked Ishtar.

"I wanted to make an offering of thanksgiving to the gods. So I prepared some gifts to please you, O Queen of Heaven, the Morning and Evening Star."

Gilgamesh clapped his hands, and a half dozen servants carried two huge horns forward.

Gilgamesh affectionately announced in the manner of a royal proclamation that Ishtar knew was more mockery, "I grant these horns of the Bull of Heaven, filled with sweet oil, for you to savor."

The servants carried them up to Ishtar. She gestured for her own servants to receive them. She did not bother to give even a fake smile. She just stared blankly without response. She was boiling with bile.

Gilgamesh continued with his biting mockery, "And also, this grateful offering, procured by Enkidu himself, for your pleasure to consume."

He moved aside. Enkidu signaled for a retinue of fifty slaves to bring in the huge amputated fifth leg of the Bull of Heaven that he had chopped off.

They eased it down on the floor. It took up most of the room. The hierodules and harlots had to move back to allow it room. The flesh was already rotting and filled the room with a sickening stench.

Enkidu stood before Ishtar and bowed in reverence. Ishtar could see close up now that Enkidu was very sick. He could barely keep himself straight.

"Feeling unwell, poor Enkidu?" Ishtar whispered.

He hissed back, "I know what you did. And if I could vanquish you, I would do to you what I did to this leg. I would drape your guts around your neck."

It dawned on Ishtar with a bit of unexpected surprise that the curse she uttered at Gilgamesh on the wall of Uruk must have taken effect. She had not engaged in proper ritual or used any sorcery in conjunction with her utterance. She had spit it out in a moment of anger, but evidently it had worked. This was a much better affliction than she had thought of. It would be more of a punishment to leave Gilgamesh alive and well to watch his beloved Enkidu suffer the curse. And if Enkidu died, all the better for the despair of utter loneliness that would torture Gilgamesh for the rest of his life. Such a living hell was much more damage than one's own suffering and death.

She found this a good thing too, because she had been preparing to engage in the most dangerous stunt of her life as revenge on Gilgamesh. She meant to perform a necromancy ritual that would open the gates of the underworld and release the dead to rise up and eat the living. Now she would not have to do that, because this would be a far worse punishment for the Scion of Uruk, or as she liked to call him, the Gadfly of Sumer.

Ishtar watched as Enkidu stumbled his way back to Gilgamesh at the door. She could see it coming, so she gave a little blowing wisp just as he collapsed to the floor, unconscious.

Gilgamesh ran to him shouting, "What is wrong, Enkidu?"

Enkidu could not speak. His eyes were upturned, he was white as death, and cold and clammy to the touch.

Gilgamesh looked up at the grinning Ishtar. "What have you done to him?"

She gave a gesture of her hands as if to say, "Nothing."

Gilgamesh picked up his friend and left the room like an Anzu in flight.

CHAPTER 33

Enkidu lay in his bed delirious and barely coherent. Shamhat took care of him. Gilgamesh did not leave his side. He helped her put wet rags to Enkidu's forehead and used various herbs passed down as healing essences. He brought in the diviners to read omens and the sorcerers to create healing potions. But nothing helped. Gilgamesh suspected it was a curse by Ishtar. But he could not prove it. And she denied it.

He considered going to Ishtar and throwing himself on her mercy to plead for the life of his one and only friend. It was a kind of madness he entertained, being at the end of his desperation. He considered all possibilities: selling his soul to Ereshkigal of the underworld, trading places with his comrade, even killing himself to join Enkidu. But the momentary madness passed when Gilgamesh realized there was nothing he could do.

After several days, Enkidu became more conscious. Gilgamesh asked him, "What did Ishtar say to you?"

"She did not curse me," said Enkidu. "She looked surprised when I met her and she surmised I was not well. Then she looked at you curiously. It was as if she had been expecting you to suffer, not me."

"Can a curse be diverted? Do you remember any other strange happenings?" asked Gilgamesh. Shamhat sat right next to him, listening raptly.

Enkidu had a hard time concentrating. He gathered his wits. "Yes. When I attacked the Bull of Heaven, he snorted upon me and I was drenched in his slime. At that moment, I felt strange, but I soon forgot it because we had a Bull to kill."

"True enough," said Gilgamesh. "It would not surprise me that that chaos monster from the Abyss would have spittle filled with disease and evil."

Ninurta remained ever vigilant and ever silent by the door.

Suddenly, Enkidu blurted out, "I curse the mighty cedar door we made for Enlil. I curse the day I cut it down and carried it to the Euphrates, and drifted it to Nippur. And I curse the hunter who found me in the wilderness."

Gilgamesh thought it strange that such an emotional outburst of cursing come from an otherwise rational man.

Enkidu looked at Shamhat's sad face and added, "I curse you, Shamhat. I curse the day you civilized me."

Shamhat could not believe what she was hearing. Enkidu kept going, "May you never bear offspring. May you never be received by proper women."

A tear slid down Gilgamesh's cheek. Shamhat was already weeping a river. "My sweet love, my Enkidu, my husband, why do you speak to me this way?"

Gilgamesh became angry, "She saved you! Why do you curse the woman who brought us together? You are a fool descending into chaos."

Enkidu could not help it. He knew his end was near and he could not face it. He finally understood what all of Gilgamesh's fuss was about. His brooding contemplation about the "mysteries of the cosmos" were not the silly waste of time Enkidu had thought. Gilgamesh was not needlessly introspective as Enkidu had supposed. The king had been the wisest of men, after all. He had looked into the depth of the Abyss and faced the truth. Without something beyond this world, everything was a worthless delusion. Nothing had meaning, and every apparent blessing was only a mocking curse.

Enkidu now faced that oblivion.

He decided to make one last act of love to his wife. He said, "I am sorry, my Shamhat, my wife, my life. I do not want to die and yet this is my demise. Forgive me. I bless you instead. May you have a long and blessed life with many children."

It was too late. The damage could not be undone with an insincere retraction calculated to make her feel better. Even though she brushed it aside in order to care for his ailing body, the seed of bitterness took root deep in her heart. She had lived a life of abuse at the hands of men. She thought she had found one truly worthy and good man. And now he had failed her as well. He had overshadowed her potential, and controlled her destiny. At his darkest moment of pain, he abandoned her. Despair waited for her as his own death did for him.

Enkidu turned to Gilgamesh and held up his hand. Gilgamesh saw it was now clutching the gold amulet of adoption from Ninsun. It was the only thing he had carried with him through every adventure, every battle, every exploit in the face of death. It was his birthright. "If you are my brother, then pray for me to the gods. If they are not who they claim, my king, then we are all doomed."

"I will pray for you, my brother and friend," said Gilgamesh. But in his heart he thought, *We are all doomed.*

Enkidu dropped back into unconsciousness.

That night, Gilgamesh prayed and entreated and supplicated to the gods. He sought not merely Shamash, but also implored Enlil, Enki and Anu for their mercy.

As had happened previously, no response was forthcoming, because none of the gods could hear him.

By the twelfth day, Enkidu's body had wasted away to an emaciated skeleton of his former self. His eyes were sunken into his scrawny face. Shamhat remained tirelessly by his side, cleaning him and trying to get him to drink or eat anything. The best she could do was wet his mouth. He lay in a deep sleep from which he could not waken.

Suddenly, as Gilgamesh and Shamhat tended to him, he awoke. His eyes snapped open and he stared at Gilgamesh.

Shamhat shrieked in surprise.

Enkidu spoke in a hoarse croak, "I had a dream."

Gilgamesh knew his friend was not entirely in his right mind, but he tried to treat him with dignity. He knew the end was near.

"What did you see?" asked Gilgamesh.

"I was standing between heaven and earth. And the heavens thundered and the earth gave reply. And a man like an Anzu thunderbird stood before me with paws of a lion and claws of an eagle. He struck me and crushed me underfoot like a mighty wild bull."

Gilgamesh and Shamhat looked at one another trying to understand it.

Is that me? thought Gilgamesh. *Am I responsible for his death?*

Enkidu continued after a raspy cough. "I called out to you to save me, but you could not. You were afraid."

So it was not me, thought Gilgamesh.

"He tethered me like a captive bird and brought me down to the House of Dust, to the Land of No Return."

Gilgamesh swallowed. This was not a dream. This was a vision. Shamhat clutched Enkidu's hand.

Enkidu did not look at them. He stared into the void and kept speaking, "In the depths of Sheol, I saw crowned heads who ruled the lands since days of yore. I saw Etana. I saw Lugalbanda your father. I saw Sumerian kings from distant days. But I also saw Humbaba the Terrible and the dread shades of Sheol, always consuming, never satisfied. Both young and old, rich and poor, king and commoner, good and evil, hero and villain, all end in the dust of death."

Enkidu looked at Shamhat and he smiled. It was a moment of connection with the past. Their eyes penetrated one another and she knew this would be her last touch of the soul of the one man she had ever loved and would ever love. In mere moments her world would end.

Enkidu glanced at Gilgamesh as if he was surprised to see him. "My king," he said.

"Do not call me king," said Gilgamesh. "I am your friend. I am not king where you are going."

"Oh, but you are," said Enkidu. "I saw you as king of the shades. You will sit in judgment over the dead in Sheol."

Gilgamesh did not reply. He only smiled. He knew it was a delusion of Enkidu's own desire to procure for his beloved friend the significance that eluded him. He knew that in Sheol there was no significance. It was not a place of distinction for kings. It was the Land of Forgetfulness.

Enkidu said, "Remember me, my friend. Do not forget all we have been through."

"I will not forget," said Gilgamesh. "Your name will live on in the memory of the living." He said what he knew Enkidu wanted to hear. But he knew it was a lie.

"I have become as nothing," concluded Enkidu. He summarized his life that his memory reviewed. "If I had died in battle, I would have glory. I would have a name. But instead I have faded away in disgrace. I have ended most ingloriously."

Gilgamesh could say nothing, because there was nothing to say. Enkidu was right. All their journeys and hardships together, all their labors and adventures, their victories and triumphs — all of it was in vain, because Enkidu would be no more. Soon enough, Gilgamesh would follow him into the darkness, where his memory that kept Enkidu alive would also be consumed in nothingness. They would end where all men ended, and where no man's works mattered.

The thought crossed Shamhat's mind that this was the sad, pathetic state of the male gender. They were obsessed with "glory" and "fame" instead of love and acceptance. They sought a transcendent meaning in the abstract beyond, and completely ignored the imminent meaning of human relationship all around them. They entered Sheol alone.

She thought to herself, *But do we not all enter Sheol alone?*

Enkidu closed his eyes and breathed his last.

Shamhat wailed in the traditional way. It was deep and guttural because in the depths of her being, she felt a turn, so simple, yet so profound that she knew she was not the same person in that instant.

She would never again allow her destiny to be controlled by a man. She would never love again.

Gilgamesh wept.

Ninurta breathed the slightest sigh of relief. None of them knew that Ishtar was not the one who had inflicted Enkidu, nor was it the Bull of Heaven. It had been Ninurta. He had poured a slow-acting poison into Enkidu's dinner wine, intending to take away from the king the one connection to humanity that kept him from accomplishing the purpose of the gods. After all, Ninurta had been charged with making sure Gilgamesh performed their secret goal.

Enkidu had been the one impediment in the way of that goal. He simply had to be taken out of the way.

CHAPTER 34

Ishtar laughed. She could not believe her good fortune. Revenge upon this insolent king was sweeter than death itself, more thrilling than pillaging and plundering, more cathartic than a bloodbath. Her enemy would be imprisoned in a living torture of loneliness and mourning that would haunt him until he took his own life in despair. Who knows? Maybe she could milk this misery for years or decades. She looked out of her temple window to the king's palace across the way and giggled with anticipation of the next palace servant who would return to her with gossip of what was going on inside that house of despair.

For six days and seven nights, Gilgamesh kept Enkidu's body in the palace walls without funeral or burial. Enkidu remained in his bed, still sleeping peacefully under his sheets.

The corpse caused such a stench that Shamhat had to move into another section of the palace to avoid perpetual nausea. Ninurta stood outside the door, instead of inside the room with the revolting odor. Servants wore linen cloths over their mouths and noses to keep from gagging as they came and served the king, who lay at the foot of Enkidu's bed like a dutiful hound pining for its dead master.

Ninsun came to the door every day to keep an eye on her son. But she could not find the courage to enter for she held a secret so dark that if Gilgamesh discovered it, would only crush the soul of her son, who thought nothing could crush him more than he already had been.

Tears streamed down her face as she heard Gilgamesh babbling about the mourning of everyone from the elders of Uruk to the rivers and forests to every gazelle, lion, panther, leopard, deer, and jackal of the steppe. He even said that the river Euphrates from which they drank and along which they strode was a stream of tears for him. Then he recounted his tales of adventure to his dead companion, as if Enkidu were alive and laughing along with a beer in his hand.

"Remember that clodhopper of the Cedar Forest?" said Gilgamesh to the corpse. "Some Rephaim giant he was. We killed him, you and I, and we cut off his head, one, two, three. Do not mess with the Scion of Uruk and the Denizen of the Steppe! We showed those gods we were afraid of nothing. We showed them." He laughed the laugh of madness and continued his storytelling.

"And how about that Bull of Heaven? He was no match for the Wild Bull on the Rampage and his Wild Born. Three hundred soldiers could not touch that stinking bovine, but we took him out with an axe and a dirk to the brain, did we not?"

By the seventh day, Gilgamesh had ripped off his royal robes and paced to and fro, naked and unwashed. He refused meals and soon become gaunt. He did not shave, so his beard grew in and his hair grew long. Some of it he would tear out with his hands when overcome by emotion. He was transforming into a Wild Born himself. It was a strange form of empathy and identification. It was madness.

On that dawning day, Gilgamesh stopped mumbling to himself. He thought he saw Enkidu move his head. Was he seeing things? Was he truly mad after all?

Gilgamesh slowly approached Enkidu's corpse. He stared at the emaciated face. Would the gods bring his Enkidu back from the dead? Was it possible?

There it was again. The head did move ever so slightly. But it did move. As he drew near, he could see the almost imperceptible twitching of musculature beneath his cheeks. The process of resurrection must be a difficult one of struggle to revive the once dead body parts into life again.

Gilgamesh bent close, inches away from Enkidu's face. Suddenly he saw the nose twitch.

Then a maggot fell out of the nostril onto his cheek, wriggling and writhing in search of more flesh to consume.

Gilgamesh backed up in horror. Enkidu was not coming alive, he was being eaten inside by maggots and worms.

Suddenly, Gilgamesh returned to reality. The fetid stench overwhelmed him. He turned and vomited on the floor beside the bed. He looked up and saw his mother Ninsun at the doorway watching him.

He could bear it no longer. He went back to Enkidu's body, and pulled a linen sheet over his face like a veil. Then he ran to the window and, still naked, climbed down to the street below.

He ran all the way to the walls of the city that had been torn down by the Bull of Heaven. Laborers worked to rebuild the broken structure. He climbed up and over the rubble. The workers cowered in fear and watched the naked wild Gilgamesh dart off into the grasslands of the steppe.

By the time Ninurta realized what had happened, it was too late to follow Gilgamesh as his dutiful bodyguard. He looked out onto the landscape, but Gilgamesh had disappeared into the wild. Ninurta spit in anger. If word got out about this, he would be chastised by the assembly for incompetence. He decided to hide away, so that he could not be indicted by his obvious separation from the king. Everyone would assume he was with Gilgamesh.

CHAPTER 35

Ninsun had the body of Enkidu removed and placed in a temporary crypt, until she could find her son to oversee the funeral. He may have had a fit of madness, but she believed he would come back. When he did not, she sent some soldiers to search for him. They came back empty-handed. Then she realized that she knew exactly where he would be. And she knew that she was the one who would have to go to him.

She set out for a secret location in the steppe where she used to take him as a child, to play in the grass alongside the river. The recent traumatic events had distracted Ishtar's attention, particularly from Ninsun. The queen mother had been virtually forgotten in the bustling mayhem. She slipped out alone, without anyone really noticing her absence.

When she reached the hidden haven, the familiar spot lay overgrown with weeds and new trees. It had been many years since she had come to this special place, this sacred space. She sat down by the river and put her feet in the water as she used to do. She sang the lullaby she used to sing for her precious Gilgamesh, remembering how it would lull him to sleep in her arms.

"Sleep come, sleep come,
sleep come to my son,

sleep hasten to my son!
Put to sleep his open eyes,
settle your hand upon his sparkling eyes,
as for his murmuring tongue,
let the murmuring not spoil his sleep."

Her voice lilted across the grass and through the trees with haunting melody. Soon, she sensed a presence behind her. She turned.

It was Gilgamesh. He was a mass of tangled hair and bushy beard, naked as an ape. He had reverted from civilized man to Wild Born. Strangely enough, he had with him the animal skins his mother had given him when he was a child, the ones he used to hunt with. They draped over his shoulder.

His mother's soothing voice had drawn him in and brought him back to his senses. At least momentarily.

"Hello, Gilgy," she said. It was her special nickname for him, another lure to draw him nearer.

He stepped closer, cautious, but trusting. He hesitated because she was crying and he did not know why. He tilted his head as a dog might, when trying to figure out what it was observing.

She kept saying over and over, "My son, my son. You are my son."

Finally he touched her shoulder and whispered, "Mother."

She looked up at him.

He sat beside her as he used to do, putting his feet in the water.

She said, with all the love of a mother, "My child, why? Why do you run? What are you afraid of?"

Gilgamesh sighed. "Death," he said.

He paused.

"I lost my only friend in the entire world, and I realize that I too will end up like Enkidu."

"We all end up like Enkidu," she said.

"I thought I could cheat death," he said. "I thought I could find eternal life. First it was through indulgence and power, but that only led to the insatiable hunger of tyranny. Then I hoped to become famous and make a name for myself, so I conquered the giant Humbaba and even the mighty Bull of Heaven. But it does not matter, because even if these achievements become legendary, even if they are inscribed in tablets of epic, they too will ultimately fade into oblivion in distant days and in far off years. Of what value are glorious stories to those of whom they speak? What legends are in Sheol? Darkness is infinite and the dead do not see the radiance of the sun. Fame and glory are but illusions of vanity. They are wisps of smoke that are here and gone. When I met the gods and conversed with them face to face, I learned that the gods gave eternal life to only one man, Atrahasis, to mock the rest of us. I soon realized that all I had was Enkidu, my friend, my brother, thanks to you. But now that has been taken from me, I see that all is vanity and emptiness. All of life is one big cruel jest of the gods to give us hope, only to dash it to pieces in an eternal void of meaninglessness."

Ninsun broke out bawling like a baby.

Gilgamesh held her.

"Why do you cry?" he asked.

After a moment, she was able to gather her strength to speak.

"I have a confession to make, Gilgy," she said. "Ishtar was going to force me to do so, but I wanted to tell you myself, without compulsion."

She swallowed. Her voice went small. "I am not a goddess."

Gilgamesh stared at her blank-faced. He was not sure what she had said. "You are not a goddess?" he repeated.

"No, I am not a goddess," she said, waiting for it to register with him.

"But father was a human," he said.

"Yes, he was," she affirmed. "He was only declared to be a god through apotheosis at his death." Apotheosis was astral deification, the exaltation of a king at death to the status of deity, accompanied by their ascension into the stellar host of heaven. The gods were identified with stars.

"But I am two thirds god, one third man," said Gilgamesh. "How could that be?"

She still could not bring herself to tell him.

"You yourself cut off my extra fingers and toes when I was an infant," he complained.

"That is true," she said. She realized that he had figured out that he was a Naphil born of god and man.

She dropped the axe. "But you are my *adopted* son."

He refused to understand it. "I am not your son?"

"You *are* my son," she said firmly, "but not of my flesh. You are from the line of Cush, son of Noah."

It still confused him. He became like a child again with his mother. "But how?" he asked.

She explained to him, "The man that the gods called Atrahasis, was actually Noah ben Lamech. He was the one the gods chose to protect from the Great Deluge. He and his sons and their wives were the eight that were saved by the boat. One of those sons, Ham, had a wife who had been impregnated by the god Anu. That child, Cush, was born and though he was not himself a giant, he carried the blood of giants in him. He was rejected by his own family, and traveled south to rebuild the cities of Uruk and Eridu and others. When you were born a giant, Cush secreted you in my palace to grant you the chance to thrive and fulfill your destiny as a Gibbor, a mighty leader amongst men. He swaddled you in those magic animal skins that you wear now and have worn all your life on the hunt. They were the original coverings that the creator god made for Adam and Havah, the first pair. They were handed down through the line of Seth to Enoch and eventually were stolen by Cush. Lugalbanda and I adopted you as our own and I claimed to be a goddess so your identity would not be compromised."

Gilgamesh brushed hair out of his eyes. It was all coming clear to him now; why he never felt quite at home anywhere, including in the palace of Lugalbanda and Ninsun. He had always felt different, special, an outsider.

"So I am not your child. I am more alone in this vast emptiness than I had even imagined I was," he said.

"No!" she reprimanded him. "You *are* my son and the son of holy Lugalbanda. You are more our offspring than a natural born child, which we would have had no choice over. But we *chose* you and we loved you as our own. You will always be our son."

She held open her arms as she usually did. Gilgamesh could not restrain himself. He embraced her with a deep love that transcended flesh and blood.

Even as he held her, his thoughts were adding up more bits of information. He said, "So this Noah, who has eternal life, is my ancestor. I am in his lineage."

"Yes," she said. "You are a descendant of Noah ben Lamech."

He said, "Enlil told me Noah was on a distant island called 'the Land of the Living.' Is this true?"

She nodded. "That is why he is called Noah the Faraway or Utnapishtim the Distant. He and his wife Emzara have hid away on the Isle of Dilmun in the Southern Sea."

"Can you tell me how to get there?" he asked.

She said, "I know how to get you to the one who knows how to get there."

Gilgamesh said, "Noah is the only one that the gods have granted eternal life, and he is my great-grandfather."

He paused and proclaimed, "I will find my ancestor Noah ben Lamech, and I will procure the secret of eternal life from him."

He had made up his mind. It would be his final adventure. The journey toward which everything else that he had accomplished previously was but mere prelude. If he could manage to persuade his ancestor, Noah the Faraway, to grant him the secret knowledge of the gods, then he too would become immortal, everlasting. He would conquer the ultimate enemy, death.

"But first, I must bury Enkidu," he said.

"First," she said, "you must cut your hair and get some clothes on your naked bottom. You are embarrassing yourself."

Gilgamesh laughed with her, and then he said, "Thank you, Mother."

Ninsun's heart melted with happiness. No matter what happened to her now, no matter how she fared before the wrath of Ishtar and the gods, she was happy. After all, he had learned of the lies of his heritage, and after the pain of discovering his abandonment by Cush, and after the adoption by Lugalbanda, Gilgamesh still called her *Mother*.

CHAPTER 36

The funeral of Enkidu was an elaborate affair. Gilgamesh cut his hair and cleaned himself up to oversee the administration of the ceremony. His madness was over.

He wanted to give Enkidu the honor of a king. As the king's adopted brother, he had the legal right to it, but as a mighty warrior and peer of Gilgamesh, he deserved it.

Gilgamesh called together a blacksmith, a goldsmith, and a lapidary jeweler to craft a golden statue of Enkidu with a beard of lapis lazuli and gem laden skin of gold. Black obsidian, red carnelian, and white alabaster were incorporated into this image of his incomparable friend.

Gilgamesh had a herd of fatted cattle and sheep slaughtered and piled them high in the open before the temple of Ishtar on behalf of his friend.

A procession of slaves carried the body in its sarcophagus on a portable throne. Behind them followed gifts that Gilgamesh had prepared to lay in Enkidu's tomb for the underworld: a chair and staff of lapis lazuli, jewelry of silver and gold, an obsidian knife with sharpening stone, his mighty battle axe, and a table of precious wood laid out with carnelian bowls of honey, lapis bowls of butter and flasks of oil. Gilgamesh thought to himself that these accessories were of no help to the dead, but only served to comfort the living in their delusion of hope. But even that, he told himself, was something if it would help ease his grief.

They walked the processional way, performed services in the temple of Shamash, and buried the body in a palace family tomb. Gilgamesh ironically noted that Shamhat was the first to leave the crypt. Gilgamesh, with Ninurta his newly returned shadow, was the last to leave. His mourning was over. Enkidu was dead, and with him, friendship, love, and hope.

But Gilgamesh was alive.

• • • • •

Ishtar stormed through her temple, flinging servants and prostitutes out of her way like rag dolls. When she crashed through her palace doors, she hit them with such force that they ripped off their hinges with shattering splinters. One of the flying doors crushed a guard to death.

Ishtar did not even stop to notice. She was infuriated and concentrated on finding that despicable tramp, the Queen Mother.

She had been trying on a new outfit, when the sleazy courtier alerted her to intelligence he gathered from the royal palace. As she marched through the street, she thought her long silk robe flowing behind her was a nice touch. It enhanced the ethereal majesty she affected in her wardrobe. Her skin had been colored white with black lips and eye shadow, the pallor of the undead. She painted high arching eyebrows to amplify her facial expression. A large neck ruff embroidered with golden thread circled her head and framed her face like a work of art. She was a work of art. This particular theme was purity so it was all white. She loved to create irony and was particularly aroused by the image in her mind's eye of a queen's white purity awash in the blood and gore of slaughter.

She entered the temple of Shamash and stomped her way to the rooftop, where she found Ninsun engaged in offerings to Shamash.

"Where is he, Cow?!" she yelled.

Ninsun stared up at her fearfully.

Ishtar sensed a presence and turned to see the quiet muscular figure of Ninurta standing in the shadow of the pillars. In that instant, she suspected Gilgamesh was gone. He had left the city. But where and why? Was Ninurta here to face her down, keep her from following Gilgamesh?

"I thought I smelled excrement," said Ishtar. "Ninurta, you really must stop hiding in the shadows like a cockroach. Unless, of course — you want to *be* a cockroach, in which case I am sure my sorcerers could help you out with some incantations and magic potions."

Ninurta stepped out silently into the light. He strode toward Ishtar.

Ishtar tightened with readiness and a slight grin. So this was it. He was finally going to challenge her in a duel of power. This upstart may be a mighty warrior, but he had nowhere near the experience of Ishtar. She had cut through a myriad of warriors and tread through oceans of blood to get to her position as the fiery goddess of war. She had an uncontrollable temper, but when it came to battle, she was an invincible champion of technique, precision, and skill. In the assembly of the gods, she was uncontested.

Just try me scrapper, she thought. *Give me the excuse.*

He walked right past her, not challenging her. Both clenched their teeth. Their eyes followed each other like serpents ready to strike. He walked up to Ninsun and stood beside her.

I will have my day, blowhard, mused Ninurta. *And then you will know wrath. But my day is not yet here.*

"I see," said Ishtar. "The calf of Uruk is gone on a secret mission, so guard the cow."

Ninurta did not speak. His power was his silence. Words were wasted on enemies. Silence maintained advantage.

Instead, Ninsun responded, "Gilgamesh is on a clandestine quest of utmost importance and secrecy. He will reveal his undertaking and purpose upon his return."

"How formal and proper of you," hissed Ishtar. Then she stopped and brightened with realization.

"You told him, did you not?" said Ishtar.

Ninsun would not answer, but she did not have to. This little imposter had outwitted her and told Gilgamesh before Ishtar could force her to do it.

"You did. You told Gilgamesh about his lineage."

Ninsun cast a nervous glance at Ninurta, who remained as inexpressive as a stone statue.

Ishtar added slyly, "And about your façade of deity?"

Ninsun had already been so completely humiliated by Ishtar in her own city and temple that this mockery was mere redundancy.

Ishtar announced with sarcastic melodrama, "And now he has gone on a journey to seek the Land of the Living in search of his ancestry and eternal life." It was too easy for her to figure that one out.

Ishtar approached Ninsun. Her extravagant robe dragged on the floor giving her the appearance of floating in the air.

Ninurta placed his hand on his sword hilt.

"Stay your sweaty nervous hand, guard dog," said Ishtar. "I am not in the mood."

Ninurta stepped closer, his face an impenetrable wall of stone, his sword arm a steel trap ready to spring.

Ishtar leaned close enough to whisper to Ninsun with a triumphant grin. "Your orphan amputee is in for a big surprise." It was a reference to Gilgamesh's amputated fingers and toes.

Ninsun did not understand what Ishtar meant. What kind of surprise? Was it all a lie? Was he walking into a trap? Ninsun was afraid to betray her fear. She tried to be casual in her concern. "What are you talking about, 'surprise'?"

Ishtar stepped back and laughed. "Why do you not ask your dog?" Ninsun looked to Ninurta.

He said nothing.

Ishtar leaned back in. Ninurta followed with readiness. Ishtar hissed, "You are safe now, Lady Cow. But I have no more use for you. And the day will come when you will no longer be protected, and I will gut you."

Ninsun gulped and felt nauseous.

Ishtar thought for a moment and then added with a chuckle, "With delightful pleasure."

She turned and walked away, her robe train following behind her like a long flowing cape. At the entrance pillar, she stopped for one glance back at Ninurta and whispered too softly for humans to hear, "You and I will dance later, big boy."

But with their preternatural hearing, the gods could pick out the softest of sounds at a great distance. Ishtar's whisper did not go unheard by its target.

CHAPTER 37

Gilgamesh had left before the dawn with only a dirk in his belt and the clothes on his back. He was on a long perilous journey. He would need all his strength and the lightest load he could carry for the feat before him. It would be the mightiest of all his accomplishments because it was a contest with his largest nemesis yet. He was going to outrun the sun.

Ninsun had told him of the legends of Dilmun, the Land of the Living, that resided where the sun rises at the mouth of the rivers. The mouths of the Tigris and Euphrates poured into the Southern Sea. That sea opened up into seas that circled the earth. The poetic reference to the sun rising was a way of saying a place of dawning glory faraway.

It was a magical island, considered to be an abode of the blessed, where Noah ben Lamech and his wife had retreated to live out their immortality, awarded by the gods. It was described as an Edenic paradise. Some thought it was the original Eden.

Gilgamesh had read of this Land of the Living, where the sweet waters came up and mixed with the bitter waters of the ocean. It was written that in Dilmun, "the croak of the raven was not heard, the bird of death did not utter the cry of death, the lion did not devour, the wolf did not rend the lamb, the dove did not mourn, there was no widow, no sickness, no old age, no lamentation."

Gilgamesh had wondered if this was the Garden called "Edin" of Sumerian myth, where the gods bestowed eternal life to all who lived there. He could not know that the original Eden had been completely covered over in lava up in the Ararat mountain range. He was ready to sacrifice everything to find his great-grandfather and obtain the immortality that alone could quench his thirst.

Ninsun had explained that the only way to find Noah was to find his boatman, Urshanabi, who could take him to Noah across the Waters of Death. But Urshanabi could only be found by traversing "the Path of the Sun," a long underground passageway beneath the earth that began at the twin mountain peaks of Mashu, and passed through a pitch black subterranean tunnel of Sheol. The dead could not escape Sheol, but if a living being like Gilgamesh could follow the pathway without wavering to the right or to the left, and do so before the sun could complete one revolution around the earth, he would safely arrive near the location of Urshanabi's boat crossing.

Gilgamesh chuckled to himself. He remembered how Sinleqiunninni, his scholar sage and librarian, had gone off on another long jackal trail of words when describing the fabled Path of the Sun.

"Actually," the scholar had said, using one of his trademark sentence openers that was an indication he was about to correct someone again, "the Path of the Sun is not technically the *real* path of Shamash under the earth. You see, commoners in their ignorance lack nuance in their reasoning and simply think that it is the 'literal' path of the sun. But as a wisdom sage, I can tell you that the assured results of elite scholarship know that the sun travels around the solid firmament above and sets in the West, where it circles beneath the earth through its underworld tunnel eastward, where it rises behind the far mountains at the edge of the world. But the Path of the Sun that you are taking begins at the twin peaks of Mount Mashu within traveling distance, to the east of Uruk, not the far edge of the world.

Secondly, Mount Mashu is said to guard the rising of the sun, but in point of fact, if you begin your run where the sun rises, then you will be running against the sun's circuit toward the west and will only have twelve hours before the sun sets and meets you in the beginning of its tunnel beneath the earth. Additionally, you are traveling westward, which is in the opposite direction of the magical land of Dilmun which lies eastward in the South Sea. Therefore the fact that you have twenty-four hours to run your course *and* the actual tunnel does not match the true path of the sun, obviously implies that 'Path of the Sun' is a poetic metaphor that is lost on uneducated and ignorant literalists who..."

"Sinleqi!" interrupted Gilgamesh with impatience, "Shut up, will you? I got the point."

Sinleqiunninni stopped with a gasp. Gilgamesh wondered if the scholar had even taken a breath during that entire monologue.

Gilgamesh summarized, "I am passing through a pitch black tunnel in Sheol, and I have twenty-four hours to make it or else."

Gilgamesh realized he was not done. "Which leads to my next question. And please try to answer only what I ask in as few words as possible."

"Yes, my lord," replied Sinleqiunninni.

"What happens if I do not make it?" asked Gilgamesh. "Will the shades attack me? Just 'yes' or 'no.'"

"But my lord--," said the scholar.

"Just yes or no," insisted the king.

"Yes *and* no," said Sinleqiunninni.

Gilgamesh sighed with a frustrated roll of his eyes.

Sinleqiunninni blurted as quickly as he could, "No, they will not attack you if you do not stray into their crevices at the tunnel's edges. Yes, they will eat you if you do."

Gilgamesh raised his brow and gave his scholar a smile.

"See, now, that was not too hard was it? Well done, scholar."

"However," Sinleqiunninni tried to add.

"Ah-ah-ah-ah-ah," said Gilgamesh with his finger in the air to stop him.

The scholar obeyed and gulped his words.

Privately, Gilgamesh gulped at how hard his task was going to be without getting eaten alive.

•••••

By the time Gilgamesh made it to Mount Mashu, he had discovered the one last thing he should have let his long-winded scholar tell him: the gateway to the Path of the Sun was guarded by monsters.

CHAPTER 38

The rustling of a brush woke Gilgamesh. He had fallen asleep inside a cave entrance that he found after running many leagues to Mount Mashu without stopping to rest. He was practicing for his twelve double hour run through the underworld. He had managed to kill a couple of lions with the intent of carrying some food with him for the grueling journey ahead.

He grasped his dagger and slid into the shadow of a crevice in the rock wall. He heard the scraping of clawed feet approaching on the rocks, and with it, a male and a female voice.

They were bickering.

The male voice was gruff and spoke with a rural accent as if he had not been in the city — ever. The female voice was raspy and badgering.

"Oh, for Enlil's sake, will you please just simmer down some?" said the male voice.

"Simmer down? You do not tell me to simmer down," snapped the female voice. "I ask you to do one little thing, go and get us some food, and you cannot even do that, without me having to leave our post to help you do your job!"

"Nag, nag, nag," complained the male voice. "Is that all you can do?"

"Well if you did your job, I would not have to nag," nagged the female voice. "And now all we have is this mangy dog that is not fit for an appetizer."

Gilgamesh saw the bickering couple enter the cave. He gasped with horror. They were Scorpion People. Abominable hybrid beings that he had heard of in fables of dark antediluvian days, but had never actually seen. They had the lower bodies of scorpions with stinger tails and eight arachnid legs, and the upper bodies of humans, male and female. But where their hands would be on their arms were scorpion claws, large powerful pincers.

He had heard that before the Flood, the gods had experimented with dark occultic arts in an attempt to interbreed nature with itself. To unite opposing poles of being. They had created soldiers with canine and avian heads, Scorpion People and other crossbred creatures. He did not know just exactly what the point was behind it all and whether this had something to do with the arrival of the Deluge of judgment. Had the gods reinstituted their diabolical cross-breeding plans or were these just rejects from a dying line of those ancestors?

The female dragged a diseased dog carcass by the hind leg and plopped it against the wall. It must have been dead for days. It was rotting with maggots and flies all about it. Gilgamesh felt vomit rise in his throat. These mongrels of miscegenation were the sentinels of the Path of the Sun.

"Now do I have to also gut it and clean it for you or can you at least do that simple task?" she asked with contempt, as she began making a fire.

The Scorpion man rolled his eyes, sighed. He took the dog by the throat, thrusting his other claw into the belly to clip through it like a pair of scissors. Its rotting guts poured out on the floor. The Scorpion Man licked his claw and crunched a few maggots.

Gilgamesh gathered his wits. He stepped out into the light of the fire.

The Scorpion Man saw him first and just stared at him. At nine feet tall, Gilgamesh was a good bit taller than their approximate height of about six feet. Also, Gilgamesh was a Gibbor warrior, a mighty king who had conquered the Rephaim Humbaba and the Bull of Heaven.

He felt confident, but who knew what these occultic chimeras were capable of? Maybe they had magic powers from the gods. After all, the gods would not post sentries who were not capable of defending their turf. Their grumpy personalities must have been a disarming façade hiding some very vicious creatures ready to sting and claw to death their adversaries.

Then again, they could not hunt well enough to find their own food.

The Scorpion Woman turned to see the Scorpion Man standing frozen in position. She blurted out, "Will you please stop piddling around like a statue and get your…"

She stopped when she saw Gilgamesh standing with his dagger in hand. She backed up a couple of steps in shock.

Gilgamesh did not allow them time to strategize. He proclaimed, "I am King Gilgamesh, Scion of Uruk, Wild Bull on the Rampage, slayer of Humbaba and the Bull of Heaven, the mighty king who has no equal."

The Scorpion Man finally spoke, "That is one mighty long list of epithets. Do you have a shorter name that is easier to remember?"

"For Enlil's sake, Girtablu," barked the Scorpion Woman, "It is King Gilgamesh."

Girtablu smiled as recognition slowly crept over his expression, and said, "We know you. He whose body is flesh of the gods is our visitor."

The woman, Sinnista, corrected him, "Only two thirds of him is god. A third of him is human."

Gilgamesh, feeling a bit for the chastised of his gender, decided to help out Girtablu, "That is just a myth. I am really a half-breed. Like you are."

Girtablu and Sinnista grew cold. A pall of tension descended upon the cave.

"We would appreciate it," said Sinnista, "if you would refrain from such derogatory comments about 'half-breeds.' It is offensive and it's *kindism*."

"Kindism?" asked Gilgamesh.

Girtablu jumped in to help clarify, "It is the human tendency to judge animal beings by their created 'kind' and then to place them on a hierarchy of superiority with man being on the top, of course, and lowly scorpions being inferior or of lesser value. It is used to justify oppression and the exploitation of the 'other.'"

"But I was not implying such a value distinction," said Gilgamesh. "I am a mixture of kinds myself."

"That is just what a Kindist says," argued Sinnista. "I will bet some of your best friends are also half-breeds too, are they not?" she added sarcastically.

Now I know why the gods appointed these two as guards of the Path of the Sun, thought Gilgamesh. *They will quarrel anyone to death who tries to get past them*. But at least he knew now that his life was not in danger with these maladjusted nitpickers.

"Never mind," remarked Gilgamesh. "I wanted to offer you the lions I captured and cleaned."

He stepped over to the fire and took a burning log for light. He moved just a few feet back into the cave to show two large lions hanging and drying out over the rocks.

Gilgamesh added, "I ate some of their meat already, but you can have the rest of them for yourselves."

Girtablu glanced at Gilgamesh and smiled as if to say, "You would do that for us?"

Sinnista piped up, "See, Girt? He was able to capture two lions and he only had a dagger. Look at what you could achieve if you only applied yourself."

Girtablu rolled his eyes for Gilgamesh to see and mimicked her mouth gestures to him like a chicken clucking without the noise. Gilgamesh smiled.

"So what is your journey?" asked Girtablu.

"I seek Urshanabi, the boatman of Noah ben Lamech," answered Gilgamesh. "I am told he is at the end of the tunnel of the Path of the Sun."

"You want to travel the Path of the Sun?" exclaimed Girtablu.

"It has never been done before," added Sinnista.

"There is a first for everything," said Gilgamesh.

"But you only have twelve hours to make it to the other side," said Girtablu.

"I thought it was twelve double hours," said Gilgamesh. "That is what the legends say."

"Well, the legends are wrong," said Girtablu. "It only takes the sun twelve hours to traverse the sky and enter its channel beneath the earth. You can see it with your own eyes. Or do you cling to blind faith in your legends against the observable facts?"

Gilgamesh's heart dropped. Now he only had half the time he thought he would have to traverse the tunnel. It seemed to just keep getting worse.

"Very well, I have only twelve hours," said Gilgamesh.

"In utter darkness that even torches cannot penetrate," added Sinnista.

"I know," repeated Gilgamesh. He had heard that the darkness of some parts of Sheol was so thick, all earthly light was consumed in the blackness. Although he thought it was called "outer darkness," not "utter darkness." Maybe it was just the rural accent of this yokel.

"And if you stray to the right or to the left, the shades will eat you alive," said Girtablu.

"I know, I know," exclaimed Gilgamesh. "But what I do not know is how I will be able to run that straight line through the tunnel without being able to see where I am going."

"Oh, that is easy," said Girtablu. He extended his large claws on either side of Gilgamesh's ears and clacked them with a smile. "You follow the sound."

"Girt," interrupted Sinnista, "We are supposed to be guarding the Path of the Sun, not giving away its secrets."

"WOMAN!" shouted Girtablu. He was fed up. She had gone too far. "Do you really think this half-breed..." Sinnista's eyes widened with shock, "Yes, I said *half-breed*, will be able to beat the sun?"

"Thanks for the vote of confidence," muttered Gilgamesh.

Girtablu continued his rant at Sinnista, "This will be entertaining. So shut up, sit down, enjoy the show, and leave me be, you pestering billy goat!"

Sinnista was dumbfounded at the tongue lashing. He had never stood up to her with such firmness. She deferred to his display of strength.

Even Girtablu was a bit surprised at his outburst. But he rather liked it. Maybe he would act more like a scorpion and wear the claws in the family from now on.

He turned back to the giant king and asked him with an annoyed look on his face, "Are you married?"

Gilgamesh shook his head no.

"Lucky you," Girtablu muttered.

Gilgamesh asked him, "What exactly do you mean 'follow the sound'?"

Girtablu's eyes narrowed and he began to speak with the kind of expressive gestures that an actor in a theatre performed. Gilgamesh could tell he loved telling stories.

Girtablu explained, "The Path of the Sun is the only segment of Sheol that the shades will not transgress. It is the Path of the Sun, for Shamash's sake! I would not either. But once they know you are there, they will surround you in every nook and cranny, every crevice, every godforsaken hole that opens to Sheol. And they will wait for you to get too close to their gnashing monstrous chops, and when you do, you are shade bait."

Gilgamesh was not encouraged by the news. In fact, he was growing increasingly discouraged, wondering why he ever chose this crazy idea in the first place.

Girtablu continued with his excitable and expressive storytelling, "But that is their weakness," he grinned widely. "They cannot stop chomping!"

Gilgamesh's eyebrow rose. He was beginning to catch on.

"Their foul smelling, chattering little chompers create a tunnel of sound."

Gilgamesh smiled. Of course. He should have thought of that. He remembered the tales of the shades that he had heard as a child. Their bodies were animated by worms and maggots, and they had faceless faces with huge sets of double teeth that clattered with endless hunger. The phrase, "The mouth of Sheol is never satisfied" brought to mind not only the inevitability of death, but also the eternal lack of satisfaction in that state.

Girtablu interrupted his reminiscence, "Be like a bat. Turn off your sight and invest every ounce of your mind into your ears. Listen. And simply follow the tunnel of sound as you would a tunnel of sight."

"Girtablu and Sinnista," announced Gilgamesh, "I thank you for your aid. I will never forget this day. I will return and lavish you with all the gold, carnelian, and lapis lazuli you could desire."

"Some cooking utensils and spices would suffice," retorted Sinnista.

"You are still going to die," concluded Girtablu with a casual resignation toward Gilgamesh. "Because there is no way you can make it in twelve hours."

"I have a running stride of nine feet. They do not call me Wild Bull on the Rampage for nothing," said Gilgamesh with a smile. "You just wait and see."

He shared a meal with the chimerical couple and listened to their life stories, interrupted by hair splitting and quibbling over petty details. His mind drifted to Sinleqiunninni. He had been right about the discrepancy of twelve double hours he had pointed out to Gilgamesh. But all in all, he was amused and fell asleep to the sound of the cackling fire.

CHAPTER 39

Gilgamesh awoke before dawn. The Scorpion couple led him to the entranceway of the Path of the Sun, lit only by their hand-held torches.

The cave entrance dropped steeply down to intersect with the huge round tunnel below. Exactly where the sun came out past his entrance he could not figure out. He would not bother himself with minor operational details. He had a race to run.

The steep descent into the underworld sent a chill down Gilgamesh's spine. He held a torch for light and looked into the opening. He could not see very far down. It was as if the blackness was as thick as bitumen and swallowed up any attempt to shed light on its corners and crevices.

Gilgamesh stretched his body in preparation for his run. He was in a race against time, and he was going to push his body to its limit like he had never done before. He wore only a loincloth, made from the magical animal pelts, to support his private area from the exertion. Anything else, be it sandal or tunic, would be an added weight to slow him down. He even pulled back his hair and shaved his beard off to maintain minimal air resistance.

He took his last bite of lion meat and a swig of water from his water skin.

"Wish me luck," he said to the couple.

Girtablu remarked, "If you make this before the sun enters and burns you alive or before the shades catch you and eat you alive, then I will mend my ways and build Sinnista her dream cookery."

Sinnista slapped him playfully and said, "That is not fair. You are sure to win that bet."

Gilgamesh took a second look at Girtablu and Sinnista. They had a strange peaceful look about them, as if the constant tension between them was momentarily released. It was not their normal disposition. They were even holding claws.

Then he realized what the change was. They probably had marital relations last night for the first time since the gods know when.

He smiled and said to Girtablu, "Better get your tools together, because I am coming back to visit and make sure you eat crow."

A hopeful look crossed Sinnista's face and she smacked her lips. Clearly, crow sounded tasty to her.

A tiny beam of orange began to break the sunrise. Girtablu turned and held his claws to his mouth and bellowed with all his might, "COME AND GET HIM, YOU SLOBBERING TEETH HEADS! BREAKFAST IS READY!"

Gilgamesh gave Girtablu a dirty look.

"What?" said Girtablu. "You need them for the sound."

"I know, I know," said Gilgamesh. "But you do not have to make it sound like I do not have a chance."

"You do not," he said.

"How about something more positive?" said Gilgamesh.

"Okay," said Girtablu. "I for one, will be sad to see you gone."

Gilgamesh shook his head at Sinnista, who smiled with sympathy.

Gilgamesh leapt into the darkness and began his descent into Sheol.

He did not carry a torch. It would have been useless. The darkness would swallow the light anyway. Soon Gilgamesh could hear the sounds of munching, grinding teeth and the soft hisses and whines of hunger pangs gathering around him. This was it. He had reached the Path of the Sun through Sheol.

He stopped. Closed his eyes. It made no difference. He could not see a thing anyway. He opened them, and listened. He concentrated on the growing sounds around him. Teeth clicking, clattering, chomping, and grinding. Together with the moaning and soft wails, they began to blend into an aural tunnel that his ears could hear as clearly as his eyes would see with light.

Amazing, thought Gilgamesh. *Girtablu was right.*

And there was no time to waste.

He began to run.

He paced himself. He had only twelve hours, but if he pushed himself too soon he could burn out, which would lead to a collapse and then a *burn up* by the sun. Persistent concentration on the sound tunnel was an added mental pressure that sapped his endurance. It was a challenging feat to balance the interests of all these factors against the sun dial that moved relentlessly toward his death.

The ubiquitous darkness around him made him lose all sense of time and place. He had only his breathing to trust. He knew the tempo of breathing he had to maintain to make it out in time, and he trusted his discipline and training. He would not eat anything for the entire twelve hours. He would only sip water occasionally from his water skin, because it tended to offset the cadence of his breathing and synchronized footsteps. The fact is, if he made it out in time, he could very well collapse dead at his feet from dehydration or exhaustion.

Soon the sound of his breathing and the sound of the shades craving his flesh created a rhythm that absorbed him and he lost himself.

He did not know how long he had been running. He did not know how far he had gone or how far he had to go. He only knew he was on time because his breathing.

In, out, stride, stride, in, out, stride, stride.

He guessed he was maybe three quarters of the way there. Nearing the home stretch.

Then it happened. The unforeseen. It was not a monster, it was not a shade, or a villain of evil. It was a rock. A simple rock. Of all the scenarios they had discussed, dealing with a piece of rock that had loosened from the tunnel ceiling and fallen to the ground in a simple random occurrence was not one of them. Of course, rocks loosened all the time and fell to the ground all the time. But not here, not now. It would be of no consequence to the huge sun rolling through the tunnel burning up everything in its path. But to a demigod who could bleed and break it was big enough to hurt, and it was of grave consequence.

It was the size of a large mikku ball like the one he had made out of the Huluppu tree. He could not have seen it. He could not have heard it. It was not making sounds like the shades all around him.

His foot hit it in midstride. He launched forward in a fall. He would have scraped his face off had it not been for his hands flailing out in front. He hit the ground with a huge thud and slid twenty feet. He thought he blacked out for a second, but could not tell since he was surrounded by impenetrable blackness. He felt his shin. It was not broken, but it was bruised badly. He tried to get up and a shaft of pain split through him like lightning. He screamed out.

Then he heard the shades. Their hunger suddenly became like the sound of a hive of wasps. They were all around. He could no longer hear the tunnel. He could only hear their grinding, gnashing, gnawing teeth all around him like a bubble and he was inside it. How did that happen? Had he fallen down a hole into the recesses of Sheol?

No. They would be upon him by now. He had to gather his wits and concentrate. Focus on the sound. His head started to clear, though his shin continued to throb. He stood up, trying to tune his hearing to the agony trying to consume him. He knew he had tumbled away from the center of the tunnel and must be very close to one of the walls, deathly close. He could smell the fetid reek of their decay inches away.

He thought he sensed a clear path ahead of him. He was about to move forward, when he was checked by his Naphil sense, that preternatural awareness of danger that had protected him many a time on the steppe with lions, wolves, and bears. He exhaled and relaxed, forgetting his time constraints just long enough to achieve full aural awareness.

He could now hear two pathways, a large one to his left and this smaller one right in front of him. He realized that the shades had almost tricked him. They knew of his audible reliance, so the denizens of Sheol had cleared away from a portion of the wall to create the illusion of a clear pathway. If he had run into the empty wall, thinking it was the tunnel, they would be upon him.

He stepped back into the center of the tunnel and got his bearings. He could hear the tunnel again.

He started to run again. Or rather, to limp, as the pain shot up his leg with each step. It was going to destroy his concentration. He had to overcome this. He had no option. He may have already lost everything.

He turned the sharp pain into a new part of the rhythm. In, out, step, PAIN, in, out, step, PAIN.

It took him a few cycles, but he finally achieved the cadence he needed again with his newly altered rhythm of pain. Then, because he had lost time, he picked up the pace and took no water for the rest of the run. Every single choice, every single action now, from an irregular stride to a drink of water meant life or death.

It may already be too late.

He had been running a long time. Just when the pain began to fade into his being, he saw a tiny ray of light coming in ahead of him. He still did not know how far he had to go. It was not the kind of encouragement that is usually given to someone when they see the light at the end of a tunnel. This light meant he was too late. The sun was arriving at the setting end of the Path of the Sun where it would enter the tunnel and roll over him, vaporizing him into ash. Seeing the light meant the sun was ahead of him. It was beating him. He was going to lose.

He did not pray to Shamash, even though he was the sun god. He had already proven to Gilgamesh to be entirely incompetent and unreliable. The thought suddenly struck him that he was pursuing Noah the Distant, so why not pray to Noah's god? But who was it? Ninsun had never told him who Noah's patron deity was. He had only heard references to the Creator. Was it Nudimmud or Qingu? It could not be Nintu or Mami because they were creatresses. There were too many to even try a process of elimination. He thought he would just wing it and throw out a cry for mercy to an unknown god.

He prayed silently, because he could not afford the energy to pray out loud. *God of Noah, I do not know who you are, and whether you are even capable of doing anything wherever you are. But I ask you just this once, if you are there and if you are real, allow me safe passage I pray, that I might seek the wisdom of your child, Noah ben Lamech.*

It was a desperate plea. A last resort. Could this god even hear the thoughts of his heart? Shamash proved incapable of doing so. That inept and posturing little twerp.

Then he saw it, the circle of the tunnel exit, a rim of light that grew rapidly in size as he approached nearer and nearer.

Then it was huge and he was at the opening. He dove out into the light.

A flash of a fireball entered the tunnel, burning his loincloth and singeing some of his hair.

He did not actually see the fireball enter the Path of the Sun. It probably would have burned his eyes out of their sockets. But he marveled at how close he had come.

Was that an answer to prayer? He thought. *But how could a god who was not addressed by name know who was being addressed? I did not even know who I was addressing.*

The lack of omniscience of the pantheon had persuaded him that he had deluded himself. When a man reaches the end of his rope and there is nowhere else to turn, he will try all options, even fantasy ones. Any gods will do. What an ironic coincidence it was that he happened to pray just as he was unknowingly near the end of his own achievement. It must have been his own oneness with his surroundings that allowed him the prescience. He would have to remember that one for a good story to his posterity.

He looked around him. He had rolled right into a garden of delights. Lush foliage, and brilliance like that of gemstones glowed all around him.

Because there *were* gemstones all around him. The trees must have been trees of the gods. They were made of carnelian and lapis lazuli. Instead of thorns and brambles, there were rubies and amber.

He saw that the trees bore fruit that were good for food and they were a delight to the eyes. He took of the fruit and ate. But when he saw the glistening pool of sweet spring water, he dove in without hesitation and began to gulp its life-saving waters. He could feel his vitality return to him with each swallow.

He laughed and swam and drank.

CHAPTER 40

Gilgamesh did not know how long he rested in the precious garden. He lost track of time. Was it days or weeks? His strength revived. The pain in his bruised leg seeped away. His beard had grown back. But he knew he had to leave. As much as he could have stayed there forever, it would ultimately become a false paradise, a temporary respite of pleasure before an eternity of pain.

What awakened him from his blissful slumber was not an innate righteousness or wisdom. It was the fact that he became aware that someone or some*thing* was watching him.

It was not human, that much he knew. Humans had a distinct presence, unlike animals or gods. They were simpler and less aware of their own embeddedness within their environment. They were sloppier in their movements and their scent was more sour than animals, probably because of their consumption of milk and cheese products made from goat and bovine milk. This one smelled more like barley.

He first noticed his visitor when he had emerged from the pond one day and put on his sole loincloth pelt after drying himself in the sun. A brief wave of melancholy came over him as he thought to himself that Enkidu would love this place. The big lunk would be beside himself with Wild Born glee at the sights, smells, and sounds of a world without city. He still missed his dear friend and Right Hand. But then he smiled, thinking of Enkidu running around like a crazy hyena and finding a most stunning beauty at a drinking hole probably much like this one.

He felt a chill penetrate his nerves.

He did not see anything. It was not a noise. It was not a smell. It was an overwhelming sense of incarnation. Like something that inhabited its flesh with such superiority that it had an effect on everything near it. The sensation defied logical explanation. He had only noticed such sensation in the presence of the assembly of gods. But what god would hide itself? No, this must be a predator. Something that liked to toy with its prey before assaulting and slaughtering it.

He got up, trying to avoid giving the appearance of his knowledge of the intruder. He sought out a tree branch large enough to wield as a pike or spear and small enough to break from its roots. He had no weapon, since he had left his dirk and everything but his loincloth at the cave of the Scorpion couple. In the excitement of his discovery of the oasis, the thought of protection had escaped his mind.

How did I ignore such obvious shortsightedness? He thought. *Was I enchanted? Am I under a spell?*

Maybe this garden was not a paradise of delight after all, but a trap of illusionary peace intended to distract the victims with sensory pleasure. It would blind their instinct of self-preservation, making them ripe for the picking.

The loud, snapping crunch of the branch breaking off in his hands echoed throughout the garden.

Whatever you are, come and get it, thought Gilgamesh.

He may be half-naked half-human, and made of flesh, but he was a Gibbor, a mighty warrior and hunter and he could kill with skilled ferocity. He was the Wild Bull on the Rampage.

Come and get it.

But when he marched back to the pond in fighting posture, he realized it was gone. Fled.

The coward, he mused to himself. Of course, it was not necessarily a coward, but such was the kind of thinking that poured through the mind of a warrior when all his senses became flooded with preparation for battle. It was like he became a different person, from prey to predator, from victim to victor.

He bellowed with a mighty warrior cry, "I AM GILGAMESH, MIGHTY SCION OF URUK!"

It was the shout of an alpha male claiming his superiority and ownership of territory, an instinctual reaction.

It could very well cost him his life.

The one thing he had over whatever was hunting him was his anonymity. The thing did not know his identity or his experience triumphing over giants and monsters. It did not know that Gilgamesh was half man and half god. If this thing was sentient with human or godlike intelligence, Gilgamesh had just given away his secret. He had spilled the porridge like a boastful adolescent boy.

Son of Ishtar, he cursed to himself. Why did I not just tell it how to defeat me while I was at it? Oh, and you can find me sleeping without the protection my guardian Ninurta between the hours of midnight and dawn.

He hit himself in the head and muttered, "Moron."

He had to move on, and he had to leave *now*. He took the time to rub the tree branch on a rough rock to scrape a point into both ends of his newly acquired javelin.

While I am at it, he thought, *I might as well make two.*

So he made a second sharply pointed javelin. No more surrendering to the blindness of pleasure and the ignorance of illusory security. He would go nowhere anymore without some form of defense.

He left the garden refreshed and renewed for his quest to find Noah the Distant and Faraway.

•••••

He did not know where he was. The surroundings were not familiar. But he recognized the sound of an ocean in the near distance. He had traveled many lands and seas, but he did not remember anything like where he was at this moment. The Path of the Sun seemed to play with his sense of spatial location. Maybe he was in a magical land not on any of the maps of his map makers.

He tread a path toward the sound of the ocean. No matter where one was in the world, a coastline could help pinpoint one's location.

The sea that spread out before him was as foreign to him as the mysterious land. He wondered if this was the Southern Sea. It appeared as if the Path of the Sun may have gone under the sea and emptied him out somewhere on the coast. He could not put it all together. He thought maybe the reality was as contradictory as the mythology of it was.

His attention was caught by the appearance of a large dwelling just south of his position on the beach.

He knew his next destination.

CHAPTER 41

By the time he reached the structure, he had surmised that it was a tavern. Of all the luck in the world! Gilgamesh had not had a good barley beer in ages. He hoped that they were heavily stocked with dark bitter beer, his favorite. He was salivating just thinking about it.

The door was barred shut. The tavern was locked down and boarded as if it was under siege. Where was the tavern keeper? Was it abandoned? Had he stumbled upon the equivalent of an illusory oasis in the desert only to die from a thirst for beer?

"Ho, hurrah!" he shouted. "Is anyone home?"

Funny, he thought, *how much of Enkidu I have absorbed into my own soul.*

"I say again, is there anyone there?"

"Go away!" came a voice from above on the roof.

He looked up and saw a woman's veiled face peering down at him.

"And who might you be, my lady?" said Gilgamesh.

"I know who you are, Gilgamesh the hunter," she shouted back. "Slayer of wild bulls you are!"

Gilgamesh was taken aback. "How do you know my name?" he asked.

She ignored his question. “You made straight for my gate,” she yelled.

Then it hit him. His eyes lit up with recognition and a slight smile even pursed his lips.

“Was that you in the garden?” he asked her. “Were you the one spying on me?”

“I am Shiduri the ale-wife of this tavern, and I do not countenance troublemakers!”

“Well, Shiduri, the ale-wife, you did not answer my question,” he said with a lighthearted amusement. “Are you a peeping ale-wife, getting your jollies watching kings swim naked?” His words were more of a tease than an accusation.

“You are a king?” she asked. Now, she was the one confused.

“King Gilgamesh in all his naked glory,” he sported.

“I was not peeping on you,” she complained, trying to defend herself.

He said, “I take it you are a respectable woman, due to the veil, or is that a disguise you wear when peeping?”

Women who frequented taverns and ale houses were usually scandalous or slaves and they were forbidden the veil in such places. Only virtuous women wore them.

“I was not peeping!” she shouted back indignantly. She then showed her bow, with arrow drawn and aimed at him. “And for your information, I could have killed you where you lay. I am not afraid to defend myself and have done so on occasion.”

Gilgamesh laughed with genuine amusement. He threw his spears aside and opened his hands wide as a gesture of diplomacy. He could dodge any standard hunting arrow launched by a woman.

He said slyly, “I have no doubt of your training in the art of self-defense, considering the patrons of such establishments. But I am getting weary of this exchange. Now, either you come down here and unbar your door with traditional kindness to a stranger, or I will kick it in and take my fill. It is your choice."

He listened for her response. But he could not see her little head poking out from the rooftop anymore. She was hiding.

"Shiduri?" he shouted. "My patience is…"

His shout was interrupted by the sound of the door being unbarred from within. He sighed with eager anticipation of his long overdue imbibing of lager.

The door creaked open and Shiduri stood timidly in the crack of an opening.

"Forgive my impertinence, King Gilgamesh," she offered. "Surely you respect my caution."

"Impertinence forgiven," said Gilgamesh. "You have nothing to fear from me, Shiduri. All I really want from you is your list of brews available for consumption."

After he had an assortment of spirits dark and light sloshing in his belly, Gilgamesh began to feel a little more carefree and light-headed.

Shiduri stood across from him at the bar refilling when needed and probing his heart like the woman she was.

"My friend Enkidu once drank a keg without nary an effect on him. He even outdid the goddess Ishtar in a drinking contest of sorts. Although I suspect she was feigning a bit. He knows how to hold his drink, that Wild Born."

Gilgamesh's eyes were tearing with the memory of his loyal Right Hand and friend. But he was talking as if Enkidu was still alive. The alcohol had loosened him up and he was imbibing in the past as if it were the present.

"You two are close," she said.

"Closer than a wife," he said quickly. "I do not mean in that way," he qualified to her smile.

"He has a wife to die for. And he almost did when he challenged me at his wedding to her. Ah, Shamhat. Harlot turned queen. You remind me of her a little bit."

Shiduri's eyes went wide with surprised offense.

"The second queenly part, I mean," he corrected himself. "Although Shamhat would never peep in on me swimming."

She slapped him playfully.

He grinned and boasted, "Together we cut off the head of Humbaba the Terrible, Guardian of the Great Cedar Forest. We survived the presence of the assembly of the gods. We slaughtered the Bull of Heaven and defied the goddess Ishtar, that treacherous vile snake."

Shiduri's eyes watered with empathy for him. She said softly, "Why is there sorrow in your heart, mighty Gilgamesh? Your face is sunken, your cheeks are hollow, your mood wretched and wasted like one who has traveled a long road."

Gilgamesh stared out into oblivion. "Because my friend Enkidu, whom I love has turned to clay."

She put her hand on his with sympathy for his loss.

"I am so sorry," she said.

He continued, "I did not give him up for burial. For six days and seven nights, I wept over him. I reminisced with his corpse until a maggot fell out of his nose. It was too much for me to bear. So I went mad and roamed the wild. But not because of my mourning for him. It was mourning for me. Because I shall too soon be like him. I will also lie down, never to rise again through all eternity."

In that moment, it all came clear to Shiduri. His following of the Path of the Sun, his crisis of meaning and confrontation with death. His craving for immortality.

"You are searching for Noah ben Lamech," she said.

He glanced up at her through his bleary eyes. He half whispered as if in the presence of the holy, "Ale wife, do you know the road to Noah ben Lamech?"

She said nothing. She searched his eyes.

He grew impatient. "What is the landmark? Do you know the landmark? Give it to me, please, Shiduri. I will cross the ocean if need be. I will face death itself."

Shiduri spoke with wisdom, "You will cross the ocean if you seek Noah ben Lamech. But since days of old, none has ever done so. The crossing is perilous."

Gilgamesh was all ears now. He had reverted to the kind of listening he had engaged in before traveling the Path of the Sun through the underworld of Sheol.

"And then there are the Waters of Death," she said ominously.

He did not care about any danger. He had already faced death a hundred times.

He looked deep into her eyes and said, "I have nothing else to live for."

Without ceremony, she said simply, "Down the shore, you will find Urshanabi the boatman of Noah ben Lamech. He will take you to him across the waters."

Gilgamesh continued staring into her eyes.

She added, "But beware the Stone Ones."

Stone Ones? He thought. But the moment was too holy to ruin with a stupid question like "who are the Stone Ones?" So he chose instead to embrace the sacredness.

"Are you a goddess?" he asked. He remembered how he had sensed her presence in the garden and was sure it was not human. Was this a goddess of wisdom who graced his presence?

But she did not answer him.

Instead, she slowly moved around the bar to stand above his stooped over seated figure. She pulled his face up to meet hers.

She whispered to him, "Death is your destination, Gilgamesh. Play the day, dance the evening. Enjoy your family. That is all you can have."

She kissed him on his forehead.

He wept, broken before this goddess of kindness.

CHAPTER 42

Gilgamesh hid in the forest watching Urshanabi cutting lumber, no doubt for the building of a new boat for his shoreline pier out on the water. It was a simple pier, made for the purpose of a sole black boat tethered to its posts.

Memories of the previous evening intruded on his thoughts. The ale wife Shiduri would not tell Gilgamesh what she was, goddess or other, but one thing was certain, she was beyond human.

He hid now because of what she had said. *Beware the Stone Ones*. A warning meant danger, and all he had for his protection were his two crude spears and a woman's short sword that Shiduri had given him, along with some new clothes.

He saw four of them in the brush.

Apparently, they were called Stone Ones because they were made out of stone.

They were taller than him, maybe ten feet high, and without his weakness of flesh and bone. He had heard of these things in the past. They were creatures that had come out of the western Levant and were called *golemim* in the plural, and *golem* in the singular. They were soulless bodies made from mud or rock, much like the original Man was made from the earth. Unlike the original Man, a golem did not have the breath of God in it. Instead, it was animated through a magical incantation that was written on a parchment and stuffed into the mouth. Since they were mute and did not breathe, the parchment would not fall out. Take the parchment out and they "died," or rather, ceased to move. Since they had no soul, they could not really die. And since they had no flesh, they could not feel pain either. They were like animated yet lifeless statues made of earth. They were perfect for the slave labor they were engaged in. Gilgamesh thought it would be of great use to have an army of these things, if he could only get his hands on the incantation that created them.

The golem Stone Ones chopped trees. They were so powerful, they could fell timber in a couple of strokes with their huge axes. How could he fight these moving blocks of stone if provoked? His spears would be of no use against them. They were larger than he was, stronger than he was, could not feel pain, and did not have a breath to extinguish. These walking boulders were intimidating, even to the mighty Gilgamesh.

Urshanabi stood by the log pile, supervising his work crew. He looked like death itself, tall and gaunt but with a round little pot belly that stuck out from his skeletal figure. Gilgamesh thought he must have frequently patronized the tavern of Shiduri for her fine variety of beers.

Urshanabi impatiently ordered his Stone Ones about, like a cruel master handling disobedient dogs. He yelled at them, cursed, and paced back and forth, irritated. He even kicked one in anger, only to hop around in pain, nursing his stubbed toes.

Despite this unstable scenario, Gilgamesh decided he would avoid a fight. He would pursue his interest through the fine art of negotiation. As king, he may have had a past of being oppressive to his people, but he changed when he saw the injustice of it. And when it came to royal diplomacy with other city-states, he was quite proud of his ability to inspire compromise. The incident with King Agga was one example of avoiding a very bloody and costly battle and getting what he wanted. Gilgamesh was not merely a master warrior, he was a master negotiator.

So he set his javelins in the brush, stood up with his hands open in surrender, and approached Urshanabi with a deferring posture.

He called out, “Urshanabi! I come with the blessing of Shiduri the ale wife! My name is Gilgamesh!”

Urshanabi looked at Gilgamesh at first with surprise, then with confusion. He pointed at him, and yelled at the top of his lungs, “STONE ONES! KILL!”

It shocked Gilgamesh. No consideration, no thought, just the command to kill. Who would do such a thing to an unarmed surrendering man?

There was no time to think. The Stone Ones were upon him.

The first one swung its mighty axe. Gilgamesh ducked and it buried itself in the tree behind him. The blade sank deep into the wood from the tremendous force of the blow, and wedged tight. The Stone One struggled to pull it loose.

Just as it yanked it free, another Stone One collided with it in full force. The two of them crashed to the ground in a pile of rubble. The thought flashed through Gilgamesh’s mind that he was watching a moving earthquake. It was like monumental boulders crashing into each other.

This surprised Gilgamesh even more. The charging Stone One did not have quick enough faculties to slow down or steer clear of its comrade in time. Evidently, its lack of soul meant a corresponding lack of brains.

These things were stupid.

And once they fell apart, they were useless. It was like chopping off the head of a shade.

He got an idea. He found the axe in the rubble and lifted it. The other two Stone Ones approached him with their axes and backed him up against a tree.

Gilgamesh was experienced with a battle axe, very experienced.

The Stone Ones were not as stupid as Gilgamesh had thought. They began to attack with synchronized swings of their axes. They worked in tandem. The first one took the top of the tree off right where Gilgamesh's head had been. He ducked just in time. The second one swung low to lop off his legs. Instinctively Gilgamesh leapt off the ground and did a backward somersault over the newly made tree stump behind him.

They kept coming like unstoppable automatons. They did not tire like Gilgamesh did. He was now breathing hard, dodging and jumping backward. He did not know how much longer he could keep this up. They were wearing him down.

He had to make his move.

He tried to break the rhythm of the attackers by blocking with his axe instead of dodging.

Unfortunately, their strength was incredible. He could feel their hits ring through his whole body to its core. He almost lost his grip on his own axe. This strategy would not work for long.

Urshanabi, the little creep, moved near enough to keep shouting invectives at Gilgamesh as he fought, though he was careful to stay out of reach. Gilgamesh did not know what would wear him down first, the axes of the rock warriors or the annoying tongue of their shrill commander.

"Die, you piece of Mesopotamian filth! Kill him! Kill him NOW, you stupid blockheads! Why have you come for me, mercenary?!"

Gilgamesh yelled back, "I did not come to kill you!" He dodged another swing, and clanged his short sword against the other.

"Well, why are you here?!" shouted Urshanabi.

"Call them off and we can talk!" Gilgamesh shouted back. Clang! Another near miss. He was tiring. He might not take these warriors out so easily after all.

"Oh, sure," yelled Urshanabi, "that is just what you want, so you can kill me and drag me back for the bounty!"

So that was the reason for his hostile reaction. He must have been hiding out from justice. After all he had been through, Gilgamesh was about to be killed at the screeching commands of a two-bit outlaw.

Another dodge. This time, he felt the blade nick his chest and draw blood.

The swing threw the Stone One off balance just a little. Gilgamesh saw his last chance to strike before succumbing to fatigue and their blades.

He stepped inside the Stone One's swing and brought his blade down on the shaft of the other axe. Connection! The shaft cut in half.

Gilgamesh spun around in a full circle to maximize his impact and brought the blade right at the neck of the Stone One. If he hit it anywhere else, it would have shattered the blade with a mere chip off the old rock. But the neck was the thinnest part of the earthen warrior.

The blade connected with a resounding CRUNCH and severed the head from the body. It also mangled Gilgamesh's blade into a useless crumpled piece of metal. The impact was so hard, he fell to the ground.

The now lifeless body of the Stone One broke apart, falling down upon him like an avalanche. He rolled.

The Stone One crashed to the ground, shaking the earth and missed crushing Gilgamesh by inches.

Gilgamesh looked up. The last Stone One stood over him with blade raised high, swinging down to cleave him in two.

Instinctively, Gilgamesh rolled again. The blade buried itself deep into the ground by his head.

The Stone One had not anticipated the gnarly tree roots in the earth. His blade became instantly entangled in the pliable maze.

Gilgamesh jumped to his feet while the Stone One struggled to wrench his axe free. He swung himself onto the back of the Stone One. It tried to reach behind to grab him, but its arms were too bulky, rock not being very flexible.

The creature spun in a circle, trying to grab him. Gilgamesh saw they were headed straight for a tree. He was going to be crushed like a bug.

He hung on with one arm and maneuvered the remains of his crumpled blade with his other. It would be utter foolishness to think he could cut the throat of a golem made of stone, especially with the damaged sword.

He dug the blade into its mouth and leveraged the lips open. The Stone One spun further, whirling violently. He hit a tree. Gilgamesh lost his breath. He felt a couple of his ribs crack under the impact. He screamed out in pain and almost lost his grip.

He held on. The Stone One reached up and grabbed Gilgamesh's sword wrist. It meant to rip his limb off his body. Gilgamesh reached around its neck with his other hand and felt inside the mouth of the monster.

His probing fingers touched the parchment, grabbed it and yanked it out of the mouth.

The Stone One froze instantly, its hand still grasping Gilgamesh.

It worked. Pulling the written spell out of its mouth had sucked the life out of the creature. It was living stone no more. Now, it was just stone.

Gilgamesh wrested his hand from its grip and jumped down to the ground. He grabbed his bruised back in pain. He gasped in a few breaths. Then, with a huge growl, he heaved and pushed the Stone

One onto the ground on its face with a thud, breaking it in several pieces.

Gilgamesh looked at the spell. It was high level sorcery that he could not fully understand. He folded it and tucked it away in his belt pouch for future use.

He turned and glared at Urshanabi. The man stood staring back at him in fear, no longer hurling invectives as fast as his mouth could move.

Gilgamesh trounced over to Urshanabi, and complained, "What *were* you thinking? I told you I was coming in peace! I said I had the blessing of Shiduri! Do you not listen to people?"

Urshanabi looked downcast at the forest floor. "I am sorry," he said. "I am a tad hot-headed and impulsive."

"A tad?" exclaimed Gilgamesh. "I almost got crushed to death by your blockheads! You call that a 'tad'?"

"I was afraid!" blurted Urshanabi. "You are a Gibborim! Should I not fear for my life?"

Gilgamesh stopped. He had a point.

"How can I make it up to you?" asked Urshanabi.

"Oh, you will make it up to me," said Gilgamesh. "You will take me to Dilmun to the Land of the Living where Noah ben Lamech lives."

Urshanabi sighed. "That, I am afraid, is no longer possible."

"What do you mean no longer possible?" said Gilgamesh. "You are Noah's boatman and your boat is docked on the shoreline."

"Yes, you speak the truth," said Urshanabi, "but you just destroyed the only oarsman capable of getting us to Noah: the Stone Ones."

Gilgamesh sighed. The day was *not* going well.

Urshanabi explained, "You see, in order to travel to Dilmun, we must cross the cosmic sea for three days. But the waters that surround the island are called the Waters of Death."

"I have heard of them," said Gilgamesh.

"For any human, touching the Waters of Death is instant death. A mere splash of the water while rowing will kill you. So, I always took one Stone One to be my oarsman through the Waters of Death. They were not humans, so they could not die."

"Well, that is just great, boatman," said Gilgamesh. "You had better put that impulsive nature to good use and give me one good reason why I should not crush your skull for your incompetence that just ruined my search for immortality."

"Wait," interrupted Urshanabi. "You are seeking immortality?"

"Yes," said Gilgamesh.

"Is that why your face looks sunken, your jowls hollow, and your mood wretched?" said Urshanabi.

Sunken face? thought Gilgamesh. You should talk, skeleton man.

"My friend, Enkidu, whom I loved deeply," started Gilgamesh. He stopped himself. "I am not going to rehearse for you my reasons. Noah ben Lamech is my distant relative and I seek an audience with him. Now, how are you going to help me get there?"

Urshanabi thought for a moment, then brightened up.

"I have an idea," he said. "Go into the forest and cut me three hundred punting poles, each, one hundred feet long."

Punting poles were used to propel a boat along in shallow waters.

"Since no human hand can touch the Waters of Death, then you can use each pole once to propel the boat forward, and leave it in the water. That way, you need never touch the deathly seas."

It was genius. It would get Gilgamesh to his destination.

And it was a lot of hard work.

"Three hundred?" complained Gilgamesh. He had just exerted every ounce of energy he had taking down four rocky brutes and now he would have to cut down, trim, and furnish three hundred poles with two broken ribs and no strength left?

Urshanabi gestured to his own scrawny figure and said, "I would help you, but I think you would be waiting a long time before I would be of any benefit."

Gilgamesh chortled in agreement. He picked up an axe and was about to embark on his new exhausting task, when Urshanabi dropped a big egg on him.

"But you had better hurry. It takes three days for us to get there and the new moon arrives in four days."

"So, what is the problem?" asked Gilgamesh.

"It is spring tide season. At the full moon, the tide will be so low, we could get stranded in the Waters of Death. We would be unable to get out and wade the waters without perishing."

"But do not tides change from low to high every twelve hours?" said Gilgamesh.

"Not in Dilmun," said Urshanabi. "In Dilmun, it's every fifteen days."

Gilgamesh gave him a skeptical look.

Urshanabi turned defensive. "It is a magical island. Do not blame me."

Gilgamesh sighed and said, "Well, it does not surprise me. I have had one pain in the rear end after another. And I am sure they are not going to stop after this."

CHAPTER 43

It took Gilgamesh a little longer than he had hoped to cut down his punting poles and trim and furnish them for the trip to Dilmun and the Waters of Death. He shackled Urshanabi to a tree to insure that he did not try to run away. Unfortunately, Gilgamesh ended up wishing that he *had* run away, because his relentlessly croaking critical voice was insufferable. He critiqued almost every move Gilgamesh made. First, his chop was sloppy. Then, his poles were not trimmed straight enough. After that, he was not applying a thick enough varnish of bitumen on them. Finally, Gilgamesh decided to muffle Urshanabi's mouth so he could finish his task in peace. He stuffed some leaves between his lips and wrapped a piece of cloth around his mouth to keep them from coming out.

When he finished piling the poles on board the craft, he released Urshanabi and ungagged him.

Before Urshanabi could begin a new string of complaints, Gilgamesh held up his finger to his face to warn him and said, "Urshanabi, I am done with your belligerent faultfinding. You will not speak unless spoken to or I will cut out your tongue. Am I understood?"

Urshanabi nodded his head yes. He trembled because he knew Gilgamesh would do it.

"Now, how many days did you say we have before low tide?" asked Gilgamesh.

Urshanabi was afraid to answer.

"It is all right. I spoke to you," said Gilgamesh, trying to calm his fears.

Urshanabi kept it concise, as he thought of losing his most valued appendage to the blade. "Three."

Gilgamesh had taken a full day to accomplish his task.

Gilgamesh smiled. "Well done, boatman. A single word answer, and *that* without complaint or provocation. I am proud of you."

Gilgamesh slapped him on the back. His larger than life personality was contagious. Urshanabi gave a half smile and caught the breath that was almost knocked out of him.

"I packed the beer and food as well," said Gilgamesh.

Urshanabi raised his hand like a humble schoolboy.

"What?" smiled Gilgamesh.

Urshanabi said darkly, "It is a five day row."

"I thought you said three days," said Gilgamesh.

"For a Stone One who does not have to rest," said Urshanabi. "You did not stipulate."

They were already a day behind when Gilgamesh began his task and it had taken him the better part of a full day to cut, trim, and finish all three hundred punting poles now in the boat.

He thought to himself for a moment. He could not stand fifteen days with this unbearable bellyaching malcontent, waiting for the next high tide. Keeping him gagged for those fifteen days would only breed bitterness and revenge that would backfire on Gilgamesh. He would simply have to push himself to the limit, double his efforts and row a five day trip in three days, while suffering complete exhaustion from the previous two days of fighting Stone Ones, breaking ribs, and cutting three hundred punting poles.

"Well, it should not be too difficult," said Gilgamesh. "We had better get cracking."

They pushed off to sea in the fifty-foot long "square boat." It was crescent-shaped with high prows both forward and aft. It contained a large comfortable canopied throne lounge in the center, obviously for the self-important Urshanabi to be rowed around by his stone crew. The boat was made of fresh water reeds, tightly bound and covered in and out with bitumen pitch for sealant against the water. The sturdy sea-worthy vessel had been reinforced in order to support the extra weight of a single Stone One as oarsman on each trip. The punting poles lay on both sides, with their extended lengths sticking out the back of the boat into the air.

Urshanabi got in and sat on his throne.

Gilgamesh pulled off the canopy and rolled it up.

He quipped, "So sorry to inconvenience you with the perilous rays of the sun, but we are going against the wind so this canopy will slow us down."

Urshanabi just gulped and nodded. He was just grateful that Gilgamesh did not trust his scrawny muscles to any of the rowing.

"By the way," said Gilgamesh, "how will we know when we have arrived at the Waters of Death?"

Urshanabi answered, "When the island is in sight, and the waters glow."

Gilgamesh sat and held the oars. He took a deep breath and sighed.

He began to row.

And row.

And row.

He reached a kind of meditative state that helped him to dissociate from his body of pain into flights of fancy, not unlike what he had done in the Path of the Sun with his bruised shin. He rowed for almost eighteen hours straight before he took the first of only two half-hour naps.

Urshanabi woke him and he began to row again without pause. He had become like a Stone One, a soulless automaton of work. The thought passed through his mind that this was not much different from what every life amounted to anyway. Live, work, eat, and die. The dreams and hopes and pursuits of human passion amounted to a temporary hallucinogenic state of imagination before it ended — for everlasting unto everlasting.

They arrived at the Waters of Death with about six hours left before low tide would strand them to their deaths. They could see the island of Dilmun, he reckoned the distance was still far. All around them the water glowed an iridescent greenish-blue. It was the normal color of water, but with a shining that almost dared one to dive in. The shining waters guarding the Land of the Living reminded Gilgamesh of the stories he had heard in his youth of the shining Cherub guarding the Garden of Eden.

Gilgamesh stopped rowing before they hit the glowing waters. He put the oars away. The act of rowing caused too much splashing for them to be able to make it to the island alive. He pulled out his first punting pole and said the Urshanabi, "Is there anything else I need to know before I place this pole in the Waters of Death and jeopardize my life?"

"Just do not let the water touch your hands," said Urshanabi. "Leave the pole behind you without raising it out of the water, and use the next one."

"Easily spoken, not easily done," said Gilgamesh. "You better pray to Enki, because your life depends on my life."

"I do not mean to be critical, but we are still behind time," said Urshanabi. "We have got about three hours left, but we need about six."

"Now see, Urshanabi," said Gilgamesh. "That is the difference between you and me. You avoid the impossible because it cannot be done. I seek the impossible because it cannot be done."

"I guess that explains your search for eternal life," said Urshanabi.

Gilgamesh smiled and put his first pole in the water with the words, "It does indeed."

Urshanabi had been wrong. Gilgamesh once again caught them up on time with double speed. But it was not time that they would run out of, *it was punting poles*. Gilgamesh had come within a mile of the island of Dilmun and he had but two poles left in the boat. He stopped. These would glide them another few hundred feet or so. Then they would be stranded in the Waters of Death with no means of propulsion. They would not make it after all. Urshanabi had miscalculated.

Gilgamesh glared at him.

"You think I want to die out here with you?" said Urshanabi. "I thought three hundred poles were more than enough to make it through the waters. Even these changing winds cannot push us far enough in time. Can we please put the canopy back up, so at least I can die without a sunburn?"

Gilgamesh lightened up. "You are right. The winds have changed. They are now at our back. Now, see, Urshanabi, within your own words lay the solution to our dilemma, but you could not see it because you refuse to face the impossible."

It confused Urshanabi. He watched as Gilgamesh rummaged through the bottom of the boat and pulled out the large canvas canopy that he had taken down at the start of their journey.

Gilgamesh took Urshanabi's dagger from him and cut some holes in the ends of the canopy. Then he cut some lengths of rope and began to tie the canopy to one end of a punting pole. When he finished, he did the same thing with the other side of the canopy on the other punting pole. And he kept the dagger.

Gilgamesh smiled and said, "We cannot punt our way in, but we can sail."

Urshanabi filled with hope.

Gilgamesh said, "Urshanabi, grab the tiller. There is not much time."

Urshanabi grabbed it and began to steer while Gilgamesh held up the makeshift sail. It caught the wind and they began to glide over the Waters of Death.

Gilgamesh had to lean into the wind with all that was left in him. His arms stretched out wide, holding the poles. The wind created a driving air pocket that sailed them toward Dilmun.

CHAPTER 44

They arrived at the small port harbor of Dilmun just as the waters were beginning to draw back into the sea.

It struck Gilgamesh how oddly crammed the port was with boats and ships from all over the world. From the Indus Valley to Egypt, their styles spoke of the universal appeal this paradise had over the minds of mankind. But there were no people. Anywhere. It was like a ghost harbor.

The beach also was crammed with older decaying ships, all the way up into the tree line.

"What is this?" asked Gilgamesh. "Where are all the people? This is Dilmun?"

"Yes," said Urshanabi as he tied up the boat to the dock. He walked past Gilgamesh to lead him to his destination.

Gilgamesh complained, "Well, it looks more like the Land of Ghosts than the Land of the Living."

Urshanabi said, "Now you are beginning to sound like me."

"You never told me about this," said Gilgamesh.

Urshanabi gave a wry jab, repeating Gilgamesh's own words to him, "I am to speak only when spoken to."

Gilgamesh rolled his eyes, a victim of his own temper.

"Okay, Urshanabi," snapped Gilgamesh, "I grant you the royal privilege to explain to me what in Sheol is going on here?"

As he finished his words, they arrived at the peak of a hill overlooking a vast expanse of barren land. It was a graveyard, a gargantuan necropolis. It was larger than anything Gilgamesh had ever seen before. Miles and miles of "tumuli" burial mounds and other tombs, completely filling the land as far as the eye could see. There were hundreds of thousands of them.

"Welcome to the abode of the blessed, the Land of the Living," said Urshanabi.

"You mean the Land of the Dead," said Gilgamesh.

The only sign of life was a handful of tomb builders, laying stone for underground burial vaults. Several small lines of priests at various locations carried sarcophagi in funerary processions. Smoke and incense trailed their handheld censors. Small troupes of minstrels played dirges.

"On Dilmun, death is worshipped as a religion," explained Urshanabi. "Everyone comes to the island hoping to find eternal life."

Gilgamesh felt a shudder go through him. Was he just another fool in pursuit of the unattainable?

Urshanabi continued, "They believe that by entering Sheol through this paradise, they will have a better chance at blessing in the underworld. The island is an antechamber to the spirit world. The island's inhabitants perform the ceremonies for a fee, paid with the possessions of the client. Thus, Dilmun has become a trade center for the world."

"Where are the living?" asked Gilgamesh.

Urshanabi said, "Over the hills on the south of the island. But you are not here to meet them."

Gilgamesh nodded. "Take me to Noah."

They traveled along the shoreline of the island until they reached a small, beautiful jungle full of life. It was a real oasis on this false oasis. It was a pocket of life on an island of death. Gilgamesh could hear insects, birds, and monkeys screaming out their instinctual tones.

When they walked inside the jungle boundaries, they were besieged by a world of foliage and plant life Gilgamesh had never seen before. Huge palm trees spread across the ceiling of foliage, creating a canopy over a moist interior. Animals ran around without concern for their human presence. They came to a huge waterfall of crystalline water, spilling over into a bubbling river alive with visible schools of fish.

Now, this is more like it, he thought. *This is the kind of beauty that one could conceive of as Paradise.*

Urshanabi found a small clearing with a modest couple of huts and a small garden beside them.

Gilgamesh glanced at Urshanabi, who nodded to him.

When he looked back, he saw a man and woman step out of the hut to greet them. A very old man and woman. They were a bit bent over. The man had a cane to steady himself. The woman held onto him, but he could not tell whether it was to help the man or keep herself steady.

Gilgamesh's eyes teared up. He had traveled so long and so far, and had suffered so many hardships, all in pursuit of the impossible. It all came flooding back into him like the waterfall behind them.

The old man and old woman recognized Urshanabi, so they were not afraid. But they did not know who this nine foot tall giant was, stumbling toward them, bawling his eyes out.

They stepped back in caution. Urshanabi gestured to them not to fear.

Gilgamesh dropped to his knees yards from them. He could not make it the rest of the way. It was as if his strength had failed him. The old man and woman closed the distance with their hobbling pace.

They arrived at the kneeling weeping giant.

Gilgamesh muttered, softly, painfully, “Grandfather.”

Noah ben Lamech, well over nine hundred years old by now, reached down and lifted the head of the blubbering giant.

Emzara clutched Noah’s arm and started to weep sympathetically.

Noah said simply, “Son of Cush.”

Then he sniffed and wrinkled his nose, and added, “You stink to high heaven.”

Gilgamesh’s crying turned to laughter. Through all the exertion of his mighty strength in battle and in toil, since his evening with Shiduri the ale wife over a week ago, he had failed to wash his body or his clothing. It was true. He stank to high heaven.

Emzara added, “Let us get you washed up and in some clean clothes.”

CHAPTER 45

Gilgamesh sat in the humble little hut of Noah and Emzara. He had cleansed his body in the waterfall and washed his matted hair as clean as could be. Emzara threw his old clothes out to sea, and they draped a royal robe over him as a sign of honor and dignity as their guest. It was a bit small for his giant nine foot frame, but it did the job.

Urshanabi sat next to Noah. Emzara prepared a drink from water and tea leaves that she presented first to Noah with an affectionate whisper, "My Utnapishtim."

Noah reached up and kissed Emzara, whispering back, "My Naamah."

So this is where the names came from, thought Gilgamesh. *Someone overheard their nicknames.*

She poured Gilgamesh some tea. Noah asked him, "Your face looks sunken and hollow, like one who has traveled a long distance with great sorrow in your heart."

"I have been told that a lot," said Gilgamesh. "Is it that obvious?"

Noah and Emzara nodded timidly.

"I have traveled too far and too wide," said Gilgamesh. "And I am weighed down with despair."

He proceeded to tell Noah and Emzara of his life. How he had been raised by Ninsun the goddess queen of Uruk, and how he was told he was a child of Lugalbanda and Ninsun. How he had become an oppressive king whose pride was humbled by a Wild Man from the steppe. About Enkidu, who taught him how to suck the marrow out of life and became his only true friend. He spoke of how together, they killed the giant Humbaba, and the great Bull of Heaven, how they stood in the assembly of the gods and defied Ishtar the goddess of war, and how Enkidu died and shattered Gilgamesh's world.

"Death has haunted me my entire life," said Gilgamesh. "No matter what I do, no matter what I achieve, it all comes to nothing in the end because I too will turn to clay and will be gone forever. But when I learned that I was a son of Cush from the line of Noah ben Lamech, I understood why I felt so different, and why I felt I had a destiny to fulfill. I hoped and prayed to the gods to find you because you were the only man to be given immortality from the gods."

Noah and Emzara exchanged looks of surprise. Immortality? The truth was much more mundane than such legends.

Gilgamesh continued, "I have traveled through Sheol and back to find you. I have scourged myself with sleeplessness, I have filled my sinews with endless pain, to find you, with the hope that I too could have the eternal life that you alone attained. I even considered that I may have to fight you to gain the gift of the gods."

Noah murmured with sadness, "My son." It seemed to him a sad lie of wasted pursuit.

Suddenly, Gilgamesh's countenance turned dispirited. "But now I see you and my hand is stayed. For you are old and weary. Your form is no different than mine. You are just like me. Your flesh appears weak and near death."

Gilgamesh looked to Noah expectantly. Noah gave a glance to Emzara that indicated a deep sorrow and resignation.

He turned to Gilgamesh and said, "Gilgamesh, everything you know to be true is a lie."

It took a moment for the extremity of the statement to sink into Gilgamesh.

Everything?

Noah said, "I will tell you the truth, but I warn you, you will not like it. It will require a challenge in your soul that all men must face, but few are willing to accept. And your response will determine your eternal destiny."

Emzara gave a slight smile as she watched her husband speak. He had always been one for bluntness in his talk to the point of insensitivity. She used to struggle with it. She wished he would ease a person into the truth rather than blast him with it. Uriel the archangel used to chide him for it with smooth, subtle sarcasm. That was so long ago. Over the years, she had learned to love Noah and to live with his ways, as he had learned to love her and live with her ways. She had also learned that sometimes, barefaced brazen truth was exactly what was needed.

Noah continued, "Emzara and I do not have immortality. That is a false myth. We came to Dilmun to escape our shame of the moral descent of our family. As you now know, this is not the Land of the Living, it is the Land of the Dead. The truth is we will die. This flesh and blood will not inherit the kingdom of God. I am sorry to say, my son, that you have exhausted yourself with pointless toil. Filling your sinews with endless pain and sleepless nights has merely hastened your demise, brought you nearer to the very death you seek to overcome. Man is one whose life is snapped off like a reed in the marsh. He is like a mayfly, born in a numberless swarm only to die mere moments later. It is only the swarm that lives on. No matter who you are, great king, or lowly peasant, beautiful young woman or mighty Gibborim warrior, death will hack you down. It is the way of all mankind."

Gilgamesh listened silently. He could feel the rage slowly rising in him with every word Noah spoke. It was all for nothing. He had sought the one last chance to attain immortality and it had ended in death. He had come to the end of his journey, to the end of his rope. There was nowhere else to go. But he still refused to accept it.

One word came out of Gilgamesh's mouth. One word that held back the volcano of anger bubbling inside him, "Why?"

"Because all humanity has turned its back on the Creator. For although they knew God, they did not honor him as God or give thanks to him. And they worshipped and served the creation rather than the Creator who is blessed forever. When our forebear Adam disobeyed the Creator, he and his beloved were exiled from the Garden and from the Tree of Life, that would have been the source of continued renewal to live forever. As Adam's descendants, we are exiled from our Creator. The immortality you seek, lies in him and in his Chosen Seed."

"I have never heard of such a story," complained Gilgamesh.

"I did not expect that you would," said Noah. "Cush was a rebellious son who sought to defy his own heritage, deny his Creator, and create his own cosmos of power, and the narrative to go with it."

Gilgamesh protested, "I have seen the assembly of the gods in Mount Hermon. Anu the father sky god, Enlil the lord of the air, and all the others. Ninurta, my protector and storm god awaits me in Uruk. Who is this Creator you speak of?"

Noah answered, "His name is Yahweh Elohim and he is the one who created you and me, and all things."

Noah had used the covenant name of the Creator, Yahweh Elohim, that distinguished him from all other claims of deity. He was the true and Living God among the gods.

Noah continued, "The gods you speak of are *Bene ha Elohim*, Sons of God from the divine council of Elohim's heavenly host. They are Watchers of mankind. But they fell to earth in rebellion and set up their 'assembly of gods' as a mockery of God's own divine council. They have sought to draw worship away from the Living God unto themselves and to corrupt the bloodline of the coming king."

"Coming king?" interrupted Gilgamesh. This struck him where it most hurt. Gilgamesh had sought to be the greatest king. "Who is this king?"

"I do not know," said Noah. "But the plan of the Watchers was to mate with human beings and corrupt that bloodline. Their progeny was the Nephilim, demigod giants who they sought to engage for their nefarious purposes. The Nephilim and their allies are the Seed of the Serpent at war with the Seed of Eve our mother."

Gilgamesh was stunned by the implications. "My mother told me I was a Naphil as well. But you are saying that I am a Seed of the Serpent? Am I so cursed? Am I beyond redemption?"

Noah said, "I do not know that either, Gilgamesh. There is much about Elohim that I do not understand and have even wrestled with over my long life. He seems to do things that we humans do not understand nor approve of. But he is the Creator, and not we ourselves."

Gilgamesh erupted, "What kind of a Creator creates a vessel purely for destruction, and others for nobility at his whim?"

Noah did not answer that. Instead, he said, "The Nephilim had spread upon the land, and the inhabitants had turned to worshipping the Watchers instead of Yahweh. But the Watchers also corrupted creation through their diabolical cross-breeding. They sought to unify what God had made separate. To eliminate all distinction, so that creation itself might become a part of God. Yahweh saw that the wickedness of man was great on the earth and that his heart was fixated on evil. All flesh was corrupted and the land was filled with violence. It grieved Yahweh's heart, and he regretted that he made man. So he sent the Deluge to blot out all life from the face of the land. But only after telling me to build a large boat to save the animals and my family. Elohim was returning the land to chaos in order to recreate the cosmos and begin anew."

Gilgamesh interrupted again with irritation, "But he did not kill all the Nephilim. You said yourself that I was born through the very line of Cush. Why would he allow this so-called 'Seed of the Serpent' to survive? What kind of puppet game is he playing with this world?"

"I am sorry," said Noah. "I just do not know. Perhaps you can be the first Naphil who repents, who turns back to Yahweh and humbles himself before the Most High God."

Gilgamesh would not accept such tyrannical pompous despotism. "Most High God? I am the Scion of Uruk, Wild Bull on the Rampage. I have defied kings and gods. I have made a name for myself through my own exploits. Who is this suzerain who seeks to sublimate me as vassal, while damning me without my approval? Where is he hiding?"

"Alas, I do not know that either," said Noah. "Yahweh has been silent in this post-diluvian world. I do not know his plans."

Gilgamesh said, "For being the Chosen Seedline, you do not know very much. Do you have *any* answers?"

"I have faith," replied Noah. "Faith in my Creator that he will do as he promised and one day put the world to rights. How he will do so he has not revealed, nor is he obligated to."

Gilgamesh said, "Well, I do not approve of this invisible Yahweh and his unyielding demands upon me. Repent? I say explain himself if he requires such subservience. What is more, if he creates me as a Seed of the Serpent, then what right has he to claim judge over my actions? Am I not a servant of his will?"

Emzara tightened with fear. She could see Gilgamesh was increasing his anger with each accusation. Urshanabi knew just how powerful and dangerous Gilgamesh was. He started to tremble.

Noah noticed this and changed the subject. "Gilgamesh, there is a word we have for such incorrigibility and defiance."

"Do you?" said Gilgamesh.

Noah told him the special word in its original tongue and said, "It means 'to rebel.' Do not be so."

Gilgamesh said nothing. He tucked that special word in the back of his mind because he was drawn to it. Drawn like a crocodile to flesh or a sea dragon to chaos. A strange word that he had never heard before. But he knew that he would use it one day as a badge of honor, in the face of a tyrannical god who had the gall to create a world founded upon suffering, and who then demanded allegiance.

Emzara tried to keep her eyes from tearing up. She sniffled. She had the uncanny ability to see the end of a person based on his behavior. She could see Gilgamesh's end and it was terrifying.

Urshanabi dreaded the fact that he would have to bring this seething ingrate back to the mainland on his boat. He wondered if he would be drowned at the end of it all, out of spite. Maybe that would not be so bad after all, since Urshanabi had been released from employment as Noah's boatman. He had disobeyed his orders not to bring anyone to Noah without prior approval.

Noah challenged Gilgamesh. "What would you do with immortality should you gain it?"

Gilgamesh thought for a moment. Then he pronounced, "I would rule the world. The cosmos would be mine."

"And what would you do to those who defied you?" asked Noah.

Gilgamesh looked at him with contempt. He knew exactly where he was going with that line of questioning. He was trying to force Gilgamesh to admit he would do the same exact thing he condemned Yahweh for doing. He was not going to fall into that lion trap. He changed the subject.

"I did not come here without a plan of my own," said Gilgamesh. "Yahweh is not the only potentate who does not reveal his secret machinations."

Gilgamesh was referring to the plan that Enlil and the assembly of gods had commissioned him to participate in. He was not about to unveil that plan and suffer the possible leak of intelligence to his enemies who would seek to stop him and cut him down. Now that he had discovered that the immortality he sought was out of his reach with Noah and his god, then the only other option he had left was to follow through with the plan of the gods.

"What plan are you talking about?" asked Noah.

Gilgamesh answered, "Let us just say that there is more than one way to achieve immortality. More than one god who can bestow eternal life."

"The gods you worship are imposters," said Noah. "Whatever they offer you is in their own interest."

Gilgamesh replied, "And your god's offering is not?"

"Do you really think they will not discard you when they are through using you?" said Noah. "They will chew you up and spit you out."

"The gods are not the only ones who have contingency plans," said Gilgamesh.

"Then let me offer you this," said Noah. "If you consider yourself worthy of immortality, then show your power over the simplest of weaknesses: sleep."

Gilgamesh looked at him with surprise.

Noah added, "If you can stay awake for seven days, then I will tell you where you may find a magic plant that rests in the ocean of the Abyss, one that will return your youth to you. It is called 'plant of heartbeat,' or as I like to call it, 'Old-Man-Has-Become-Young-Again.'"

Emzara jerked a look at him and blurted out, “Noah!”

Urshanabi rolled his eyes. This contest was going to continue on after all.

Noah ignored Emzara. He added, “You will not achieve immortality, but it will return you to your prime of youth and allow another lifetime to accomplish all the glory you seek.”

Finally, Emzara pulled on his arm to get his attention. She could no longer stay silent.

“What are you doing, Noah?” she exclaimed. “That secret was ours for safekeeping. You know the devastation that could cause.”

Gilgamesh interrupted them, “I am sorry you have such little faith in me, great-grandmother.” He turned back to Noah. “ I accept the challenge.”

Noah was no fool. He had appealed to Gilgamesh’s biggest weakness, his vanity, and Gilgamesh had fallen for the bait. A man puffed up with pride, be he human or demigod, was a man about to fall. Noah knew, all too well, something about pride. And now he maneuvered that self-knowledge into an advantage.

CHAPTER 46

Gilgamesh was shown to a small hut for rest. He just meant to sit down and prepare for his next exploit of staying awake for seven straight days and nights. He sat down on his bed and quickly realized that he had better not lay down or he would pass out instantly. He had just pushed his body to the extreme limit of endurance that no man had ever done before. This would not be so easy a task.

His eyelids immediately grew heavy. Even though he was not allowed to sleep, he thought he would just shut his eyes for a moment to rest them. But when he did, all the physical exertion of the previous couple of weeks came crashing down on him. He immediately fell backwards on the bed. It jarred him awake and he jerked up again.

He stood back up. The bed called him in a phantom voice to sleep. He felt like he had a second wind, refreshed and ready for this next trial, after all.

Then he noticed something beside his bed that had not been there only moments before, when he sat down. Seven loaves of bread at various stages of decay sat on separate platters. He looked more closely and noticed that they were each progressively more decayed than the previous, as if one had been baked each day for seven days and laid out in order to rot.

He felt a presence at the door. He turned to see Noah with Emzara and Urshanabi, standing over him as if in judgment.

"How did these loaves get here?" asked Gilgamesh. "I blinked my eyes for one moment and when I opened them again, they were here as if by magic. Are you a sorcerer of some kind?"

"I baked those loaves, one each day for seven days," said Emzara.

Gilgamesh did not follow. "When?" he asked.

"For the seven days you have been sleeping," said Noah.

"But I just closed my eyes for a moment," said Gilgamesh.

"You slept for seven days," countered Noah, with an authority in his voice that Gilgamesh knew declared he was not lying.

He added, "Instead of staying awake for seven days, you slept for seven days. Your body caught up on all the sleep you deprived yourself of — almighty god."

That last sting sarcastically mocked Gilgamesh's vanity.

Gilgamesh boiled, "You *are* sorcerers. You put a spell on me."

Emzara said, "I am a baker. I baked seven loaves of bread as you slept, Gilgamesh."

He knew they were right. His head spun, but not with confusion. Seven days of sleep had brought back his wits and his sharp ability to strategize on the fly.

Gilgamesh stood up to his nine foot height. He strode up to Noah, grabbed his robe, and lifted him up to his own face. Noah's feet dangled in the air.

Urshanabi stepped back in fear.

Emzara grabbed his arm. "Please, Gilgamesh, no," she pleaded.

Gilgamesh stared into Noah's eyes with animosity. "You *will* tell me where the plant is," he ordered.

Noah just stared back. Gilgamesh looked down at Emzara, still pulling at his arm.

He dropped Noah and grabbed Emzara's head in his hands. She froze, a mouse caught in the paws of a giant feline.

Gilgamesh looked over at Noah and reiterated his command with a whisper that was more venomous, more terrifying than the shout of a war goddess. "You will tell me where the plant is, or I will crush your beloved's life out of her."

It did not require any thought. Noah immediately barked out, "I will tell you!"

Gilgamesh did not release her. He waited expectantly for more.

Noah said to Urshanabi, "Take him past the Waters of Death, to the mainland, by way of the black coral beds. One hundred feet out from the beds, near the ledge of the Abyss."

Urshanabi nodded with recognition.

Noah then said to Gilgamesh, "It is surrounded by deadly coral that will kill anything that touches it. It will be like withdrawing a flower from a pit of snakes."

Gilgamesh released Emzara. Noah ran to her, clutching her for all his life.

Gilgamesh said with disappointment, "There certainly are a lot of deadly elements in these waters."

Noah did not tell him of the far greater terror just over the crevice of the Abyss. He thought it fair to let him find that one out for himself.

Gilgamesh sighed and turned to leave. He would not waste any more time. "Come, Urshanabi." He turned back with one last look at Noah. "And if it is not there, I will return for blood."

Gilgamesh and Urshanabi left them. Noah and Emzara embraced each other.

"What will become of this monster?" asked Emzara. "With such rejuvenation, he could destroy everything. What is this secret plan? Is it another war of gods and men?"

Noah watched them walking away. A dark pall of realization swept over him. He said, “It is time for us to return to the land between the two rivers. Elohim’s work with us is not yet done.”

She looked up at him. She knew what he meant and dreaded it. She also knew that their lives were in the hands of Elohim, had *always* been in the hands of Elohim. From the moment their tribe had been slaughtered, to her captivity in Uruk, and Noah’s descent into Sheol, God had delivered them at the last moment from the hands of Inanna and her minions. He had brought them safely through the waters of the Flood. He would take care of them now.

It had taken many years for her to heal from what their son Ham had done to her. His violation was not only depraved in a personal sense of defilement, it was an act of evil that she knew would result in a generational curse that only began with the fruit of that unholy violation: Canaan.

CHAPTER 47

Gilgamesh and Urshanabi made their way back to the mainland. The Waters of Death were far behind them. When they were still a league out, Urshanabi stopped Gilgamesh from rowing. He indicated that they were by the black coral beds, the location of the magic plant of heartbeat that Noah had told him about.

Urshanabi said, “We drop anchor here.”

Gilgamesh corrected him, “No, I will be the anchor.”

Urshanabi watched as Gilgamesh released the rope from the two anchor stones and tied it around his waist. Then he tied the anchor stones to his own feet, to weigh him down and carry him to the bottom.

Gilgamesh picked up the two huge weights. He glanced at Urshanabi and said slyly, “Do not go anywhere now.”

He took a huge gulp of air and leapt off the side of the boat. He let the stones pull him to the bottom of the ridge near the coral reef.

As a demigod, Gilgamesh had extraordinary lung capacity. He did not need as much air as a human to stay conscious. He could stay below for as long as fifteen minutes with ease, and twenty or so if needed for survival.

When he reached the bottom, the stones hit and shook the ridge. He reached down and lashed his feet directly to the blocks, so that he could use them as stilts. This would enable him to walk on the deadly coral without it touching his skin.

He immediately began walking the bottom toward the coral bed. His footsteps echoed down the crevice with each weighted step. They were heavy. He used a lot of his energy up just to get to the coral bed.

His footsteps created a vibration that sent fish of all kinds scattering. The vibrations also echoed down into the crevice of the Abyss, where it roused other creatures of the deep.

He reached the coral and stepped upon the bed. His steps crushed the deadly reef material beneath his feet. If the poison of the reef did not kill the organism that came into contact with it, the razor sharp edges would cut it, making it bleed to death. He was safe from the deadly poison and cutting edges. He imagined how like a Stone One he was at this very moment.

Then he found the plant. It looked like the thorny dog-rose plant that existed on land. It was surrounded by just enough coral to protect the plant and yet absorb nutrients. There was also just enough space for Gilgamesh to get his arm through to grab the plant.

He moved with caution, knowing that the slightest miscalculation would cost him his life and leave his body to be eaten by fish in the depths of the sea. His heart beat faster.

The plant of heartbeat, he thought. *The coral of death. Ironic that opposites could grow so close together.*

He had to pull it out of the sediment. If he jerked the plant too suddenly from its bed, he would surely touch the razor coral just inches from his skin.

He pulled with the most controlled force he could. It came out easily. The roots were not deep. Thank the gods.

Slowly, he drew his hand out, narrowly avoiding the edges of the killer coral.

He did it. He got the plant out without touching the coral.

Strange, he thought. *Of all the dangerous, death-defying deeds I have achieved, this was the only one that went easily without a hitch.*

As he backed away from the coral, his resounding footsteps caused more rumbling thuds. They ran through the rock bed, down into the crevice.

It provoked one of the roused creatures of the deep.

Gilgamesh paused, suddenly aware of a change. He felt the water all around him go very cold. Then he realized that the water had not changed. It was his Naphil extra sense. Danger was coming. Very big danger.

He was near the ledge of the crevice. He felt a wave, undulating out of the Abyss, push him back. Something gargantuan was moving up the crevice at a fast pace.

Gilgamesh was almost out of air. He did not want to see what was coming. He cut the ropes tying his feet to the blocks, and cut the anchor rope. He began to swim furiously for the surface.

He would not be fast enough to outrace the monstrous sea dragon that surged out of the crevice of the Abyss. It was the size of several large ships, it had seven heads, and it came straight for him.

It was Leviathan, sea dragon of chaos.

Its body was covered with armor like potsherds. Its mighty two-pronged tail propelled it through the water with powerful force. Each of its seven mouths, filled with monstrous rows of gleaming fangs, prepared to slice through him faster than the coral he just avoided. Gilgamesh had known of the existence of the creature, but had believed that it was only a metaphor for the powers of chaos that the gods would suppress when they established their order. He had not thought it was real.

But it was real.

And it was almost upon him.

He turned around. He saw the creature and all his senses came alive. He grabbed his dagger with futility, knowing that he was going to die.

Instinctively, he dropped the plant from his hand. It slowly sank through the waters. He positioned himself to get at least one good stab in a skull or an eye before being crushed in the jaws of death.

But the strangest thing happened. The sea dragon suddenly changed its course. It glided completely beneath Gilgamesh. One of the heads caught the sinking plant in its jaws. it kept going without attacking Gilgamesh.

It had seven heads, any one of which could easily have snapped him up without even slowing down. But they did not.

Gilgamesh felt as if it knew who he was and was on its own mission to steal the plant. Maybe it had been waiting in the crevice for just such an opportunity because its size was too big to retrieve the plant without being cut and poisoned by the coral. No matter how colossal it was, it was still a creature whose life could be poisoned to death.

Gilgamesh tumbled in the undertow of the wake created by the immense submarine creature passing him by.

Its waving double tail slapped him and shot him upward like a jet stream.

Urshanabi sat in his boat, leaning over the side watching it all happen below him. He froze in terror, doing nothing. He would not have been able to do anything anyway.

Gilgamesh burst out of the water high into the air. It snapped Urshanabi out of his trance.

Gilgamesh yelled, “HO, HURRAH!” He plummeted back to the sea with a splash.

The spine-covered back of Leviathan broke the water nearby in its speedy departure.

Urshanabi thanked the gods that Leviathan had overlooked his little boat. It could have exploded into splinters with a flip of the creature's tail.

Gilgamesh dragged himself from the water onto the boat. He tried to catch his breath while the shocked Urshanabi screamed at him.

"What happened down there? Where did it come from? Why did it not eat you? Where is it going? Did you get the plant?"

Gilgamesh looked at him. "Urshanabi, shut up," he coughed.

Urshanabi obeyed.

Gilgamesh said, "I retrieved the plant. But that monster must have felt the vibrations of my heavy stone footsteps on the sea bottom and it came out of the Abyss. It took the plant, but it did not take me. It was as if it knew who I was and it was ordered not to kill me."

"Ordered by who?" asked Urshanabi.

"How should I know?" snapped Gilgamesh. "It did not come up to me and tell me what was on its mind, fool."

Urshanabi thought for a moment. "I know that the gods had bewitched it to do their bidding before the Flood. Noah told me as much. The goddess Inanna used enchantment spells to capture it and release it upon the enemy in the War of Gods and Men. But that was many years ago. Could they still have some kind of sway over it?"

"Well, I intend to find out," said Gilgamesh. "Set me on a course back to Uruk at the mouth of the rivers."

CHAPTER 48

Gilgamesh had been gone a long time from his mighty city-state of Uruk. In that time, Ishtar rebuilt the portions of her temple and complex demolished by the felled Huluppu tree. She wasted extravagant expense on the complex. It had taxed the treasury, but she did not care. It was one way to get revenge on Gilgamesh for the humiliation he had paid her. A king without sufficient financial resources was not a loved king.

She had much of her own to plot and scheme for the future. Her access to Ninsun was limited, thanks to the bodyguard protection afforded her by Ninurta, that overgrown brooding bully. She knew that once Gilgamesh got back, that God of Broccoli would return his attention to his true ward, the king. Ishtar would then have Ninsun all to herself.

She had developed a playful way to ridicule Ninurta, calling him derogatory titles that could technically be considered legitimate. Thus, she could not be accused of provocation. She would refer to him as "Mighty Cucumber Deity" or "God of Weeds," all legitimate parts of the world of vegetation over which he ruled. She could see it annoyed him. That was her goal. It would all add up. One day, he would lose control, and she would have the advantage.

But Ishtar was restless. The assembly of gods had hidden away at Mount Hermon and had left her out of their secret plans. Uruk had a history of greatness, but she felt its time waning. Other kings vied for position and power. Kingship would move to other city-states as it naturally did. Uruk was still the city of Anu, its patron deity, and she was only considered an escort of the sky god. No matter how glorious she made her temple complex, she would still be only an escort of the patron deity of the city and not the supreme being. She wanted her own city to rule over. She wanted more power.

She wanted more of everything.

On her roof, Ninsun prepared for another sacrifice to the seemingly absentee Shamash. Ever since her confession to Gilgamesh of his adopted status, Ninsun could barely live with herself. She had thrown herself even more deeply into her religion to salve the pain. She had loved Gilgamesh with all her heart and soul. He was her child. Spirit was thicker than blood. She knew him better than he knew himself. She knew that Gilgamesh would go to the ends of the earth to find the truth and to attain eternal life, even if it killed him to do so.

He had gone on a quest to the ends of the earth to find his ancestor, Noah the Distant and Faraway in the magical island of Dilmun. She suspected that he would learn the full truth from Noah. But just what the full truth was, Ninsun did not know herself. All she knew was what she already told Gilgamesh: he was the bastard son of god and human, rejected by his true ancestor, the great Flood survivor, and given in secret adoption to avoid the curse that no doubt followed him. It would crush him. If he made it back alive to Uruk with this self-revelation, she feared he would either go mad with despair and kill himself, or go mad with bitterness and lay waste to the world.

So Ninsun found herself spending many hours in prayer every day for her son. She sought the penance that would grant her forgiveness for her failure to protect him from the truth. She could not shake the guilt.

Ninurta spent much of his time with Ninsun, protecting her until Gilgamesh returned. He suspected he was the only thing keeping Ninsun alive and safe from the vengeance of Ishtar. Not that he cared one whit for the cow's worthless life. But he was commissioned to tend to the safety of King Gilgamesh in order for the assembly's plan to take proper shape in proper time. The King commanded that he protect her while he was away on a personal journey.

Though Ninurta was a god, and Gilgamesh the son of a god, the assembly had nevertheless established that they would be accountable to the rule of human kings, who were the covenanted heirs of dominion over the earth by Elohim's own decree. If the gods would seek to take over that right of inheritance, then surely Elohim the Creator would intervene drastically again as he did previously with the Deluge. But as soon as Gilgamesh returned, he would leave this pathetic blubbering fool and reconvene to the side of his liege the king. That order, Gilgamesh could not contravene.

When the herald's trumpets announced the arrival of the long-gone king of Uruk, everyone in the city stopped what they were doing. Bakers baking bread, mothers feeding their children, workers in the fields tending harvest, Sinleqiunninni in the basement arranging clay tablets, and Ninurta overseeing Ninsun, all left their tasks.

Ninurta whisked away from the pillared rooftop of Ninsun's palace to meet Gilgamesh at the gates.

Ninsun turned and saw her protection vanish like a vapor. She knew her end was near. But she was not about to go down without a fight. She would not let Ishtar have the pleasure of triumph. She had been preparing for this moment for a long time. She readied herself for defense.

At the sound of the herald's trumpet, Ishtar put down a goblet of blood that she was drinking. A smirk crossed her face, and she left her cup unfinished. She had things to do, things she had planned for. The first thing to attend to was to properly attire herself for the arrival of the king. She had carefully calculated that her outfit should be both regal and aggressive. It should display a queenly sense of religious authority, but also carry an edge of political defiance. She chose leather and bones for her tunic. Over that, she draped a grand purple flowing robe with wide semicircular neck ruff that screamed "Queen of Heaven." She had no time for elaborate make up, so she clouded her face deathly white with powder and ratted out her hair into an exploding bush, placing a gem-studded tiara on top.

Simply delicious.

The next thing to do was *not* to greet the king at the gates. That would be too subservient. Let *him* come to *her* temple. Her next business was to visit the Queen Mother's palace. She knew Ninurta would no longer be leaving the stench of his presence surrounding the shrew Ninsun.

Gilgamesh and Urshanabi approached the city gates. Since he had been released from employment by Noah, Urshanabi decided to take his only other offer of being Gilgamesh's boatman on the river Euphrates.

Urshanabi was overwhelmed with the glory of the walls of Uruk. The sevenfold gate was magnificent. They stepped through each chamber as the doors slid open to allow them into the next, until they opened up to the city entrance crowded with citizens cheering their king.

"You are quite beloved," said Urshanabi to Gilgamesh.

Gilgamesh muttered back to him with disdain, "They have no idea who I am, the mob of simpletons. They cheer the victor who gives them bread. They will turn on me as easily. They will not be happy with what I plan to do."

Urshanabi knew Gilgamesh had been forever changed by his encounter with Noah ben Lamech. A root of bitterness had taken hold. He had rejected the god of Noah and that deity's demands upon him. Gilgamesh's soul seemed to radiate a darkness he had not possessed when the traveling king first confronted Urshanabi in the forest.

Gilgamesh saw Ninurta waiting for him, beside a golden chariot harnessed to a team of grand black stallions. He grinned. Ninurta could tell that Gilgamesh had in him a dark new determination he had never seen before. He had a diabolical edge on his lips.

So this new quest was worth it after all, Ninurta thought with smug satisfaction.

Gilgamesh pronounced, "Ninurta, I have missed you. But the time has arrived for our agreement."

Ninurta smiled. Finally, this useful demigod was ready.

They mounted the chariot and pranced down the Processional Way with pomp and regality.

Ishtar moved swiftly through the halls and stairways of the royal palace. She reached the rooftop and slowed down. She wanted to make sure she would achieve maximum effect with a restrained glide toward Ninsun, like that of a snake slithering toward its rodent prey. She wanted Ninsun to feel the full impact of fear, knowing her death approached her.

She stepped out of the shadows of the pillars, into the light. The cheering crowds could be heard at the gates, echoing through the city.

Ninsun stood at the ledge, watching the triumphal entry of her magnificent son. A tear of pride and happiness flowed down her cheek. He was so magnificent, so godlike.

But she did not want to be ordered by Ishtar, so she turned around to confront her predator.

Complete ease covered Ninsun's face, throwing off Ishtar's stride for a second. This was not a victim in fear of her obvious demise. Did she have a hidden weapon?

Ishtar shook it off and said with a seductive tone, "My fat little cow, pretender to deity, I see you are prepared for burial," said Ishtar.

Ninsun had dressed up in her finest high priestess garb. She had on a pure white linen toga with a trimming of colorful patterns of painted gold and silver. A large necklace of shells draped on the skin above her breasts. She had large, gold, double earrings, and strands of golden willow leaves studded with lapis lazuli and carnelian interwoven into her long hair. She was crowned with the horned headdress of deity. On her back, she wore a special cape made of vulture's feathers to give the appearance of relaxed wings. Standing next to the large golden gong that was a call to worship, she looked radiant and divine.

Ishtar said, "I love your earrings, and nice touch with the winged robe."

Ninsun smiled and said, "I know who you are, Azazel, and you are destined to lose. You will not have victory over me."

How did she know my true identity? thought Ishtar.

Ninsun raised the hammer and hit the gong. It rang through the land. She immediately stepped up on the short ledge of the rooftop and cast herself off.

Ishtar's eyes went wide, then narrowed with anger.

You cowardly bovine, she thought, *how dare you steal my opportunity to kill you.* She realized she had better flee or she would be blamed. No sense in unnecessary complications.

Down in the triumphal entry, everyone turned toward the palace temple of Ninsun at the sound of the gong. Gilgamesh saw the lone figure of his mother cast herself off the ledge of the rooftop. Her body plunged to her death in the garden below.

He knew who it must be, but he showed no shock. He was now too calculated to let his defenses down. He immediately searched the rooftop for a malefactor, but saw none. It was a suicide. He had anticipated Ishtar murdering her, but it was perfectly sensible to him for Ninsun to beat Ishtar at her own game, considering she had no other options once Ninurta was gone from her side.

He snapped his reins and yelled for his stallions to race his chariot toward the palace garden. The citizens followed their king without thinking.

When he got to the garden, he saw his mother laying peacefully on her back. She lay in a garden plot of white roses, stained red with her blood. She stared at the heavens as if in search of the gods.

Without shedding a tear, Gilgamesh got off the chariot. He walked right past her toward the palace entrance, unexpectedly shouting to his servants, "Clean this mess up."

Another impediment out of the way, he thought.

He was truly a changed man.

They scurried to obey.

Urshanabi followed him around to the front of the building. Gilgamesh mounted the steps and faced a crowd of servants.

He barked to the head servant impatiently, "Fetch me Sinleqiunninni, I have much to do. Hurry!"

The servant ran off. Then Gilgamesh pointed at a lowly brewer servant and told him, “Go tell Ishtar that the king has arrived and wishes an audience with her in my throne room tomorrow morning.

“But, sire,” sputtered the servant. He could not finish his exclamation of surprise. It was so obviously out of protocol to send a lowly servant, and a brewer at that, to make a call on the goddess. It was clearly an insult, on top of another insult of holding her off until morning, placing her in secondary importance.

Gilgamesh yelled at him, “NOW!”

The servant gulped and bowed and ran off, wondering what his fate would be with the goddess.

Then Gilgamesh stopped as if he had forgotten to make a point. He turned to Ninurta. “Thank you for watching over my mother while I was gone. At least it kept you occupied.”

Ninurta nodded silently and followed Gilgamesh to the throne room.

CHAPTER 49

Within the hour, Sinleqiunninni led a host of scribes into the palace throne room to greet the king. They brought their clay tablets and styluses as ordered by Gilgamesh and set up their tables in an orderly fashion.

Sinleqiunninni bowed to Gilgamesh. He spoke with trepidation, "My lord, I am loathe to report that the palace finances have been raided by Ishtar to rebuild her palace. We are perilously depleted of wealth."

"I do not care," said Gilgamesh, to the scholar's astonishment. "I want you to organize a cycle of shifts with your scribes. I have some stories to tell."

"He who saw the Deep," said Gilgamesh. He paused. He was dictating to the first shift of scribes recording his exploits in cuneiform on clay tablets in his throne room.

"On second thought," said Gilgamesh, "maybe you should start with 'Surpassing all other kings…'"

But he stopped again. He could not make up his mind. He gestured to one half of the room.

"Very well, this half write 'He who saw the Deep' and this half write, 'Surpassing all other kings.' If I cannot make up my mind, I might as well have several versions and see which one does better."

Gilgamesh told his stories all night long. The scribal school perspired, trying to keep up. He told episodes of his journeys to different shifts. The first shift heard about his oppressive start and the quest for significance. The late shift heard his contest with Enkidu and friendship. Another shift, the story of Humbaba and the Cedar Forest. Still others, his journey to seek eternal life from the survivor of the Great Flood, Utnapishtim, on the island of Dilmun.

Of course, he embellished all his stories. But the story of his meeting with Noah was very different than the reality. That one he completely fabricated from the tales of Atrahasis and the Flood that he had heard as a child. He changed Noah's name to Utnapishtim and completely ignored everything Noah had actually told him. Instead, he repeated the concocted tale of a man who was told by the god Enki to build his ridiculous boat cube because Enlil was going to flood the land. He spoke of how Utnapishtim had been given immortality by the gods. There were just enough details in his tale to ring true with what really happened, but just enough contrived details to point away from the truth and toward what Gilgamesh wanted the world to believe.

By the time he had finished, he had multiple episodes copied by many scribes on separate tablets. Then he commissioned Sinleqiunninni to create a single version that combined them all into a simpler storyline with an entertaining plot.

Gilgamesh concluded, "And I want you to carve my exploits on a stone of lapis lazuli and place it in a wooden chest to be buried in the foundation of the walls of Uruk."

Sinleqiunninni sighed. "Your majesty, in order for proper story structure to be maintained, I may have to change some details from your episodic tales in order to make them fit. You may not realize, there are storytelling principles that have been discovered by the poets that are necessary for a good story to hold an audience with amusement. Surely, you…"

"Scholar, shut up!" interrupted Gilgamesh. "Just make it happen."

Then, Gilgamesh went to take a nap.

CHAPTER 50

The next morning, Ishtar arrived in the throne room to find a seated Gilgamesh. His ever-present bodyguard Ninurta stood beside him, holding a mighty battle axe that looked like something out of the pit of Death — because it was from the pit of Death.

Ninurta's eyes followed Ishtar's every movement as she approached the throne.

Ishtar noticed Shamhat standing where the king's Right Hand normally stood. Evidently, Gilgamesh meant to honor the memory of her dead husband by granting her station. She was adorned in an ambitiously ornamented dress, reminiscent of her harlotry days. She was flaunting.

Ishtar wore what could only be considered warrior garb of battle skirt, sandals, shield and dagger, axe, and sword on her belt. She took off her gilded helmet. She looked Ninurta up and down with disdain.

She spoke first to Ninurta, a counter insult to Gilgamesh. "Greetings, majestic Lord of Turnips."

Ninurta's jaw clenched. Of all the outrageous extremes of her behavior toward him, it was ironic that this simple verbal mockery was the one thing that got under his skin like no other.

And she knew it. It delighted her to no end.

She turned to Gilgamesh and said, "King Gilgamesh, may we place behind us all petty offenses of the past. Welcome home, Scion of Uruk, Snorting Bull on the Rampage."

The verbal jab at Gilgamesh did not work on him, as it did with Ninurta or Enkidu before him. The proper title was Wild Bull on the Rampage, not "Snorting Bull." Gilgamesh took it in stride, chuckling as if at a joke.

"Is there a war somewhere I ought to be aware of?" asked Gilgamesh, with a touch of sarcasm.

"No," said Ishtar. "I am just feeling a bit — feisty this morning."

"Well, I called you here for a reason," said Gilgamesh.

Ishtar gestured to Shamhat and replied, "Judging by your escort's hasty replacement of mourning clothes with festive apparel, I would guess your intent was celebratory."

Shamhat narrowed her eyes at the insult toward her.

Gilgamesh said, "Ninurta and I will be leaving Uruk for good."

Ishtar's eyebrows raised with curiosity. "Oh?"

Gilgamesh said, "You may have the city to yourself. Choose a puppet king and do whatever perverted manipulations you want with him."

Ishtar said, "Where, may I ask, are you and the Prince of Pumpkins going?"

A snarl escaped Ninurta's lips.

"North," said Gilgamesh.

She stared at him. He was not going to reveal much. She could see in his eyes a dark resolve she had never seen before.

"I take it your journey to find yourself some immortality did not end with satisfaction."

"I know what I must do, now," he said. "I know my destiny."

Now it was her turn to surprise him.

"Well, I do not want Uruk," she said. "Its days are over. It is rotting flesh on a Sumerian carcass. It is not the future, and you know it. Do not treat me like a fool, Gilgamesh. I could crush you in an instant."

Ninurta gripped his blade and stepped forward.

"Slow down there, Mighty Chickpea," she said, raising her hand. He growled. She mewed back like a cat.

She turned back to Gilgamesh. "I have a counter offer for you instead."

Gilgamesh looked at her. He did not expect it would go easy. He knew he would have to negotiate. This goddess was cunning.

"I am listening."

She smirked and said, "I happen to know that you are gathering all the offspring you have sired through your royal exploits of *jus prima noctis* in your naughty boy years."

Gilgamesh glanced angrily at Ninurta.

Ishtar said, "You are not the only one with palace spies, after all."

Gilgamesh had secretly sent a security force of soldiers to go throughout the city and claim royal prerogative over his illegitimate children. Most of them were adults by now, and they were giants as well. They were *Elioud*, also called *Elyo*, the second generation of giants breeding with normal humans. Many were already warriors.

Ishtar continued to dig, "You are amassing armed forces to take with you, leaving Uruk a husk of protection, with its mighty walls as its only defense. I do not know what the assembly of the gods has commissioned you to do, but I know it is something big, something very big. Now, despite the confidence and bravado of Lord Lettuce Head here, you know full well that I am about the only one in heaven and earth who can become a thorn in the side of your ambition."

Gilgamesh's teeth clenched. She alone certainly could be the fly in his ointment if she chose to be. And he knew she had already chosen.

She continued with a sense of glee, "Let us face it, you know that I am very talented at chaos and destruction. I *am* the goddess of war after all. So the sole pursuit of my every waking moment would therefore be the overthrow of your designs, however grandiose they may be. And why not? Can you blame me? What else is there for me to live for?"

"So what do you want in order to leave me be?" asked Gilgamesh. He knew she was far too sophisticated for mere threat. She was not threatening him, she was persuading him, by building the logic to her counteroffer. If he knew the inevitable, he would be more able to negotiate realistically.

"I want my own city," said Ishtar. "You are no doubt going north to build a new kingdom. If you build me a city further north of yours, then I will have the power I wish to thrive in, and I promise not to interfere in yours. In fact, I will represent your interests in the northern regions and you can consolidate your power over the whole of Mesopotamia, south *and* north."

Then she added a finishing touch of wit, "We would be pals. Allies, if you prefer."

Gilgamesh considered her offer.

Ninurta leaned close to the king's ear and whispered some advice. He did not trust this dragon one bit. He knew her schemes and devices. He knew what she really wanted.

Gilgamesh shook his head to Ninurta. He really had no other choice. Ishtar would surely engage in unending terrorism to foil the plans of the assembly, to foil his plans. He intended to build several cities up north anyway. Each of them needed a patron deity. It was not that much of a sacrifice on his part to give her one of them for her own little fiefdom. He wondered what she was not telling him. What nefarious double cross she might be scheming over, what small wording she might place at the bottom of the covenant that he could not read. It was never so simple with Ishtar. There were always hidden agendas and ulterior motives and unintended consequences. She could not be trusted.

But he had no other choice. She would thwart his plans before he made his forces strong enough to defy her.

"Accepted," said Gilgamesh.

She brightened. Ninurta sighed.

Then he added, "On one condition."

Her eyes narrowed. She knew this king would not be so easily outmaneuvered.

"That you preside over my funeral," said Gilgamesh.

CHAPTER 51

The funeral of Gilgamesh was extravagant. Citizens packed the Processional Way, weeping and tearing their clothes, and throwing dust over their heads. Ishtar, dressed up in her funerary best, led the funeral procession. Her black costume of leather and satin, with a flowing robe and horned headdress of deity, looked spectacular. She painted her face death white with black lipstick and heavy black eyeliner. She felt ravishingly dead as she led the procession out of the city toward their destination at the Euphrates River bed.

A large, empty golden chariot drawn by four stallions rolled behind Ishtar. Next followed a small band of minstrel singers playing a dirge on their instruments and singing with a low chant like sorrow.

Then came a portable throne bearing Gilgamesh's huge sarcophagus, carried on poles by dozens of slaves. It was inlaid with gold and carnelian and lapis lazuli.

Trailing behind the sarcophagus was a long line of mostly female palace servants, richly adorned with gold and silver jewelry and wreaths of gold leaves, carrying small cups in their hands. They included the cup bearer, the barber, the gardener and other palace retainers, grooms and musicians. Lastly, a series of oxen plodded along, drawing carts of wealth and goods for Gilgamesh to take with him into the afterlife.

Gilgamesh sat above the sevenfold gate of the city, watching the funeral train parade below, through the gates and out into the plains. He had exhumed Enkidu's body from his tomb and arrayed his decayed corpse with garments fit for a dead king, including the golden family amulet that Enkidu treasured as his birthright. He had Enkidu's body placed into the sarcophagus intended for Gilgamesh. He had concluded that this was the perfect substitution. Enkidu could be king and experience all the pomp and circumstance he deserved as a great man, the adopted son of Lady Wild Cow Ninsun, high priestess of Shamash, whose sarcophagus followed behind Gilgamesh's, on a more humble funerary cart.

Gilgamesh had taken some time alone with Enkidu's corpse during the preparation period. He looked close into the sunken sockets of Enkidu's skull, saturated with spices and herbs to preserve the flesh for its destination. He knew Enkidu's destination was not an afterlife. His destination was the grave. All the journeys and all the quests he had shared with this great warrior of the steppe were now distant memories that had faded in his mind. He was no longer that man. He had faced the future and he had changed. He was not burying his friend for the afterlife. He was burying his past, along with any shred of mercy, friendship, and compassion that he once toyed with. This would be the last bit of sentiment that he would allow to endanger his position of power ever again.

The funeral procession approached the tomb by the river. Gilgamesh had a workforce of laborers temporarily divert the Euphrates so that they could build his stone tomb below the riverbed itself. It would be a way of discouraging tomb raiders. It would symbolically unite him with the great river that, along with the mighty Tigris, fed the life of the Fertile Crescent for millennia past, and would continue to do so for millennia to come.

The entire population of Uruk followed the parade out to the tomb and gathered around for the mourning ceremonies. Thousands filled the plains with rapt attention as the entire funerary procession marched into the mammoth tomb and down a long sloping passageway. Inside the stone crypt they took various compartments as their residence. Even the oxen and their carts had a large room for sequestering.

Copper helmeted guards stood by the inside doors. The retinue of over one hundred royal servants gathered around the sarcophagus of their king and the tomb was sealed. They drank poison from the little cups they carried. They lay down in an orderly fashion and fell asleep, never to waken. They would enter Sheol with their king — rather, the one they thought was their king.

The oxen were given the poison to drink as well and the room of gathered wealth was sealed forever into the earth.

Up above the tomb, Ishtar presided over the ceremonies with Gilgamesh's successor, one of his royal sons, Ur-Nungal. He would rebuild the Urukean armed forces to maintain rule over the southern region, including Uruk, Ur, Eridu, Larsa, and others.

The ceremony bored Ishtar to death. It was all so much wasted ritual for her. She wanted to get on with her kingdom building. Her duties at the tomb were done, so she left the mourning ceremonies behind her, to meet with Gilgamesh high upon the city walls.

As the mourning for Gilgamesh continued out by the river, Gilgamesh himself oversaw the departure a contingent of several thousand soldiers, leaving the city to march north up the river. He stood on the parapet of the city gates, Ninurta to his right and Ishtar to his left. They watched the soldiers marching away from their beloved city to start anew upriver. Gilgamesh's royal giant progeny led the marching mass and said goodbye to their past forever.

As Gilgamesh gazed over his corps of marching loyal soldiers, and then sought the far edge of the horizon. He spoke words he knew would change the world.

"We will travel several leagues upriver to our new home. I shall build a city in the north for the esteemed goddess of sex and war. You shall be Ishtar of Nineveh."

Ishtar smirked with satisfaction.

"It will be a new world with new gods," added Gilgamesh. "Ninurta, you shall be called by a new name, Marduk."

Marduk nodded with acceptance.

Gilgamesh stared out as if into the Abyss itself. "Together, we shall build a city and a temple-tower, with its top in the heavens and its roots in Sheol. We will make a mighty name for ourselves, that will resound in eternity."

"What will be that name?" asked Ishtar.

"Babylon," said Gilgamesh. "Gate of the Gods."

Ishtar mused, "Mighty Gilgamesh, potentate and god."

"Gilgamesh is dead," he replied. He looked again at the distant funeral by the riverbed. "I am reborn, as you once were from the grave."

Gilgamesh remembered the word that Noah had used, had warned him against becoming. He embraced it deep in his soul with consuming rage.

That word would become his name.

He said with a slow, burning pause…

"I am Nimrod.

"I am Rebel.

"I am Empire."

EPILOGUE

Leviathan swam through the waters of the Abyss toward its destination. Its seven heads pointed in earnest, its body wriggling and twisting in perfect synchronization to maximize its speed. It moved like one colossal muscle of power and destruction. It retained the magic plant it had taken from the swimming demigod in the water, holding it in one of its mouths. It had not eaten the plant. Leviathan did not need it, but something else did.

It journeyed up an underwater cavern to a small lake opening not too far inland from the gulf of the Southern Sea. It knew the exact location. It had been waiting a long time for the right moment to accomplish its goal.

It came through an opening, into the small lake that had been created by breaking through to the water table. It glided along the bottom, looking for its object.

Then Leviathan found it. A huge skeleton of rotted flesh with skull and teeth sticking out of the rock sediment at the bottom.

Leviathan, with its cunning intelligence, knew exactly what it had to do. It placed the magic plant into the jaws of the great skeletal carcass and pushed the jaws shut, grinding the plant into its mouth.

Leviathan swam in slow circles around the skeleton, waiting.

Suddenly, the huge skeleton shuddered.

Its flesh began to regenerate, its organs recomposing.

The skeleton was coming back to life from the dead.

As the musculature filled out with new flesh, the mass convulsed in a spasm that broke it free from the sediment, a broken body hanging limp in the water.

More muscle and more skin and more armored scales reconstituted on this enormous creature of the deep. It was larger than Leviathan and more monstrous in its bulk and muscle. Its thorny spines and hardened scales were almost impenetrable.

Finally, its brain began functioning. The spine shivered as if hit by lightning. It opened its eyes. Its immense jaws yawned with hunger and the creature shook its tail to move.

It was swimming.

It was alive.

It was reborn to chaos.

Up above at the surface of the small lake, the citizens of Uruk went about their business, unaware of the resurrection that had just taken place in their flooded clay pits.

They would never know. The two dragons of the deep left through the cavernous hole that led back down into the Abyss.

They were free again to rule the waters together. Free to wreak havoc and destruction in the cosmos.

They were Rahab and Leviathan.

• • • • • •

Chronicles of the Nephilim continues with the next book, Abraham Allegiant.

If you liked this book, then please help me out by writing an honest review of it on Amazon. That is one of the best ways to say thank you to me as an author. It really does help my exposure and status as an author. It's really easy. In the Customer Reviews section, there is a little box that says "Write a customer review." They guide you easily through the process. Thanks! — *Brian Godawa*

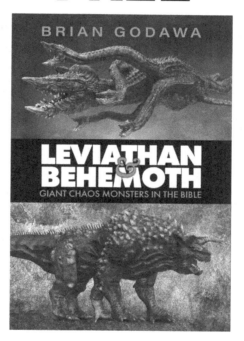

APPENDIX
GILGAMESH AND THE BIBLE

The Biblical fantasy novel *Gilgamesh Immortal* is a retelling of the ancient Babylonian *Epic of Gilgamesh*. This narrative of the heroic journey of its protagonist, is a myth imagined around a supposedly historical figure, King Gilgamesh of Uruk, the fourth king of the first Dynasty of Uruk. His name is mentioned in an ancient *Sumerian King List* as reigning after "the flood swept over" the land, and scholars place him in the third millennium B.C. But the truth is, even this is not sure, and nothing much is known about this great hero except what we have in the epic, which was first uncovered in 1849 by Austen Henry Layard in the library of Ashurbanipal at the excavations at Nineveh in modern Iraq.

Since that time, many other older fragments have been discovered in other locations around the Middle East that seem to indicate that the epic had been pieced together and rewritten from much earlier unconnected individual Gilgamesh episodes from Sumer. Jeffrey Tigay documented this editorial process from the extant clay tablets in *The Evolution of the Gilgamesh Epic*.[1] Tzvi Abusch concluded that at least three major versions of the epic can be documented as retellings of the story that embody the social, political, and religious concerns of the ever-changing national identity of Babylonia, from the older heroic age of individualistic kings into the more "civilized" existence of the state-governed city.[2]

---

[1] Jeffrey H. Tigay, *The Epic of Gilgamesh*, Wauconda, IL: Bolchazy-Carducci, 1982, 2002.
[2] Tzvi Abusch, "The Development and Meaning of the Epic of Gilgamesh: An Interpretive Essay, *Journal of the American Oriental Society*, Vol. 121, No. 4 (Oct. - Dec., 2001), pp. 614-622.

Gilgamesh Immortal was drawn from the various versions of the epic narrative as well as the original Sumerian Gilgamesh episodes now found in several published editions of the poem.[3] Upon first blush, some readers may question a novel about a non-Biblical character in a saga of Biblical heroes. But patient reading yields a powerful revelation of interconnectedness of these ancient Near Eastern narratives. When I was researching for the novel, I was amazed at how many elements of the epic fit within the storyline of the *Chronicles of the Nephilim*, so much so that very little was altered in terms of story structure, characters, and plot of the original Gilgamesh story. Of course, the context and meaning is reinterpreted through the Biblical paradigm, but readers of *Gilgamesh Immortal* will nevertheless be introduced to a prose edition of the epic poem that is fairly representative of the original plotline.

The epic is relevant for the primeval history of *Genesis* because it sets the stage for a lost and rebellious Mesopotamian world in which God chooses his lineage to bring about the promised Seed. The time after the Flood before the Tower of Babel seemed to be a time where God was distant from humanity, "giving up" the pagans who did not honor God "over to their lusts," "foolish hearts," and "futile thinking," to "worship and serve the creature instead of the Creator" (Romans 1). What better way to capture that hiddenness of God than to tell a pagan story that embodies the hiddenness?

The Gilgamesh epic was a national story that embodied the worldview and spirit of Babylonia which would be the ultimate enemy of God's chosen seedline. As readers of the novel discover, it depicts

[3] The three I found most helpful in studying the epic were A.R. George, *The Babylonian Gilgamesh Epic: Introduction, Critical Edition and Cuneiform Texts*, Vol. 1, Oxford University Press, 2003; Benjamin Foster, transl. ed., *The Epic of Gilgamesh: A Norton Critical Edition*, New York: W.W. Norton, 2001; and the Maureen Gallery Kovacs Translation at http://king-of-heroes.co.uk/the-epic-of-gilgamesh/maureen-gallery-kovacs-translation/

the origin of a very important character who embodies that rebellion against God which would ultimately lead to the scattering of the nations and their allotment ("giving over") to the sovereignty of the rebellious Sons of God (Deut. 32:8-9).

Death and the Meaning of Life

The Epic of Gilgamesh is the oldest extant hero story excavated from ancient archaeological mounds in the Middle East, yet it reads ike a modern novel or movie in its story structure and hero's journey. Moderns fancy themselves as more intellectually sophisticated than ancient man, yet they are often ignorant of the fact that their notions of existential angst and individual identity that they think is the erudite offerings of modern existentialist philosophers like Kierkegaard, Sartre, and Nietzsche, were wrestled with millennia before the chaotic narcissistic spasm of the modern period.

Gilgamesh is a ruler who is two thirds god, one third human, yet that humanity means he is ultimately mortal. He seeks significance and immortality because of the dread of death and its apparent blanket of meaninglessness on a world without a clear vision of the afterlife. He begins as a godlike oppressive king who lives in debauchery of power, only to discover his equal in the tamed "Wild Born" Enkidu. He makes a friend of this champion and proceeds to pursue acts of heroism in the killing of Humbaba, the ogre guardian of the cedar forest of the mountain of the gods in Lebanon.

With the aid of his loyal Enkidu, he brings back the head of the monster with such hubris that he defies the goddess Ishtar's proposal of marriage. He spurns her promise of deification because he knows it will only lead to slavery in the Netherworld, not glorious immortality. When he overcomes the Bull of Heaven sent by the vengeful Ishtar, he becomes even more filled with pride, until his mighty equal Enkidu is struck dead with sickness from the gods. This brings him face to face with the fact that no matter how heroic or powerful he becomes, he too will die like all men. Death is both the great equalizer and the great destroyer of significance and meaning. The age of heroes does not bring lasting glory after all.

So he seeks an audience with Utnapishtim the Faraway (Noah), the survivor of the Flood and the only human granted immortality along with his wife, who are now far removed from normal humans in a distant mystical island. Gilgamesh figures he might wrest from Utnapishtim his secret of eternal life from the gods. But when he discovers that death is intrinsic to human existence and the special gift will never be granted to another human being, he returns to his beloved city of Uruk and finds his final fame in building the mighty walls and city, which will continue after he is long dead. In the end, man can only find lasting glory in being a part of something bigger than himself that continues on when he is gone. For Gilgamesh that something bigger is the city-state.

Gilgamesh's ruminations of death, meaninglessness, and despair will be familiar to Bible readers in the similar ruminations of another king in the book of Ecclesiastes. Called *Qoheleth* or "the Preacher," this king of Jerusalem writes about all of life being a vapor because death destroys all human pursuits. He tells of seeking pleasure, wealth, and wisdom, only to conclude that none of it brings lasting meaning because death turns it all upside down. The Preacher speaks of enjoying the simple pleasures of life like a wife, good food, and hard work because the pursuit of power and glory is ultimately worthless and defeating, the equivalent of striving after wind.

A side by side comparison of passages from the Gilgamesh Epic and the book of Ecclesiastes illustrates a profound congruity between the wisdom writings of the Old Testament and Babylonia.

GILGAMESH EPIC	ECCLESIASTES
Do we build a house for ever? Do we seal (contracts) for ever? Do brothers divide shares for ever? Does hatred persist for ever in [the land]? Does the river for ever raise up (and) bring on floods? [4]	There is no remembrance of former things, nor will there be any remembrance of later things yet to be among those who come after. (Ecclesiastes 1:11) A generation goes, and a generation comes, but the earth remains forever. All streams run to the sea, but the sea is not full… (Ecclesiastes 1:4–7)
Since the days of yore there has been no permanence; The *resting* and the dead, how alike they are! Do they not compose a picture of death, The commoner and the noble, Once they are near to [their fate]?[5]	For of the wise as of the fool there is no enduring remembrance, seeing that in the days to come all will have been long forgotten. How the wise dies just like the fool! (Ecclesiastes 2:16)
[You,] kept toiling sleepless (and) what did you get? You are exhausting [yourself with] ceaseless toil, you are filling your sinews with pain, bringing nearer the end of your life. (Tablet X:297-300)[6]	And what gain is there to him who toils for the wind? Moreover, all his days he eats in darkness in much vexation and sickness and anger. (Ecclesiastes 5:16–17)
Man is one whose progeny is snapped off like a reed in the canebrake: (Tablet X:301)[7]	For who knows what is good for man while he lives the few days of his vain life, which he passes like a shadow? (Ecclesiastes 6:12)
the comely young man, the pretty young woman, all [too soon in] their very [prime] death abducts (them). (Tablet X:302-303)[8]	The wise person has his eyes in his head, but the fool walks in darkness. And yet I perceived that the same event happens to all of them. (Ecclesiastes 2:14)
No one sees death,	For man does not know his time…

[4] *The Ancient Near East an Anthology of Texts and Pictures.*, ed. James Bennett Pritchard, 92-93 (Princeton: Princeton University Press, 1958).

[5] *The Ancient Near East an Anthology of Texts and Pictures.*, ed. James Bennett Pritchard, 92-93 (Princeton: Princeton University Press, 1958).

[6] A.R. George, *The Babylonian Gilgamesh Epic: Introduction, Critical Edition and Cuneiform Texts*, Vol. 1, Oxford University Press, 2003, p. 697.

[7] George, *The Babylonian Gilgamesh Epic*, p. 697.

[8] George, *The Babylonian Gilgamesh Epic*, p. 697.

no one sees the face [of death,] no one [hears] the voice of death: (yet) savage death is the one who hacks man down. (Tablet X:304-307)[9]	so the children of man are snared at an evil time, when it suddenly falls upon them. (Ecclesiastes 9:12)
At some time we build a household, at some time we start a family, at some time the brothers divide, at some time feuds arise in the land. At some time the river rose (and) brought the flood, the mayfly floating on the river. Its countenance was gazing on the face of the sun, then all of a sudden nothing was there![10] (Tablet X:308-315)[11]	For everything there is a season, and a time for every matter under heaven: a time to be born, and a time to die;... a time to love, and a time to hate;... a time for war, and a time for peace. (Ecclesiastes 3:1–8) Vapor of vapors, says the Preacher, ...All is mist and vapor. (Ecclesiastes 1:2)
Oh, Enkidu, a team of two will not perish. He who is lashed to a boat will not sink, No one can tear asunder a three-ply cloth.[12] (Gilgamesh and Humbaba A)	Two are better than one, ...For if they fall, one will lift up his fellow...a threefold cord is not quickly broken. (Ecclesiastes 4:9–12)
Thou, Gilgamesh, let full be thy belly, Make thou merry by day and by night. Of each day make thou a feast of rejoicing, Day and night dance thou and play! Let thy garments be sparkling fresh, Thy head be washed; bathe thou in water. Pay heed to the little one that holds on to thy hand, Let thy spouse delight in thy bosom! For this is the task of [mankind]!"[13] (Tablet XI)	Go, eat your bread with joy, and drink your wine with a merry heart, for God has already approved what you do. Let your garments be always white. Let not oil be lacking on your head. Enjoy life with the wife whom you love, all the days of your vain life that he has given you under the sun, because that is your portion in life. (Ecclesiastes 9:7–10)

The natural question that arises is whether or not the Biblical author got his ideas from Babylonia, or the reverse, or whether they

[9] George, *The Babylonian Gilgamesh Epic*, p. 697.

[10] George, *The Babylonian Gilgamesh Epic*, p. 697.

[11] George, *The Babylonian Gilgamesh Epic*, p. 697.

[12] v. 130-133, Benjamin R. Foster, Ed., *The Epic of Gilgamesh: A Norton Critical Edition*, New York: Norton and Company, 2001, p. 109.

[13] *The Ancient Near East an Anthology of Texts and Pictures.*, ed. James Bennett Pritchard, 90 (Princeton: Princeton University Press, 1958).

both used a common source background. Regardless of which way the influence flows, the Gilgamesh Epic and Ecclesiastes certainly display a striking exchange of ideas. The last verses of Gilgamesh Tablet XI and Ecclesiastes 9:7-10 show a thought for thought progress of thinking that surely suggests a deliberate cultural exchange of ideas.

But the differences are perhaps just as profound and striking as the similarities. First and foremost is of course the polytheism of Gilgamesh that is dutifully overturned by the monotheism of Ecclesiastes. Jewish ethical monotheism was a hostile unbridgeable chasm between the worldviews of Israel and her surrounding pagan neighbors, a chasm between Abraham's bosom and Hades.

But an equally profound separation lies in the anthropocentric (human-centered) paganism of Gilgamesh versus the theocentric (God-centered) optimism of Qoheleth. While both affirm a kind of meaningless despair that death brings to the human condition, Gilgamesh concludes with resignation that the best one can do is a substitute immortality of glory in the perpetual life of the state, a rather modern humanistic proposition for an ancient.

But the Preacher argues that we are to eat, drink, and be merry, not merely because tomorrow we die (9:10), but because it is a gift from God (3:13), and that "for all these things God will bring you into judgment (11:9)," because "whatever God does endures forever" (3:14). So eternal life *is* found in connection with God in Ecclesiastes because not even the *polis* or city of the ancient world lasts forever like God does, and the individual life rooted in God is a life rooted in transcendence.

> Ecclesiastes 12:13–14
> The end of the matter; all has been heard. Fear God and keep his commandments, for this is the whole duty of

man. For God will bring every deed into judgment, with every secret thing, whether good or evil.

Echoes of Eden

The thematic existential pursuit of meaning and transcendence is not the only thing in common between the Babylonian epic and Biblical Scriptures. Echoes of Eden resound in the journey of Gilgamesh that scholars have long pointed out reflect a literary correspondence with the Bible.

When Enkidu enters the Gilgamesh story, he is a "Wild Born" untamed man who lives as an animal in the steppe with a hairy naked body, wandering the hills, feeding on grass and upsetting traps set by the hunter for his mammalian kin. He was in fact created by the goddess Aruru as a foil to the "civilized" oppression and "fierce arrogance" of king Gilgamesh over the city of Uruk.[14] Theirs is the perennial conflict between rural and urban human identity. The city dweller may be "civilized," yet he can be barbaric and cruel compared to the "noble savage" who is the only redemption for such oppression.

In the Standard version of the Babylonian epic, a hunter tries to stop Enkidu from ruining his traps by seducing him with a harlot named Shamhat. Enkidu is drawn to her with instinctual lust and he is ultimately tamed by his sexual satisfaction with the female, who then civilizes him with clothes and human etiquette.[15] It is the ancient classical paradigm of human nature: The sensuality of Woman tames the savagery of Man.

But this civilizing of human nature is also depicted as a loss of innocence required for human maturity. Suddenly, Enkidu's eyes are

---

[14] George, *The Babylonian Gilgamesh Epic*, pp. 543-544.
[15] Tablets I and II, George, *The Babylonian Gilgamesh Epic*, pp. 549-561.

opened, "he had reason, he was wide of understanding." His psychic link with the animals is broken, and Shamhat says to Enkidu, "You are just like a god."[16]

This little episode and its mythic metaphor of human growth and separation from the animals through loss of innocence has obvious parallels with the Garden of Eden in *Genesis* 3. Eve, seduced by the serpent, influences Adam to eat of the fruit of the tree of the knowledge of good and evil which "opens their eyes" and they "become like God" losing their innocence.

Critical scholarship has noted these parallels and has prioritized the Babylonian account, which results in twisting the Biblical account into a humanistic parable that subverts Original Sin into Original Wisdom, where it was a good thing to disobey God and take control of human destiny. God becomes the villain and the serpent becomes the hero of this interpretation in that the serpent helps mankind escape dependency on a jealous deity fearful of man taking his place and making him unnecessary. Liberal scholar James Charlesworth, quoting another liberal scholar suggests that to "characterize him [God] as villain is not impossible, in view of 3:8 (the Garden is for his own enjoyment), and vs. 23 (where he feels 'threatened' by the man!) As villain, he is the opponent of the main program."[17]

Charlesworth then concludes that,

> "The story of the serpent in our culture is a tale of how the most beautiful creature [the serpent] became seen as ugly, the admired became despised, the good was misrepresented as the bad, and a god was dethroned and recast as Satan. Why? It is perhaps because we

---

[16] Tablet I: 202, 207, George, *The Babylonian Gilgamesh Epic*, pp. 551
[17] James Charlesworth, *The Good and Evil Serpent: How a Universal Symbol Became Christianized*, New Haven: Yale University Press, p. 309.

> modern humans have moved farther and farther away from nature, cutting the umbilical cord with our mother earth?"[18]

But this critical hermeneutic is autobiographical projection of fashionable modern prejudice against the Judeo-Christian depersonalization of nature. It completely misunderstands the polemical nature of most Biblical interaction with its pagan environment, and misunderstands the Gilgamesh story as well. Similarities in stories illustrate a common subject, but differences express a contrast of meaning.

Charlesworth surveys iconography on archaeological artifacts in Bronze Age Canaan to accurately describe ancient Canaan as a "serpent cult civilization."[19] Canaan was the land promised to the Israelites by God. They were commanded to devote all the giant clans and their cities to complete destruction because of the connection of the giant Anakim clans to the antediluvian Nephilim (Numb 13:32-33).[20]

> Joshua 11:21–22
> And Joshua came at that time and cut off the Anakim [giants] from the hill country... Joshua devoted them to destruction with their cities. There was none of the Anakim left in the land of the people of Israel.

[18] Charlesworth, *The Good and Evil Serpent*, p. 419.
[19] Charlesworth, *The Good and Evil Serpent*, p. 100.
[20] See the appendix "The Nephilim" in *Noah Primeval* for the explanation of the expulsion of the giant clans from the Holy Land. They are essentially the Seed of the Serpent at war with the Seed of Eve. Brian Godawa, *Noah Primeval*, Los Angeles, CA: Embedded Pictures Publishing, 2012, pp. 307-326.

I have explained elsewhere that the creation story of Genesis follows the ancient Near Eastern paradigm of justifying territorial and governmental control over a region. When a kingdom would assert its authority or power, it told a creation story of how its deity established order out of the primordial chaos and laid claim on the land.[21] The Babylonian creation story Enuma Elish does this with its ascendency of the Babylonian patron deity Marduk as king over the assembly of gods, and the Genesis account does this for Yahweh's people as inheritors of the Promised Land. "The earth" in Genesis 1, is better translated as "the land" in Hebrew and, as John Sailhamer has pointed out, is most likely a literary reference to the Promised Land of Canaan.[22] Since the Old Testament is filled with a history of Israel constantly falling away from Yahweh and worshipping the false gods of Canaan, it makes perfect theological sense that the Tempter in the Garden that draws Israel's forebear Adam away from obedience is the symbol of Canaan, the serpent.

There is no meaningful way that serpents could be interpreted as a hero or positive symbol in Genesis 2-3 in context with the Israelite worldview. And the serpent is not a positive symbol in Gilgamesh either.

Another episode in the Epic of Gilgamesh that carries overtones of the Genesis creation story is on Tablet XI. After Gilgamesh encounters Utnapishtim (Noah) and discovers he cannot attain eternal life, he leaves dejected. But Utnapishtim feels sorry for him and decides to tell him about the location of a magic plant that is able to

---

[21] Brian Godawa, "Biblical Creation and Storytelling: Cosmogony, Combat and Covenant," http://godawa.com/Writing/Articles/BiblicalCreationStorytelling-Godawa.pdf.

[22] Bruce R. Reichenbach, "Genesis 1 as a Theological-Political Narrative of Kingdom Establishment," *Bulletin for Biblical Research* 13.1 (2003), pp. 47-69. See also, John Sailhamer, *Genesis Unbound: A Provocative New Look at the Creation Account* (Sisters, OR: Multnomah, 1996).

make one young again. Gilgamesh journeys to find the plant, and then see what happens next:

> At thirty leagues they pitched camp.
> Gilgamesh found a pool whose water was cool,
> he went down into it to bathe in the water.
> A snake smelled the fragrance of the plant,
> [silently] it came up and bore the plant off;
> as it turned away it sloughed a skin.[23]

The notion of a plant that rejuvenates and a serpent "stealing" the opportunity of renewed youth has long been connected to the Genesis account of the rejuvenating effect of the Tree of Life being withheld from Adam due to the serpent's deception. But they also both contain etiological explanations of snake biology, Genesis for the serpent crawling on its belly, and Gilgamesh for the snake shedding its skin. These echoes of Eden reaffirm the negative character of the serpent as one who spoils the opportunity for renewed life, not the positive agent of human maturity.

Noah and the Flood in the Epic of Gilgamesh

Perhaps the most fascinating connection that the Epic of Gilgamesh has to the Bible is in the presence of a Noah character and his story of the Great Deluge. Scholars have written endlessly on this topic ever since the first translations of the account were available in the late nineteenth century. A comparison of the two stories yields, yet again, some significant similarities that indicate a common origin, yet

---

[23] Tablet XI:302-307, George, *The Babylonian Gilgamesh Epic*, p. 723.

some even more significant differences that indicate divergent meaning.

As mentioned earlier, extant tablets prove that the Gilgamesh epic had gone through a literary evolution. One very distinct change involves the addition of the Flood story that probably did not exist in the oldest Babylonian version of the epic poem, but does exist in a later Babylonian version. This has prompted Tigay to suggest, and most scholars now agree, that an additional Akkadian story of the Flood called Atrahasis was used as a source to add to the Gilgamesh cycle. And a third and older Sumerian version called The Deluge may also have had some influence on Gilgamesh.[24]

But what about the Genesis story of Noah's ark? While it is virtually unanimous among scholars that Genesis was written and edited over time using multiple sources, the more extreme view of this has been adopted by the scholarly establishment that has sought to divide the Old Testament, and in particular the Flood story, into contradictory sources that have been woven together from an older "Yahwist" source and a newer "Priestly" source, all with opposing agendas.

This radical view is falling from favor with the advent of literary and form criticism and because of the complete absence of manuscript evidence to support the remote speculation of such radical redaction.[25] What is coming more to light is the genius of composition that exists in the final canonical literary form that virtually defies categorizing of

---

[24] Tigay, *The Epic of Gilgamesh*, pp. 214-240.

[25] See Umberto Cassuto, *The Documentary Hypothesis and the Composition of the Pentateuch,* Skokie, IL: Varda Books, 1941, 2005; Duane A. Garrett, *Rethinking Genesis: The Sources and Authorship of the First Book of the Pentateuch*, Baker, 1991; John H. Sailhamer, *The Meaning of the Pentateuch: Revelation, Composition and Interpretation,* Downers Grove, IL: Intervarsity, 2009; "The New Literary Criticism," Gordon J. Wenham, Vol. 1, *Genesis 1–15*. Word Biblical Commentary. Dallas: Word, Incorporated, 1998, pp. xxxii-xlii; Victor P. Hamilton, *The Book of Genesis, Chapters 1–17*. The New International Commentary on the Old Testament. Grand Rapids, MI: Wm. B. Eerdmans Publishing Co., 1990, pp. 12-38.

specific sources. For example, Gordon Wenham has pointed out the complex literary poetic form of "chiasmus" used in the Flood narrative. Chiasmus is a kind of mirroring literary structure that builds the plot with increasing succession, to the middle of the story, where the thematic message is highlighted, only to conclude the second half of the story in a reflective reversal of the first half.

At the risk of overwhelming the reader, here is the literary structure of the Genesis Flood narrative as detailed by Wenham, emphasizing the superior originality of authorship over alleged source material.[26]

[26] Gordon J. Wenham, "The Coherence of the Flood Narrative," *Vetus Testamentum* 28, no. 3 (1978), p. 338.

Genesis vi 10-ix 19

A Noah (vi 10a)
B Shem, Ham and Japheth (10b)
C Ark to be built (14-16)
D Flood announced (17)
E Covenant with Noah (18-20)
F Food in the ark (21)
G Command to enter ark (vii 1-3)
H 7 days waiting for flood (4-5)
I 7 days waiting for flood (7-10)
J Entry to ark (11-15)
K Yahweh shuts Noah in (16)
L 40 days flood (17a)
M Waters increase (17b-18)
N Mountains covered (19-20)
O 150 days waters prevail ((21)-24)
P GOD REMEMBERS NOAH (viii 1)
O′ 150 days waters abate (3)
N′ Mountain tops visible (4-5)
M′ Waters abate (5)
L′ 40 days (end of) (6a)
K′ Noah opens window of ark (6b)
J′ Raven and dove leave ark (7-9)
I′ 7 days waiting for waters to subside (10-11)
H′ 7 days waiting for waters to subside (12-13)
G′ Command to leave ark (15-17(22))
F′ Food outside ark (ix 1-4)
E′ Covenant with all flesh (8-10)
D′ No flood in future (11-17)
C′ Ark (18a)
B′ Shem, Ham and Japheth (18b)
A′ Noah (19)

Early Biblical criticism tried to reduce the Biblical Flood narrative to a derivative of the Babylonian version, but that theory is now thoroughly discredited.[27] Archaeologist P.J. Wiseman uncovered the existence of a "toledoth" formula in the repeated Genesis phrase, "these are the generations of," that indicates original source material of inscribed clay tablets rather than a hodgepodge of Yahwist,

[27] Bill T. Arnold and David B. Weisberg, "A Centennial Review of Friedrich Delitzsch's 'Babel und Bibel' Lectures," *Journal of Biblical Literature*, Vol. 121, No. 3 (Autumn, 2002), pp. 441-457.

Priestly, and other contrary sources.[28] Whatever narrative congruity exists between the Bible and the Gilgamesh Epic, their genetic ties are not found in being a derivative of one another.

In *Gilgamesh Immortal*, while I do write of Gilgamesh visiting Noah and his wife on a distant island, and I do have Noah tell Gilgamesh the story of the Flood, just as he does in the Epic of Gilgamesh, I bring a subversive twist to the scenario. The story that Gilgamesh inscribes onto clay and stone is not the one that Noah told him. Why? Because Gilgamesh is not a repentant follower of Noah's god, Yahweh Elohim, the God of the Bible. So it would make sense that if he rejects the living God, he would reject the living God's metanarrative and replace it with his own that would exalt himself or his biased religious construction. So the version we read in the Epic of Gilgamesh today is the deliberately fabricated version of a rebel against Yahweh. This is the nature of all subversive storytelling as I have indicated in previous appendices of the *Chronicles of the Nephilim*.[29]

So what is the storyline of the Flood in the original Gilgamesh Epic?

In Tablet XI of the epic poem, Utnapishtim, the Gilgamesh Noah, explains that because of some unexplained sin of man, the pantheon of gods decide to send a Deluge to kill all of mankind. But the god of the waters of the Abyss, Enki (or Ea) defies the decision and sneaks away to give a dream to Utnapishtim, a wealthy man who lives in the

---

[28] P. J. Wiseman, D. J. Wiseman, Ed., *Ancient Records and the Structure of Genesis: A Case for Literary Unity* Thomas Nelson, 1985.

[29] One of the major premises of *Chronicles of the Nephilim* is that pagans replace the narrative of the Biblical God with their own mythical constructs that justify their prejudices and protect their consciences from moral repentance. Their accusations that Biblical religion is a fairy tale concocted to control others is a projection of their own hubris to control others by negating transcendent authority.

city of Shuruppak in Mesopotamia. Through the dream, he tells him to tear down his house and build a large boat to save "the seed of all living creatures." He gives him the dimensions of the boat and instructions of how to build it.

Utnapishtim is to lie to his neighbors when asked about the large boat by explaining that he is going to move downstream to the city of Eridu. When he finishes the boat, he loads on it all kinds of animals as well as all his extended family members and some skilled craftsman.

The gods then start a storm of wind and rain, led by the storm god Adad, that devastates the land with such force, even the gods get scared and hide up in heaven like frightened dogs with their tails between their legs. The blowing wind and gale force downpour lasts six days and seven nights until "all the people are turned to clay."

The boat finally runs aground on Mount Nimush, and after seven days, Utnapishtim lets out a dove to see if it can find a perch, but it does not and returns to him. He waits and sends a swallow, and then finally a raven that does not return, indicating enough dry land to get out of the boat.

Utnapishtim then offers a sacrifice to the gods, who "smell the sweet savour" and "gather like flies around the sacrificer." But when the great god Enlil arrives, he is angry to discover Utnapishtim survived the destruction. When he finds out that Enki had leaked the plan to Utnapishtim, they quarrel. But the crafty Enki denies violating the will of the gods because he did not tell Utnapishtim *directly*, but through a dream.

Enlil resigns himself to the trickery and decides to bestow immortality on Utnapishtim and his wife, so they would be like the gods, but placing them "at the mouth of the rivers" to dwell faraway from normal mankind.

Utnapishtim then explains to Gilgamesh that the gods will not assemble for his benefit to bestow upon him eternal life. He is destined to die like all humanity. To prove the impossibility, Utnapishtim tells Gilgamesh to stay awake for six days and seven nights to prove his worthiness of becoming immortal by exercising power over the stepchild of death: sleep. Gilgamesh cannot do so and he is sent on his way with the consolation prize of finding a magic plant that will restore his youth. As stated before, the serpent then steals that plant away from him.

Wenham has listed seventeen major correlations between the Genesis Flood and the Gilgamesh Deluge that indicate a strong genetic connection between the two narratives:

1. Divine decision to destroy
2. Warning to flood hero
3. Command to build ark
4. Hero's obedience
5. Command to enter
6. Entry
7. Closing door
8. Description of flood
9. Destruction of life
10. End of rain, etc.
11. Ark grounding on mountain
12. Hero opens window
13. Birds' reconnaissance
14. Exit
15. Sacrifice
16. Divine smelling of sacrifice

17. Blessing on flood hero[30]

But Alexander Heidel's classic *The Gilgamesh Epic and Old Testament Parallels* has teased out the differences between the two that shed light on their radically divergent meanings.

To begin with, the name for the Flood hero in Gilgamesh is Utnapishtim, which means, "he saw life," an apparent free rendering of the Sumerian *Ziusudra*, that meant "he found everlasting life." In the Flood story most likely borrowed for the Gilgamesh Epic, his name is Atrahasis which means "exceedingly wise." In Genesis, Noah means, "rest."[31]

The Sumerian Noah, Ziusudra, was a priestly king of the city of Shuruppak, the tenth in line of the prediluvian Babylonian kings. In Gilgamesh, Utnapishtim is not a king, but a wealthy citizen of Shuruppak. The Biblical Noah is the tenth prediluvian patriarch, but beyond this, we only know he was pious in that he "walked with God" and found favor in his sight.[32] In Genesis, only eight people were in the ark with the animals; Noah, his three sons, and all their wives. In the Sumerian Deluge and Gilgamesh, Noah's extended family also came along with some craftsmen, and a boatman.

Heidel then points out the theological differences between the narratives regarding the cause of the Flood and the possibility of redemption for humanity.[33] In Atrahasis, the "noise" of man's overpopulation and "cries of rebellion" awaken Enlil from his sleep to send several plagues and famines without satisfying results before

---

[30] Wenham, "The Coherence of the Flood Narrative," p. 346.

[31] Alexander Heidel, *The Gilgamesh Epic and Old Testament Parallels*, Chicago, IL: University of Chicago, 1946, 1963, p. 227.

[32] Heidel, *The Gilgamesh Epic*, p. 228.

[33] Heidel, *The Gilgamesh Epic*, p. 230-232.

he conspires to send a flood to drown out their rebellious noise.[34] In Gilgamesh, the gods send the Deluge because of an undefined sin of mankind (Tablet XI:180). Utnapishtim lies to his neighbors about the ark because the gods do not want man to know what they are about to do.

Contrarily, in Genesis, the Flood is very clearly a righteous judgment upon an earth that was "corrupted and filled with violence." "The LORD saw that the wickedness of man was great in the earth, and that every intention of the thoughts of his heart was only evil continually." God gives man a "period of grace" of one hundred and twenty years with which to repent and obey God (Gen 6:5-6). Though this purpose is not stated explicitly in Genesis, two other passages in the New Testament seem to indicate this notion of God providing such opportunity.

> 1 Peter 3:19–20
> [In the spirit] he went and proclaimed to the spirits in prison, because <u>they formerly did not obey, when God's patience waited in the days of Noah, while the ark was being prepared</u>, in which a few, that is, eight persons, were brought safely through water.

> 2 Peter 2:5–6
> if he did not spare the ancient world, but preserved <u>Noah, a herald of righteousness</u>, with seven others, when he brought a flood upon the world of the

---

[34] Bernard Batto points out this distinction that is often missed by scholars. The noise and din "indicate the cries of rebellion of humankind against the authority of the deity. In the prior revolt by the lesser gods Enlil's sleep was also interrupted by a similar outcry from the rebel gods. The humans are thus portrayed as carrying on in the spirit of the slain rebel god out of whose flesh and blood they were created." Bernard Batto, "The Sleeping God: An Ancient Near Eastern Motif of Divine Sovereignty," *Biblica* 68 (1987), p. 160.

> ungodly... making them an example of what is going to happen to the ungodly;

Surely, there is an assumption, sometimes explicit, but always implicit throughout the Old Testament that if man repents, God will stay his hand of planned judgment. But the notion that Noah actually "preached" words to the condemned is not necessarily in the text. Some Evangelicals assume that Noah as "herald of righteousness" means he preached sermons like the Apostles in Acts. But this assumes too much. For the context of the New Testament passages are about Noah's *example to us* "of what is going to happen to the ungodly" of Peter's current era.

Jesus in his Olivet sermon uses Noah's *example* as a sermon illustration for his coming judgment as well.

> Matthew 24:37–39
> For as in those days before the flood they were eating and drinking, marrying and giving in marriage, until the day when Noah entered the ark, and <u>they were unaware until the flood came</u> and swept them all away, so will be the coming of the Son of Man.

Noah's preparation for the Flood was a *declaratory action* that spoke louder than words, and apparently, it was not understood by those who were "unaware until the flood came and swept them all away."

Another passage sheds light on the notion that Noah's *act* of building the boat in anticipation of the Flood was itself the "proclamation."

> Hebrews 11:7

> By faith Noah, being warned by God concerning events as yet unseen, in reverent fear constructed an ark for the saving of his household. By this he condemned the world and became an heir of the righteousness that comes by faith.

Though God always seems to give a generation under condemnation an opportunity to repent, he does not always do so with sermons of words, but certainly with examples of actions.

The ark also provides an example of significant difference between the narratives. The length of Noah's ark was 450 feet long, 75 feet wide, and 45 feet high, with a displacement of approximately 43,300 tons. It had three levels to contain the animals, that on the surface of the account is structurally feasible. Utnapishtim's vessel however, was not so amiable to reality. According to Babylonian measurements, it was supposed to be a square cube of 200 feet on all sides and was divided into seven levels, displacing approximately 228,500 tons, making it a rather questionable sea worthy craft.[35]

In the Biblical story, it is well known that the flood began with rain coming down from the heavens and waters coming up from the deep. The rain storm lasted 40 days and 40 nights, and then after 150 days, the waters began to abate until the earth was dry enough to leave the ark about 360 days or 1 year after the start of the flood. In the Babylonian versions, the flood storm lasts only 7 days and 7 nights, followed by an unspecified number of days for the waters to dry up before Noah leaves the ark.

[35] Heidel, *The Gilgamesh Epic*, pp. 232-236.

Upon leaving the boat, Ziusudra, Utnapishtim, and Noah all build altars and offer sacrifices of thanksgiving and appeasement unto their gods. But the theological incongruity between the accounts is spelled out in the divine reactions. In Gilgamesh, "The gods smelled the savour, the gods smelled the sweet savour, the gods gathered like flies around the sacrificer" (Tablet XI:161-163). Of this passage, Andrew George writes,

> The simile used to describe the gods' arrival is famously the image of hungry flies buzzing around a piece of food. This imagery implies a somewhat cynical view of gods, even more disrespectful than the earlier simile likening them to cowering dogs.[36]

Heidel adds a dimension to this zoomorphic (animal-like) denigration of the gods when he suggests that the gods had been without food sacrifice from humans for so long that they were hungry like a bunch of flies dependent on parasitic hosts. Enlil then starts to quarrel with Enki for revealing the secret to Utnapishtim, wherein Enki defends himself with trickery by arguing that he did not reveal it directly to Utnapishtim, but through a dream, thus freeing him from blame.

Contrary to the Babylonian zoomorphic simile of the gods, the Bible engages in anthropomorphism (human-like) in that man is created in the image of God and thus sacrifice is understood in the priestly terms of atonement for sin (Lev. 1:9). God "smelled the pleasing aroma, the LORD said in his heart, 'I will never again curse the ground because of man (Gen. 8:21).'" Heidel explains

---

[36] George, *The Babylonian Gilgamesh Epic*, pp. 518.

> The propitiatory character of the sacrifice is brought out quite clearly in the biblical narrative, where the ascending essence of the burnt-offerings is called a "soothing odor," or, literally, an "odor of tranquilization." One purpose of Noah's sacrifice, as seems to be indicated by what follows, probably was to appease the wrath of God which had been kindled by the sins of mankind and which Noah had just witnessed. But at the same time it was undoubtedly an offering for the expiation of his own sins and those of his family.[37]

Whereas the Babylonian anthropomorphic descriptions of their deities tended to reflect human weaknesses (hunger) and sin (quarreling), the Biblical account depicts the human-like character traits of God in terms of relationship (propitiation and atonement).

In the Babylonian versions, Noah and his wife are blessed with eternal life after Enlil gives in to Enki's defensive arguments. They are then taken to a distant place, "at the mouth of the rivers," probably referring to the Persian Gulf, into which the Euphrates and Tigris rivers opened up. In Gilgamesh, this was the mythical and distant "place where the sun rises," in the Sumerian version it was the island of Dilmun, now considered by most scholars to be in the area of the Bahrain islands.

The Biblical version is theologically motivated by God's covenantal nature. God blesses Noah, and then grants him the original charge given to Adam to multiply and fill the earth, and to exercise dominion over the creatures (Gen 9:1-3). As the flood was a return to

---

[37] Heidel, *The Gilgamesh Epic*, p. 255.

the chaos waters before creation, so the world of Noah is a new creation with a new Adam. And God reinforces his value of the created image of God in man, by bringing special attention to capital punishment for murdering man, made in the image of God.

The rainbow becomes God's covenant promise to stay his hand from Deluge judgment, unlike the Gilgamesh Epic, that has a secondary mother goddess claim that a necklace strung with flies will, "remind her of the hungry gods buzzing around [Utnapishtim's] sacrifice, and ultimately of her special responsibility to her human children"[38] (Tablet XI:165-169).

Comparison and Contrast

The value of comparative religion lies in achieving a better understanding of the historical and cultural context of ancient writings like the Bible. Too often, both religious believers and unbelievers approach the text with their own preconceived modern worldview or political agenda that they project upon the text in order to "use" it for their own purposes, positive or negative. Christians have been guilty of forcing poetic passages into the straightjacket of a hyper-literalistic hermeneutic, or imposing our notions of historical accounting or scientific accuracy upon ancient writers who just did not write with our post-Enlightenment modern scientific or historical worldview.

I addressed the Mesopotamian cosmology in the Bible in an appendix of *Noah Primeval* to make the point that the Biblical authors were men of their times that could not have possibly been writing Genesis as a scientific treatise on the origin of the material universe, simply because they did not write creation texts with that intent. They wrote them as theological/political documents. When we impose our

---

[38] George, *The Babylonian Gilgamesh Epic*, pp. 518.

own modern categories upon the Bible, we are engaging in the worst sort of cultural imperialism, denying the human side of the divinely inspired text.

But it works the other way as well. Modern notions of literary evolution get imposed upon the Bible by detractors who wish to discredit the narrative by reducing it to one of a variety of myths that evolve over time. This modern prejudice also ignores the polemical thrust of much ancient literature that interpreted historical events with divergent meanings, or engaged in retelling narratives through contrary theological lenses. This is not the syncretism of evolutionary plagiarism, but the subversion of worldview polemics.

Another aspect of storytelling where this subversion occurs is in the changing names of characters and locations in ancient narratives. As indicated earlier, the Flood hero has different names depending on which era and culture is composing the text. Some of this comes down to simple translation between languages. *Utnapishtim* in Akkadian may simply be the Babylonian translation of the Sumerian *Ziusudra*, which both mean "finding long life" or something similar. Others may be derivative. Some scholars argue that the name *Noah* can possibly be derived from the middle element of *Utnapishtim*, as one rendering has it: Ut**n'ah**pishtim.

Other cases illustrate outright changes of names to fit the story to the culture's paradigm and differing deities. An important Sumerian text, *The Descent of Inanna into the Underworld*, was literally rewritten by the Babylonians as *the Descent of Ishtar into the Underworld* to accommodate their goddess Ishtar.[39] The Babylonian creation epic, Enuma Elish tells the story of the Babylonian deity

[39] Stephanie Dalley, trans., *Myths from Mesopotamia: Creation, The Flood, Gilgamesh and Others*. New York: Oxford University Press, 1989, 2000, 2008, p 154-162. The Sumerian version can be found in Jeremy Black, trans., *The Literature of Ancient Sumer*. New York: Oxford university Press, p 65-76.

Marduk, and his ascendancy to power in the Mesopotamian pantheon, giving mythical justification to the rise of Babylon as an ancient world power in the early 18th century B.C.[40] And then when King Sennacherib of Assyria conquered Babylon around 689 B.C., Assyrian scribes rewrote the Enuma Elish and replaced the name of Marduk with Assur the name of the Assyrian chief god.[41]

The Bible contains the renaming of people that often occurred in the ancient Near East with the intent of expressing destiny or identity. Faithful readers are familiar with Abram's name changed to Abraham to become the "father of many," or Jacob ("supplanter") to Israel ("striving with God"), or Saul of Tarsus being changed to Paul, as a possible Romanizing of his mission to the Gentiles.

But the Hebrew writers of the Bible also engaged in the renaming of enemies for polemical purposes. Thus *Baalzebul*, the god of Ekron, whose name meant "lord of the heavenly dwelling," was renamed *Baalzebub* by the author of 2 Kings 1:2-6, which means the derogatory, "lord of the flies."[42] The wicked queen of Tyre, whose name *Izebul* meant "where is the Prince Baal?" was renamed by the Jews as *Jezebel*, which is a slurring wordplay on dung (2 Kings 9:37).[43] Genesis 11:9 even explains its polemical renaming of the city of Babylon ("Gateway of the Gods") to Babel ("Confusion of Tongues") .

I sought to capture this historical environment of changing names and concepts throughout the series of *Chronicles of the Nephilim* by

---

[40] Alexander Heidel, trans., *The Babylonian Genesis*. Chicago, Ill: University of Chicago, 1942, 1951, 1963; 14.

[41] C. Jouco Bleeker and Geo Widengren, eds., *Historia Religium I: Religions of the Past.* Netherlands; E.J. Brill, 1969; p 134. Richard J. Clifford. *Creation Accounts in the Ancient Near East and in the Bible*, Catholic Biblical Quarterly Monograph Series 26. Washington D.C.: Catholic Biblical Association of America, 1994; p 7-8.

[42] "Baalzebub," *The International Standard Bible Encyclopedia, Revised.* (*ISBE*) Edited by Geoffrey W. Bromiley. Wm. B. Eerdmans, 1988.

[43] "Jezebel," *ISBE.*

having characters, locations and measurements change in ways that reflected history. Thus, locations like Erech, Aratta, and Shinar in *Enoch Primordial* (and the Bible) become the later known Uruk, Ararat, and Sumer in *Gilgamesh Immortal*. The Watchers change their names to Mesopotamian deities, Inanna changes her name to Ishtar, Ninurta to Marduk, and Gilgamesh changes his name, reflecting an important historical theory of the origins of Babylon. Even measurements begin as ancient calibrations like cubits and leagues in *Noah Primeval*, but eventually become the more modern familiar measurements of feet and miles by *Gilgamesh Immortal*. I wanted to give the reader the same experience of real world changing identities, times, and cultures.

There is both continuity and discontinuity within comparative religion, that captures both the common understanding as well as the polemical differences that separate and change meaning. A comparison of the Gilgamesh Epic with the Bible bears this out as Heidel concludes,

> As in the case of the creation stories, we still do not know how the biblical and Babylonian narratives of the Deluge are related historically. The available evidence proves nothing beyond the point that there is a genetic relationship between Genesis and the Babylonian versions. The skeleton is the same in both cases, but the flesh and blood and, above all, the animating spirit are different.[44]

[44] Heidel, *The Gilgamesh Epic*, p. 268.

Uncovering Noah's Nakedness

One additional significant element of *Gilgamesh Immortal* requires explanation. In the novel, Noah's son Ham rapes his own mother Emzara that results in the curse of the fruit of that maternal incest: the child Canaan. This brutal scene is not mere voyeurism of depravity, it is the very theological foundation upon which the rest of the *Chronicles of the Nephilim* are based. And that foundation is not imagined fantasy, it is the actual Biblical basis of the Jewish claim on the Promised Land of Canaan, as odd and controversial as it may seem. But as previous discussions have shown, Genesis is no stranger to odd and controversial stories.

Here is the text from the Bible:

> Genesis 9:20–27
> 20 Noah began to be a man of the soil, and he planted a
> vineyard. 21 He drank of the wine and became drunk
> and lay uncovered in his tent. 22 And Ham, the father
> of Canaan, saw the nakedness of his father and told his
> two brothers outside. 23 Then Shem and Japheth took a
> garment, laid it on both their shoulders, and walked
> backward and covered the nakedness of their father.
> Their faces were turned backward, and they did not see
> their father's nakedness. 24 When Noah awoke from his
> wine and knew what his youngest son had done to him,
> 25 he said, "Cursed be Canaan; a servant of servants
> shall he be to his brothers." 26 He also said, "Blessed
> be the LORD, the God of Shem; and let Canaan be his
> servant. 27 May God enlarge Japheth, and let him dwell
> in the tents of Shem, and let Canaan be his servant."

Literalists have a difficult time with this passage for several reasons. They do not like to admit the fact that Noah becomes a drunk after being the worlds' greatest Bible hero of that time. They read Genesis 6:9 that says Noah was a righteous man, blameless in his generation, and that he walked with God as being a description of Noah as some kind of moral perfectionist one level less than Jesus. But as explained in the appendix of *Noah Primeval*, they miss the fact that righteousness was having faith, not moral perfection. Secondly, having faith was not perfect faith because all Biblical heroes falter in their faith. Thirdly, "blameless" was a physical Levitical reference to genetic purity (as in "spotless" lamb) that was most likely a reference to being uncorrupted by the fallen Sons of God. Fourthly, walking with God did not mean being sinless. Noah was a sinner with imperfect faith and obedience as every believer is. His broken humanity is how we identify with him and draw our inspiration.

The real problem for literalists who do not consider the ancient Near Eastern poetic language of Genesis is in concluding that an entire nation was cursed simply because one of its forefathers saw his dad without clothes on! While it is certainly possible that ancient Mesopotamians had some holy taboo about a parent's nakedness that we are simply unfamiliar with, there is nowhere else in the Bible that affirms the absurdity of such a taboo.

There are however, several places that explain the concept of "uncovering a father's nakedness" as a figurative idiom for having sexual intercourse with his wife.

Bergsma and Hahn's masterful article "Noah's Nakedness and the Curse of Canaan (Genesis 9:20-27)" elucidated for me the notion that I used in my novel that Ham had forced maternal incest with his mother, Noah's wife.[45] They explore the different scholarly explanations of "uncovering Noah's nakedness" and disprove them: voyeurism, castration, and homosexual paternal incest. There are simply no references in the Bible anywhere that reinforce any of these interpretations.

The only one that is reaffirmed and makes sense is that Ham's uncovering his father's nakedness was an idiom or euphemism for maternal incest.

They explain that the definitions of uncovering nakedness in Leviticus 18 are tied to the practices of the Canaanites (sound familiar? Canaan is cursed?). And the Biblical text itself explains that in a patriarchal culture, uncovering a man's nakedness was an expression that actually meant uncovering his wife's nakedness.

> Leviticus 18:7–8
> You shall not uncover the nakedness of your father, which is the nakedness of your mother; she is your mother, you shall not uncover her nakedness. You shall not uncover the nakedness of your father's wife; it is your father's nakedness.

Likewise, they explain, "Lev 18:14, 16; 20:11, 13, 21 all describe a woman's nakedness as the nakedness of her husband."

They then prove that "seeing nakedness" and "uncovering nakedness" are equivalent phrases and are the usual expressions of sexual intercourse in the Holiness Code of Leviticus (18:6; 20:17). It could not be more explicit than Deuteronomy 27:20:

---

[45] John Sietze Bergsma, Scott Walker Hahn, "Noah's Nakedness and the Curse on Canaan (Genesis 9:20–27)", *Journal of Biblical Literature* 124 (2005): 25, ed. Gail R. O'Day, 25 (Decatur, GA: Society of Biblical Literature, 2005)..

> Deuteronomy 27:20
> 'Cursed be anyone who lies with his father's wife, because he has uncovered his father's nakedness.'

Biblically, "uncovering a man's nakedness" was an idiom for having sexual intercourse with his wife. What then of Shem and Japheth walking backward so as not to see Noah's nakedness? Surely, this is not a reference to avoiding maternal incest, but a literal covering of Noah's body with a cloak? In that case, the literal and the figurative collide in a metaphor of meaning. The authors explain the apparent incongruity this way:

> *The brothers' actions play on the broader meaning of the phrase.* Not only did the brothers not "see their father's nakedness" in the sense of having intercourse with him, but also they did not even dare to "see their father's nakedness" in a literal sense. Where Ham's act was exceedingly evil, their gesture was exceedingly pious and noble.[46]

The final clincher to making sense of this bizarre passage is the curse of the son Canaan. Throughout Genesis 9, Ham is oddly and repeatedly referred to as the father of Canaan. It is a strange repetition that draws attention to itself and is finally climaxed with Canaan being cursed instead of Ham for Ham's dirty deed. Well, if Canaan was the fruit of that illicit union of maternal incest between Ham and Emzara, it makes perfect sense within that culture that he is cursed. It may not sound kind to our modern ears, but it is perfectly consistent with that

---

[46] *Journal of Biblical Literature* 124 (2005): 33, ed. Gail R. O'Day, 33 (Decatur, GA: Society *of* Biblical Literature, 2005).

Biblical time period. Ham sought to usurp his father's patriarchal authority through maternal incest which was "uncovering his nakedness." The fruit of that action, the son Canaan, is a cursed man. And that cursed man is the forefather of a cursed nation.

The writer of Genesis, whether Moses or a later editor, was clearly showing the origins of the evil curse on the land of Canaan that they were about to take from the Canaanites. Canaan was cursed to be a servant of the Shemites, or Semites of Israel, and that is a justification of their conquest of the Promised Land.

In short, the Canaanites are the Seed of the Serpent at war with the Israelites, the Seed of the Woman, and they deserve to be dispossessed of their land by the God whom their ancestors rejected and by whom they were cursed. Of course, there is much more to the story than that, for there were giants in the land of Canaan as well, giants that were the descendants of the Nephilim, the original Seed of the Serpent. But you will have to wait for the novels *Joshua Valiant* and *Caleb Vigilant* to see how that all fits together.

For additional Biblical, historical and mythical research related to this novel, go to www.ChroniclesoftheNephilim.com under the menu listing, "Scholarly Research."

If you liked this book, then please help me out by writing an honest review of it on Amazon. That is one of the best ways to say thank you to me as an author. It really does help my exposure and status as an author. It's really easy. In the Customer Reviews section, there is a little box that says "Write a customer review." They guide you easily through the process. Thanks! — *Brian Godawa*

GREAT OFFERS BY BRIAN GODAWA

Get More Biblical Imagination

Sign up Online For
The Godawa Chronicles

www.Godawa.com

Updates and Freebies
of the Books of Brian Godawa
Special Discounts,
Weird Bible Facts!

CHRONICLES OF THE NEPHILIM

Nephilim Giants, Watchers, Cosmic War.
All in the Bible.

www.Godawa.com

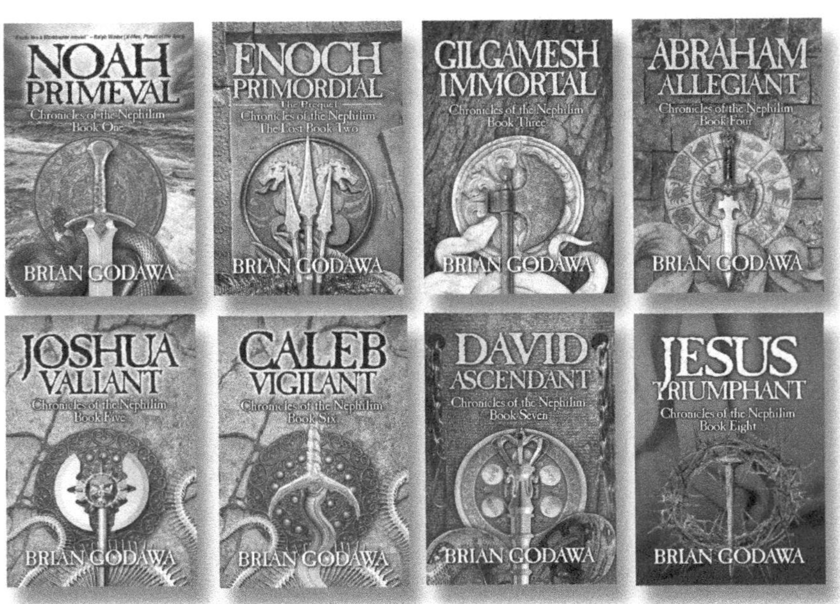

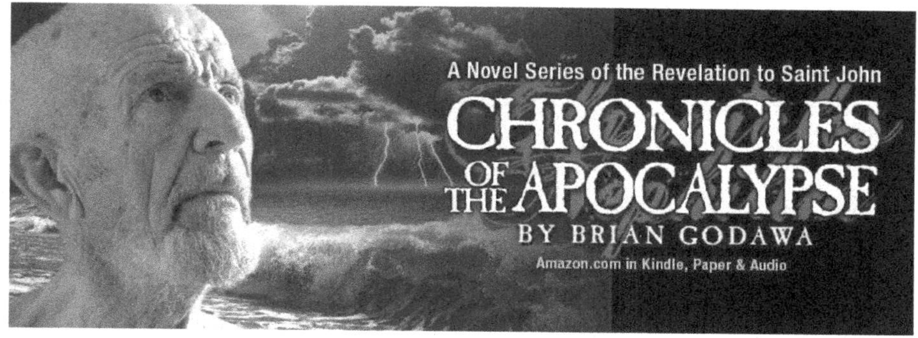

A Novel Series About the Book of Revelation & the End Times. A Fresh Biblical View.

www.Godawa.com

CHRONICLES OF THE WATCHERS

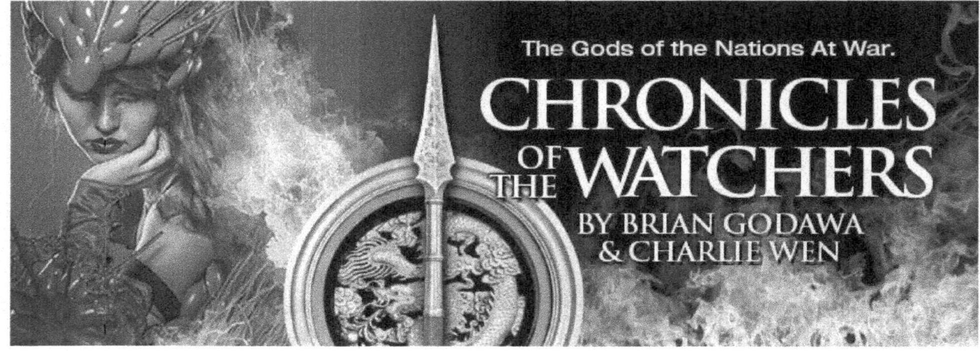

A Series About the Watchers in History.
Action, Romance, Gods, Monsters & Men.

The first novel is *Jezebel: Harlot Queen of Israel*

www.Godawa.com

VIDEO LECTURES

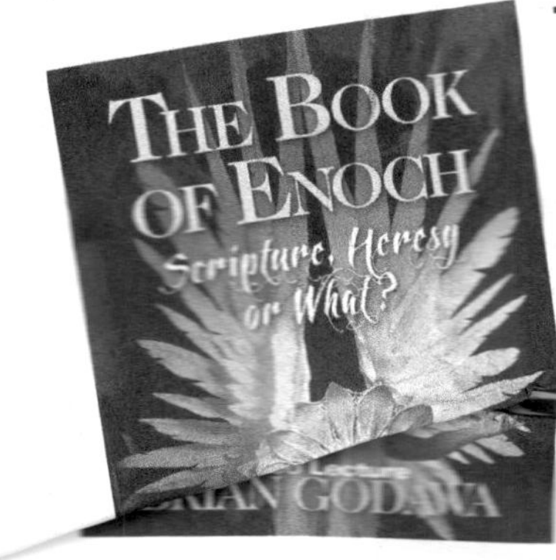

The Book of Enoch: Scripture, Heresy or What?

This lecture by Brian Godawa will be an introduction to the ancient book of 1Enoch, its content, its history, its affirmation in the New Testament, and its acceptance and rejection by the Christian Church. What is the Book of Enoch? Where did it come from? Why isn't it in the Bible? How does the Book of Enoch compare with the Bible?

Available on video.

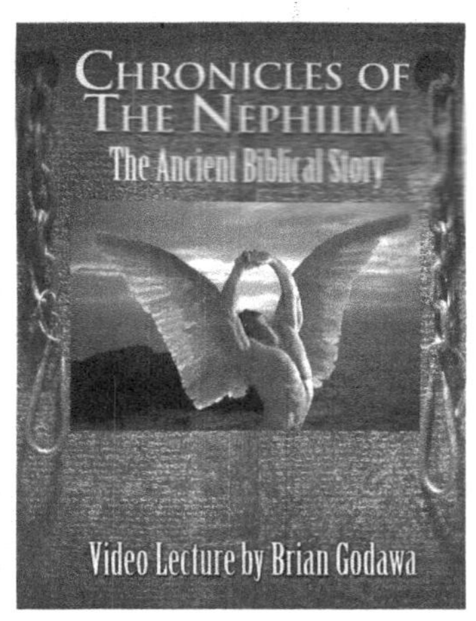

Chronicles of the Nephilim: The Ancient Biblical Story

Watchers, Nephilim, and the Divine Council of the Sons of God. In this dvd video lecture, Brian Godawa explores the Scriptures behind this transformative storyline that inspired his best-selling Biblical novel series Chronicles of the Nephilim.

Available on video.

To download these lectures and other books and products by Brian Godawa, just go to the STORE at:

www.Godawa.com

GOD AGAINST THE GODS

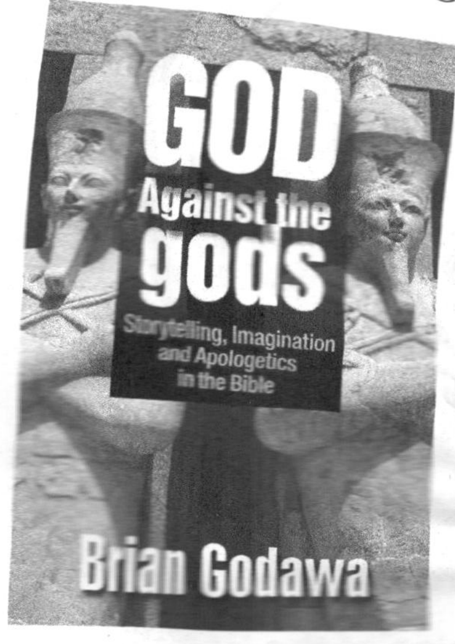

How God Captures the Imagination

This book was previously titled *Myth Became Fact: Storytelling, Imagination & Apologetics in the Bible.*

Brian Godawa, Hollywood screenwriter and best-selling novelist, explores the nature of imagination in the Bible. You will learn how God subverts pagan religions [illegible] creativity, and redee[illegible] your imag[illegible] imagery and worldview. [illegible] approach to glorifying God and defending [illegible]

Demonizing the Pagan Gods
God verbally attacked his opponents, pagans and their gods, using sarcasm, mockery, name-calling.

Old Testament Storytelling Apologetics
Israel shared creative images with their pagan neighbors: The sea dragon of chaos and the storm god. The Bible invests them with new meaning.

Biblical Creation and Storytelling
Creation stories in the ancient Near East and the Bible both express a primeval battle of deity to create order out of chaos. But how do they differ?

The Universe in Ancient Imagination
A detailed comparison and contrast of the Biblical picture of the universe with the ancient pagan one. What's the difference?

New Testament Storytelling Apologetics
Paul's sermon to the pagans on Mars Hill is an example of subversion: Communicating the Gospel in terms of a pagan narrative with a view toward replacing their worldview.

Imagination in Prophecy & Apocalypse
God uses imaginative descriptions of future events to deliberately obscure his message while simultaneously showing the true meaning and purpose behind history.

An Apologetic of Biblical Horror
Learn how God uses horror in the Bible as a tool to communicate spiritual, moral and social truth in the context of repentance from sin and redemptive victory over evil.

For More Info

www.Godawa.com

THE IMAGINATION OF GOD

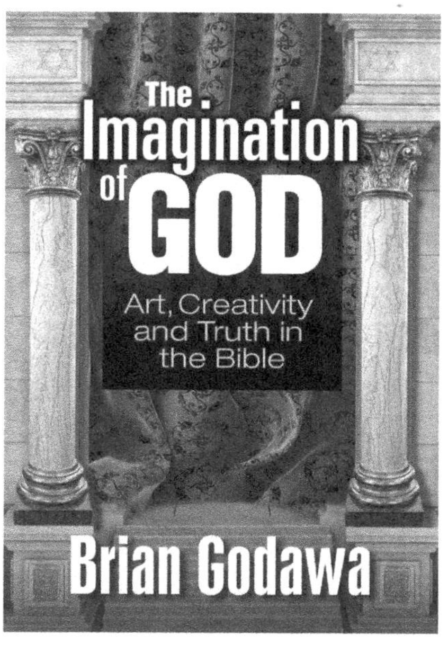

Art, Creativity and Truth in the Bible

In his refreshing and challenging book, Godawa helps you break free from the spiritual suffocation of heady faith. Without negating the importance of reason and doctrine, Godawa challenges you to move from understanding the Bible "literally" to "literarily" by exploring the poetry, parables and metaphors found in God's Word. Weaving historical insight, pop culture and personal narrative throughout, Godawa reveals the importance God places on imagination and creativity in the Scriptures, and provides a Biblical foundation for Christians to pursue imagination, beauty, wonder and mystery in their faith.

This book was previously released with the title, *Word Pictures: Knowing God Through Story and Imagination.*

Endorsements:

"Brian Godawa is that rare breed—a philosopher/artist—who opens our eyes to the aesthetic dimension of spirituality. Cogently argued and fun to read, Godawa shows convincingly that God interacts with us as whole persons, not only through didactic teaching but also through metaphor, symbol, and sacrament."

— Nancy R. Pearcey,
Author, *Total Truth: Liberating Christianity from its Cultural Captivity*

"A spirited and balanced defense of the imagination as a potential conveyer of truth. There is a lot of good literary theory in the book, as well as an autobiographical story line. The thoroughness of research makes the book a triumph of scholarship as well."

— Leland Ryken, Clyde S. Kilby Professor of English, Wheaton College, Illinois
Author, *The Christian Imagination: The Practice of Faith in Literature & Writing.*

For More Info
www.Godawa.com

ABOUT THE AUTHOR

Brian Godawa is the screenwriter for the award-winning feature film, *To End All Wars,* starring Kiefer Sutherland. It was awarded the Commander in Chief Medal of Service, Honor and Pride by the Veterans of Foreign Wars, won the first Heartland Film Festival by storm, and showcased the Cannes Film Festival Cinema for Peace.

He also co-wrote *Alleged*, starring Brian Dennehy as Clarence Darrow and Fred Thompson as William Jennings Bryan. He previously adapted to film the best-selling supernatural thriller novel *The Visitation* by author Frank Peretti for Ralph Winter (*X-Men, Wolverine*), and wrote and directed *Wall of Separation,* a PBS documentary, and *Lines That Divide*, a documentary on stem cell research.

Mr. Godawa's scripts have won multiple awards in respected screenplay competitions, and his articles on movies and philosophy have been published around the world. He has traveled around the United States teaching on movies, worldviews, and culture to colleges, churches and community groups.

His popular book, *Hollywood Worldviews: Watching Films with Wisdom and Discernment* (InterVarsity Press) is used as a textbook in schools around the country. His novel series, the saga *Chronicles of the Nephilim* is in the Top 10 of Biblical Fiction on Amazon and is an imaginative retelling of Biblical stories of the Nephilim giants, the secret plan of the fallen Watchers, and the War of the Seed of the Serpent with the Seed of Eve. The sequel series, *Chronicles of the Apocalypse* tells the story of the Apostle John's book of Revelation, and *Chronicles of the Watchers* recounts true history through the Watcher paradigm.

Find out more about his other books, lecture tapes and dvds for sale at his website **www.godawa.com**.

BLANK PAGE

BLANK PAGE

BLANK PAGE

BLANK PAGE

BLANK PAGE

BLANK PAGE

BLANK PAGE

BLANK PAGE